The Shadowhunter's Codex

ALSO BY

CASSANDRA CLARE

THE MORTAL INSTRUMENTS

THE INFERNAL DEVICES

THE
Shadowhunter's Codex

BEING a RECORD of
the WAYS and LAWS of the NEPHILIM,
the CHOSEN of the ANGEL RAZIEL

AS COMPILED BY
CASSANDRA CLARE
and JOSHUA LEWIS

Twenty-Seventh English Edition, 1990
First Revision, 2002
Alicante, Idris

Second Revision, 2007,
Clary Fray, Brooklyn, NY, USA
THIRD REVISION, 2007, SIMON LEWIS, BOOK STOLEN FROM CLARY
WHILE SHE TRIES TO STUDY, FUNKYTOWN, USA

WALKER
BOOKS

Fourth Revision, 2007, Jace Wayland
Gives Book Back to Clary and Glares at Simon, USA

First published in Great Britain 2013 by Walker Books Ltd
87 Vauxhall Walk, London SE11 5HJ

This edition published 2015

8 10 9

This book has been typeset in Dolly

Printed and bound by CPI Group (UK) Ltd, Croydon, CR0 4YY

British Library Cataloguing in Publication Data:
a catalogue record for this book is
available from the British Library

ISBN 978-1-4063-6546-7

www.walker.co.uk

CONTENTS

Welcome and Congratulations. You have been chosen to become one of the Nephilim. Soon, if you have not done so already, you will drink from the Mortal Cup, taking into yourself the blood of angels, and you will become one of the "Shadowhunters," named for the founder of our order. Our eternal work is the battle against the forces of darkness that encroach upon our world. We also keep the peace in the Shadow World—the hidden societies of magic and magical creatures wrought by the demons we fight—and keep it hidden from the mundane world. And this now is also *your* charge. You are protector, defender, knight errant in the name of the angels. You will be trained to fight demons, to protect mundanes, to negotiate the complex landscape of the Downworlders—werewolves, vampires, and the like—that you will encounter. Your life will be spent in the pursuit of the angelic against the demonic. And when you die, you will die with glory.

This may appear an intimidating description of the Shadowhunter's life, but we must emphasize the sacredness and the weight of our mission. Joining the Nephilim is not like becoming a mundane policeman, or even a mundane soldier. "Shadowhunter" is not *what you do*; it is *who you are*. Every aspect of your life will change to accommodate the holy assignment you have been chosen for.

This Codex serves to assist you in acclimating to the new world into which you have been thrust. Most Shadowhunters are born into this life, raised and immersed in it constantly from birth, and thus many things about the world that are second nature to them will be new to you. You have been recruited out of your mundane life, and you will quickly encounter much that is confusing and dangerous. This book is designed specifically to reduce your confusion and, ideally, to keep you alive long enough to become a full Shadowhunter in good standing in your local Institute.

It goes without saying that it is against the Law for the Codex to be shared with any persons other than Shadowhunters and mundanes in the process of Ascension (see "Intermarriage," page 187).

WHAT IS A SHADOWHUNTER?

The Nephilim are the appointed warriors on Earth of the Angel Raziel. We are appointed specifically to control and preside over the demonic in our world, both demons and the supernatural creatures born of their presence among us. A thousand years ago Raziel bestowed on us the tools to accomplish this task. These tools are:

—The Mortal Instruments, by which we may know truth, speak with angels, and make more of our own kind

—The country of Idris, in which we may live safely away from both demons and the mundane world

—The Book of Raziel (or "Gray Book"), with which we may make use of the magic of angels to protect and augment ourselves

These were gifts given by Raziel to the first Nephilim, Jonathan Shadowhunter, and so after him we call ourselves Shadowhunters.

Yeah yeah yeah.
Get to where I learn kung fu!

SURE IS CONVENIENT THAT HE WAS NAMED THAT ALREADY. IT MAKES A GOOD NAME FOR THEM.

THE SHADOWHUNTER OATH

There have been many versions of the oath that is spoken by new Nephilim when they drink from the Mortal Cup and join our ranks. The one currently in use was created a little more than a hundred years ago, as part of the reforms that swept through the Shadow World around that time. It replaced an older oath whose language was very martial in tone and that focused mostly on the fact that Shadowhunters are good at killing things. Typically at that time the oath was spoken in one of several holy languages—Latin, Sanskrit, Hebrew, et cetera—and thus was treated more as a formality to execute rather than words to listen to and reflect upon.

The oath follows. You should commit it to memory. At the time you are made a Shadowhunter, you will need to recite it without any prompting. Many new Shadowhunters have complained that this is an unnecessary burden, to which we respond that half-angelic soldiers against the dark forces of the world should not be fazed by the need to memorize a hundred words.

I hereby swear:

I will be Raziel's Sword, extending his arm to strike down evil.
I will be Raziel's Cup, offering my blood to our mission.
I will be Raziel's Mirror; when my enemies behold me, let them see his face in mine.

I hereby promise:

3

I will serve with the angels' courage.
I will serve the angels' justice.
And I will serve with the angels' mercy.

Until such time as I shall die, I will be Nephilim. I pledge myself
in Covenant as a Nephilim, and I pledge my life and my family
to the Clave of Idris.

It's not like that—there's a zillion laws you're agreeing to follow. It's covered by the "in Covenant."

Would think the oath would be longer?

SHADOWHUNTER NAMES

Most Ascending mundanes like yourself give up their family name in favor of creating a traditional Shadowhunter name. By tradition most Shadowhunter family names are compound, like "Shadowhunter" itself—in this case, "shadow" + "hunter." Jonathan Shadowhunter's name was, obviously, not actually "Shadowhunter"—such a coincidence would beggar belief. NM, my complaint has been anticipated. Codex 1, Me 0

What Jonathan Shadowhunter was called, before he was made the first Nephilim by Raziel, is lost to history; we do not even know from what country he came. He was given the name Shadowhunter by Raziel (often found written as separate or hyphenated words, as in "Shadow-Hunter," earlier in history) as a symbol of his transformation. According to many tellings of the story, Raziel told Jonathan, "I grant you the light and fire of angels, to illuminate your way in dark, for you and your companions will be Hunters of the Shadows." Like Masters of the Universe™ Not much like them no.

There is a kind of poetry in the selection of a Shadowhunter family name; combining just any two things into a name is not enough. Your name should try to reflect something about who you are, or where you're from, or what you hope to be. In order to stimulate ideas of your own, we here supply a list of appropriate English words that can be combined to make names. Simply select

That coincidence—beggars belief. A 60 ft tall angel appears to you, apparently does not beggar belief.

Wait till you meet Jonathan Universemaster

4

two of them and put them next to each other. Usually they will sound better in one order than in the other order.

NOTE: USE YOUR JUDGMENT. Your name must be approved by those evaluating your petition for Ascension. Do not try to name yourself Dragonrider or Firedance or Elfstar. Nephilim are meant to be inconspicuous. Obviously things such as Hammerfist or Bloodsteel should also be avoided.

ALDER	GOLD	SCAR
APPLE	GRAY	SHADE
ASH	GREEN	SHADOW
ASPEN	HALLOW	SILVER
BAY	HAWK	STAIR
BEAR	HEAD	STARK
BLACK	HEART	STORM
BLOOD	HERON	THRUSH
BLUE	HOOD	TOWER
BOW	HUNTER	TREE
BRANDY	KEY	WAIN
BROWN	LAND	WALKER
BULL	LIGHT	WATER
CAR	MAPLE	WAY
CART	MARK	WEATHER
CHERRY	MERRY	WELL
CHILD	NIGHT	WHEEL
COCK	OWL	WHITE
CROSS	PEN	WINE
DOVE	PINE	WOLF
EARTH	RAVEN	WOOD
FAIR	RED	WRIGHT
FISH	ROSE	YOUNG
FOX	SCALE	

What is your Shadowhunter name?

fairchild.

Can't believe you actually wrote that in.

DEFINITELY EITHER STORMWALKER
OR NIGHTRAVEN—WHAT DO YOU THINK?

BLOODSUCKER *fits.*

NOT COOL BRO

THE SHADOWHUNTER'S GLOSSARY

Shouldn't that be "glossarie"?

The world you are entering is a secret one. It is kept hidden from the vast majority of the mundane world, who do not know even that our kind exist, much less the many varieties of ~~monster~~
\^ HANDSOME INDIVIDUAL
among whom we are responsible for keeping peace. Naturally, the denizens of that world may make common reference to places and things with which you are not yet familiar. We thus provide this handy short guide to some of the more common terms, which will be explored in more depth in later chapters as warranted.

Well, thank goodness.

PEOPLE AND PLACES

We are called *Nephilim* or *Shadowhunters*. We are the children of men and *angels*; the Angel *Raziel* gave us our power.

Our primary mission is to eliminate *demons*, who come in a large

Hey.

I don't know you. I can't guess who you might be. But I'm done with this Codex now, and I think it's time I pass it on.

Okay, I've written all over it. And ... drawn all over it. But I think it's better than a fresh clean Codex, because I've corrected some stuff and added some things. I think it's more true, has less of the political stuff the Clave puts in to make themselves look good.

So this is yours now. Whoever you are. If you need to find this, you'll find it.

Anyway, welcome. This is the Codex. I always thought it was like this great tome of wisdom, but it's more like an army field manual—how you teach someone to be a Shadowhunter when you're already being chased by demons. So I'm not the usual reader. Luckily, Jace has added some notes too. He's taking my training a little too seriously, by the way. I think it's because everyone already thinks we're just pretending to train and actually making out. So, he's Jace, he has to prove them wrong. Hence real serious training. Which is why I am writing this with an icepack on my hip, by the way.

Simon has appeared to announce that the Codex reminds him of a Dungeons & Dragons manual. "Like, you know, it tells you the rules. Vampires are weak to ... fire! They bite you for 2d10 damage with their vicious fangs!" Now he is making a bitey face at me. He kind of looks like a hamster. Seriously, I love Simon, but he is like the worst vampire ever.

Simon, you don't have to make pretend fangs with your fingers. You have actual fangs.

Why Do People Become Shadowhunters, by Magnus Bane

This Codex thing is very silly. Downworlders talk about the Codex like it is some great secret full of esoteric knowledge, but really it's a Boy Scout manual.

One thing that it mysteriously doesn't address is *why* people become Shadowhunters. And you should know that people become Shadowhunters for many stupid reasons.

So here is an addition to your copy.

Greetings, young aspiring Shadowhunter-to-be —or possibly already technically a Shadowhunter. I can't remember whether you drink from the Cup first or get the book first. Regardless, congratulations. You have just been recruited by the Monster Police. You may be wondering, why? *Why of all the mundanes out there was I selected and invited to this exclusive club made up largely, at least from a historical perspective, of murderous psychopaths?*

Possible Reasons Why:

1. You possess a stout heart, strong will, and able body.
2. You possess a stout body, able will, and strong heart.
3. Local Shadowhunters are ironically punishing you by making you join them.
4. You were recruited by a local Institute to join the Nephilim as an ironic punishment for your mistreatment of Downworlders.
5. Your home, village, or nation is under siege by demons.
6. Your home, village, or nation is under siege by rogue Downworlders.
7. You were in the wrong place at the wrong time.

8. You know too much, and should be recruited because the secrecy of the Shadow World has already been compromised for you.

9. You know too little; it would be helpful to the Shadowhunters if you knew more.

10. You know exactly the right amount, making you a natural recruit.

11. You possess a natural resistance to glamour magic and must be recruited to keep you quiet and provide you with some basic protection.

12. You have a compound last name already and convinced someone important that yours *is* a Shadowhunter family and the Shadowhunteriness has just been weakened by generations of poor breeding.

13. You had a torrid affair with a member of the Nephilim Council, and now he's trying to cover his tracks.

14. Shadowhunters are concerned they are no longer haughty and condescending enough—have sought you out to add a much needed boost of haughty condescension.

15. You have been bitten by a radioactive Shadowhunter, giving you the proportional strength and speed of a Shadowhunter.

16. Large bearded man on flying motorcycle appeared to take you away to Shadowhunter school. (Note: Presence of flying motorcycle suggests bearded man may be a vampire.)

17. Your mom has been in hiding from your evil dad, and you found out you're a Shadowhunter only a few weeks ago.

That's right. Seventeen reasons. Because that's how many I thought of. Now run off, little Shadowhunter, and learn to murder things. And be nice to Downworlders.

variety of species and forms. We also seek to keep the peace among several populations of demihumans, known collectively as *Downworlders*. These groups are *werewolves, vampires, faeries,* and *warlocks*. We preside over a treaty known as the *Accords* that ordains how we and all of these groups may interact, as well as each group's rights, responsibilities, and restrictions. The Accords are revised and signed every fifteen years by representatives of the Nephilim and all Downworlder groups.

We have our own secret country, which is hidden in Central Europe and is known as *Idris*. Its capital city—indeed, its only city—is named *Alicante*, and that is where the Council resides, and where Clave meetings are held (see below).

Most Shadowhunters spend their younger years as warriors. The exceptions are the members of our two monastic orders, the *Silent Brothers* and the *Iron Sisters*. The Brothers serve as our keepers of lore and knowledge: They are our librarians, our researchers, our medics. They reside in the *Silent City*, a place deep underground, many of whose levels are kept secret even from normal Shadowhunters. The Sisters design and forge our weapons; they are the keepers of *adamas*, the holy metal given by Raziel for our use. They reside in the *Adamant Citadel*, which is even more hidden than the Silent City; except for a single receiving chamber, it can be entered only by Iron Sisters. *Obsessed with secrecy? A little?*

CLAVE, COUNCIL, CONSUL, COVENANT

The *Clave* is the collective name for the political body made up of all active Nephilim. All Shadowhunters that recognize the authority of Idris—and this should be all of them in the world who remain Shadowhunters—make up the Clave. When Shadow-hunters reach adulthood at the age of eighteen, they declare their allegiance to the Clave and become full Clave members, with rights to contribute to any Clave issue under discussion. The Clave keeps and interprets the Law, and makes decisions about the guidance of the Nephilim through history as it unfolds. *What if you don't declare allegiance?* *That's called "leaving the Shadowhunters." It'll be covered later.*

Smaller, more regional groups of Shadowhunters, for instance the Shadowhunters of a specific country or sometimes of a particularly large city, are collected in what are called Enclaves in most of the world, and Conclaves in the Americas and Australia. These regional groups coordinate their own local decision making and organizational structures as they see fit, although the Clave as a whole is responsible for placing Shadowhunters in charge of specific Institutes. The Clave may intercede in cases where an Enclave or Conclave is organized in some way that is against the spirit of the Nephilim as a whole (for instance, in cases where some individual Shadowhunter has tried to seize dictatorial power over nearby Downworlders, as with the infamous cult of personality and human sacrifice declared by Hezekiah Short in the Mayan ruins of southeastern Mexico in the 1930s).

The term "Clave" comes from the Latin *clavis*, meaning "key," and its use in such terms as "Enclave" and "Conclave" refers abstractly to the idea of an assembly "under lock and key"—that is, meeting in secret. The Clave is, so to speak, the great secret of the Nephilim; with the key of the Mortal Cup, one earns entrance to its chambers.

The *Council* is the governing body of the Clave. Once, there were few enough Shadowhunters in the world that in matters of impor-tance the entire Clave could be canvassed for their opinion, but it has been many hundreds of years since this was the case. The Council does, however, in representing the larger Clave, retain the power to recall any Shadowhunter to Idris at any time. Today local Enclaves choose representatives to sit on the Council, which deals with matters of immediate import that are not large enough for the entire Clave to become involved in. Enclaves may decide for themselves how to appoint their Council representatives. Most times this is accomplished with a simple vote or by the Conclave head appointing a chosen delegate; sometimes the Conclave head sits on the Council herself. Some regions have more colorful means of appointing their representative. For instance, in eighteenth-century France under the Sun King, the Council delegate was appointed by means of a dance competition. The Saint Petersburg Enclave to this day holds a massive annual chess tournament; the competitor who loses the most matches is named the Council delegate.

The *Consul* is the highest appointed official in the Clave. He is something like a prime minister rather than like a king or president; he wields little executive power but rather serves to preside over the Council, to officially tally its votes, and to help interpret the Law for the Clave. He also serves as an adviser to the Inquisitor, and is intended to be a consulting mentor for the heads of Institutes. His only real source of direct power is his authority to call the Council to session and to adjudicate disputes between Shadowhunters. The Nephilim do not have such uncivilized mundane notions as political parties; the Consul is voted into office by the Council and, like most prime ministers, can be put out of office by a vote of no confidence.

Tying all of these entities together is the *Covenant*, another name for Nephilim Law. It provides the rules of conduct for Shadowhunters and Downworlders; it is by the right of Covenant that the Nephilim enforce their Law in Downworld. (There have been times and places where that rule of Law has been held in place by force rather than by Covenant, but we happily live in more enlightened times today.) The Covenant protects the rights of Shadowhunters to enforce civilized relations among the Clave, Downworld, and the mundane world, and also protects the rights of Downworlders so that they may not be maltreated by Shadowhunters.

It is the Covenant also that guarantees that the Shadow World remains shadowed from the mundane world. Nephilim are sworn by Covenant never to reveal the truth of the world to a mundane, unless such a revelation cannot in any way be avoided. All Downworlders who have signed the Accords agree to the same. Demons are the great unpredictable force in keeping the Shadow World secret, but so far demons have decided that secrecy is best for them as well.

This description makes the Covenant sound simple, but its fine print is more or less the entire legal system of the Shadowhunters, specifying not only the criminal code that the Nephilim and various Downworlder communities have agreed to abide by, but also how that criminal code may be prosecuted, how trials may be run, and so on. This means both Shadowhunters and Downworlders may refer to the Covenant to claim some specific right. For instance, Shadowhunters may swear upon the Covenant to keep information confidential that has been shared with them in an investigation.

The Covenant long precedes the Accords; the Accords can be seen as a kind of Bill of Rights, amendments to the Covenant that are agreed to be taken as the law of the land by all of the Shadow World.

DISCUSSION QUESTIONS AND THINGS TO TRY

1. What do you notice about the kinds of words that are used to make up Shadowhunter names? What do they have in common? What might this say about the Shadowhunters' identity and what family names are supposed to represent?

SIMON NIGHTRAVEN NEEDS NO DISCUSSION QUESTIONS.

It's not your book, Simon. YOU DON'T NEED DISCUSSION QUESTIONS EITHER, CLARY HORSEPHONE.

2. Do you know who your local Council member is? Do you know who runs your local Institutes? Find out!

Yes. Yes. Okay. WHO

That's not what it says!

SEE ME

3. Try: Introducing yourself to a Silent Brother! Their appearance may be intimidating, but you will find them to be friendly and patient. (Note: Do not try to introduce yourself to an Iron Sister at this time.)

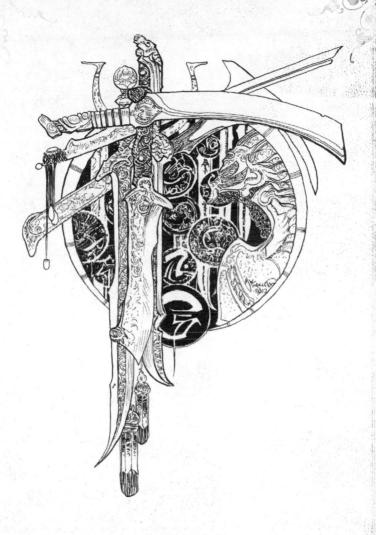

CHAPTER ONE

TREASURY

ARMS

CHOOSING A WEAPON

Shadowhunters do not use firearms, and typically we fight in close quarters. We also usually fight in short, improvised confrontations rather than in planned battles. As such, the basic armaments of the Shadowhunters are those hand-to-hand weapons that humans have used for thousands of years. Each of these come in endless variations, and you will need to tune your training to the specifics of your locale. Here we endeavor to lay out the categories of weapons and briefly discuss their pros and cons.

You should plan to quickly achieve a basic competence in each of these categories. Remember that demons are infinite in type and variety; a Shadowhunter never knows when she might face a foe against whom her preferred weapons are totally useless. You should, however, also give thought to what kind of weapon you might choose to specialize in. Some feel called to the longsword, while others will have a natural gift with a bow and arrow. Finding the intersection of your interest and your talent is a major goal of your early training.

 Any decently stocked Institute should have on hand a selection of all of the weapons mentioned here, in addition to other basic useful combat tools such as: binding wire of silver, gold, and/or electrum; wooden stakes in oak and ash; amulets of protection; assorted holy symbols for major world religions; and basic magic implements (chalk, iron filings, small vial of animal blood, etc.). A truly well-stocked large Institute might add to that list such specialty items as lead swords, holy trumpets, bone staves, etc., depending on location.

> Did you know?
> Shadowhunter weapons are Marked with runes. While only seraph blades can cause permanent harm to demons, angelic Marks on other weapons will at least slow a demon's recovery from a wound. Without these Marks, demons easily shrug off the effects of our physical weapons.

SWORDS

Swords are long hilted blades used to wound both by piercing and by slashing. Variants range from light and flexible blades wielded in one hand, such as the rapier, to heavy blades such as the Scottish claymore that require two hands to wield and whose blades may well be taller than a person. And more or less all possible stages in between are represented. Generally Shadowhunters have a preference for speed and agility in fighting, and so most who prefer swords specialize in one of the smaller one-handed versions. There are, of course, exceptions. Note that if you have never wielded a sword before, you may be surprised by how quickly your arm will grow tired, even when using a light blade. If you have never used a sword before, you can get an early start on training by practicing simply holding a sword out in front of your body, parallel to the ground, for a length of time. You will be ready to start actual combat training when you can keep the sword steady for thirty minutes.

KNIVES AND DAGGERS

These smaller blades are less tiring to hold, and frequently two are wielded at the same time. The trade-off is, of course, that they have a shorter reach than a sword, requiring you to be closer to your foe. They are also far easier to conceal than a sword. Seraph blades are typically wielded using techniques associated with dagger fighting, so you will want to grow proficient with these weapons no matter what. *Thank you, Codex, because I didn't know what a knife was.*

You may also learn to throw knives and daggers, but it's a very difficult skill to pick up, and daggers are usually more difficult and expensive to create than arrows, considering that you may lose them after a single use. Still, many Shadowhunters favor the throwing skill for its showy nature. *HAHA JACE THROWS KNIVES BECAUSE OF HIS SHOWY NATURE.*

We were all 14 once. You'd have learned it too if you could have.

MACES, AXES, HAMMERS, ETC.   *Touché, whatever your last name is.*

Those who do not seek subtlety in their combat may wish to consider specializing in a weapon in these categories, whereby the enemy is simply bludgeoned with a heavy block of metal, possibly sharpened. You will come across few creatures that cannot be successfully defeated by the application of sufficient blunt trauma. The main advantage of these weapons is that, while one can learn finesse in wielding them, they tend to be effective even when that finesse is lacking. All the wielder requires is brute strength and room to swing. *Oh please please please Clary. Tiny girl with a gigantic hammer. So anime!*

The main disadvantages of these weapons are that, for one, they can be difficult to conceal, and for another, they depend on the enemy's skin being less strong than the material of the weapon, which is usually true of Downworlders but may often be untrue of demons.

Flails and morning-stars, in which the aforementioned heavy chunk of metal is attached to the handle by a chain and thus can

In real life tiny girl with gigantic hammer has gigantic forearms.

17

be swung around to build up more momentum, add more force to your blows in exchange for a higher risk of accidentally walloping yourself or the person standing next to you.

POLEARMS, PIKES, SPEARS, LANCES

There are almost as many variations on these as there have been human armies in history, but they all have the same basic structure: a sharp blade at the end of a long sturdy stick. Traditionally these have been used in mundane warfare to give a fighter a longer reach than normal—which can be useful when fighting a foe on horseback (or giant lizard-back, in the case of some demons), a demon covered in tentacles, a demon with obscenely long arms, and so on. Today, however, fighting from horseback is obsolescent, and the annoyance of carrying a sharp six-foot-long pole around is rarely worth the trouble. You are most likely to see these carried by Shadowhunter guards as ceremonial weapons; you are also likely to find that these guards have other weapons on their person that they would wield instead in case of action.

BOWS AND CROSSBOWS

These are the definitive Shadowhunter weapons for long-range fighting. They are lightweight and easy to carry, and you can bring a large number of arrows with you with little trouble. Often Shadowhunters will carry arrows with several different arrowhead materials, useful for fighting different kinds of creatures. (We recommended color-coding the feathers for ease in identification.)

Like sword fighting, archery is a complex and difficult skill, and you will need to train diligently to be able to use it in a real-life scenario. Shadowhunters almost never fire arrows from an entrenched stable position, like someone defending a castle from a siege. Expect to have to arm, aim, and fire your bow while in the middle of total chaos. Do not expect your archery instructor to let you take a bow with you into combat until you have demonstrated some serious skill.

IMPROVISED WEAPONS

The Nephilim are trained in the use of weapons, and our weapons are a vital part of our combat methods. It is important to always remember, however, that a Shadowhunter without fighting weapons is not helpless. The fight against demons is a desperate one, and weapons can be improvised from the environment—a tree branch, an andiron, a handful of pebbles thrown in the face of a foe. Then too the Shadowhunter should always remember that her own body is a weapon. She has been trained to be faster and stronger than mundanes, and in the panic of battle should remember her strength and make use of it. A weapon does not win a battle; the Nephilim wielding the weapon does.

EXOTIC WEAPONS

There are, of course, as many nonstandard and exotic weapons as there are human cultures, and you may find that your local Nephilim have some combat specialties  outside the common weapon types. These may include whips, sword canes, obscure weapons of martial arts traditions, household objects modified to double as blades, and so on. These rarer "specialty" weapons are not forbidden or discouraged from use. Indeed, a Shadowhunter is likely to be more effective with a weapon toward which they feel an affinity than with one forced into their hand by the dictates of training protocols.

Two specific exotic weapons are worthy of note here, one angelic, one demonic.

The *aegis* is a dagger that has been seethed and tempered in angel blood. They are incredibly rare, as one would imagine, since angel blood is not easily come by. There are only a small number of these in the hands of the Shadowhunters, and they are kept by the Iron Sisters and are not permitted to reside in an Institute. They are available for requisition in the armory, but the requestor should be prepared with a very good reason for the request. The Iron Sisters are not usually pleased to give them out.

The *athame* is a ceremonial, double-edged dagger, usually with a black handle and carved with demonic runes. It is used in demon-summoning rituals to draw blood or carve lines of magical force and is only for ritual use. The weapon loses its power if used in combat. It is one of the four elemental tools of the neo-pagan mundane religion Wicca; as such there are many false *athame* floating around. Warlocks can of course tell the difference on sight, but mundanes cannot. This can sometimes lead a mundane to accidentally possess a genuine *athame*, which is a great danger.

SERAPH BLADES

There is a legend told of the first seraph blade, which may or may not be true. The legend dates to the earliest days of the Iron Sisters, when they were few in number and the Adamant Citadel was merely a single *adamas* forge and a set of protective wards. In those days the paths from the mundane world to the volcanic plains of the Citadel were not as hidden and guarded as they are now, and it is said that a demon, a Dragon—for in those days Dragon demons were not almost extinct—found its way to the location of the Citadel. There was only a single Sister there working at the forge, and she was caught unawares and unarmed, having placed her faith in the impossibility of the Sisters' forge being found by the enemy.

Laughing and threatening, the Dragon stepped through lava beds as though skipping across shallow streams. In terror, the

Sister cast about her for a weapon, but all she had to hand were irregular jags of *adamas*, recently extracted from ore and waiting to be worked. She seized one and held it between her and the approaching Dragon like a pikeman preparing to receive a charge. Her hand trembled; she was afraid not for her own life but for the continued existence of the Iron Sisters: If the demons could travel here, surely they would overrun the Citadel soon enough.

Panic-stricken, she called out prayers to the forces of good. As the Dragon was upon her, she loudly abjured it in the name of Michael, the slayer of Sammael, general of the armies of Heaven. Promptly the *adamas* jag lit up, blue and brilliant with heavenly fire. The Sister's hand burned where she clutched it, but with all her strength she thrust her makeshift lance and pierced the Dragon in the soft flesh under his jaw. She expected it to wound the Dragon and nothing more—but perhaps it would buy her enough time to flee.

Instead the *adamas* spear bored through the neck of the Dragon as if through paper, and around the spear burst flames of seraphic fire. The Dragon screamed and burned, and as the Sister watched, the demon staggered away from her, damaged in a way she had never seen a demon damaged before. Across the lava moat surrounding the Adamant Forge, the Dragon was overcome, fell to the ground, and burned for an hour.

The Sister fell to her knees in exhaustion and watched the Dragon's carcass slowly fade from the world. She could then have rested—no one would have blamed her—but she was an Iron Sister, and by the time her fellow Sisters found her a few hours later, she had deduced the nature of the power she had uncovered and had drawn up on vellum the first blueprints for the seraph blade.

Iron Sisters: surprisingly badass.

Today seraph blades, or angel blades, are the fundamental weapon in Shadowhunter combat. They are as clear as glass, usually double-edged, and normally about two feet in length. Being *adamas*, they are incredibly finely honed and are capable of holding their edge indefinitely. They are thus potent weapons against any foe. Their true power, however, is revealed when they are named—when a Shadowhunter holds them and invokes the name of an angel. The spirit of that angel is said to then inhabit the blade for a time, and the weapon will glow brightly with heavenly fire, like the flaming sword of the angel who guards the Garden of Eden.

This heavenly fire is very potent against demons. Most demons can heal themselves from mundane injuries in our world fairly quickly, just as werewolves and vampires can. We Mark our mundane weapons (see sections below) to make them more potent, but even so, the best we can do with them is damage demons enough that they must retreat to lick their wounds, as it were. Only the seraph blade can *permanently* damage a demon, so that it must withdraw for more significant and lengthy healing or must return to the Void to repair itself.

After a time the power of an activated seraph blade will be exhausted, and it will need to be refreshed by the Iron Sisters in order to be used again. Depleted seraph blades can be brought to the weapons room of your local Institute for regular recycling.

Iron Sisters are badass at recycling!

Note that the seraph blade is a viable but drastically overpowered weapon in a fight against a mundane. Downworlders are harmed by them in much the same manner as demons, but mundane flesh pierced by a seraph blade will burst into flame and may consume the mundane entirely. *The Clave has officially deemed this awesome.*

Shadowhunters will not be so burned by seraph blades, given our angelic blood, but even so, activated blades can severely burn the wielder's hands, and you should not touch a seraph blade until you have been Marked with the rune of Angelic Power. (Typically this is placed either at the base of the throat or on the inside of each wrist.) A Shadowhunter who has been stabbed by a seraph blade will *not* burst into flames, but it should be remembered that seraph blades are still blades and can kill a Shadowhunter by more terrestrial means, like any other sword or dagger.

By the way, most Shadowhunters think we have to name seraph blades just because Jonathan Shadowhunter thought it was important to make everyone memorize a lot of angel names. That guy was hard-core.

It does mean you rule at Angel Trivial Pursuit. Also Angel Scrabble.

MATERIALS

You'll find weapons made of all kinds of materials in your local Institute, chosen for their magical properties.

ADAMAS

Adamas is the heavenly metal granted to the Shadowhunters for our use by the Angel Raziel. The metal is silver-white and translucent, and glows slightly (although this glow may not be visible in broad daylight). It generally feels smooth to the touch, like glass but notably warmer and heavier. It is the hardest substance the Nephilim know of, and cannot be worked by mundane means. The Iron Sisters use seraphic Marks unknown to non-Sisters to shape the metal; to craft weapons and steles from it, the Sisters use forges that take their fire from the heart of a volcano.

IRON

This element is toxic to faeries. You will often encounter the term "cold iron" in reference to the fey; this is just regular iron. The term "cold iron" refers to the fact that it is cold to the touch, which was at one time believed to be associated with its magical properties. Iron takes enchantment and blessing very well. It's generally believed that it is the large quantity of iron in human blood that causes its affinity for enchantment. It is especially worth mentioning that meteoric iron, the nickel-iron alloy that makes up many meteors, is a particularly good conductor of magical energy.

STEEL

This type of iron alloy is usually *not* toxic to faeries. It is the purity of iron that grants its power over the fey. Steel does, however, hold a sharpened edge very well, and thus the Shadowhunter will normally spend a large amount of time training with steel weaponry to learn how to put one of those sharpened edges through a demon.

SILVER

Silver is a metal with which all Nephilim are intimately familiar. Using a weapon made of silver is one of the only ways to permanently injure a werewolf, who will heal from a wound made by any other material. The element is toxic to vampires and causes them to experience pain, headaches, nausea, and so on, though it will not kill them. Silver is a potent conductor of magical energies, behind only gold and *adamas*, and as a result the fey also use a large amount of it in both their arms and armor, and also in their decorative arts. Shadowhunters have the unenviable task of learning to wield both steel and silver weapons, which differ noticeably in weight, and the Shadowhunter must in fact learn to switch between them quickly.

GOLD

This metal is poisonous to demons. It is also an excellent conductor of magical energies, although it is rarely used to make weapons or tools, since in its pure form it is one of the most soft and pliant metals. Interestingly, it has both strongly positive and strongly negative associations in religious ritual. On the one hand its rarity, resistance to corrosion, and beauty has caused it to be used to symbolize high esteem, power, and the light of Heaven. On the other hand its expense and rarity has made it a symbol of greed and of the profanity of material wealth, as opposed to the sacredness of spiritual wealth. Thus, one will find gold used in sacred and powerful religious decorations and also in some of the darkest of demonic rituals.

ELECTRUM

Electrum is an alloy of gold and silver that can be found naturally in the earth. It has been known and used since the time of the pharaohs of ancient Egypt. Its lack of purity means that it is rarely used in specific rituals, but it is considered a good conductor of magic. It combines the mystical abilities of both silver and gold, in lesser strength than either pure metal but at significantly less expense than pure gold and without some of the disadvantages.

COPPER

This element is used mostly as an intensifier for other materials. It is thought to help bring the abilities of other metals into better alignment with the wielder, and thus is often used decoratively, or to form hilts or handles of silver weapons, for instance.

DEMON-METAL

Demon-metal is a noble metal (that is, one resistant to corrosion) that is believed to originate in the Void, and cannot be found naturally in our universe. It is black in appearance but is believed to be transparent and glowing with black demonic power. It is something like the demonic equivalent of *adamas* in that it creates wounds that cannot be easily healed by seraphic Marks and require much more involved medical attention. You will find it sometimes used to forge weapons or armor wielded or worn by demons themselves. It is incredibly rare to find it in the hands of Downworlders or humans.

ROWAN

The European rowan tree has long been known to have magically protective properties. It has been used in Europe to ward off malevolent spirits and enchantments for thousands of years. These properties, along with the tree's density and strength, have made it a common choice for the staves of druids and other priests, and it is commonly used in the construction of Institutes and for arrows wielded by Nephilim.

ASH

The wood of Yggdrasil, the world-tree of Norse mythology, is believed to be the source of the so-called Mead of Poetry, the mythological beverage that would magically transform the drinker into a scholar. It has properties similar to that of rowan but is notably easier to work. It is also often used in a similar way to iron—it is believed to have a similar affinity with humans. (Norse mythology also cites it as the wood from which the first human was created.)

OAK

The oak tree is often considered the "most mundane" of woods, and from this very fact it draws its power. It has great strength and hardness and is therefore frequently the material of choice for wooden weapons. Stakes for vampire slaying, for instance, are traditionally crafted out of oak, which is believed to help guide the wielder's hand to the source of demonic magic, in order to eliminate it. *Jace is considered the most awesome material to make a Shadowhunter out of.*

I AM BOTH GROSSED OUT AND CONFUSED.

HOLY WATER Batman!

You probably already know of holy water. In fact the use of
water as a weapon against evil is well-explored in myths and
legends. Water is the substance that, more than any other,
defines and sustains life in our world. It can be made, with
the application of ritual, to take into itself something of
the angelic, to become not merely the water of life but
holy water. Holy water has proved to be a useful weapon
against demonic powers: It is severely toxic to demons and
also to vampires. It can be used to flush out the beginnings
of vampire infection, to save someone who has ingested
vampire blood. (See the Bestiaire Part II, Chapter 4, for more
details.) Faeries, on the other hand, can stand its presence
and its touch but will be made severely weakened and ill if
they can be fooled into drinking it. (Interestingly, werewolves
are not affected by holy water at all, just as they are not at all
negatively affected by other mundane religious objects.)

That actually interesting! Ask Luke about.

Many mundane religions include this notion of
seraphically aligned water, and it is from the mundanes' holy
men and women that the Nephilim acquire the majority of
our holy water. As part of our relationships with mundane
religions, we maintain connections with monastic orders
across the globe. One of these orders' responsibilities is to
bless water and other objects for the Nephilim. The orders
connected to the Nephilim tend to be among the more
secretive monastic orders, often those sworn to silence, and
the relationships are often kept up by Silent Brothers and
Iron Sisters.

How we collect, store, and distribute all this holy water to the
Institutes and to Idris is a fascinating hydrodynamic engineering
problem that will not be gone into in this text. Those who are

interested in more depth are encouraged to visit the Silent City, where the research Brothers there will be more than happy to supply you with the multivolume handwritten tomes they have created specifying the processes, for perusal at your leisure.

No need to be sarcastic, Codex.
I think that's sincere, actually.
Wow.

— ARMOR AND OTHER TOOLS —

Black for hunting through the night
For death and mourning the color's white
Gold for a bride in her wedding gown
And red to call enchantment down.
White silk when our bodies burn,
Blue banners when the lost return.
Flame for the birth of a Nephilim,
And to wash away our sins.
Gray for knowledge best untold,
Bone for those who don't grow old.
Saffron lights the victory march,
Green will mend our broken hearts.
Silver for the demon towers,
And bronze to summon wicked powers.

—Old Nephilim children's rhyme

SHADOWHUNTER GEAR

One's first set of Shadowhunter gear is, for most Shadowhunters, an important moment in their training—the time when they begin to first *look* like other Shadowhunters. When you wear gear, you become part of a tradition joining Shadowhunters across hundreds of years; our gear has remained basically unchanged since modern textile methods came into being.

Battle gear is crafted of a well-processed black leather, created by the Iron Sisters in their Citadel, stronger than any mundane leather and capable of protecting the skin from most demon venoms while still allowing for swift and free movement. Nephilim on regular patrols or similar excursions may choose to wear only the basic gear, but those preparing for battle will often add bracers and greaves, traditionally of electrum (see "Materials" page 23).

Both the gear and accessories such as bracers are typically Marked, both with runes of protection and strength and with more decorative symbols. These might include family crests, Marks commemorating battles, names of angels invoked as protectors, and so on.

The standard Shadowhunter gear involves, for both men and women, simple flat-soled shoes and sturdy, closely fit trousers. For most of Nephilim history gear differed between men and women—men would wear with the above a closely fit waist-length shirt and sometimes a jacket, whereas women would wear a long belted knee-length tunic. This tunic was always a less practical choice, and was worn historically to maintain the standards of modesty and decorum that were required of women as they moved through mundane society. In the past fifty years or so, the use of this tunic has faded in favor of more unified, unisex gear worn by male and female Shadowhunters alike.

THE PROBLEMS OF TRADITIONAL ARMOR

Many new Shadowhunters through the years have arrived at their first day of training proudly clad in their family's ancestral plate armor, as if they were going off to fight the Hundred Years' War. (Obviously this problem was at its worst during the actual Hundred Years' War.) In truth this kind of heavy armor is not very useful to Nephilim; standard fighting gear is preferred, and the specifics of the gear are less important than one's weaponry. The mundane world went through a complicated "arms race" through the Middle Ages regarding armor. Both weapons and armor gradually improved in effectiveness, with new weapons designed to pierce armor, and then new armor designed to withstand those weapons. Armor reached its apex with a somewhat ridiculous full suit of steel intended to stop a blade or an arrow, and became rapidly irrelevant with the advent of artillery and firearms in mundane warfare.

Shadowhunters never participated in this silly exercise. First, Shadowhunters have always, by necessity, prioritized such attributes as freedom of movement, detailed assessment of the environment, and swiftness over raw strength of material, and as a result were rarely tempted by heavier, bulkier armor. Second, the fact is that mundane armor is designed to protect the wearer from the attacks of other mundanes. We, on the other hand, frequently face foes who wield magic, and who might on any given day attack us with fire, with excoriating acid, with bolts of demonic lightning, with venoms and poisons of all kinds. We know of no material—including *adamas*—that can keep a Shadowhunter safe from all of the devices at the disposal of our demon foes. We therefore have always had to learn to avoid harm by our wits and reflexes, since no amount of steel covering our bodies would truly keep us safe.

THE EVERYDAY CARRY

Shadowhunters do not typically travel heavily loaded with equipment. What they take with them on patrols or investigations must not slow them down very much, or compromise their agility. Thus they typically prefer small tools, lightweight and easily kept in a pocket. Most Shadowhunters will find a set of tools that they will take with them everywhere; it is worth some time considering what tools you find useful to keep on hand. Some common tools are here suggested, and described in detail where necessary.

TYPICAL SHADOWHUNTER EQUIPMENT
—Gear
—Primary weapon
—Two seraph blades

SLING? LIKE WITH A ROCK? REALLY?

—Ranged weapon (e.g., crossbow, sling) (Optional)

—Stele *You're kidding. Lame. Okay. Custom lesson from Jace here. Yes, take all that stuff.*

—Witchlight *Actually, carry two witchlights. Some other stuff that I always carry with me on patrol: chalk. A multi-tool with screwdrivers and two knives and a corkscrew and*

—Sensor *all that. A sturdy watch. A strong folding utility knife. A butane lighter. A phone.*

If you are also carrying a backpack, I recommend throwing in nylon rope, a small crowbar, binoculars,

THE SENSOR *a basic first aid kit, a spare stele, two extra seraph blades. Oh, and rubber gloves.*

The Sensor is a common Shadowhunter device for detecting demonic activity. Sensors have varied in design over the years, but today the Sensor is usually a small handheld oblong made of a black metal. It bears some resemblance to a modern cellular phone or other handheld mundane communication device, but where that mundane device would have control buttons and switches labeled in a mundane language, the Sensor is labeled in Marks whose meaning must be learned. The original Sensor was invented in the late 1880s by Henry Branwell and for a time revolutionized the pursuit and capture of demons. *It's a tricorder.* **What? What is** *a*

Every so often you'll be very glad you have them.

Unfortunately, the Sensor is somewhat limited in what it is able to sense. It functions as a frequency detector, tuning in to the vibrations that demons create as they pass through the magical ether. These vibrations vary by demon species and change in intensity based on the intensity of demon activity (number of demons, demonic magic in use, etc.). In theory it is possible to create a "frequency table" matching specific demon species to specific frequencies, and in fact much ink and time was spilled in the years following the invention of the Sensor, creating endless tables for "translating" specific demon signals. In the field Shadowhunters almost never have time to consult a table, and it is usually faster and easier for them to learn from experience to recognize demon types by sight. These tables are now considered mostly a historical curiosity. *But we have wasted your time by telling you about them anyway.*

tricorder? Three . . . cords?

These days Sensors are designed not to be manually tuned (though most can be so tuned if the user demands it) but to scan

31

up and down continuously for all demon activity and offer some educated guesses about the causes of any frequencies that appear. Modern Sensors may have mapping systems, proximity alarms, and other colorful features.

The Sensor often baffles new Shadowhunters, mostly because of its control buttons, which are labeled in angelic runes. This is done to allow the device to be used universally around the world, as the Shadowhunters do not share a single common language other than the language of Raziel and the Gray Book.

SENSORS THROUGH THE YEARS

That title makes me sleepy just looking at it.

I have never in my life been bored enough to actually read this sidebar.

The first Sensor used as its warning mechanism a standard mechanical metronome, which in the proximity of demons would begin to clack rhythmically, its speed increasing as the demon and Sensor grew closer together. This metronome sat atop a large wooden box clasped in copper, the copper having been elaborately inscribed with Marks, and a variety of Marked and un-Marked mechanical works inside did the sensing and ran the metronome. The whole contraption sat atop a heavy cart with four wheels that had to be pushed around, since the metronome had to be kept level with the ground at all times and could easily be disrupted by unexpected movements. Various experiments took place through the early twentieth century to try to make the Sensor self-propelled and able to follow a Shadowhunter, patrol an area independently, and so on. These experiments never resulted in any usable innovation, and more often resulted in a dangerously mobile demon-powered cart that might at any moment charge the nearest Shadowhunter with unknown intent, clacking madly because of its extreme proximity to its own sensing apparatus. This failed branch of Sensor evolution fell away from the tree entirely in the 1960s when modern rune miniaturization magic made it possible to create Sensors that could be carried in a trouser pocket.

The Shadowhunter interested in its history can find older models displayed in libraries and museum collections of older Institutes.

Did you know? *No!* *The Codex has a different definition of "interesting" than me* Interestingly, the standard runic labels on the Sensor were originally intended as a temporary measure. In his classic memoir of 1910, *A Whoops and a Bang: The Shadowhunter of the Modern Age*, Henry Branwell hypothesizes a single Mark that could be used to cause the buttons of a Sensor (or anything else) to appear in the native language of the person holding it. Such a Mark is not known to exist, but Branwell was at that time enthusiastically arguing for the use of warlock magic in collaboration with Nephilim Marks to create new and more complex effects, an unpopular position both then and now (although see the Grimoire, Chapter 6, for a discussion of the history of the Portal). This course of Branwell's experimentation, however, was disrupted when in 1914 he began a long collaboration with the Iron Sisters, the results of which remain secret to this day. The Mark of Translation remains uncreated, and the Sensor remains covered in runes whose meanings must be committed to memory.

SENSOR TECHNICAL SUPPORT
FREQUENTLY ASKED QUESTIONS

The Sensor is a complex tool, and many Shadowhunters struggle with the nuances of its use. Here we attempt to answer those questions that arise most frequently.

Yes, that is what "Frequently Asked Questions" means, thank you.

Can the Sensor be modified to detect werewolves, vampires, and other Downworlders?

It cannot. The Sensor is attuned to the presence of demon energy; while Downworlders all have some demonic magic in them, they are not demons and do have normal human souls. Therefore they will not register on a Sensor.

Can the Sensor be modified to detect only certain kinds of demons?

Yes! This is a lesser-known but useful function of the Sensor that requires no modification. The buttons can be manipulated, using the Marks, to isolate only demons who match a certain set of qualities.

Can the Sensor be modified to detect a specific Greater Demon?

No.

Can the Sensor be modified to detect where I left some object?

No.

When will my Sensor support the Flash rune?

The Flash rune referred to here causes a burst of bright holy light, and rumors have existed for years that the Sensor was going to be modified to be able to successfully hold the Flash rune. Unfortunately, the Flash rune currently causes the Sensor's normal function to slow down and often stop working entirely. As yet, the only Sensors available do not support Flash, and only the Iron Sisters know whether they ever will.

Help, my Sensor's buttons are all labeled in runes.

Those are Marks.

I haven't learned these runes yet!

We might recommend a trick long known to Shadowhunters, involving drawing your own labels on the
Sensor buttons with a felt-tip marker.

My Sensor is vibrating!

That is within the normal bounds of Sensor operation.
When a Sensor is overloaded with the proximity of
demon energies, it will begin to vibrate with intensity.
This was long considered a deficit in the design of
Sensors, but the advent of modern technology has
caused many Shadowhunters, especially those more
familiar with the mundane world, to regard the
vibration as a useful feature.

Unlike the mundane tools that vibrate, the Sensor
can become so overloaded with demon energies
that it can ignite and explode. Therefore, caution
is advised.

**My Sensor has vibrated so much that it has ignited
and exploded.**

You will, unfortunately, need to requisition a new Sensor
from your Institute. Also, there is a tremendous quantity
of demonic energy in your immediate vicinity. You must
make sure to evaluate your immediate circumstances
before trying to examine your Sensor; it is possible that
you are about to be devoured by either a Greater Demon
or a Portal to Hell.

So if you had a human who'd drunk a lot of Greater Demon blood when he
was a baby, would he set off a Sensor?

Who would do such a terrible thing.   Just hypothetically.

If you already know this guy, track him down!   GOD, GET A ROOM, YOU TWO.

Sensors are for demons you don't already know personally!   Good point.

35

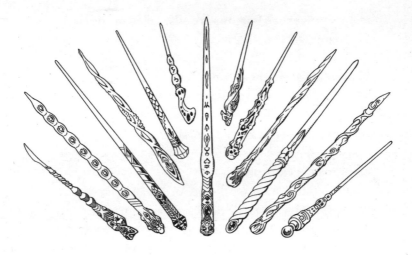

THE STELE

The stele (pronounced in English 'steh·lay) is listed here among the tools of the Shadowhunter but could just as easily be mentioned among weaponry; it is the fundamental tool of the Nephilim, the device by which Marks, our only magic, may be inscribed. An elaborate decorated stele is often the first tool given to a young Shadowhunter at the beginning of her studies.

The stele is a wandlike instrument, made of pure *adamas*. It is inert when not in use but when taken up glows and warms with the magic of the Marks. It is longer than modern writing instruments, usually a foot long or more, and as a result contemporary Shadowhunters will require practice to be able to draw runes with facility when using one.

All steles are functionally identical, but of course there is wide variation in their design. Many have handles inscribed with family crests and the like, some are studded with gems— the only requirement for a working stele is that it include an unbroken rod of *adamas* of at least a certain length. On the other end of the spectrum are the narrow practice steles given to child Nephilim to learn runic manuscription on sheets of parchment.

The first stele is believed to have been a rough oblong of *adamas* used by Jonathan Shadowhunter to inscribe the first Marks on his own skin. The stele designs have become refined over the years. Some scholars see a link between the stele and the Jewish *yad*, the ritual pointer used to avoid physically handling the parchment of the Torah when reading from it, but no direct connection can be made, although it is probable that the earliest Iron Sisters were inspired by such designs. *Represent!*

Demons are not harmed by exposure to a stele, but they will typically recoil from one, as they will recoil from all *adamas*.

WITCHLIGHT STONES

One of the great secrets kept by the Iron Sisters is the precise manner by which *adamas* is extracted and purified from its ore. What we do know, however, is that the presence of *adamas* affects the rock from which it is extracted, and though it is simple rock, it gives off a pure white glow, as though reflecting the light inherent in the *adamas*. These "sister stones" of *adamas* are broken up and polished by Iron Sisters, and Marked to make their glow a property that can be turned on and off at the will of the Shadowhunter holding them. Most rune-stones are basic and interchangeable, and rarely do Shadowhunters get attached to a particular stone over any other. All Shadowhunters carry a witchlight stone, to remind them that light can be found even among the darkest shadows, and also to supply them with actual light when they are themselves literally among dark shadows.

The great advantage of witchlight stones is that their glow never fades or dissipates, for no fuel is being consumed in creating their light. Such a stone can, however, be destroyed by pulverizing it into dust, whereupon the angelic light absorbed into it will dissipate; thus one never finds "witchlight sand" or the like.

The largest single witchlight crystal in the world can be found in the Silent City in the form of the Angelic Colossus, a representation of the Triptych, the familiar motif of Raziel ascending from the water wielding the Mortal Instruments. The crystal stands roughly thirty feet tall, and it guards (and lights) the entrance to the Silent Brothers' living quarters. The Colossus is rarely seen by anyone other than the Silent Brothers, however, and those interested in large installations of witchlight are encouraged to visit the Institute of Cluj, where the renowned Vampire Arch forms the threshold to the Institute. For many years it was thought that humans infected with vampirism were sensitive to natural and holy light and would recoil from it; the Arch was built under the belief that it would protect the Institute from infected humans. We now know this not to be true, but the Arch remains as a symbol of the Cluj Institute's dedication to the Angel.

Or maybe they just like hurting vampires a lot.

Definitely that. Those Cluj guys are crazy.

See this is why you are a useful teacher. I get the inside scoop.

I BELIEVE I MENTIONED SOMETHING ABOUT YOU TWO AND A ROOM A FEW PAGES AGO?

DISCUSSION QUESTIONS AND THINGS TO TRY

1. What's your everyday carry? What might you add to it to cover your new Shadowhunter responsibilities?

   Wallet, watch, phone, stele, pencils, sketchbook, waterproof fine-tip pen for inking, pencil sharpener, witchlight, mint lip balm.

   I HEAR CHAPPED LIPS ARE A LEADING CAUSE OF DEATH IN SHADOWHUNTERS. MY TURN! WALLET, WATCH, PHONE, BASS PICKS, PENS, NOTEBOOK, DICE OF VARIOUS KINDS, LITTLE CLOTH THINGIE TO CLEAN GLASSES WITH—EXCEPT I DON'T WEAR MY GLASSES ANYMORE, HUH. I GUESS I DON'T NEED TO CARRY THE CLOTH AROUND ANYMORE—SUPER-NERDY POCKETKNIFE. Aaaand lip balm.

   Don't even lie. You reek of strawberry right now.

2. What weapon might you like to specialize in? What about it draws your attention?

   Alas! MY SECRET SHAME REVEALED!

   Go ahead, say "rapier wit." I know you want to.

   RAPIER WIT FINE YES THAT IS WHAT I WAS GOING TO SAY BECAUSE I AM SO FUNNY. Poor Simon.

   Anyway, I have no idea of an answer to this question, and frankly, Codex, this kind of question is the least of my problems right now. I would like to specialize in not being nearly killed yet again.

   I WOULD LIKE TO SPECIALIZE IN BEING AN IMMORTAL INVULNERABLE KILLING MACHINE WHO CRAVES THE BLOOD OF THE LIVING.

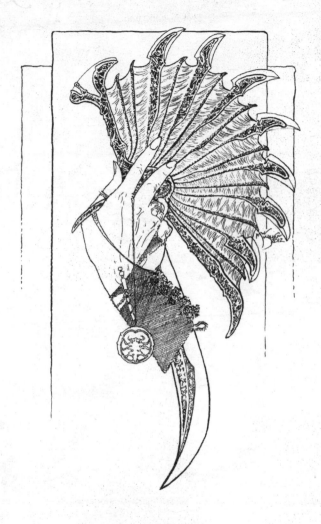

CHAPTER TWO

THE ARTS

COMBAT TRAINING

Once you have familiarized yourself with the tools of the Shadow-hunter, you must begin to learn the Shadowhunter's arts: combat, stealth, agility, endurance.

It surprises most new Shadowhunters to learn that there is no single set of skills that define us as warriors. We are found all over the globe, just as demons are found all over the globe. As such, there are as many varieties of Shadowhunter combat style as there are varieties in the mundane world. Typically you will undergo training in several different fighting styles, often selected from across human culture, and you will naturally find the styles that most appeal to you and with which you are most effective. You will be likely to study Western combat style, Eastern martial arts, and often stylized combat sports such as fencing or judo. There is a vast common ground of physical ability and prowess underlying almost all of these styles, and so as a new Shadowhunter you should expect to spend plenty of time on basic training to enhance your strength, speed, flexibility, and so on, before you have so much as picked up a weapon.

Marks may be used to enhance physical traits, but this is not typically done during training, and Marks cannot substitute for the muscle memory that the body learns through repetition and practice.

Our emphasis on learning from a wide range of sources is supported by a tradition whereby when Shadowhunters advance to majority at eighteen years old, they often travel and spend time in residence at an Institute well away from their home. There is great variation in local Shadowhunter cultures, both in philosophy and in specific techniques. Shadowhunters who have grown up in Idris are especially encouraged to travel, since the protected environment of Alicante may not prepare them for the harsh realities of the mundane world.

The newly made Shadowhunter, too, should seek to travel during her training, if at all possible. There is no obvious occasion to mark as there is with born Shadowhunters becoming adults, so talk with your Institute head or local Enclave about scheduling.

A PHILOSOPHY OF WAR

The first Shadowhunters, including Jonathan himself, dreamed of a world where someday their people would not need to be warriors. David the Silent, especially, loathed fighting and violence, and he wrote eloquently of the Nephilim's main mission to "discover Peace upon all the World." It's believed that the Silent Brothers were, in fact, founded with the primary mission of reversing the great evil acts of Sammael and Lilith, and closing our dimension again to demons. This philosophy continued to guide the Silent Brothers for hundreds of years. Brother Christopher de Sevilla could still write, in 1504, that the Nephilim's job was to "obsolete ourselves" by "driving the horde back and sealing the doors behind them."

The fact, however, is that a thousand years of work and research has brought us no closer to understanding how Sammael and Lilith accomplished their great Incursion, much less to discovering how it can be reversed. The thread of hope that the endless demonic horde could be turned back has frayed and is now so thin in Shadowhunter culture as to have nearly disappeared. Most believe today that if the

RECOMMENDED WEEKEND TRAINING
SCHEDULE FOR: CLARY FAIRCHILD

Just a proposed regimen for your weekend to keep you in good shape for next week. (Get ready for stick fighting!!!)

8-9 a.m.: Wake up. Eat breakfast (lean protein, light carb, NO CAFFEINE).

9-9:30 a.m.: Calisthenics @ home

9:30-10 a.m.: Yoga @ home

10 a.m.-12 p.m.: Language study (Greek, Latin)

12 p.m.-1 p.m.: Lunch

1 p.m.-3 p.m.: Intense cardio (running, probably)

3 p.m.-4 p.m.: Study demon weaknesses and appearances in textbook Demons, Demons, Demons.

4 p.m.-6 p.m.: Practice kata (your choice of martial arts school)

6 p.m.-7 p.m.: Dinner

7 p.m.-11 p.m.: Study (suggestions: history of faerie abductions, poisons and their antidotes, werewolf clan markings)

11 p.m.-12 a.m.: Free time!

12 a.m.: Sleep

WEEKEND TRAINING SCHEDULE FOR: ME

8 a.m.: Woke up.

9 a.m.: Woke up again; got up this time. Breakfast (bagel, scallion cream cheese, tomato, coffee w/milk). Calisthenics (walked briskly to deli and back).

10 a.m.–10:15 a.m.: Yoga. Very centering.

10:15 a.m.–11 a.m.: Language study (Looked through Latin textbook, watched last forty-five minutes of Gladiator. Fight scenes very inspiring. Took some notes.)

11 a.m.–12 p.m.: Took sketchbook to Prospect Park lawn. Simon brought lunch (noodles I like from place right by his house). Drew kids playing cricket on lawn. Studied cricket technique for potential application in combat. Drew gladiators playing cricket. Synthesis.

12 p.m.–1 p.m.: Lab: Interviewed vampire re: vampire history and culture, vampire combat techniques, etc. Very edifying.

1 p.m.–2 p.m.: Urban exploration (Took subway into Manhattan.)

2 p.m.–4 p.m.: Literary research (Visited comic book store, bought several volumes of long illustrated study of medieval combat in Japan.)

4 p.m.: Healthy midafternoon snack (smoothie)

4 p.m.–7 p.m.: Watched research film in multiplex.

7 p.m.–9 p.m.: Dinner, tiny Korean place on Thirteenth, soup. (Soup is healthy! Critiqued fight techniques seen in movie—very unrealistic.

9 p.m.–10 p.m.: Orienteering (subway home)

10 p.m.–12 a.m.: Talked on phone with primary Shadowhunter trainer, updated him on status. Planned training regimen for following day. Exchanged positive affirmations.

12 a.m.–2 a.m.: Read illustrated study of medieval Japanese combat. Cultural exchange with vampire re: illustrated study, vampire's current boredom. Fell asleep, practiced difficult "balance phone on face" technique for indefinite period of time before it fell onto the floor and woke me up.

2 a.m.: A refreshing, well-earned sleep.

demonic tide is to be turned, it will be Heaven's doing, not ours. Our role is to stand behind the open gates and turn them back one by one. And so we fight.

SUBJECTS OF NEPHILIM STUDY

This Codex intends to provide you, the newly minted Shadowhunter, with the basic knowledge you will need to survive and understand your new world and your new people. We cannot possibly provide a full course of training in these pages, and mere written instruction, without the help of a skilled instructor who could not only demonstrate techniques but evaluate your abilities, would be a disservice to the training you deserve.

Instead we here provide the outlines of a general course of Shadowhunter training, along with touchstone goals for beginners, for more intermediate students, and for those seeking true expertise. It can be difficult for new Shadowhunters to understand their own training progress. We do not have ranks, promotions, "belts," levels, merit badges, or anything of the kind. Most of your fellow Nephilim have lived in our warrior culture their whole lives, and the qualities of the well-tempered Shadowhunter have been part of their upbringing. These suggestions therefore should not be taken as rigid requirements but rather as guidelines that may help you understand your progress as you train.

One final note for the especially ambitious Shadowhunter: No one can be an expert at all things. As you train, one of your goals will be to find those elements of Shadowhunter life that you wish to pursue more closely, because of either your natural aptitude in them or your interest in deeper study. All Shadowhunters should first aim to achieve at least beginner competence in all of these categories before seeking more advanced study.

MONOMACHIA (HAND-TO-HAND COMBAT)

Beginner: Basic competence ("black belt" equivalent) in at least one Eastern martial art or Western fighting tradition. Ability to reliably fend off two to three simultaneous attackers.

Intermediate: Competence in three to five mundane fighting traditions. Ability to reliably fend off five to eight simultaneous attackers.

Expert: Competence in more than ten mundane fighting traditions. Ability to reliably fend off an arbitrarily large army of demons.

RANGED-MISSILE COMBAT

Beginner: Competence with standard set of ranged weapons—longbow, crossbow, sling, thrown daggers, javelins, big heavy rocks.

Intermediate: Competence with above while blindfolded.

Expert: Competence with above while blindfolded and lying down.

STEALTH

Beginner: Ability to pass undetected through darkened alley or room.

Intermediate: Ability to pass undetected through darkened alley or room filled with small breakable objects precariously balanced atop other breakable objects.

Expert: Ability to pass undetected through open terrain in broad daylight.

BLENDING AND CONCEALMENT

Beginner: Ability to pass as a mundane in a typical public scenario ("driving a car," "shopping for food," etc.). Please see *Mundanes Do the Darndest Things*, 1988 edition, in your local Institute library, for suggestions.

Intermediate: Ability to pass as a mundane at a small cocktail party or reception.

Expert: Ability to pass as a mundane in the midst of a mundane demonic cult performing a human sacrifice.

AGILITY AND GRACE

Beginner: Basic competence at acrobatics, tumble, trapeze, gymnastics, etc.

Intermediate: Competence at above skills while wearing thirty kilograms of gear and several heavy weapons.

Expert: Competence at above skills while wearing thirty kilograms of gear, several heavy weapons, a blindfold, and iron manacles.

ENDURANCE

Beginner: Competence at improvised survival skills in typical harsh environments (e.g., high desert, drifting ice floe).

Intermediate: Competence with above in extreme environments (e.g., inside a building that is on fire, free-falling from an airplane at high cruising altitude, in outer space, in Hell).

Expert: Ability to withstand torture by Greater Demon while in above harsh or extreme environments.

TRACKING

Beginner: Knowledge of tracking runes; ability to identify telltale signs of animal or demon activity and maintain pursuit.

Intermediate: Ability to maintain pursuit while also evading similar pursuit by different animal or demon.

Expert: Ability to maintain pursuit while in harsh or extreme environments (see Endurance, above).

ORIENTEERING

Beginner: Intuitive grasp of altitude, cardinal direction, time of day, weather conditions, etc.

Intermediate: Ability to find way to known safe location when dropped into arbitrary environment.

Expert: Ability to find way to known safe location when dropped into extreme or harsh environment (see above).

OBSERVATION AND DEDUCTION

Beginner: Basic forensics knowledge; ability to "read" the scene of a crime and reconstruct events there with high probability of accuracy.

Intermediate: Ability to reliably identify revealing details of a scene that mundane law enforcement would typically overlook.

Expert: As above, but while blindfolded.

LANGUAGES

Beginner: Knowledge of several mundane languages, preferably a mixture of living languages spoken near your geographical base and ancient languages used in religious writings (e.g., Sanskrit, Hebrew, ancient Greek, Sumerian).

Intermediate: Knowledge of the above and at least two demonic languages.

Expert: Knowledge of the above, at least four demonic languages, and ability to intuit basic meanings from written or spoken language never encountered before.

DIPLOMACY

Beginner: Ability to talk your way out of being eaten by a demon or killed by angry Downworlder horde.

A Quick Evaluation of Me and 48 My Friends By the Above Scale:

Alec: Intermediate, Expert, Intermediate, Intermediate, Expert, Intermediate, Intermediate, Beginner, Intermediate, Beginner, Intermediate.

Isabelle: Expert, Intermediate, Beginner, Beginner, Expert, Expert, Intermediate, Intermediate, Intermediate, Intermediate, Beginner.

Me: Beginner, Beginner, Beginner, Expert (I am very good at blending in with the mundane world!), Serious Beginner, Beginner,

Intermediate: Ability to talk your way out of being eaten by Greater Demon or killed by angry Downworlder political leadership. *Intermediate, Intermediate, Beginner, Expert (I am counting runes here, okay!),*

Expert: Ability to talk your way out of being eaten by Greater Demon or killed by angry Downworlders that letting you go was their idea.

Expert (at least compared to the rest of this group).

WHY DON'T NEPHILIM USE FIREARMS?

Guns are rarely used by Shadowhunters because, for our purposes, they normally do not work correctly. Etching Marks into the metal of a gun or bullet prevents gunpowder from successfully igniting. Considerable research has been done into this problem, with little success. The prevailing theories today prefer an alchemical explanation, contrasting the heavenly source of our Marks with the demonically allied brimstone and saltpeter that make up classic gunpowder, but this explanation does not, unfortunately, hold much weight. Demonic runes have the same impeding effect on guns as our own Marks, and the problem remains even with the use of modern propellants, which do not contain these supposedly "demonic" materials. This remains one of the great unexplained mysteries of runic magic, and researchers continue to pursue explanations and solutions to this day.

Me: Expert, Intermediate, Expert, Expert, Expert, Expert, Expert, Expert, Expert, Beginner.

Me: Vampire, Vampire, Vampire, Vampire, Vampire, Vampire, Vampire, Vampire, Vampire, Vampire, Vampire.

49

Guns can, of course, be successfully used to harm vampires and (with silver bullets) werewolves, but shots must be made with pinpoint accuracy. The risk of collateral damage and the difficulty of scoring a direct hit, combined with the understanding that Shadowhunter weapons will be overwhelmingly used to fight demons rather than Downworlders, has led to a general rejection of firearms as part of the Shadowhunter arsenal.

Finally, it is to the advantage of the Nephilim to have our weapons forged and built by the Iron Sisters as much as possible. Modern gunsmithing involves elaborate industrial machining that our traditional weapons don't require, and if we were to have the Iron Sisters forge firearms, that would drastically change the Iron Sisters' need for resources and equipment.

—— THE TRADITION OF THE ——
PARABATAI

> *Whither thou goest, I will go;*
> *Where thou diest, will I die, and there will I be buried:*
> *The Angel do so to me, and more also,*
> *If aught but death part thee and me.*
> —The Oath of the Parabatai

The tradition of the *parabatai* goes back to the beginnings of the Shadowhunters; the first *parabatai* were Jonathan Shadowhunter himself and his companion, David. They in turn were inspired by their coincident namesakes, from the biblical tale of Jonathan and David:

"And it came to pass ... that the soul of Jonathan was knit with the soul of David, and Jonathan loved him as his own soul... Then Jonathan and David made a covenant, because he loved him as his own soul."
—1 Samuel 18:1–3

Out of that tradition Jonathan Shadowhunter created the *parabatai*, and codified the ceremony into Law.

David the Silent was not at first a Silent Brother (See Excerpts from *A History of the Nephilim*, Appendix A, for more details). At first there were no Silent Brothers; earliest Nephilim hoped that their more difficult and mystical roles could be integrated into their warrior selves. Only as time passed did it become clear that the work of David would take him ever toward the angelic and farther and farther from his physical form. David and his followers set down their weapons, exchanging them for a life of mystical contemplation and the pursuit of wisdom.

Before this time, however, Jonathan and David fought side by side as the first *parabatai*. Tradition tells us that the ritual they performed, where they took of each other's blood and spoke the words of the oath and inscribed the runes of binding upon each other, was the second-to-last time that David was known to shed human tears. The last time was the moment when the *parabatai* bond was broken, as David took the Marks that made him the first Silent Brother. This is a bromance of very heavy-duty proportions. You have no ide

Today *parabatai* must be bonded in childhood; that is, before either has turned eighteen years old. They are not merely warriors who fight together; the oaths that newly made *parabatai* take in front of the Council include vows to lay down one's life for the other, to travel where the other travels, and indeed, to be buried in the same place. The Marks of *parabatai* are then put upon them, which enable them to draw on each other's strength in battle. They are able to sense each other's life force; Shadowhunters who have lost their *parabatai* describe being able to feel the life leave their partner. In addition, Marks made by one *parabatai* upon another are stronger than other Marks, and there are Marks that only *parabatai* can use, because they draw on the partners' doubled strength.

The only bond forbidden to the *parabatai* is the romantic bond. These bonded pairs must maintain the dignity of their warrior bond and must not allow it to transform into the earthly love we call Eros. The late Middle Ages were littered with Shadowhunter-troubadours' songs of the forbidden love of *parabatai* pairs and the tragedies that befell them. The warnings are not merely of heartache and betrayal but of magical disaster, impossible to prevent, when *parabatai* become romantically linked.

Like the marriage bond, the *parabatai* bond is broken, normally, only by the death of one of the members of the partnership. The binding can also be cut in the rare occurrence that one of the partners becomes a Downworlder or a mundane. Per above, the bond dissolves naturally if one of the partners becomes a Silent Brother or Iron Sister: The Marks of transformation that new oblates take are among the most powerful that exist and overwhelm and dissolve the *parabatai* Marks of binding just as they overwhelm and dissolve more ordinary warrior's Marks.

A Shadowhunter may choose only one *parabatai* in his lifetime and cannot perform the ritual more than once. Most Shadowhunters never have any *parabatai* at all; if you, newmade Nephilim, find yourself with one, consider it a great blessing.

— HOW TO REPORT A DEMON —

- If you are not sure you can handle the demon yourself, do not engage it in battle or even in conversation.
- Remember such things as the number of demons, exact location, their current activity.
- If you know the demon's species (or name, in the case of a Greater Demon), report it; if you *don't* know the demon's species, remember possible identifying features such as:
  - » Skin color (gray, green, purple-black, iridescent) and texture (scales, hide, bony spikes, fur)
  - » Presence of slime, color of slime
  - » Number of eyes, mouths, noses, arms, legs, heads
  - » Size (compare to other things of similar size rather than trying to estimate actual measurement—e.g., "about as big as a grizzly bear")
  - » Noises (languages spoken, high-pitched voice versus low-pitched voice)

>> Gender markings (very rare except with Greater Demons)

>> Noticeable strengths (eats rocks or metal, ability to cling to walls and ceilings, etc.) and weaknesses (sensitive to being harmed by frostbite, compulsive need to count individual grains of spilled rice, overweening pride)

>> Obvious sources of physical danger: fangs, talons, claws, spines, constricting body, acid blood, prehensile tongue, etc.

· Bring your thorough report to your local Institute, which will evaluate the threat and decide on next steps. You can assist by searching for the demon you've seen in *Deutsch's Demonfinder*, the definitive resource cataloguing demons based on their physical characteristics. (It is, however, quite possible that the Institute already knows of the demon you're reporting, in which case the investigation may be quite short.)

CHAPTER THREE

Bestiaire Part I:
DEMONOLOGIE

Demons, the great trespassers into our universe, are the reason why the Nephilim exist. They are the shadows that we hunt. Though our work managing and maintaining the careful balance among Downworlders and mundanes often feels like the majority of our responsibility, it is secondary. It is the work we do when we are not fighting demons. The primary task of the Shadowhunter, the mission granted us by Raziel, is to eliminate the demon scourge by returning the demons, once and for all, to the Void from whence they came.

——— WHAT ARE DEMONS? ———

The very word "demon" is problematic. Its etymology in English has nothing to do with evil spirits at all; it is used to describe these creatures only because of translation confusions in the early days of Christianity, many years before the Nephilim began. We use the word "demons" to describe the creatures we fight because Jonathan Shadowhunter used the word, based on his own religious history. Most human belief systems have some concept that represents what we call demons: Persian daevas, Hindu asuras, Japanese oni. To keep terminology uncomplicated, we refer to them as demons, as do most Nephilim.

Demons are not living beings in the sense that we usually understand. They are alien to our universe and are not sustained by the same kind of forces that sustain us. Demons do not have souls; instead, they are powered by a roiling demon energy, a vitalizing spark that maintains their form in our dimension. When demons die, this energy is separated from its physical body, and that body will be yanked quickly back into its home dimension. To human eyes, this disappearance can take many forms, depending on the species of demon. Some explode into dust, some fade from view, some crumple into themselves. In all cases, however, no remnant of the demon's physical self remains in our world. (Warlock rituals exist that can "preserve" demonic physicality in our world, allowing one to keep, say, a vial of demon blood without its vanishing when its demon source is dispatched.)

WHAT DO DEMONS WANT WITH OUR WORLD? WHY DO THEY COME HERE?

We do not really know. Nephilim folklore says that demons are originally *from* our world, before they were banished (see Excerpts from *A History of the Nephilim*, Appendix A), so perhaps they are seeking to take it back for themselves. On the other hand, our stories also tell us that the demons were destructive and wicked from the beginning—that is why they were banished. So they may instead represent the spirit of evil in our world, in some fashion.

At an individual level, demons seem to come to our world in order to wreak havoc. Sometimes they come in search of power— power over other creatures, more powerful magic, and the like— but that power seems to have no ultimate purpose beyond its own existence, other than to wreak more havoc upon our world.

Many have argued for more philosophical origins of the demons' hate for our world—that they hate our ability to create, for instance, which they lack. This argument is often used to explain why demons create warlocks: It is the only act of creation of which they are capable, and even that they must accomplish by stealing our own act of creation from us.

But we must, for now, throw up our hands and admit that it remains a mystery why demons come to our world. All we can say for sure is that they are here to do us violence, and that they have no interest in truces or treaties.

WHAT DO DEMONS "REALLY" LOOK LIKE? DO THEY LOOK LIKE UGLY MONSTERS EVEN WHEN IN THEIR OWN DIMENSION?

The relationship of demons' bodies in our world to their "reality" in their own is a secret we may never discover. We believe that demons have no choice about the physical form they take in our world, but other than that, their true form is a mystery. We do not know if terms like "appearance" even apply in the Void from whence they come. One popular theory holds that when a demon travels to a dimension, a body is created for that demon that can survive in that dimension, and that this is the reason that demons are the only creatures that can move freely between worlds. This is mere conjecture, of course.

HOW DO I RECOGNIZE A DEMON IN THE WILD?

Recognizing demons, unless they are shapeshifters, is normally not difficult. Demons always take on monstrous forms in our world, and can usually be discerned by the uncanny, nauseating feeling that billows around them like a dark aura. In the rare cases of uncertainty, positive identification can be made via the demon's violent reaction to holy items and places or via a Sensor's violent reaction to the demon.

In addition to their general hideousness, demons often carry with them a scent of death that can be very strong. Shadowhunters asked to describe it usually reach for terms like "rotting," "spoiled," "brimstone," "burning hair," and the like. The effect can be debilitating to the unprepared Shadowhunter.

> I AM ACTUALLY FEELING KIND OF BAD FOR DEMONS HERE.
>
> Is THAT WRONG? *Yes.*

WHAT IS THAT DISGUSTING BLACK LIQUID THAT APPEARS WHEN YOU CUT THEM?

Like other living creatures, demons' bodies are kept fresh by a vital fluid, but this is not the usual red blood of our world. Instead, they contain a supernatural ichor. The term "ichor" refers originally to the golden blood of angels, and comes from the ancient Greek word for the blood of their gods. Demon blood is also ichor, but as it is infused with demon energies, it is black and viscous, thinner than blood but totally opaque. Ichor is not dangerous to touch, but it is somewhat toxic to humans if it gets into the blood via a wound or other means. It is unlikely to harm any Shadowhunter who has the usual range of protective Marks, but care should be taken.

CAN DEMONS SPEAK HUMAN LANGUAGES?

Most common demons cannot speak human languages. A good number of species are, however, able to parrot human speech that they have heard. This is often a sign that a demon has been summoned rather than coming to our world on its own; the demon will be heard to repeat, often obsessively, words and phrases spoken to it by the summoner.

There are a number of demon languages—possibly an infinite number of them—but a number that we have identified and that warlocks and, more rarely, Shadowhunters interested in demon research may learn. The two most common are known to demon philologists as Cthonic and Purgatic. It is worthwhile to at least be able to recognize these two languages in their written and spoken forms, and perhaps to memorize a few frequently used phrases, such as "Hello," "Good-bye," "I am a Nephilim," "In the name of Raziel I abjure thee," "Begone, fiend," and so on.

DO DEMONS POSSESS PEOPLE?

Despite the mundane obsession with demons taking possession of their bodies, actual demon possession is very rare and requires a very powerful Greater Demon. This is lucky, because it is one of the most powerful magics that demons possess. Usually the only way the connection between the possessor and the possessed can be broken is by killing the demon, which more often than not kills the hapless mundane victim as well. If you encounter a possession, *do not* try to handle the situation on your own. Do not try to negotiate with the possessed as if they are political hostages. The possessed are not merely corrupted by demonic influence but are fully controlled. They become like passengers in their own bodies, able to experience everything that the demon is doing but unable to exert any will to act independently at all. (Mercifully, the possessed usually retain no memories of their actions while inhabited.) You may restrain the victim, preferably with help from other Shadowhunters, and then you should contact the Silent Brothers and allow them to remove the subject to the Silent City, where they will perform magics that you are better off not witnessing.

WHY ARE DEMONS SO EAGER TO DESTROY US?

It's believed that demons have an intrinsic hatred of us as a result of their envy of the life of our dimension. Theirs, as far as we can tell, is a dead dimension, a dimension devoid of life, and they desire to consume us and our world to take that which they themselves do not (or, perhaps, no longer) have. Demons are able to sense the presence of life nearby; in fact, they will often use this sense to track down their prey.

DID YOU KNOW?

One of the great unsung heroes of the Nephilim is Gregory Hans, a seventeenth-century Silent Brother who discovered the correct combination of Marks to both enhance a Nephilim's senses and exclude the smell of demons from that enhancement. Generations of Shadowhunters thank him. (Note that under standard demonic glamour, those who are susceptible cannot smell a demon any more than they can hear or see one. All the senses, thankfully, are negated.)

— HOW DO WE KILL THEM? —

The most important weakness of demons is, of course, their vulnerability to angelic power and heavenly fire. Like the Downworlders they brought into being, they cannot easily be harmed by normal earthly weapons, or at least not permanently harmed. For this reason you will find even the most basic Shadowhunter weapons to be Marked to strengthen them against demons, and you will find the seraph blade (see Treasury, Chapter 1) to be the most important of your tools in combat.

In addition to being repelled by direct seraphic energy, most demons can be warded off with holy symbols of all kinds. Very powerful demons, however, such as Greater Demons, may be caused only discomfort by the presence of holy symbols, rather than actual harm, so a Shadowhunter should not depend exclusively on these symbols to protect themselves.

Like vampires, demons cannot stand the direct force of sunlight upon their bodies. Note that—just as in the case of vampires—this does not mean that demons are not active during daylight hours. They can stand our artificial lights with no ill effects. And unlike vampires, who often attempt to live undetected among mundanes, demons have no need to pretend to tolerate sunlight. It is possible to destroy a demon with light, but the Shadowhunter will need to somehow entrap the demon in a situation where sunlight cannot be escaped, which can be difficult. A seraph blade to the throat or heart is usually a more reliable attack.

Finally, one great advantage that we have in our fight against demons is that they are unable to perceive the difference between mundanes and Shadowhunters, and unable to sense the working of angelic magic. This enables us to hide from them using glamours until such time as we are ready to fight them. Demons can, however, detect the presence of other demons and Downworlders.

This section summarized for your convenience:
We don't know a thing about either of these.

THE VOID AND THE DEMON CITY OF PANDEMONIUM

Well, that is a time saver, thanks.

We know little about the Void, the home of demonkind. Many names have been used in literature to refer to the home of the demons—all mundane religious terms for Hell, and other abstract terms such as "Chaos" and "Abyss," for example—but in modern times we have settled on "Void" as both descriptive and ecumenical, and, oddly enough, the Greater Demons who have manifested in our world in modern times have also used the term.

The geography of the Void remains a mystery to us. It often appears that demons have no real homes and are present everywhere at all times. One can, for instance, summon any demon for whom a summoning ritual is known, and all of these demons will appear reliably and in roughly the same amount of time, whatever kind of demon and wherever the summoner may be. On the other hand, certain species of demons tend to "naturally" occur in certain parts of our world—the Rakshasas of the Indian subcontinent, for example, or the Gorgons of Greece. Plenty of theories have been advanced as to why this might be, but the fact is that we do not understand why certain demons have an affinity for certain locations. The fact that some demons do have an affinity for a location is to our advantage, though. Those Shadowhunters posted in certain places will become experts in fighting particular kinds of demons and for the most part will not have to know everything about all demons but will be able to locally specialize.

One may generally assume that the number of different demons in the Void is, for all intents and purposes, infinite. At the very least, it's believed that there are hundreds upon hundreds of millions of different types, and while Shadowhunters have fought demons for the entirety of our thousand-year history, it's unlikely that we've encountered more than the tiniest percentage of them. It's speculated that there are many demons who are incapable of manifesting themselves materially in our world at all.

A constant in our communication with those demons who can speak human language is their references to the city of Pandemonium, the supposed great nexus of demons at the center of the Void, if a void can be said to have a center. No human has, of course, ever visited that city and returned to tell the tale, so it is impossible to make any definite statements about it and what it is like, or even to say whether it can be described as a physical entity in the manner of our cities at all. About the only thing we can say about Pandemonium definitely is that it is very, very large— staggeringly larger than any of our human cities, and possibly larger and more populous than Earth. Research on Pandemonium has been limited, largely because most Nephilim consider that there are enough demons present in our world without going to find still more of them.

DEMONS VERSUS GREATER DEMONS

We do not know if there are actually "Greater Demons."

There are specific demons that we refer to as Greater Demons, and they have some aspects in common: human-scale intelligence, personalities, names, and an inability to be permanently destroyed by us with any weapon available. We know this because of a long recorded history of Greater Demons who have been "killed," only to return later, intact and unharmed. Void Theory tells us that the destruction of the Greater Demon's physical body sends the Greater Demon snapping back to the spaces in the Void, where its ethereal body exists. There the Greater Demon must spend time carefully accruing power in order to rebuild its physical form.

But it's important also to remember that this is mostly speculation. It may be the case, for instance, that no demons, Greater or otherwise, can be permanently killed by us, but since we can't discern individuals among the demons that have subhuman intelligence, we cannot tell if a demon we believe we have killed actually returns later. Attempts have been made at various points in history to

65

"tag" individual demons for tracking, usually with terrible results. Killing demons is difficult enough; catching a small number alive in order to tag and track them has proven impossible.

It is possible, therefore, that "Greater Demon" simply means "any demon with humanlike intelligence," rather than the term indicating some firmer distinction between Greater Demons and regular demons. More research will be needed to discover the truth; luckily, the endless torrent of hideous un-life from beyond the Void shows no sign of slowing, and research material will likely never be in short supply.

—— DEMONS, DEMONS, DEMONS ——
Now with additional demons!

I. SOME GREATER DEMONS

LILITH

Unlike her dark consort, Sammael, Lilith is still alive and has been known to appear on Earth. Pray that you never meet her.

Lilith is known by many names, even when considering only the Jewish tradition from which most of her folklore is sourced. This does not count the many other entities in other mythological traditions that are similar in form or function and may or may not be the same demon. Lilith's other names in Jewish folklore include: Satrina, Abito, Amizo, Izorpo, Kokos, Odam, Ita, Podo, Eilo, Patrota, Abeko, Kea, Kali, Batna, Talto, and Partash.

Jewish tradition says that for her disobedience she was punished by being made unable to bear children. Many versions of the tale paint an even more brutal picture in which Lilith actually *is* capable of birthing infants, but all of them die upon birth. As such she is associated with the harming and weakening of human babies, and much of our knowledge of Lilith comes from Jewish mystical tradition designed to protect newborns from Lilith's influence, with amulets and incantations.

SAMMAEL

Apart from his foundational role in the Incursion, not much is known about Sammael. He is thought to have been the great Serpent by which humanity was tempted and fell from grace. But his physical shape is a mystery, for Sammael has not been seen on Earth in many hundreds of years.

Traditional tales state that for his crime of softening the veils between the human world and the Void, he was hunted and murdered by the archangel Michael, commander of the armies of Heaven. This story comes to us through mundane religious tradition, but is often repeated and is clearly believed by the demons of Pandemonium themselves. Since Sammael has not been seen in our world for so long a time, no rituals survive to summon him.

ABBADON

The Demon of the Abyss. His are the empty places between the worlds. His is the wind and the howling darkness. He is a nine-foot-tall rotting human skeleton.

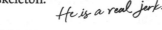
He is a real jerk.

AZAZEL

Lieutenant of Hell and Forger of Weapons. Like most of the greatest of Greater Demons, he was an angel at one time. He is said to have taught humanity how to make weapons in the times before history, where previously weapons making had been knowledge held only by angels. This great transgression caused him to fall and become a demon. The irony of a demon being responsible for giving humanity the knowledge necessary to fight against demons is not lost on the Nephilim; we assume that it is not lost on Azazel himself either. As the Book of Enoch has it, "And the whole earth has been corrupted by the works that were taught by Azazel. To him ascribe all sin."

HUNGER

The demon known as Hunger is an obese devil-like humanoid figure covered in hard, bony scales and a variety of chomping fang-lined mouths all over his body. Hunger is made to devour everything he encounters, usually in as messy and grotesque a fashion as possible.

MARBAS

A blue demon, half again the size of a man, covered in overlapping blue scales, with a long yellowish tail with a stinger on the end. Scarlet eyes, lizard's features, and a flat snakelike snout.

MRS. DARK

A large creature of hard, stonelike skin, apparently female (although what gender means in the realm of demons is unclear). She is horned, with twisted limbs and clawed hands. She can also be identified by her glowing yellow eyes and her triple row of mouths lined with greenish fangs. She is of the Eidolon (see separate entry on page 70).

II. SOME COMMON DEMONS

BEHEMOTH

The Behemoth is a formless monstrosity of a demon. It is roughly oblong and could be described as sluglike in its movements, but with less coherence of shape. It is large, much larger than a human, and slimy. Double rows of teeth line the length of its body. The Behemoth devours everything in its path, including people.

DRAGON

Dragon demons are the closest thing in the modern world to the ancient myths of dragons. They are large, flying, fire-breathing lizards, and are quite intelligent. They come in a variety of shapes and colors. They are formidable foes; luckily, Shadowhunters are likely to never encounter them, since they are almost extinct. They are not to be confused with Vetis demons, which are like dragons but are not Dragons.

DREVAK

Shadowhunters know well the appearance of Drevaks, weak demons in frequent use by Greater Demons or evil warlocks as spies or messengers. They are smooth, white, and larval, resembling a giant version of a mundane grub or maggot. They are blind and do their tracking by scent.

    Their shapelessness and lack of intelligence does not mean they are not dangerous; instead of teeth their mouths contain

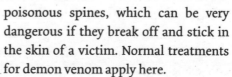

poisonous spines, which can be very dangerous if they break off and stick in the skin of a victim. Normal treatments for demon venom apply here.

DU'SIEN

The Du'sien is one of the lesser-known shape-shifting, or Eidolon, demon species (see below). Its true appearance is abstract, like an irregular blob of greenish-gray jelly with a small glowing black core. They cannot mimic other creatures with the detail that many Eidolon can, and their command of human language is weak. They are thus often found disguised as "generic humans," members of a crowd, rather than impersonating specific individuals.

EIDOLON

"Eidolon" is not the name for a specific species of demon. Rather, it is a comprehensive term for a variety of shape-shifting demon species. Shape-shifting demons come in many different original shapes, and many different sizes and strengths. Since there are dozens of these species, Shadowhunters typically use the term "Eidolon" to refer to shape-shifting demons in general. It is, in other words, usually more useful to note a demon's shape-shifting ability than the minor details of their original form.

Eidolon demons make up the majority of demon parents of warlocks, for obvious reasons. (See the "Warlocks" section of Part II of this Bestiaire for an explanation if the reasons are not obvious to you.)

In addition to the danger posed by their nearly perfect ability to camouflage themselves, Eidolon also have a marked advantage over other demon species: When shifted into the form of a human, they are somewhat protected from the destructive light of the sun. A shifted Eidolon demon still cannot stand in direct sunlight but can endure the diffused light coming through heavy clouds, fog, rain, and so on, with only minor discomfort.

FACEMELTER

Self-explanatory.

HELLHOUND

A demonic corruption of the dog, just as many demons are corruptions of the forms of men and women. Typically hellhounds appear as vicious canines much larger than any mundane dog, with red eyes, coarse black wirelike fur, and a murderous temperament. They have a similar intelligence to mundane dogs and are used by demons for similar purposes—tracking and hunting. (Obviously there are many uses for mundane dogs, such as herding and companionship, that hellhounds are never used for, since demons are incapable of concepts such as companionship.) Like with dogs, hellhounds' jaws are their most dangerous weapons, but unlike with dogs, their tails end in a set of spiked nail-like protrusions, similar to a mace.

HYDRA

A medium-size multiheaded demon, vicious but not intelligent. Known for its multiple heads, at least three but often many more. The Hydra can be distinguished from other multiheaded demons by its animalistic intelligence level, the presence of heads on stalks, and its blindness—the Hydra cannot see normally and relies on sound, scent, and its sheer number of large mouths to catch its prey.

IBLIS

The Iblis demon is corporeal but not of solid form. Instead it has the appearance of a figure about the size and shape of a human but made of a roiling, fast-moving black smoke. In the part of its vapor that represents its head, it looks out onto our world through yellow burning eyes.

IMP

The common Imp is a small humanoid with the characteristics of a typical Western devil—horns, forked tail, et cetera. They are not very dangerous individually but can become a problem when encountered in swarms of more than two hundred, as is occasionally reported.

DJINN
Djinn are mentioned here because they are often incorrectly believed to be demons. They are not; they are faeries.

KAPPA
A reptilian water demon covered in a protective carapace and with a protruding beak, but otherwise the size and rough shape of a human ten-year-old child. Fond of leaping from the water to drag unwitting mundanes to their deaths.

KURI
These are spider demons, large and shiny black, with eight pincer-tipped arms, and fangs extending from their eye sockets.

MOLOCH
Somewhat confusingly, the name "Moloch" refers both to a Greater Demon known as one of the most fearsome demon warriors, a being of smoke and oil, and also to a species of lesser demons ("Molochs") that are minions and foot soldiers of the Greater Demon Moloch. Individuals of the species are man-size, dark, and made of thick roiling oil, with arms but only a formless liquid appendage instead of legs. Their primary weapon is the flames that stream from their empty eye sockets, and they are usually seen in large numbers rather than in isolation.

ONI
Human-size demons with green skin, wide mouths, and horns upon their heads.

RAHAB

These are large bipedal demons, somewhat lizardlike in appearance and movement. They are blind, with a line of teeth where their eyes should be, and a regular mouth, this one fanged and tusked, in a more usual place on their faces. They have a narrow, whiplike tail edged with razor-sharp bone. Their talons and teeth are, of course, sharp and dangerous, but their most threatening weapon is the bulb-shaped stinger on the end of their long, forked tongue.

RAUM

The Raum is an intimidating and dangerous demon, not capable of speech, but somewhat clever as an opponent nonetheless. Raums are about the size of a man but possess white, scaled skin, bulging black eyes without pupils, a perfectly circular mouth, and tentacles for arms. These tentacles are the Raum's most dangerous weapon; they are tipped with red suckers, each of which contains a circle of tiny needlelike teeth.

RAVENER

The Ravener is a classic monstrosity: a long, squamous black body with a long domed skull like an alligator's. Unlike on an alligator, its eyes are in an insectile cluster on the top of its head. It has a vicious, barbed whip tail and a thick, flat snout. Raveners possess sharp fanged teeth, which envenomate their prey with a deadly toxin. In time the poison will burn away all of the life of the victim, leaving only ash behind. The toxin is particularly terrible even among demon venoms, and there we are talking about a category that includes the poison of the Facemelter demon. (See "Facemelter," page 70.)

SHAX

These demons are known for their keen sense of smell and are sometimes summoned by warlocks to use in tracking a missing person. They must be carefully controlled, however; they are brood parasites and reproduce by wounding a victim and then laying their eggs in the still-living victim's skin.

VERMITHRALL

Most Shadowhunters will incorrectly tell you that the Vermithrall is a monstrous lumbering mass made up of thousands of writhing worms. In fact the Vermithrall are the individual worms themselves. They do, however, collect into colonies in the shape of a humanoid and attack as a unified single entity. Worse, worms separated from the main body will endeavor to rejoin it, making it very hard to permanently kill a Vermithrall.

VETIS

They are not to be confused with Dragon demons, which they somewhat resemble but are unrelated to. They are gray and scaly, with overlong serpentine arms and an elongated but humanoid body. Like Dragons, they are known for hoarding valuables; unlike Dragons, they do not have any understanding of what is valuable and what is dross, and their lairs are more closely reminiscent of large rats' nests than treasure chambers.

MUNDANE DEMONIC CULTS

Through history there have been any number of pathetic, misguided groups of mundanes who have built small cults around the worship of a particular demon or group of demons. Most of these cults are of little interest to Nephilim and serve only to clutter and confuse demonic histories, since they are based around demons that are merely imagined or invented.

Nevertheless, a minority of these demon cults have successfully raised weak minor demons. These stories usually end with the cult improperly binding the demon and the demon immediately killing all of the cult's members. In a small number of cases, a successful demon cult has endured for a short time, with the demon served by the cult members and asking little in return. These cults inevitably fade after a generation or two and are of little concern to us historically, but they may cause local trouble and require Shadowhunter intervention.

Mundane members of demon cults are often barely human by the time that intervention is needed. Their worshipped demon is likely to have consumed their humanity for fuel, to maintain and strengthen itself. This leaves behind mere shells of humans, their physical bodies in active decay and their souls worn down to a constant animalistic rage. This state is considered irreversible; killing these demon-degraded mundanes is considered an act of mercy and is thus within the bounds of the Law.

Cults have existed to serve Greater Demons, but there is little evidence that any of these have ever successfully summoned the subject of their worship. If they have, the likelihood is that they were immediately annihilated and no record exists of them to teach us of their folly.

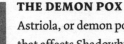

THE DEMON POX

Astriola, or demon pox, is a rare but debilitating illness
that affects Shadowhunters and is caused by inappropriate
contact with demons. The illness is not often seen, because
this kind of inappropriate contact is, luckily, not common.
Mundanes are immune to the disease; it is assumed to be
caused by the interaction of demon poisons with the angelic
nature of Shadowhunters.

The first signs of demon pox are a shield-shaped rash on
the back of the sufferer, which then spreads over the body,
creating fissures in the skin. From this point the afflicted
Shadowhunter will deteriorate physically, experiencing
fever, chills, nausea, oozing sores, non-oozing sores,
buboes, a film of black over the eyes, hair ejection, and
other similar signs of distress. In time the sores and fissures
cover the skin of the victim entirely, and they form a dark
chrysalis within which the victim transforms, painfully
and over the course of several weeks, into a demon himself.
Once the demon emerges from the chrysalis, the previously
existing person is in effect deceased, and the only end to the
torment is to kill the demon.

In earlier times astriola was invariably lethal, and not
much could be done for the sufferer but to make him
comfortable and to remove him from innocents who
might be harmed when his full demonic alteration took
place. The progress of the disease could be slowed but not
stopped, and in many cases the victim would choose not
to be treated, since by and large treatment would only
prolong his agony. Today there exist reliable cures that can
clear up demon pox in its early stages, and the illness now
causes few fatalities. It can, however, still be incurable if the
sufferer reaches a certain stage of demonification before

being treated. In addition, a fairly serious stigma is still associated with the disease, and its presence is considered sufficient evidence for the violation of the Law against consorting with demons. Thus those who are treated for demon pox today often receive this treatment while in the prisons of the Silent City.

DISCUSSION QUESTIONS AND THINGS TO TRY

1. Try: Learning a few words of Purgatic or Cthonic!
    Your local Institute should contain copies of several
    phrase books.

    I recommend the classic Learn Purgatic in Ten to Twelve Years of Misery.

    Do you plan to order lunch in a lot of demon restaurants? No. Is it worth it?

    Then no. The demons who are smart enough to have a conversation usually speak a human language.

2. For those of you with the Sight, have you ever seen a
    demon prior to your time among the Shadowhunters?
    If so, how did your mind process what you were seeing?

    Insert joke about Mrs. Thomson from seventh grade here. WELL, THERE WAS MRS. THOMSON—

    OH, YOU RUINED IT, NEVER MIND.

3. Demons are fond of promising their victims that
    which their heart most desires. What are some things
    a demon might promise you, and how might it manage
    to fulfill those desires in an ironically horrific way?
    It is worth considering these so that if a demon actually
    offers you what your heart most desires, you will not
    be taken in by its lies.

    A demon might promise me—a pony. He might manage to fulfill those desires in a horrible way by giving me a plastic toy pony, or a really angry pony that attacks people, or a pony covered in sharp spikes so that you can't ride him.

    Your homework: Figure out how to take these discussion questions more seriously

CHAPTER FOUR

Bestiaire Part II:
DOWNWORLDERS

If demons marauding across our world were the only creatures that had to be kept in check by Shadowhunters, our lives would be notably easier. Demons, except for the rare shape-shifting varieties, are usually obviously inhuman, and they are conveniently universally malevolent. In the relations between humans and demons there are no politics, no negotiations. There is just war. They attack; we defend.

But the whole of the world is not that simple. Once demons began to trespass into the lives of humans, the waters of good and evil became muddied, and the muddied waters of humanity became Downworlders. Some Downworlders—warlocks and the fey—predate the Nephilim by untold years. But the youngest Downworlders, werewolves and vampires, are a relatively recent phenomenon, the result of demon diseases previously unknown that have crept into the human race and, it seems, are with us for good.

—— WEREWOLVES ——

There wolves! *Are you going to do this in every chapter?*

The earlier of these demon diseases is lycanthropy, which is *Maybe!* believed to have first appeared in the forests of Central Europe sometime in (probably) the thirteenth century. Lycanthropy is believed to have spread rapidly through Europe and then more slowly to the rest of the world. Persecuting and publicly burning werewolves was in vogue late in the fifteenth century and early in the sixteenth century, which corresponded to a similar fashion for burning so-called witches (almost never actually Downworlders; see "The Hunts and the Schism," in Appendix A).

Lycanthropy transforms a human into a werewolf, a demi-human whose demonic infection causes them to transform into a large and dangerous wolf under the light of the full moon. Worse, werewolves in their lupine form are not merely wolves. They possess unnatural—demonic—strength and speed, and their claws and fangs are able to slash through a chain-link fence or bite through a padlock. Without help and training a werewolf can be a very dangerous creature. When lycanthropy is at its worst, a man lives what appears to be a normal mundane existence, only to become a vicious, uncontrolled, murdering beast roughly three nights each month, retaining no memory of his own evil acts.

IF YOU MEET A WEREWOLF

A werewolf who is in his or her usual human form, and not under the influence of the lycanthropic Change, is no different from any other human. You should approach any new werewolves in human form as you would anybody else. Contrary to common belief, they will not smell you or challenge you to mortal combat.

If you encounter a werewolf in wolf form, you must quickly assess the situation. If he is ignoring you, move away from the area calmly but quickly. If he is watching you, look for the signs of aggression you would look for in a dog—bared teeth, growling, hackles raised. Raise your hands to show you are not a threat. *Also try to look*

Defend yourself only if attacked, and try to incapacitate the *as little like a roast beef as possible* wolf, not kill him. A werewolf who is attacking a human is almost always responding out of terror, or is newly made and not yet in control of himself.

If you know the werewolf in question, *do not* attempt to reason with him by calling him by his human name or reminding him of all of the fun human things you have done together. Also *do not* try to give him commands like you would a dog (such as "heel" or "stay").

WHERE DID WEREWOLVES ORIGINALLY COME FROM? HOW DO THEY LIVE?

It is not known what demon, or demon species, is responsible for the first appearance of werewolves. There is a conjectured Greater Demon of origin, who is usually referred to by the placeholder name "Wolf" in literature. Despite many supposed descriptions of Wolf in medieval writing, there exists no credible candidate for who he might be. He seems to have appeared, created werewolves, and left our world forever.

New werewolves are created when a human is bitten by an existing werewolf. Approximately half the time a werewolf bite will cause lycanthropy in the victim. Many safeguards against bites are now in place, and much organizational work has been done by the Nephilim and by werewolves themselves (see the sidebar on the Praetor Lupus, page 87) to prevent unexpected attacks, which means that rogue werewolf bites are happily a rare occurrence today.

83

The job of the newmade werewolf, his new responsibility, is to gain control of his transformation, or "Change." Control in this area is more important than any other adjustment he makes to his new life. Werewolves can in fact live peaceful and calm lives among mundanes, more so than other Downworlders, with proper training and self-possession. By the regulation of the Praetor Lupus, any werewolf who cannot consciously control his or her Changing is deemed a rogue, whatever his or her other behavior. This regulation is intended to motivate werewolves to learn to control their Change—in order to get the Praetor off their backs; an accidental attack is a disaster for the Praetor and the werewolf community, and they require strong rules to prevent such a thing.

This is particularly important because newly made werewolves do not normally transition gently into their new lives. Along with the lycanthropic response often comes uncontrolled aggression and rage, suicidal anger, and depression. This raft of emotions is both terrible and potentially dangerous in the hands of a newly strengthened and powered Downworlder who no longer knows his own strength. Thus, newly made werewolves must be treated with caution. The Praetor Lupus has taken responsibility for self-policing the Downworlder community of both fledgling vampires (see "Vampires," page 88) and newmade werewolves, and can be of assistance in particularly difficult cases.

By all reports the first Change is the worst because it is a new experience, but let us be clear that the lyncanthropic Change is always a trauma. The stretching and reshaping of muscles and bones is very painful, especially the realignment of the spine. Human teeth are pushed out of the way by wolf fangs painfully tearing from the gums. This and the brain chemistry changes cause most werewolves to go into a fugue during their first Change, and they lose all memory of what they have done as wolves. This is when lycanthropes are at their most dangerous— when they do not yet have control of their Change and cannot yet retain their human mind when Changed.

Worse, most newmade lycanthropes do not yet have a pack affiliation and thus don't have access to information that would help them understand their Change. This is why we recommend mercy to new werewolves even though rogue Downworlders are technically not protected by the Accords. Newmade werewolves are literally not in control of their own faculties. The Praetor Lupus helps enormously in finding and rehabilitating these rogues, and a captured rogue werewolf should usually be brought to a local Praetor office or representative rather than to the nearest pack.

The Praetor has been very successful in their mission and

85

has made werewolves the model Downworlders of self-policing; in most parts of the world, it's rare that Shadowhunters need to be called in to deal with a rogue werewolf, a massive change since the creation of the Praetor. However, even the most controlled werewolf will still be forced into a Change by the full moon, if only on the exact night of the fullest moon. There is, therefore, no such thing as a perfectly safe werewolf.

Moreover, there is no such thing as a safe werewolf pack. There is an inherent violence at the center of traditional werewolf organization: A pack leader can be challenged to mortal combat by any member of the pack, at any time, for leadership of the pack. Apart from making the entire social structure of werewolves centered around ritual killing (an unfortunately common thread in Downworlder cultures), this also means that the werewolf population is constantly committing what mundane society would label as murder in the first degree, and such behavior may attract the attention of mundane law enforcement. Here we may find ourselves needed to perform some glamours and protections to keep the Downworlder and mundane populations away from each other.

An experienced werewolf, one in whom the Change is a well-known companion rather than an unwanted invader, can often learn more advanced shape-shifting—for instance, Changing only one hand into a wolf's paw to cut something with its claws.

Traditionally werewolves and vampires maintain an intense hatred for one another, which is believed to be inherent in their respective demonic infections, but there are places in the world where the two groups get along and are even allies, such as Prague.

Werewolves are mortal and will age and die like any other humans. They are also able to bear children, to whom they *do not* pass on lycanthropy. They can have offspring with a Shadowhunter as the other parent, and since Shadowhunter blood always breeds true, the child of a werewolf and a Shadowhunter, however rare, will be a Shadowhunter.

WEAKNESSES

In addition to their supernatural strength, grace, and reflexes, werewolves have the same unnaturally accelerated healing abilities as most other Downworlders. They cannot regenerate— if you cut the arm off a werewolf, he will not grow back a new arm—but they can recover from most mundane wounds. The only ways to permanently wound or kill a werewolf are either with the angelic fire of the seraph blade or, more famously, with pure silver. Silver is associated with the moon, and wounds made with silver weapons will cause werewolves not only permanent damage but also great pain. Any Institute will be found to have a cache of silver weapons in place for just this reason.

Showed this section to Luke, and he yelled and paced around —

THE PRAETOR LUPUS *for half an hour. I took notes.*

The Praetor Lupus is the first and largest self-policing organization of the Downworlders. It has grown from a tiny force begun in London in the late nineteenth century to a worldwide organization. The name suggests an old, even ancient, organization, but in fact the Praetor Lupus—"Wolf Guard"—was founded only 150 years ago, and its name is not ancient, but rather reflects the Victorian vogue for all things classical. The founder, Woolsey Scott, was a wealthy werewolf of London and began the Praetor in response to his brother's dying wishes. The self-declared mission of the Praetor is to track down "orphaned" Downworlders—newly made werewolves, fledgling vampires, and warlocks who have no knowledge of their people—and to help them take

It's your diligence as a student that astounds me, really. Also, definitely get Simon a satin cape. You know he wants one.

Vampires envy the danger of single rogue werewolves. Codex acts like they are like sharks in Jaws, just efficient killing machines.
Most rogue werewolves in cities are shot by cops; most rogue werewolves in woods/on farms starve, die in fights with bears, etc.
Praetor originally about saving werewolves from being killed by their condition, not saving mundanes from effects of werewolves.

The "model Downworlder" status that Codex condescendingly suggests is actually really offensive.
L. will show them where they can put their model Downworlder status. • This is why the Clave
blah, blah, blah Council blah, blah. In my day blah, blah, blah uphill both ways in the snow.
Possible Hanukkah gifts for Simon: new Tejuka box set? silly winter hat? black satin cape? blood?

control of their powers and become connected with a clan
or pack or mentor warlock.

The Clave and the Praetor have an uneasy relationship,
despite their many goals in common. The Praetor prefers
to operate without supervision and is very secretive about
their methods and their membership; this secrecy makes
the Clave uneasy, since Shadowhunters are meant to be the
chief protectors of Downworld and we believe in openness
and disclosure whenever possible. The Praetor argues, for
their part, that their goal is to save rogue
Downworlders *before* they have run afoul
of Covenant Law, and that close oversight
by the Clave would damage their ability
to protect their charges. Despite the
Accords, over the years the Praetor has
become more secretive as it has grown.

The symbol of the Praetor Lupus
is easily recognized, and is worn with much pride by its
members. The symbol is an imprint of a wolf's paw adorned
with the slogan *Beati Bellicosi*, "Blessed Are the Warriors."

—— VAMPIRES ——

DO NOT SKIP. Simon is not a textbook-level source on vampires!

Vampires are victims of another demonic infection, which turns
them into drinkers of blood. They possess retractable razorlike
fangs that are deployed when their bloodlust is roused. These
they sink into a surface vein of their victim, and then the vampire
consumes that victim's blood to his or her satisfaction. The act of
drinking blood brings a rush of energy and vitality to the vampire.
Experienced vampires can resist this rush and cease their drinking
in order to leave their victims alive and able to recover, but new

88

Showed this page to Luke. He turned purplish and told me to show it to Jordan. Notes from talking to Jordan: Praetor not actually that secretive. Secretive from Clave specifically. What Clave calls secrecy, Praetor calls not telling Clave every single thing about themselves and their operations. Claim of Clave's love of openness obviously some kind of joke. Don't need werewolves to teach me that.

You must own stroll, mosey, or hop.

vampires may have trouble controlling their urge to drink their victims to the point of death. Worse, after the initial sting of a vampire bite, the poison contained within vampire saliva dulls the victim's pain and may make the experience pleasurable for the victim. The poison acts as a muscle relaxant and a euphoric, and even a strong Shadowhunter will respond to its effects. A well-Marked Shadowhunter can, of course, retain her consciousness much longer than a mundane, but there is still a heavy risk associated with being bitten.

Unlike werewolves, vampires are considered to be "undead"; that is, their bodies are no longer alive in the sense that ours are. Their human souls reside in animated corpses, kept intact and animate by the demon disease. They cannot bear children and can create new vampires only by their infecting bite.

IF YOU MEET A VAMPIRE

Do not look the vampire directly in the eyes. Do not expose your neck or the insides of your wrists to the vampire. Do not go with a vampire you don't know to a second location strange to you. Do not drink from a goblet given to you by the vampire, no matter how much they insist it is safe. There is no need to be deferential, but they do not take insults lightly. Do not mock the vampire's hair or clothes. They place an enormous weight on whether they are being treated respectfully, and while under the Law they may not harm us, it is usually wise to avoid earning the enmity of a vampire.

Do NOT TAUNT THE VAMPIRE. Do NOT TELL HIM HIS T-SHIRT IS STUPID. Do NOT CALL HIM "THE VAMPMAN" OR "DR. TEETH" OR ANYTHING LIKE THAT.

Aw, Fangs over there makes a good point.

WHERE DO VAMPIRES COME FROM?

When two vampires love each other very much...

Vampirism is the other great result of demon infection in humans, and vampires have a well-established pedigree, as befits a people obsessed with ritual and protocol. Unlike in the case of lycanthropy, we know exactly the who, the when, and the where of the first vampires. They were created in a public ceremony for which the Nephilim have multiple written accounts, from those who claim to have been present. The Greater Demon Hecate, sometimes (and confusingly) called "the Mother of Witches," was summoned in a massive blood-based sacrifice held in 1444 at the Court of Wallachia, in what is now Romania. The then-ruler of Wallachia, Vlad III, had a great circle of prisoners of war impaled on tall wooden spikes, and in exchange for this impressive sacrifice Hecate transformed Vlad and the large majority of his court into the first vampires. *Vampire origin, surprisingly metal.*

Vampirism did not spread seriously as a disease until a few years later, when Vlad led a series of raids into neighboring Transylvania. There he and his men appear to have gorged themselves on their enemies and spread vampirism through the entire region. The city of Cluj became the site of the first vampire clan officially recognized by the Clave, and Transylvania took over as the epicenter of the vampire epidemic. For whatever reason, Vlad and his men did not create any significant number of vampires in their own home area, and vampire activity in Wallachia diminished to near silence after Vlad's death.

In a stroke of historiographical luck, the Cluj Institute in the late fifteenth century was home to a Shadowhunter named Simion. We know almost nothing about him, not even his family name—he only ever refers to himself as "Simion the Scribe"—but he provided a clear and detailed picture of the original spread of the vampire plague. He describes what can only be called an

The vampires all came forth to rock in, in.

Just no.

all-out war between the Nephilim and the earliest vampire clans, with mundanes taken from their beds and left drained in the street, vampires chained to the ground in village squares and left to burn alive in the sun, and other such horrors. Shadowhunters, especially those already experienced at hunting Downworlders, traveled to Transylvania for the sole purpose of vampire slaying; new vampires continued to appear just as fast as old ones could be killed. Within months the Cluj Institute, formerly one of the smallest and least important Institutes in Europe, had become the epicenter for the largest demonic epidemic the mundane world had ever seen. Chaos arose, as neither Nephilim nor vampires yet understood how new vampires were made or how they could be reliably killed. I AM ACTUALLY NOT FINDING THIS SECTION TO BE THE LIGHTHEARTED FUN I HAD HOPED. Reading about people like you being killed will do that.

The war ended with no clear winner. Knowledge of the vampiric disease grew, vampirism spread to other parts of Europe, and Shadowhunters returned home to sign treaties with local vampire clans and keep the peace in their own territories. Transylvania remained a devastated battleground for hundreds of years, where mortality rates for both vampires and Shadowhunters remained the highest in the world, and where the authority of the Clave was tenuous at best. Only with the unofficial end of the Schism in the first half of the eighteenth century did the battle die down, and today the Cluj Institute is, while more vampire-focused than most other Institutes, no busier or more dangerous than any other, and Shadowhunters visit not to wage war but to see the Muzeul de Vampiri, where magically animated wax figures re-create the carnage of five hundred years ago.

Exposure, the practice of binding vampires outside to be burned alive by the rising sun, was banned in the Third Accords of 1902 after the popularity of Bram Stoker's 1897 novel *Dracula* led to an enthusiasm for hunting and brutally killing innocent, Law-abiding vampires.

WHAT ARE VAMPIRES LIKE?

There is as much variation in vampires as there is in humans, of course, but generally speaking, vampires tend to be pale, sallow, and thin, as though weakened by malnourishment or some wasting disease. Contrary to this appearance, like werewolves they possess superhuman strength, grace, and speed. Also contrary to this semblance of death, their blood shimmers a bright red, much brighter than the blood of humans. Also like werewolves, vampires heal quickly from mundane injuries.

Vampires more than other Downworlders seem to have one foot in Hell already and to not be entirely present in our world. This is believed to be the reason why vampires cast no reflections in mirrors and do not leave footprints or fingerprints as they move through the world. They cannot be tracked by normal tracking magic, either demonic or Nephilimic. (Powerful vampires, however, tend to travel with mundane subjugates who can be tracked.) Vampires are comfortable in darkness; their eyes adjust to seeing in darkness and seeing in light almost instantly, much faster than the eyes of humans.

The dirt of the grave in which a vampire was buried holds special properties for that vampire. She can tell, for instance, if that grave has been disturbed, or is being trod upon, or if dirt from that grave is removed from its site. Vampires have cleverly made use of this power to communicate simple messages over long distances—for instance, breaking a container of a vampire's grave dirt could be used to alert and summon that vampire. *Should saved some of that dirt...*

The final vampire power worthy of mention here is perhaps the most dangerous: the *encanto*, or "fascination." Vampires can, with simple prolonged eye contact, convince mundanes and even Shadowhunters of almost anything, and can persuade them into almost any act. This is a skill that must be developed and practiced by vampires, and so it is typically the older and more powerful vampires that make use of it. If you live in an area particularly rife with vampire activity, you should consult your local Institute about prioritizing training to resist the *encanto*.

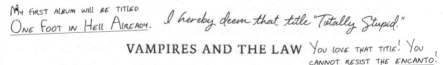

My first album will be titled One Foot in Hell Already. *I hereby deem that title "Totally Stupid."*

VAMPIRES AND THE LAW *You love that title! You cannot resist the ENCANTO!*

Many new Shadowhunters are surprised to learn that it is not against the Law for a vampire to drink blood from a human, provided that the human remains alive. This is because of the healing properties of vampire saliva. When a vampire drinks from a victim, it increases the red blood cell count in that victim, making them stronger, healthier, and able to live longer. The effect is small, but it mitigates the weakening effect of losing blood, and so a bitten human usually remains unharmed.

Nevertheless, the risk of accidentally killing a human by drinking from him too deeply, and the general sense of menace around having one's blood drained, have led most "civilized" vampires to eschew drinking from living human victims (other than subjugates; see page 98) in favor of pre-drawn blood or the blood of animals. By the Accords, vampires must abide by the same mundane laws against murder as any other Downworlders, but vampires are the only Downworlders who might commit murder for food, potentially for survival. It is notable, and admirable, that so many vampires have voluntarily committed themselves to the same respect for human life as the other signers of the Accords.

Now Simon is angry, too. He and Luke are both pacing around yelling at nobody about the Codex. Summary: "Only vampires murder for food? That is rich." It's hard being the Monster Manual.

VAMPIRE POLITICS

Like werewolves, vampires consider themselves to be on some level brethren with all other vampires, no matter what clan they are affiliated with. A vampire who raised a hand against another, except in the rare circumstance of a clan war, would be considered anathema by the vampire community, and his life would be forfeit. The Nephilim generally stay out of these matters of internal justice, although we will sometimes intervene to arbitrate conflicts between clans to stave off full-out battle. When clan wars do occur, leadership changes, as it does with werewolves: Whoever kills the head of a vampire clan becomes its leader.

Among Downworlders only faeries are more committed to notions of honor and etiquette than vampires. Vampires are often found making oaths and vows, which they take very seriously. These vows are usually written and signed in blood—not a surprise, given the vampire obsession with blood generally. These blood-oaths are binding: Vampires are compelled by the oaths' contents and cannot violate them unless the bond is broken through further, and more onerous, ritual. A vampire who has thus sworn an oath to you under these circumstances can be trusted to follow at least the letter of the oath in the strictest detail. Conversely, you should be suspicious of a vampire who is willing to make a promise to you but will not swear to that promise in blood.

I wish Simon would vow to return my Ghibli DVDs. I so vow! *In bloooooood?* Never mind!

WEAKNESSES

Obviously it would be the preference of all Nephilim to never be forced to bring harm to a vampire, but history teaches us that it is wise to know how to defend oneself against them, and what their strengths and weaknesses might entail. The Accords require that vampires turn away from their natures as hunters and predators, just as humans must choose to turn away from our own abilities to kill and harm.

Vampires are extremely vulnerable to fire. While they are much stronger and more durable in many ways than mundanes and Nephilim, their bodies are weaker and less resistant to burning than humans'. They are likely, when exposed to fire, to burst into flames in the manner of paper, dry wood, or similarly flammable objects. As such, vampires not only can be harmed by fire but can often be kept at bay by a protective boundary of fire or a burning torch.

Holy water, and other common blessed materials, such as angelically aligned swords, are harmful to vampires and will scorch and burn their flesh.

More generally, holy symbols may be anathema to vampires if the symbols hold weight with the specific vampire addressed. A crucifix may repel a vampire who held Christian beliefs before he was Turned, but a vampire who was raised as a person in a Buddhist faith would not generally respond. In the early days of vampire hunting, when there was much less migration of peoples away from their home cultures, holy symbols were more dependable as vampire repellent, but in our modern age of religious pluralism and because of the ease with which people can move around the world, it has become unwise to depend on this method.

Along similar lines, older guidebooks to the Shadow World suggest that a vampire trying to hide his demonic nature can be sussed out by his inability to speak the name of God. This is also no longer reliably true. Most vampires that as mortals did not ascribe to a religious faith do not develop an aversion to holy names as part of their Turning. In addition, older and more powerful vampires often regain the ability to speak holy names, although it's not clear whether this is because the aversion fades over time or because as the vampires age, they descend more deeply into the demonic and become able to speak God's name as a curse.

As mentioned before, vampires cannot stand the direct light of the sun. Mythology tells us that this is a facet of their status as demonic, damned creatures, that they are cursed to not be able to look at the sun that gives life to Earth. Whatever the reason, sunlight burns the skin of vampires, as does (to a lesser extent) witchlight, being light of angelic origin. Artificial light, such as that of gaslight and electric light, may cause discomfort in vampires if it is strong enough, but they are normally able to remain undamaged unless already very weak. *Also, fluorescent light is avoided as it's unflattering.*

A ray of sunlight will cause burns on a vampire's skin, but full exposure to the sun—being exposed fully to unblocked sunshine—will cause them to burst into flame dramatically, and they will be consumed and put to rest quickly. For this reason vampires are normally careful to remain dormant and inactive during daylight hours. *Unless he is a SUPERVAMPIRE, of course.*

TREATING VAMPIRE BITES Important! Note! *Why's it gotta be like that, man?*

If a vampire bites and drinks blood from a victim, no supernatural treatment may be needed. Normal Shadowhunter wound-care protocols apply—the use of an *iratze* or other healing Marks, and treatment for blood loss and shock if the draining has been severe. Mundanes also can have their blood taken by vampires with no permanent ill effects, provided the wounds are cared for and not too much blood has been taken.

The real danger lies in the case of a human who has consumed vampire blood. Even if not enough blood is consumed to cause the death and rebirth of the victim as a vampire, the smallest amount of vampire blood is enough to create in the victim an irresistible pull to vampires, which could cause that victim to become a subjugate, begging to be Turned.

The proper treatment for the consumption of vampire blood is emetic: The victim must be made to drink holy water until all of the vampire blood is out of his system. The victim is likely to be very sick during this process—he will of course cough up everything in his system, not just the vampire blood, and the presence of the blood is likely to have made him fevered and hot to the touch. This process is, however, much better than the alternative.

Even a small amount of vampire blood consumed may require the consumption of quite a lot of holy water. This is a case where it is better to be safe and consume too much holy water than too little. The victim can be assumed to be healthy and cured when the consumption of holy water no longer produces the emetic response.

SUBJUGATES

Powerful vampires will often decide that, rather than feeding haphazardly on whatever blood they can find, they would prefer a ready supply. They will then create a vampire subjugate: They will select a victim and keep him close by, drinking from him and also feeding him small amounts of vampire blood. This vampire blood will make the subjugate docile, obedient, and, in time, worshipful of his vampire master. The subjugate will cease eating food and will survive entirely on a mix of animal blood and vampire blood. He will not become a full vampire, but subjugates are kept in a suspended animation, their aging process drastically slowed (although they are not immortal and will eventually die).

A subjugate who is turned into a vampire loses his obedient and worshipful nature and becomes a normal vampire, like any other.

Most subjugates are young in appearance; vampires revere youth and beauty and tend to prefer their subjugates to possess both. (A practical consideration is also present. The younger the subjugate, the less chance that he will turn out to have diseased or otherwise problematic blood.)

Subjugates are sometimes known as darklings. Although the term is archaic, it is still used in some formal vampire rituals today. Vampires love nothing so much as formal rituals.

The culture of subjugates among vampires is that, first, they are no longer human but are something else, and therefore are not afforded the rights and respect granted to humans. Subjugation is in essence voluntary slavery; subjugates effectively consent to become the property of their vampire masters, renounce their human names, and so on. A subjugate would never introduce himself to another vampire or another subjugate, for instance; it would be his master's choice whether to communicate his name, or indeed, whether the subjugate would possess an identifying name at all.

The creation of new subjugates was made illegal in the Seventh Accords of 1962. Vampires who had subjugates created prior to the Accords were allowed to keep them. The Law also continues to allow vampires to transfer existing subjugates to other vampires. These two facts have made it almost impossible to convict vampires for creating subjugates. Vampires simply claim that their subjugates predate the Accords, and since the subjugates' identities and lives are tracked by the vampires themselves, it is very hard to prove otherwise.

FLEDGLINGS

Note: did not read. Too soon.

A human who has consumed enough vampire blood to be themselves transformed into a vampire does not, as some popular mundane stories would have it, abruptly turn from a living human in one moment to a vampire in the next. The human—who is known in vampire culture as a "fledgling"—must die, be buried, and, in being reborn, make his way out of his grave of his own power. (In the rare and sad case that a Shadowhunter is irreversibly turned into a vampire, this is the one circumstance in which her body may be buried rather than burned.)

Like a ghost, a fledgling rising from his grave draws energy and strength from the living things nearby, drawing their heat and producing a distinctive cold spot around his grave. When he has risen, he will be nearly feral and starving for the blood that will, for eternity, sustain him. This is why fledglings are the most dangerous of vampires. Sometimes a vampire clan will turn a human to a vampire purposefully, and in those cases the transition usually goes smoothly. The clan can be present for the vampire's rising, can make sure he is able to successfully rise, and can supply him with blood and take him to a safe place to recover.

This is, however, not the way that most vampires are made; most are made by accident. In those cases the fledgling is buried by his friends and family, as any other mundane would be, and rises unexpectedly, in a mundane location, desperate for blood and barely knowing himself. These are the circumstances that lead to vampire attacks and the deaths of mundanes. While such an out-of-control fledgling must be stopped, it is not the policy of the Shadowhunters to consider these fledglings rogue vampires, and thus the fledglings should be turned over either to a local vampire clan or, preferably, to the Praetor Lupus, both of which are well-equipped to take care of the fledgling's needs.

—— WARLOCKS ——

Perhaps no other Downworlders have a more complex relationship with Shadowhunters than do warlocks. The off-spring of demons and mundanes, warlocks do not have the many unifying features of werewolves or vampires, or even of faeries. The only things that can be said to be true of all warlocks are that (1) they possess a so-called warlock mark on their body that identifies them as not merely human, (2) like most hybrid species they are sterile, and (3) they possess the ability to perform magic. It is this last feature that makes them at once the most powerful of Downworlders and the most closely tied to Shadowhunters. For the whole of our history we have worked in concert with warlocks, whether as partners or (more commonly) as hired specialists, to allow us to make use of some of the demonic magic that our own powers exclude us from.

Needless to say, warlocks are rarely born from an affectionate relationship between a demon and a human. Instead they are

created through one of the two worst depredations demons visit upon our world. Most obviously, there are warlocks born from demons violating humans against their will. This was the predominant means of warlock conception in the time before the Incursion, when demons were rare and normally appeared in isolation. Today, though, demons are much less likely to manifest themselves openly, since the presence of Shadowhunters and the much larger number of Downworlders makes them more likely to be discovered and attacked. Therefore, today most warlocks are the result of a different kind of violation: the coupling of a human with an Eidolon demon (see "Demonologie," Chapter 3) who is disguised as the human's loved one.

Warlocks cannot be produced from the union of a demon and a Shadowhunter; because the angelic Shadowhunter blood and the demonic blood both normally dominate, the combination cannot create a living child. The offspring of a Shadowhunter and a demon is death.

IF YOU MEET A WARLOCK

Nothing can be generally said to be true of meetings with warlocks; these Downworlders vary in temperament and quality as much as humans as a whole. It is only noted here that it is considered impolite to stare at a warlock's mark (see page 104).

WARLOCKS AND MAGIC

All warlocks are to some extent practitioners of magic. Some inherit more magical aptitude than others, and those who cultivate that aptitude may become quite powerful among warlocks and quite useful to the Nephilim. The most gifted may find themselves able to study demonic magic in the secretive Spiral Labyrinth, the central home of warlock magical research and knowledge. Unlike Nephilim, warlocks do inherently possess magic. They have invented quite a lot of new magic, in fact, which is dutifully recorded and kept in the Labyrinth. The location of the Labyrinth is unknown even to the Nephilim, and possibly it exists in its own pocket dimension separate from our world. Its age is also unknown. According to our earliest Nephilimic writings, it was already considered ancient in the time of Elphas the Unsteady (see Excerpts from A History of the Nephilim, Appendix A). The magic by which one may travel there is one of the most closely guarded secrets in all the world, and it's whispered that a *geas* placed on all warlocks at the moment of their birth guarantees that if a warlock reveals the Labyrinth's location to a non-warlock, the result would be instant and blindingly painful death. *It is also whispered that this is completely bogus.*

The warlocks have in some ways suffered more than any other Downworlders; they have neither the clan communities of werewolves and vampires nor the sacred home of the fey, and have had to make their way in our world largely by their own individual courage and cunning. The Nephilim have not always provided a safe haven for warlocks—for example, turning on them and slaughtering them by the hundreds in the time of the Schism (see Appendix A). Today we can only mourn the loss of trust and cooperation that once existed between warlocks and Shadowhunters. Relations between the two have improved greatly since the Accords, which guarantee not only the rights of warlocks but legal permission for them to perform demonic magic when acting to assist a Nephilim investigation. It is likely, though, that the kind of mutual assistance, angelic and demonic together in the form of Nephilim and warlocks, that marked the great flourishing of magic in the Middle Ages will never again be seen. *Too bad about all that slaughtering, Clave. Not exactly making me swell with pride about my people here.*

WARLOCK MARKS

Every warlock has some feature on his body that labels him as not fully human. These marks (not to be confused with the Marks of Raziel that we use) are as varied as demonkind and range from the subtle to the glaringly obvious. A warlock's fate among the mundanes may well be decided not by himself or by his origins but by whether he is marked with, for example, strangely colored eyes or unusual height, or with blue skin or ram's horns or tiger stripes or a shiny black carapace. Any unusual feature can of course be glamoured into invisibility, but the warlock mark is present from birth, and recall that most mundanes are unaware of anything strange about their child until he is born and his mark is revealed. Even among those parents fully aware of the partially demonic parentage of their child, a warlock mark may be a deeply unpleasant surprise. These marks seem unrelated to the particular type of demon parent; it is not so much the inheritance of a demonic feature as the arbitrary mutation of the body in response to demonic magic coursing through it. *Note: Magnus's eyes.*

Hey baby, guess where my warlock mark is.

IFRITS *Never works. Trust me. Never works.*

Rarely, but sometimes, a warlock is born who, though the child of a demon and a human, has no access to demonic magic. These unfortunate souls have the disadvantages of a warlock—the warlock aspect that marks them as not fully human—but cannot perform magic. These so-called ifrits are trapped on the limens of the magical world, suffering the stigma of their inhuman marks without the benefit of supernatural power. Historically they have fallen into the underclass of the supernatural world, and are often found working on the wrong side of the Law, unable to live in the mundane world but unable to find a respectable life in the Shadow World.

Sometimes, of course, an ifrit is born with a warlock mark that can be easily hidden from public view. These "ghost ifrits" can sometimes make their way through mundane human society without complication, and as such may have no doings with the Shadow World at all. Today most ifrits with marks that are difficult to disguise acquire magical artifacts that provide them with a permanent glamour and live away from the magical world, unable to have children of their own but otherwise unremarkable to mundanes.

FAERIES

Note: The Fair Folk are not actually fair. They are big cheaters in fact.

Strange they may be, alien to us, more unknown than demons themselves, but the fey, the faeries, are Downworlders. They are people—they have souls. They are the least understood of all magical peoples, the great ancient mystery of our world. They are found in countless varieties, sizes, and types, and in all environments.

Most properly these creatures are known as "faeries," after their homeland, the realm of Faerie. They are known in literature by many other names, partly because of their enormous variety and partly because of age-old superstitions about invoking them by name. Most commonly they are called the fey, but you will also hear them named the Fair Folk, or the Kind Ones, or the Little People, or any number of other euphemisms.

UNICORN   SEELIE KNIGHT   SEELIE QUEEN   PIXIE   BROWNIES

IF YOU MEET A FAERIE

Do not sign any contracts or agree to any bargains with faeries. Faeries love to haggle but will usually do so only if they are sure they will win. Do not eat or drink anything a faerie gives you. Do not go attend their magical revels under the hills. They will paint a beautiful picture of what awaits you there, but its beauty is false and hollow. Do not tease a faerie about their height. Do not expect direct answers to direct questions. Do expect indirect answers to indirect questions.

Faeries will always exactly follow the letter of any promise they have made, but expect results delivered with great irony.

Many Shadowhunters have been taken in, despite these rules, by a belief that the particular faerie they met was simpleminded, naive, generous, and so on. This playacting is yet another ploy.

This is a little harsh. Faeries not that bad.

I don't think I agree!

WHERE DO FAERIES COME FROM?

The fey are originally the offspring of demons and angels, with the beauty of angels and the viciousness of demons. (Obviously, since angels are rarely if ever seen in our world in current times, the vast majority of faeries are the offspring of other faeries, just as most Shadowhunters are the offspring of other Shadowhunters and not born from the Cup.) The Fair Folk cannot be said to be morally aligned with either of their parent races. They are good and evil tangled up, following neither the morality of Heaven nor the immorality of Hell but rather their own capricious code of behavior. They are known for their cunning and their cruel sense of humor, and they delight especially in tricking humans—mundanes and Shadowhunters alike. They frequently seek to bargain with humans, offering someone his heart's desire but failing to mention that that desire comes with a terrible cost. They are very long-lived and become only more artful and powerful as they age.

They are the other Downworlders, along with werewolves, who can bear children. They can also have offspring with humans. These offspring will be human and not fey, but they often retain some faerielike aspects or have a penchant for certain kinds of fey magic. It's widely believed, for instance, that humans who naturally possess the Sight have inherited it from some faerie ancestor.

As with werewolves, the children of faeries and Shadowhunters will be Shadowhunters.

Although the fey are active members of Downworld, and signers of the Accords, faeries are more removed from the affairs of our world than any other known creatures except angels. They usually keep to themselves, and have their own complex politics and social structures, which only tangentially affect our world.

| OGRE | UNSEELIE QUEEN | UNSEELIE KNIGHT | KNOCKER | GOBLIN |

Commonly they are organized into courts, with sovereigns presiding over specific territories in our world and in theirs. However, there are just as many, if not more, free-ranging faeries in the world unaffiliated with any specific monarch. Just as the fey delight in manipulating humans, they delight in manipulating one another, and usually if the problems of the fey intrude into our world, it is the result of conflicts between rival courts, sometimes playful, sometimes serious and brutal.

FEY AND MAGIC

The magic of the fey is, as far as we know, unique in the world. It is very powerful but neither demonically nor seraphically allied, and it cannot be learned or wielded by any creatures other than the fey themselves. This magic is slippery and chaotic and is not easily given to structure and rules that can be learned. Nephilim Marks exist that can protect you from faerie glamours, but you should never, ever allow yourself to feel safe or at ease in the presence of faeries. Believing yourself to have the upper hand in a negotiation with a faerie is a sure sign that you are being deceived and will suffer for it in the end.

Why, then, if they are so removed from our world, do the fey continue to interact with humans as much as they do? The answer lies in genetics.

The biggest problem facing the fey in our modern world is the thinning of their blood. Over time the problem of extensive interbreeding leads to the weakening of family lines. For this reason faeries spend much of their time luring humans into their world. They pursue this in two ways: by creating changelings (see below) and by enticing adult humans into their revels. Much faerie magic exists to trap these reveling humans in Faerie forever, or at least for a long enough time that either they "go native" and forget their former lives or they can be used to produce new faerie children.

There are ways for mundanes (and Shadowhunters) to successfully join the faerie revels without trapping themselves in Faerie. A faerie could be convinced (or bargained with) to give a human a token of safe passage—usually something like a leaf or a flower. And a faerie who voluntarily brings a specific human to the revels can offer his protection and guarantee the human's ability to leave. These bargains, however, are subject to the usual faerie trickery and duplicity, and mundanes and Shadowhunters alike should beware.

CHANGELINGS

The most common contact that the fey have with mundanes is in the making of changelings. It is not dissimilar from the manner whereby the Nephilim create new Shadowhunters with the Mortal Cup, but in the case of the fey, the mundanes gain no benefit. The faeries sneak into a mundane home, take a suitable child, and replace it with a sickly member of their own race. The human child thus grows up in Faerie, able to bring fresh strong blood into the faerie lines, while the mundanes find themselves forced to parent a dying child terrified of iron. It's generally believed that the faeries exchange one of their own partly to allay the suspicions of mundanes and partly out of a twisted, and very fey, sense of fair exchange.

By some method unknown to us, mundane children raised in Faerie take on fey attributes, and can perform some faerie magic. By the same token the fey child left in the mundane world, if he survives, typically never knows his own origin. Apart from a predilection for the Sight, he may never come to know anything of the magical world at all.

By Covenant Law we are forbidden from interfering with this process of child exchange. This ruling has been debated hotly at several of the Accords proceedings over the past hundred years, but both of the children are raised in loving homes—the fey choose the unwitting adoptive parents of their offspring carefully—and no better solution for refreshing the faerie bloodlines has been found. Pragmatism leads Nephilim to prefer that the fey create changelings rather than abduct adult mundanes into their revels.

THE LAND OF FAERIE

The realm of Faerie is not one that is welcoming to Shadowhunters, and in general Nephilim should avoid spending time there.

Despite our powers and our Sight, we are still as susceptible to the lures and dangers of Faerie as most mundanes. The fey have always been clear that their signing of the Accords represents their covenant for behavior in our realm, not in theirs. Faerie is older than the Accords, older than the Nephilim, and it possesses its own magic that the Gray Book can only partly and imperfectly protect against, at best.

That said, Faerie does have rules, and those rules do not leave Nephilim helpless. A Shadowhunter who is the victim of an unprovoked independent attack by a creature of Faerie is allowed by fey law to defend herself. If the attacking creature is killed, the fey are likely to shrug and explain that the creature's decision to attack was his own, and if that decision turned out poorly, it was not the problem of other fey. (One must, of course, be careful that such an attack is not on the orders of some other creature or court; it is always worth remembering that the only thing that the fey like more than meddling in human affairs is their own internal political fights. A Shadowhunter who became a piece in one of the faeries' elaborate games of human chess would be very unlucky indeed.)

Entrances to Faerie tend to be hidden, rather than guarded, and tend to be permanently located in a single place. (The fey may close an entrance and open a new one when the original entrance has become dangerous or unworkable, or in the rare case when wars break out between fey courts and entrances must be closed or guarded.) Faerie entrances are normally found in natural surroundings rather than in man-made areas, and they are often given away by some aspect of their natural appearance that is "wrong" or "off"—a tree in an impossibly specific shape, a reflection in water that does not match the world above the reflection, an apparently empty cave from which faint music can be heard if all else is quiet.

For the most part it is wise for Shadowhunters to avoid Faerie. Though it is described as a realm and one can travel in it like in a country, it does not tolerate being surveyed and does not have a consistent layout. Seasons can change in the blink of an eye, mountains and caverns can appear where minutes before no such things were visible, and its rivers change their courses at the whim of some unknown force. No map of Faerie has ever been produced. Do not wander there; you are likely to join the untold throng of humans who have crossed the borders into the feylands and never returned.

What a surprise, that we are all mixed up with Faerie stuff that we should absolutely positively avoid. Have we as a group ever met a warning we didn't ignore?

Speak for yourself, Fangs.

DISCUSSION QUESTIONS AND THINGS TO TRY

1. What is your favorite Downworlder? Why?

   Warlocks, because they are fabulous!

   OFFENDED. ALSO, MANY WARLOCKS NOT FABULOUS. ONLY THE ONE WE KNOW.

   Vampires, because they keep bothering me. This question is stupid.

2. Do you have any prejudices about any Downworlders
   that might affect your ability to work with them? If so,
   it is important to recognize these biases and discuss
   them with the head of your Institute before you begin
   active service.

   *Vampires keep bothering me, a werewolf gives me my curfew, a warlock
   hid my memories from me, and faeries are just constantly messing with me.*

   The part where you've learned that Downworlders are a pain in the neck is accurate.

3. Have you been tested to see if you possess   *Honestly, the stuff*
   inherited faeric or werewolf blood? It may affect   *Downworlders*
   your ability to take on certain Marks. Symptoms   *have done is*
   to look for include naturally occurring Sight   *nothing compared to*
   and frequent cravings for red meat, respectively.   *what Shadowhunters
   have done to me,*

   Um, no, actually, I haven't   *so...*

   I think you're pretty safe. Both of your parents were full
   Shadowhunters, and one of them was obsessed with blood purity.

   *I bet Valentine had a werewolf grandmother or something.
   That's usually how that kind of thing turns out.*

   I just wrote a thing, but it was not
   appropriate for a textbook so I erased it.

   A ROOM. YOU TWO. GET ONE.

113

CHAPTER FIVE

Bestiaire Part III:
ANGELS AND MEN

ANGELS:
OUR MYSTERIOUS PATRONS

also terrifying

No "If You Meet an Angel" section, Codex? You are not helpful to me at all.

About angels little is known, much is conjectured, and few who might speak knowledgeably live to do so. Of all the supernatural creatures discussed herein, we know the least about angels. They are the great absent generals of our army, having left us a thousand years ago with their heavenly endorsement, basic marching orders, and enough magic to fight for ourselves. Much has been done in their name, both good and evil, even though the number of confirmed manifestations of angels in our world in the entire history of the Nephilim can be counted on one hand.

And yet their blood runs in the veins of every Nephilim, yourself included, flowing into our bodies through the transformative properties of the Mortal Cup. Angels may be absent patrons, but our patrons and spiritual parents they are, and we recognize them with our prayers, our invocations, and in the names of our most holy weapons.

In truth no one knows why angels are so distant from the events of our world. The first great heretical question of Nephilim history is one that has probably already occurred to you: If Raziel and his angels were so determined to wipe the demonic menace from our world, why not do it themselves? Like so many other questions about the nature and purpose of angels, this one remains unanswerable, and angels remain an ineffable foundation upon which our lives and our mission are built.

Writings about angel sightings through history are notoriously unreliable. The general consensus is that angels are shaped like humans, but are much larger, winged, and glowing with heavenly fire—but many authors have suggested that when angels *do* manifest in our world, they take whatever shape witnesses will recognize as angelic. Today the Clave is dubious of claims about angel appearances and mostly declines to investigate them. This attitude has been firmly in place ever since an embarrassing episode in 1832 during which a Prussian farmer and Shadowhunter, Johannes von Mainz, called the entire Clave to his farm to witness the "angel" he had summoned to his cow barn. Awe quickly turned to chagrin when some of the neighbors recognized the "angel" as Johannes's son Hans, covered in gold leaf and bellowing pronouncements in a vulgar mix of Latin, German, and what appears to have been a nonsense language of Hans's own invention. The angel's wings turned out to be a mix of goose, duck, and chicken feathers haphazardly pasted to a wooden frame. Johannes retreated to his farm in humiliation, and Hans was no longer able to so much as go into town without receiving catcalls and being pelted with feathers. Since then most Shadowhunters have been very cautious in either making or checking claims of angel appearances. *Oh, Johannes, what will we do with you?*

THE ANGEL RAZIEL

Teacher? I did an independent study, does that count?

Yes. You may skip this section. Enjoy your newfound sixty seconds.

The Angel Raziel holds, of course, a special role as the patron of the Shadowhunters and the creator of the Nephilim. His role in that creation is discussed thoroughly elsewhere in this volume; here we address what is known about Raziel himself.

Raziel is believed to be of the rank of archangel, within the heavenly chorus. In Jewish mystical traditions he is often called the Keeper of Secrets and the Angel of Mysteries. Interestingly, Jewish mysticism includes what appears to be a distorted version of the Gray Book, known as the Book of Raziel and containing a strange amalgam of kabbalistic teachings, angelology, glosses on the Jewish creation stories, and corrupted forms of demonic incantation. The book also contains a large number of runes, most of them totally invented but some of them corruptions of true Marks (but without any instruction on how they might be used or what their purpose might be). Extant copies of this text exist in both Hebrew and Latin today but only as historical curiosities. The movement during the mundane Renaissance in Europe against magic of all kinds labeled the book a dangerous work of dark magic, and its use was suppressed by mundane religious authorities, to the benefit of the Nephilim.

It is difficult to make any clear statements on Raziel's earthly appearance; we can go only from the earliest art and text describing and depicting the birth of the Nephilim. From that, we can put together, as it were, a composite sketch. We can say that the Angel is consistently depicted as many times the size of a man, as having long hair of silver and gold, as being covered in golden Marks not found in the Gray Book, and as a being whose appearances "fled from the mind and memory as quickly as they were seen." Many depictions show him with large golden wings, each feather of which contains a single golden eye.

Unfortunately, when speaking of the first meeting of the Angel Raziel and Jonathan Shadowhunter, an act of great symbolic as well as actual significance, it is difficult to divide what is intended as factual description from what is meant as allegory. Since history has not preserved a record of this first meeting—as told by Jonathan himself or even by anyone who personally knew Jonathan—all depictions of Raziel must be assumed to have some kernel of truth but also some kernel of interpretive fiction.

What is generally accepted is that Raziel is (a) huge, (b) terrifying, and (c) displeased to be dragged into human affairs, preferring for us to use the tools granted us to solve our own problems. There are many (possibly apocryphal) stories through Nephilim history of unfortunate Shadowhunters attempting to summon Raziel, only to be quickly smote and reduced to ash for wasting the Great Angel's time. The Mortal Instruments are meant to summon Raziel and provide protection so that the summoner will not, in fact, suffer a swift death. Unfortunately, Raziel is unlikely to look kindly upon those who summon him in response to a problem that is not global and truly epic. In addition, the question is merely theoretical, since the Mortal Mirror is lost to the Shadowhunters and has been for hundreds of years.

Seems obvious once you know the secret, huh?

It's a little embarrassing now, I won't lie.

OTHER ANGELS KNOWN TO THE SHADOWHUNTERS

It is a common question among young Nephilim: If angels never appear in our world, and cannot and should not be summoned here, why must we learn and memorize the names of so many of them? Shadowhunters must know the names of the angels, first because we are of their blood and so we learn their names out of respect. Also, of course, we name our seraph blades after them, and it's believed that the seraph blades are infused not just with the generic heavenly fire of *adamas* but with some of the spirit of the named angel. This is why you will rarely find seraph blades named after the most famous and powerful of angels out of worry that such angelic power might overwhelm and destroy the wielder of such a weapon.

Hereafter follows a basic lexicon of angels known to the Shadowhunters, to be used to name seraph blades. More thorough information on each angel can be found in the official angel handbook, *Be Not Afraid*, 1973, Alicante.

A handy tip: When angels say "be not afraid," you should be afraid.

Also, as I said earlier, we have to memorize angel names because
Jonathan Shadowhunter wanted us to have to memorize angel names.

They sure like to end angel names in "el." *Means "of God" in Hebrew, Clariel.*

You TWO ARE JUST ADORABLE.

Adriel	Marut
Ambriel	Metatron
Amriel	Michael
Anael	Moroni
Arariel	Munkar
Ariel	Muriel
Asmodei	Nakir
Atheed	Nuriel
Barachiel	Pahaliah
Camael	Penemue
Cassiel	Peniel
Dumah	Puriel
Eremiel	Raguel
Gabriel	Raphael
Gadreel	Raqeeb
Gagiel	Raziel
Hadraniel	Remiel
Haniel	Ridwan
Harahel	Sachiel
Harut	Samandriel
Israfiel	Sandalphon
Ithuriel	Saraqael
Jahoel	Sealtiel
Jegudiel	Shamsiel
Jehuel	Taharial
Jerahmeel	Uriel
Jophiel	Yahoel
Khamael	Zadkiel
Lailah	Zaphkiel
Malik	

*Another handy tip: Do not name a seraph blade "Raziel."
Legend says he doesn't like it.*

What would happen?

121

Just ... don't do it. Nothing good.

DO NOT SUMMON ANGELS

Wait. I'm confused. So I ... should summon angels? Is that right?

One of the lessons learned most quickly by Shadowhunters is that life is deeply unfair. Most unfair is the truth that while our vocation and mission are given to us by Raziel, we have essentially no direct access to angels or their powers [which we the editors hesitate to refer to as magic; the faculties of angels are rather beyond the ken of even the most powerful warlock, for example]. As a young Shadowhunter you may have considered that the best weapon against the demon threat might be an equal opposing angel threat, and you have thought in your idle moments of summoning an angel yourself. Perhaps you have even sought tales or grimoires on angel summoning in your Institute library.

The Shadowhunter art is an ever evolving one, and yesterday's forbidden methods are tomorrow's accepted norms. However, there is a rule that remains globally true:

You should not attempt to summon an angel to your aid.

There are several major reasons for this. The first, and least interesting, is that it is most likely a waste of your time. Angels do not respond to summonings in the same way that demons do. For one thing, they cannot maintain a corporeal form in our dimension for long, any more than other non-demon creatures can in a dimension not their own. And the summoning rituals that claim to bring angels to us are obscure, difficult, and unreliable; they have been accomplished so rarely that we don't have much evidence for what does and does not work. The risk of disaster, injury, or death from a misunderstood or misapplied summoning ritual is very high.

The second reason not to attempt an angel summoning is that there is no way to oblige an angel to cooperate with your needs. An angel cannot be *bound* in the way that a demon is bound, except by the application of forbidden and blasphemous rituals, the

122

performance of which are among the worst violations of Law that a Shadowhunter could commit.

Finally, even if a summoning is successful, you and any companions you persuade to assist you will die, and die quickly. Unlike demons, angels do not *want* to be on our plane of reality. They do not like manifesting here, they do not like helping humans, and they are not known for their mercy. They are on the whole deeply indifferent to the travails of the mortal realm. They are not merely messengers but soldiers: Michael is said to have routed armies. They are not patient or tolerant of human vicissitudes. You must put out of your head images of naked winged babies draping someone in robes. Angels are great and terrible. They are our allies, yes, but make no mistake: They are utterly alien and inhuman. They are, in fact, far more inhuman than the most monstrous demon you will encounter. Angel blood we may carry in our veins, yes, but pure heavenly fire will burn and consume us, as surely as demonic poison will.

Angels are our mystical source of power, and the origin of whatever righteousness we possess. They are not, however, our friends. *Yes, yes, ha ha, it's all very funny, this is actually important advice here.*

ON ANGEL BLOOD

What are the odds this is going to come up again?!

Nephilim are raised knowing that in their veins flows some of the blood of angels, and thus angel blood is a substance about which many stories and tall tales have been told— that it grants superior strength, that it cures any disease, that it lengthens the human life. All of these claims must be considered less than credible, if only because stories claiming the appearance of angels in our world are, to our knowledge, universally false. A Downworlder who claims to be selling angel blood, or anything derived from angel blood, is lying to you. Shadowhunters should be too smart to be taken in by such claims, but sadly over the years a number of young Nephilim have shaken in Institute infirmaries, recovering from the ingestion of whatever substances have been mixed together to give the semblance of angel blood. There are no vials of angel blood floating around that grant superpowers. None. Do not fall for this ruse. *Ahem.*

I guess this is another one where I get credit for real-life experience

I believe so, yes.

—— MUNDANES ——

Oh, I can't wait.

The mundane world is the world you know. It is the world from which, new Nephilim, you have come, and its people, the mundanes, are the people you knew and the people you yourself were, until recently when you were changed. We often speak of the mundane world as though it is a minor aspect of our lives and our world, but in truth we exist by necessity *because* of mundanes. When Nephilim say we are protectors of the world, what we mean is protectors of the mundanes. They are our charges and our responsibility. *Chumps!*

Mundanes live their lives in ignorance of the shadows surrounding them, and it is our job to protect that ignorance and, as much as possible, maintain it. As you walk the streets of your cities and towns, as you patrol, you will be surrounded by mundanes living their lives, celebrating and mourning, knocked about by happiness and sadness and anger and sorrow and joy. These emotions you see may be at odds with what you, with the true Sight, know to be the truth. Sometimes drastically at odds. Many are the Nephilim who have been shaken by their need to run down and fight to exhaustion a demon who threatens to destroy an entire town of smiling, oblivious mundanes. This is one of the burdens we bear. It is our job to bear it appropriately.

Mundanes are, of course, not allowed into Idris, or into any Institute, under normal circumstances. The Law allows for Shadowhunters to offer mundanes sanctuary if they are in imminent danger from a demon or Downworlder attack, or danger from the results of a demon or Downworlder attack. Note that the Law does not *obligate* Shadowhunters to do this. The Nephilim's holy mission is to protect mundanes, but not at the expense of our own safety. Shadowhunters must judge whether a mundane can be given sanctuary without compromising the larger secrecy, and therefore safety, of the Shadow World.

It is easy to feel contempt, and even envy, for mundanes. They are, after all, in danger from a demonic threat of which they know nothing. They go about their lives complacently; they have the luxury of not knowing the truth of the great battle of good and evil that looms over their world constantly. They have the luxury of not being in a state of constant war, of knowing that each of your friends, of your family members, is in battle every day from which, every day, there is a chance they might not return.

We urge you: Have compassion for the mundane world. It is our lot to fight for them and for them not to know of our sacrifices. This is not their fault. *Oh, come on, it's not that bad.*

THOSE POOR BASTARDS. I PITY THEM. JUST ... PITY THEM. *They want us to be kind to mundanes!*

MUNDANES WHO ARE NOT ENTIRELY MUNDANE

THEY ARE SOMEWHAT COOL. BUT NOT AS COOL AS SHADOWHUNTERS.

Lays it on a little thick though. SHADOWHUNTER DOTH PROTEST TOO MUCH, METHINKS.

There are, of course, mundanes who are not entirely mundane— *Methinks too.* whose families have, somewhere in their history, faerie blood, or werewolf blood, or even, rarely, Nephilim blood. This blood persists through generations, and these mundanes may be identified by having the Sight and by being able to see through some glamours. (Most, however, still never notice any supernatural activity, because they are not prepared to see it. An important rule of glamours: For the most part people see what they wish to see. (See "Glamours and the Sight," page 140.) Even Sighted mundanes will often look past strange appearances and explain them as illusions or misunderstandings.)

Many of these mundane-yet-Sighted families used to act as the servants and caretakers of various Institutes and wealthy Shadowhunter families; however, in most parts of the world, the practice of keeping servants has long gone out of fashion, and these families have ceased their relationships with the Nephilim. Several generations have passed since this happened in North America and Europe, and most living members of these families no longer even know that their ancestors once served the Nephilim.

Even those mundanes who do not possess the Sight may often find themselves drawn to places of magic and power, though they will not understand why. Sometimes they will find themselves compelled to make some physical mark on such a place—to build barriers separating it from the places around it, to decorate it, even to deface or vandalize it. This can be annoying to Nephilim and

Downworlders who need to make use of these sites of power, but again we urge you to have patience and pity for these mundanes. There must be some magic deep within the collective memory of all humans, for otherwise how could we (and Downworlders) make use of any magic, even with the addition of angel or demon blood? We must, all of us, have at least the *potential* to be of the Nephilim. That magic spills out into all the world, and it is part of our responsibility as Shadowhunters to maintain it.

(See also: "Mundane Demonic Cults," page 75.) JUST YOUR EVERYDAY RUN-OF-THE-MILL DEMONIC CULT.

A NOTE ON MUNDANE RELIGION

Many new Shadowhunters come to us from their own religious history and want to know which religion is "right." This knowledge is not something that Shadowhunters possess any more than mundanes do. Shadowhunters proudly originate from all points of the globe, and we naturally see and think about the Shadow World within the context of our personal beliefs.

This diversity may seem like a weakness, keeping Shadowhunters separated from one another, just as mundanes are by their beliefs. But these mundane religions have much to teach us. Encased in their mythologies and legends are practical truths about angels, demons, perhaps even Downworlders. We include all of them in our researches.

Also, mundane religion represents the moral and ethical beliefs, and spiritual insights, of our species, and we have much to learn from these as well. We ignore the teachings of the wisest of mundanes at our peril. If *all the stories are true*, we must remember that those stories have mostly been written down by mundanes.

The world's religions always have assisted, and will continue to assist, the Nephilim in our mission. Religious communities and holy buildings are universally available as havens for Shadow-hunters, and often contain secret caches of weapons and tools for Shadowhunter use. The agreements concerning these caches often go back five hundred or more years. In fact, the oldest continually operating Nephilim weapons cache in the world can be found in Milan—one of the largest mundane trade cities closest to Idris—in the Basilica di Sant'Ambrogio. The Milanese Nephilim claim that this cache was established by Jonathan Shadowhunter himself, late in his life, in what was then the new bell tower of the church.

Traditionally, entrance to caches was effected by the recitation of the so-called Martyr's Creed:

> In the name of the Clave, I ask entry to this holy place.
> In the name of the Battle That Never Ends, I ask the use of
> your weapons. And in the name of the Angel Raziel, I ask
> your blessings on my mission against the darkness.

Today most caches follow the more expedient method of opening to the presence of a Voyance rune, but the traditional method still works in most places, for those Shadowhunters who prefer a little more drama.

I actually have to memorize that, don't I. I've heard Jace say it. *Yep. You have to memorize a million Marks, too, you know.*

But that is eeeeasy *This is haaaard.*

THE FORSAKEN

THERE'S NO WHINING IN SHADOWHUNTERING!

Oh, you know that's not true.

It was only shortly after the creation of the first Nephilim that humanity came to know, to its detriment, what happens if you Mark a person who does not have Shadowhunter blood, or who has not been made a Shadowhunter by drinking from the Mortal Cup. A single Mark is likely only to cause a burning pain where

Okay. Here's my question, Codex. Why did Valentine stop using Forsaken? Why doesn't every bad guy create a giant Forsaken army?

it has been inscribed on the skin, but a number of Marks—and it does not take many—will drive a mundane to agonizing pain and mindless, insane rage. The Mortal Cup, or inherited Shadowhunter blood, steels the body against the overwhelming strength of angelic power that flows through the Marks, but an unprepared mortal will die.

They do not eat or sleep, and they ignore their injuries and wounds. As a result they are short-lived creatures, and it is only a matter of chance whether they are killed off first by starvation, exhaustion, or infection.

IF YOU MEET A FORSAKEN

Killing Forsaken is, in short, a mercy. Do not, however, take on a Forsaken one-on-one. It is easy to underestimate their strength and cunning. If necessary, flee and return with backup.

The only known method of ending the agony of a Forsaken,

other than killing him, is to make him drink from the Mortal Cup, whose power will eliminate the unfathomable pain of the Marks. Technically this will turn the Forsaken into a full Shadowhunter. There are, however, zero recorded cases in which the sufferer survived the dual shock of becoming Forsaken and then becoming Nephilim, so it is best to consider them beyond help.

WHERE DID FORSAKEN COME FROM?

We cannot know the horror of the first Forsaken, whose story is lost to history, but it must have been early in the spread of Nephilim through the world. As early as the mid-1200s, not long after the believed death of Jonathan Shadowhunter, we have notes from the Silent City suggesting that the Brothers were seeking a cure for the Forsaken. Forsaken are mentioned by that name in the first written version of Covenant Law, by the first Consul, Edward the Good and Ready, and are condemned as illegal and in fact blasphemous.

The real problem with Forsaken is that in their madness they are dangerously suggestible, and they have some affinity for the one who has Marked them. This enables the wielder of the Mark to command them. They can be made to survive for longer than normal by being ordered by their master to eat, drink, and sleep, and they can understand other simple commands. They are thus occasionally used as slave labor, but their unending rage and pain make them mostly useful only for committing violence. Forsaken are unable to build or construct anything, and they are unable to speak.

There have been surprisingly few attacks by Forsaken recorded in our history. They are certainly a threat to mundanes, but they are not actually very strong. Despots do not raise Forsaken armies, because Forsaken make terrible soldiers: They can't wield weapons, and they can't implement tactics or defend themselves. They are much less intelligent than human soldiers, and they require the same resources to maintain. They are easily neutralized as a threat by prepared Nephilim, or indeed by a powerful warlock or a significant force of werewolves or vampires. Because of all of these aspects, most Forsaken we know of were the result of errors, such as a mundane foolishly trying to turn himself into a Shadowhunter. There have also been isolated occasions in which being made Forsaken was used as a punishment, but it has always been against Nephilim Law to do so, and those Shadowhunters who were caught doing this would have been arrested and imprisoned in the Silent City for their crime.

Note that we do not see parallel "demonic Forsaken." Demonic magic, of course, has its own runes that could be theoretically inscribed on a person's flesh. In practice, though, these runes tend to produce an effect not unlike a strong demon poison. Thus we do not find, say, warlocks using them to enhance themselves; these runes cause not the mindless rage and pain of the Forsaken but the wasting collapse of the poisoned and are of no real use in practice.

Well, ten points to you, Codex. You answered my question: no Forsaken army because they fall apart and they are really stupid. Fair enough.

—— GHOSTS AND THE DEAD ——

Ghosts and spirits rarely appear in usual Shadowhunter business, but nevertheless for many Nephilim the Sight includes the ability to see, hear, and speak with the spirits of the dead. You may have it yourself! This aspect of the Sight is entirely hereditary and cannot be enhanced with Marks.

Even those Shadowhunters who cannot actually speak to or see the forms of ghosts can nevertheless usually sense their presence nearby, by noting the existence of an unnatural cold feeling. When ghosts manifest themselves in our world, they must draw energy from around them in order to maintain their ectoplasmic form, and thus suck the heat from their surroundings.

The strongest ghosts may in fact be able to manifest themselves into a close semblance of life. We can, however, always tell a ghost by its eyes: They will be hollow and empty.

Sometimes, in the case of the strongest spirits, the eyes will have flames flickering in their depths, but this is fairly rare.

The prevailing theory of ghosts is that they are trapped in our world by some wrong or crime they are seeking to resolve; they are literally "restless" and seek the talisman that will allow them to pass out of our world and into theirs fully. It takes a certain amount of strength for a ghost to be aware enough of itself and its former life to identify its talisman, and ghosts have no magical knowledge of what that talisman might be or what act might put them to rest; they are, in most cases, just guessing, and may be wrong, or too demented to accurately comprehend their situation.

WAIT WAIT WAIT, WE COULD HAVE BEEN DEALING WITH GHOSTS ALL THIS TIME TOO?
WHERE ARE THE GHOSTS? BRING ON THE GHOSTS!

You don't actually want that. New York has so bad ghosts. Trust me.

Things to ask Jace about the existence of

You left this blank. What do you want to know about?

The book leaves a bunch of things out! Like mummies. Tell me about mummie

Mummies exist. The Egyptians mummified people.
Mummies that get up out of their cursed tombs and walk around do not exist.

Do cursed tombs exist?

No. Sometimes you get a tomb guarded by a demon.

Zombies?

The voudun kind, yes—the braaaaaaiiiiinnnnsss kind,

OH, OH, I'VE GOT ONE. WHAT ABOUT A HAUNTED CAR?
CAN YOU HAVE A HAUNTED CAR?

Do you count a demon-powered motorcycle?

NO, LIKE, THE CAR TALKS TO YOU AND TELLS YOU TO KILL PEOPL

Then no.

DISCUSSION QUESTIONS AND THINGS TO TRY

Why am I even answering you? You are not a Shadowhunter. No, no leprechauns.

Elder gods?

Jace is ignoring Simon. Elder gods, Jace—same question.

1. Do you come to the Shadowhunters with existing
We'd just consider them Greater Demons, I think. religious beliefs? Try reading some of the Shadowhunter
scholars of your religion from the past, who will help
you learn how to fit your new knowledge of the Shadow

Transformers!
World into your worldview.

I don't know what those are.   *I will get right on that.*

Alien robots that turn into other things that don't look like robots!

2. Can you see ghosts? If so, try to find a haunting near you.
Someone in your Institute will know of one. Describe
your spectral experience here.

I cannot see ghosts. I am actually pretty happy about that.

Also, what about Smurfs? Also, and I am totally serious here, Santa Claus?

3. *Seriously, how much do mundanes suck? So much.*

Mundane rights!

I can't believe I am defending the Clave, but really, guys, this section is pretty good by their standards.

CHAPTER SIX

GRIMOIRE

This whole section is pretty ridiculous, by the way. Here's the short version: We don't do our own magic. We use magic from Raziel. That's the whole point. And it's not even true for you.

— AN INTRODUCTORY NOTE — ON MAGIC

Nephilim do not perform magic.

This is—far and away—the thing that most separates us from both demons and Downworlders. Demons perform magic—indeed, the vast majority of magic that you will see in the world is demonic in origin. The powers given to werewolves and vampires, too, are demonic magic. Faerie magic is the great unknown—it is very different from the magic of demons, but some believe that the two have the same origin.

Whatever the case, the Nephilim do not have any magic of their own. We use, rather, magical tools that have been gifted to us by higher powers. We cannot make new Marks. We have access only to the ones that were handed to us in the Gray Book. We can experiment with their use, but they are all the power we have been granted. Everything else that Nephilim are we have made on our own. *Most of us cannot make new Marks, that is.*

Through history many Nephilim, especially Silent Brothers, have spent countless thousands of hours trying to discover the underlying "language" and "grammar" of angelic Marks. If their constituent parts could be understood, it was believed, then perhaps new Marks could be created. These projects have inevitably led to failure. If there is an elemental grammar of Marks, then it seems that we humans are not permitted to know it, or are not capable of discovering it.

By comparison, demon magic is a much broader and more

According to Jace: weird Nephilim Pride stuff here. Most Shadowhunters don't care that much.

powerful magic in all its forms—whether wielded directly by demons or warlocks, or whether installed in the souls of vampires or lycanthropes. Faerie magic is more powerful still.

This is a lesson never to be forgotten by any Shadowhunter: We are outmatched. We are outgunned. What keeps us is our determination, our oath, our adherence to Law, our discipline, and our training.

—— WHY? ——

The great question of the Nephilim, the great mystery left unanswered by Raziel and unasked by Jonathan Shadowhunter, is this: Why have we been left with such limited powers? Why have the Downworlders been given such a range of superhuman abilities—immortality, strength, and speed beyond their physical bodies, the ability to invent and create new magic—when we have been given such limited and unchangeable weapons for our fight?

This is a question without an answer, and in fact to suggest a definitive answer is to presume to know the minds of angels. Let us, however, suggest that the Shadowhunter hold within her mind two qualities of great warriors—that of dignity and that of humility.

Dignity: Our power is that we are *chosen*. Unlike demons, born of the Void and without the free will to choose aught but evil; or Downworlders, whose powers are so often the result of accidents of birth, unpredictable events, terrible crimes; we have been selected to bear the blood of angels and lead the fight against Hell.

And humility: We are dust and ashes. We are mortal. We are vulnerable. We bleed and we die.

And in these two extremes is our great strength and our great frailty. *This: Cheesy but true! This kind of describes all people.*

We count as people!

BASIC INTERDIMENSIONAL SPACE-TIME THEORY

Do I even have to say you can skip this sidebar?

So far you know of two worlds: the mundane world and the Shadow World. But there are worlds other than these.

What. I didn't hear you. I was busy skipping this sidebar.

Our world overlaps with others, infinitely many others, that are separate from our world yet occupy the same space, in an alternate reality. These alternate realities have no obligation to hew to the same rules that our own universe follows, and so it's generally assumed that we could not survive in most of them. Not only need they not have things such as water and air and a temperature that we can stand, but they need not have the same physical laws or forms of life, and in these worlds we might disintegrate, unable to sustain our existence in a universe totally hostile to it.

Some believe Faerie to be a dimension different from our world (see discussion of the fey, Bestiaire Part II, Chapter 4), but we know for sure that the Void, home of the demons, is a different dimension. Attempts to follow demons home through their Portals back to the Void have proved to be instantly fatal to humans. It's suspected that angels come from yet another dimension, but this is mere speculation.

In truth we don't know whether the Void is a single alternate dimension—or many dimensions, or even an infinitude of dimensions whose nexus lies at

Pandemonium. In practice it does not much matter. Our vocation as Nephilim is to protect our own dimension; we will allow other universes to take care of themselves.

You shouldn't have skipped it. This is cool stuff. Space-time! Dimensions! More of this kind of thing please, thanks, love Simon.

GLAMOURS AND THE SIGHT

A glamour is the simplest magic in existence. It makes things look different from how they are. Performed correctly, it creates a perfect semblance in the mind of the observer and perfectly obscures the true shape of the thing glamoured. It is one of the few kinds of magic available to all known magic users—it is found in the Gray Book, in demonic spell books, in the researches of warlocks, and among the fey. And a glamour is the most widely and extensively used magic because of its necessity: It hides the Shadow World from mundanes, a goal that all of that world agrees upon.

Most glamours are easy to see through for any magical being, and they usually hide things only from mundanes. Vampires, faeries, and warlocks all may use more powerful glamours to hide their activities not just from mundanes but also from Shadowhunters and from one another. Faeries especially are considered the masters of glamour magic; some Nephilim theorize that everything we see of Faerie in this world is modified by a glamour in some way.

Glamours are most commonly used to put a false skin over something, as with the glamours we place on our Institutes. Nephilim also often glamour ourselves into invisibility, to move undetected through the mundane world. This is significantly easier than glamouring gear into the semblance of street clothes, weapons into the semblance of harmless tools, and so on. Similarly,

demons may glamour themselves into nonspecific forms, so that a mundane attacked by a demon will perceive it as something generic, like a dog or another random mundane.

The ability to see past glamours to a thing's true nature is often called the Sight, a term from mundane folklore. Most Shadowhunters are born with the Sight, inherited from their Shadowhunter parents. All Shadowhunters typically enhance their Sight with the permanent application of a Voyance rune, because Sight is the *only* means of seeing through glamours. Just knowing that something has been glamoured, or even knowing its true shape, does not remove the glamour effect.

This is notable because there are many folk beliefs among mundane cultures about rituals and tools that can be used to see through glamours. Some of these may successfully work to help us see through faerie glamours, by means we do not understand. These tools—clary sage, Seeing Stones, wearing clothing inside out, washing your face in a particular spring at sunrise, and so on—cannot, however, be used to see through the more common glamours used by warlocks, demons, and Shadowhunters.

Some mundanes do naturally possess true Sight, usually credited to fey blood in their ancestry, though no direct connection has ever been proved.

WHAT IS A GLAMOUR?

The origin of glamour magic is a subject that has puzzled generations of magical researchers—how is it that all of the Shadow World has access to it, and are the different versions related? There have been various theories, the most common of which historically has been that glamour magic originally belonged to the fey and was "stolen" from them by other creatures somehow. It's not clear how this could have happened, though, and so the prevailing theory today is that there are at root two types of glamours—the angelic glamours that we Nephilim use, produced by the inscription of Marks, and demonic glamours, used by everyone else. It's assumed that Raziel granted us the power of glamours, just as he granted us the power of Sight, to put us on an even footing with our foes, and to allow us to protect ourselves from mundane discovery.

I did not know this, but it turned out to be because I did not care.

ANGELIC MAGIC

THE MORTAL INSTRUMENTS

The Mortal Instruments are the greatest gifts entrusted to the Nephilim. Without them there are no Shadowhunters, no Marks used by humans, and no recourse against the demonic threat. The Instruments are venerated by Shadowhunters as our most sacred relics and are given to the Silent Brothers to keep and protect.

It is believed that the Mortal Instruments have functions beyond those that we know; old writings, especially among the Silent Brothers, speak obscurely of angelic powers essential to the Instruments that could be wielded if only we knew what they

were. These powers remain ineffable to us. Sadly, no use has ever been found for the Cup or the Sword beyond those enumerated below, and, of course, we do not know what power, if any, the Mirror might possess.

The power of dunking you in a lake and then driving you ma[...]

THE CUP   *Well done there. So glad we know about that now.*

The Mortal Cup is the means by which Nephilim are created. It is often called Raziel's Cup, or the Cup of the Angel. As our legends tell us, the Angel Raziel presented himself to Jonathan Shadowhunter and filled the cup with a mixture of his own angelic ichor and Jonathan's mundane blood. Jonathan drank from the cup and became the first Nephilim. Thereafter the Cup was imbued with angelic power, and drinking holy liquid from it would transform a mundane into a Nephilim.

The Cup is not as ornate and decorative as most new Shadowhunters assume. No jewel-encrusted chalice, it is the size of only an ordinary wineglass, and it is dipped in unadorned gold. It is carved from *adamas*, which is much heavier than glass. It is unusual that the Cup was gilded, considering the essential holiness of *adamas*— which to Shadowhunters is holier than gold.

Its *adamas* construction, however, is not the source of its power, any more than its gilding. It is assumed that the Cup is made of *adamas* because that is the angels' metal, unbreakable by any substance on earth (except the sacred fires of the Adamant Citadel). It is generally believed that Raziel could have made any cup into the Mortal Cup. It became sacred when the Angel used it as the vessel for his blood.

There have been periods of history in which the Cup was in frequent use by the Clave, but in the past fifty years this practice has mostly died out. The 1950s saw a large expansion of Shadowhunter families across the world, mostly to replenish the ranks of Nephilim lost in major world conflicts, but the Clave then saw a period of relative stability, and the current Shadowhunter families were considered sufficient to fill our ranks.

The worst use of the Mortal Cup, historically, was during the Hunts, when it was used for a form of inquisitional torture and murder. Downworlders, of course, cannot drink from the Cup and cannot bear Marks. They will typically, if given to drink from the Cup, vomit up its contents, but if they are forced to continue to drink from the vessel, it will soon burn the life out of them entirely, and they will die in paroxysms of suffering as the demonic and angelic war fruitlessly within them. (This fate is similar to that of the offspring of a demon and Shadowhunter, who cannot survive to birth.) This method of capital punishment was considered by some Shadowhunters—and, shamefully, the Clave as a whole for a time—to be not only just but merciful, since it infused the Downworlder with angelic power before death. Now viewed as barbaric and torturous, the practice fell off in most parts of the world in the early eighteenth century. It was eliminated as an official form of punishment by Consul Suleiman Kanuni in 1762 but was only made fully illegal in the Second Accords of 1887. *This is terrible! Why must you tell me these terrible things, Codex? I just wanted to learn about the Cup. At least they admit*

THE SWORD *to doing it and agree it was bad. That's a big step for the Clave.*
The Mortal Sword, often called the Soul-Sword, is the second of the Mortal Instruments. It resides in the Silent City and normally is hung above the Speaking Stars in the Silent Brothers' council chamber. When it is needed, it is typically wielded by Silent Brothers. Its primary use is to compel Nephilim to tell only truth. As Raziel said, the Sword cuts the knot of lies and deceptions to reveal the golden truth beneath. It is used in modern times mostly during trials, to compel honest testimony from witnesses, those who would have a vested interest in lying. Shadowhunters who wish to have their claims tested and proved may submit

themselves to "trial by the Sword." In this process a suitable judge—usually a Silent Brother—"wields" the sword by placing it in the hands of the deponent, where it adheres and from whence it cannot be removed until the judge wills it.

Neither Downworlders nor mundanes can be compelled by the Soul-Sword. This limit is believed to have been placed purposefully, to prevent the Shadowhunters from using the Sword as a general tool of interrogation. It is intended to maintain the integrity and honor of the Nephilim ourselves, and not to be a weapon wielded against others.

It is assumed that the Sword will not work on demons or angels, but this has never been tested. Since the fey are unable to speak untruths in the first place, its use on them would be redundant.

The Sword's shape is more or less typical of an arming sword or a knightly sword of Jonathan Shadowhunter's period. (It is believed that Raziel would have produced, in the Mortal Instruments, weapons and items that would have been somewhat familiar to Jonathan, so that their intention for use by humans would be clear.) It has a one-handed hilt and a straight double-edged blade. Unlike most Western swords of the period, it does not have a cruciform hilt but rather an elaborate design of outspread wings, emerging from the point where blade meets handle. Here the sword's heavenly origin is clear; the details of the sword are significantly more intricate and flawless than any human artisan could produce. *See, that was better. No one was unexpectedly tortured and murdered.*

Do you really think more of that is what I am saying?

THE MIRROR *Except in real life, by Valentine, using that sword. Remember?* The Mirror, also sometimes called the Mortal Glass, is the great mystery of the legend of Jonathan Shadowhunter. It is clearly the third of the Mortal Instruments given by Raziel, and it is mentioned in all Shadowhunter histories, so we do not believe that it is a later addition. No specifics, however, are given about the Mirror—where it resides, what it looks like, or even its intended function. There have been many searches for the Mirror in our history, in excavations and old libraries, through crypts and ancient Shadowhunter ruins—none of them successful. There have also, of course, been many false Mirrors that have been claimed as real, either by charlatans seeking power among the Nephilim or by naive and hopeful Shadowhunters desperate for an answer to the riddle.

Legend tells us that Raziel can be summoned by the use of the Mortal Instruments: One must hold the Cup and the Sword and stand before the Mirror. This claim must, however, remain but a story, since the Mortal Glass is lost to our knowledge, perhaps lost entirely to time. *You know what is weird? When this came out, the Cup was lost. No one knew where it was. People thought it was gone for good. No mention here at all!*

THE MARKS OF RAZIEL

Official position was "temporarily misplaced." The Codex is about as official as it gets. That is ridiculous.

The most common tools of the Shadowhunter, the source of our ability to fight the demonic Incursion at all, are of course the Marks of Raziel, the complex runic language given to us by the Angel to grant us powers beyond mundanes. You will learn these Marks for yourself—it is one of the most important tasks of your training. No one person knows *every* Mark, of course, but you will begin with the most common and useful, and will gradually learn more as they become useful or necessary to you.

Hey, we got the Cup back, didn't we? So they were right!

Learning Marks can be difficult, especially for Shadowhunters from Western countries. Many beginning students, and especially Westerners, will tend to think of Marks as a discrete set of "powers"—spells from a spell book that you have to memorize how to draw. Those Shadowhunters who are from cultures that use logographic written language, such as China, Vietnam, or the

Yes yes, you're some kind of Marks savant, you don't really need to worry about these. Check to make sure you know all of them, I guess.

All of them?

All of them.

Mayan Empire, may have an easier time absorbing the truth—that the angelic Marks are a language that we as humans cannot know in the particulars of its grammar. But we can acquire an intuitive sense of the relationships among the Marks that can make the learning experience more like becoming fluent in a language and less like memorizing a list of symbols. As with all other human talents, some Nephilim are naturally skilled at this, and some must work harder to gain competence.

We are restricted in our power in that we are permitted to use only the runes found in the Gray Book. There are demonic runes—possibly multiple different demonic runic languages— that are forbidden to us, by Law and also because they cannot work alongside the seraphic blood of the Nephilim. We cannot understand the underlying language of the Marks we have, and thus we cannot create new angelic Marks. But there are also other angelic runes, we know not how many, that have existed since time immemorial and that are, for whatever reasons, not given to us for our use. The most well-known of these is the so-called first Mark, the Mark of Cain, the first time that Heaven chose to Mark a human and provide protection. It is easy to see the origin of our magic in the first of all murderers as a dire omen, to see the affiliation as one we would prefer not to have. Yet we would argue the opposite: The Mark of Cain is a Mark of protection. It tells us that the justice of Heaven is not absolute and that this justice still contains the possibility of compassion and mercy.

Represent! Compassion and mercy! Booyah!

THE GRAY BOOK

Please never say "booyah" agai

The *Book of Gramarye* is the official name for the book of Marks that all Shadowhunters learn from. Each copy exactly replicates the contents of the original book of the Covenant in which the Angel Raziel inscribed the Marks given to Jonathan Shadowhunter. Unlike many other such holy books that claim exact replication

through history, the Gray Book's quality is maintained by a built-in check: in any given copy, all the Marks must work as drawn! This, and the continuity of Shadowhunter authority across the years, has allowed us to speak with confidence in saying that the Gray Book represents, indeed, the language of Raziel.

Preparing pages to hold the runes involves some complex magical legerdemain, which makes the process of creating a Gray Book an arduous one, always performed by Silent Brothers. Because of this complexity, the binding is often decorative and highly ornamented, to celebrate the effort involved in creating the interior. Institutes and a few old Shadowhunter families guard their Gray Books carefully and pass them down through the generations, often with much ceremony.

RUNIC MANUSCRIPTION

Learning Marks can be an intimidating process for young Nephilim; invoking the power of Heaven and likely failing the first few times is an understandably unnerving experience. The risks are, however, relatively low. In most cases poorly drawn Marks will have no effect at all and can be removed with no consequences. Most new Shadowhunters at some point perform the experiment of drawing randomly on themselves or on objects with their steles. This will cause the same "icy hot" feeling on the skin that actual Marks bring about, but no other consequences. Similarly, a mundane must be inscribed with actual Marks, and not just random stele sketching, in order to be turned into a Forsaken. One of the first tricks most young Nephilim learn, in fact, is to take advantage of the neutral character of non-Marks and inscribe an incomplete Mark on themselves, which can then be quickly completed and activated at the moment it is needed.

Only Shadowhunters can create Marks. A mundane or Downworlder can hold a stele, and it will not hurt them, but they cannot use it to create Marks; no lines will appear from the end of the stele, no matter what surface it is drawn against. Among Shadowhunters the strength of a given Mark is based on the inscribing Shadowhunter's talent for runic magic. That is, a rune to hold against pursuit will do so in relation to the strength and accuracy of its Mark.

Some Marks are applied to the bodies of Shadowhunters, and some are applied to physical objects. It is usually not dangerous to draw a body Mark on an inanimate object—a rock that has been given the Voyance rune will remain the same inanimate rock it was before. Applying object Marks to a Shadowhunter is somewhat more dangerous, as they will apply to the person's body as a physical object. This is occasionally useful. Note that Marks intended for inanimate objects, like all Marks, cannot be placed on mundanes or Downworlders, as the usual risks of madness, death, or becoming Forsaken still apply.

A Mark's power can be minimized or broken by the Mark's being disfigured. Shadowhunters should pay special attention to this potential target on their bodies; some more intelligent and well-informed foes may attempt to burn or cut Marked skin in order to deprive a Shadowhunter of the benefits of those Marks.

What happens if you Mark a dead body?

Nothing.

Really? Nothing undead or creepy?

Nope.

Well. I am disappointed

SPECIFIC MARKS

It is a common misconception that the only Marks used by Shadowhunters are those of battle. While we are warriors—and as such, conflict is part of our lives—we also make use of many Marks that speak in gentler tones. There are Marks for funerals, that tell of healing, grief, and comfort, and there are Marks for celebration, that tell of joy and gratitude. And, of course, there are the Marks that most Nephilim will never encounter, those arcane runes accessible only to Silent Brothers and other runes accessible only to Iron Sisters.

All Marks have names in the Gray Book; only the most common are typically referred to by their true names—*iratze*, for instance—rather than by informal descriptive names (e.g., "strength rune"). But the names of Marks are meaningful: They are in the language of Heaven and are, in fact, the only words of the language of Heaven we have ever been permitted to know. They are our most direct communication with the angels who gave us our lives and our mission.

There are literally thousands of Marks. We offer here a sampling of their designs and basic functions, but the Codex should not be used as a definitive source from which to learn runic manuscription. Please consult the Gray Book and your tutors for help.

Some of the Marks you will likely want to learn early in your education include:

- *The Voyance Mark*—This is the most basic and permanent Shadowhunter Mark, found on essentially all Nephilim, typically on the back of the right hand. It serves to focus the Sight and enable Shadowhunters to see through glamours and, with training and practice, to identify Downworlders on sight.
- *Opening Marks*—There are several variations on these, and it would be wise to learn a few of them before you begin

your active duty. These Marks ensure that no mundane lock, in theory, is closed to the Nephilim. Unfortunately, this also means that many demons and Downworlders will shut things away behind more magical locks.

- *The Tracking Marks*—Another set of indispensible runes for the pursuit of demons, these Marks are easy to learn to draw but difficult to use correctly. They are used as follows: An object possessed by the subject to be tracked is held in a fist in the non-stele hand. Then the tracking rune is drawn on the back of the hand. If the rune is used successfully, the Shadowhunter should see visions of the subject's location. Usually these visions will be accompanied by a knowing sense of orientation: Even if the place seen is unfamiliar, the tracker will have the knowledge of where it is, and in what direction it lies. (A common question about this process: What defines "possession" of an object? "Possession" is here defined literally. Someone is understood to possess something if they can be said to own it or if it is within the place where they live. Thus someone who has sold their house and its furnishings to a new occupant cannot be tracked using those furnishings, which are now in the possession of the new occupant.)
- *Healing Marks*—There are also several of these to be learned. The first is the *iratze*, the basic healing rune, which closes cuts and wounds in Shadowhunters. Note that this means that an *iratze* is not always the best treatment for an injury—for instance, if the Mark would cause the skin to heal over an embedded claw or thorn that needed to be removed. The *iratze* also raises the body temperature temporarily, helping to burn out infection in much the same way a fever does. This rune

TABLE OF SELECTED MARKS

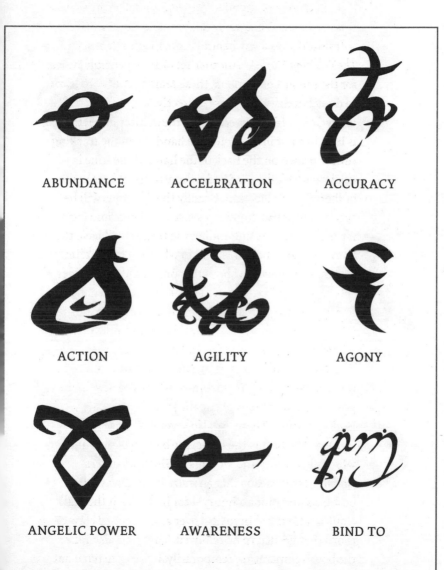

ABUNDANCE   ACCELERATION   ACCURACY

ACTION   AGILITY   AGONY

ANGELIC POWER   AWARENESS   BIND TO

TABLE OF SELECTED MARKS

BRIDGE

CALM ANGER

CLARITY

COMMUNICATION

COURAGE
IN COMBAT

CRAFT

CREATION

DESTINED

DEFLECT/BLOCK

TABLE OF SELECTED MARKS

ENDURANCE

ENLIGHTEN

EQUILIBRIUM

EXPECTATION

FIREPROOF

FLEXIBILITY

FORTITUDE

FORTUNE

FRIENDSHIP

TABLE OF SELECTED MARKS

GIFT

GOOD LUCK

GUIDANCE

HEAT

HEIGHTENED SPEED

INSIGHT/
FORESIGHT

IRATZE-HEAL

KNOWLEDGE

LOYAL TO

TABLE OF SELECTED MARKS

MANIFEST

MENTAL EXCELLENCE

MNEMOSYNE

NOURISHMENT

OPPORTUNITY

PERSEVERE

PERSUADE

POWER

PRECISION

TABLE OF SELECTED MARKS

PROMISE

PROSPERITY

PROTECTED

QUIETUDE

RECALL

REMEMBRANCE/
MOURNING

SHARING

SOUNDLESS

SPEAK IN TONGUES

TABLE OF SELECTED MARKS

STAMINA

STEALTH

STRENGTH

SUCCESS

SURE STRIKING

SUREFOOTED

SWIFT

TALENT

TECHNIQUE

TABLE OF SELECTED MARKS

TRANSMISSION

TRUE NORTH

TRUST

UNDERSTANDING

UNSEEN

TABLE OF SELECTED MARKS

VISIBLE   VISION   VOYANCE

WATERPROOF   WEDDED UNION   WINGED

is mostly ineffective against demon poisons and injuries caused by demonic runes. In these cases the injured should be quickly brought to a Silent Brother, but in the meantime it can be useful to apply a *mendelin* rune, which strengthens the victim's constitution, and/or an *amissio* rune, which slows blood loss and speeds natural blood replacement.

WARDS

You've probably heard your fellow Shadowhunters talk about the "wards" of your Institute. Wards are, put simply, magical walls. They are the simplest magic we know of, other than glamours. All Shadowhunter wards are pale reflections of the great wards of our world, the protections that largely prevent demons from entering at whim and that are believed to have been put in place by Heaven, long ago, before the measuring of the passage of time. It is these wards that were somehow "thinned" by the combined power of Sammael and Lilith, to allow the Incursion that prompted the creation of the Nephilim. Although these wards still stand, protecting us from a complete invasion, they allow a steady stream of demonkind that shows no sign of slowing and in fact may be increasing.

In the earliest days of the Nephilim, the first Silent Brothers performed rituals all over the world, intending to bolster these wards by adding our own lesser wards to their power. But wards exist at all levels of power, down through the more everyday wards we use to protect our Institutes, to simple wards that might protect a single room or even a single object, such as a locked chest. Today wards can be quite complex, and specific as to who is warded and who is allowed through.

Demonic magic, of course, has its own wards, which work similarly.

—— DEMONIC MAGIC ——

We use the term "demonic magic" to encompass all magic whose origin lies in the Void. This includes the magic employed directly by demons, which is mostly beyond our mortal understanding; the supernatural powers possessed by vampires and werewolves; and the complex but organized magic researched and performed by warlocks.

Demonic magic is by nature chaotic. Whereas the magic of Heaven is given to us whole and complete, the magic of Hell is a slippery, dangerous, growing beast. It is not known what limits might exist on demonic magic, in terms of either what it can do or how powerful its effects can become. There is much that has been discovered, and much knowledge that can be relied upon in dealings with demons (or warlocks), but never forget that—unlike our Marks, which begin and end with the bindings of the Gray Book—the edges of the demon world are full of magic unknown to us.

Shadowhunters are categorically unable to learn demonic magic, or to inscribe or even to read demonic runes. It is as if our knowledge of the Marks of the Gray Book prevents our minds from successfully being able to comprehend the Marks' demonic cousins, however we might study them. Nephilim who are expert at the reading and writing of Marks often say that trying to read demonic runes is like trying to understand someone speaking a language that sounds tantalizingly similar to your own but is too different for you to grasp the meaning.

Different kinds of demonic magic have different weaknesses—ways the magic can be neutralized—but almost all magic can be disrupted with running water. More powerful magic can sometimes overcome this, but on the other hand, larger bodies of running water are more disruptive and require more power to overcome. Thus, many powerful warlocks could successfully perform magic in the presence of a babbling brook, whereas only the most powerful in the world, or the most powerful Greater Demons, could successfully perform magic on the open ocean.

Has the Clave considered fire trucks? Just drive around the world hosing demons down?

Doesn't really work that way. You can't just spray a demon with water like it's a bad cat.

DARK MAGIC VERSUS DEMONIC MAGIC

It is important to understand that all "demonic magic" is not evil, at least not when it is used by creatures other than demons. Warlocks are in their essence human, and therefore have the same free will as all other humans. Vampires and werewolves have a demonic source for their powers but are also human and possess free will. All may choose to use demonic magic for good or for ill.

We use the term "dark magic" to refer to that demonic magic whose purpose or orientation is essentially evil. This would include such things as necromancy, the summoning of demons, the domination of an intelligent mind against its will, and so on. Dark magic is generally outlawed under the Law, although exceptions may be made for dark magic that is performed out of necessity in the course of Shadowhunter business—for example, summoning a demon in order to interrogate it.

Demons, being purely demonic and possessing none of the human about them, are considered to be performing dark magic no matter what they are doing. Technically, manifesting themselves in our world at all under their own will is an act of dark magic and is punishable under the Law.

Dark magic may be identified by some of its telltale markers. Its practice leaves behind a lingering aura that can usually be detected by a warlock, and often there is a persistent reek of brimstone and rot that even an untrained Shadowhunter can identify (although it will be typically glamoured away from mundane detection).

DEALING WITH DEMONIC MAGIC

The biggest danger of demonic magic for Shadowhunters is that, because its boundaries are soft and unclear, it can be difficult to understand the parameters of the magic one is dealing with, or what the capabilities of a magic user might be. There is no substitute for experience, of course, but we offer here some thoughts on common demonic magic and basic knowledge that may be useful for the new Shadowhunter.

DIMENSIONAL MAGIC

You will rarely encounter dimensional magic; the ability to perform it is very rare. Demons encourage the idea that they are constantly popping in and out of dimensions on a whim, but in truth none but the most powerful Greater Demons can do this. Demons travel to our dimension not through their own magic but by making use of the holes and worn spots enhanced and highlighted by Sammael a thousand years ago; as far as we know, none of the common demons have the power or knowledge to continue the thinning magic he performed. Some Greater Demons may have the power to teleport themselves to different locations within our dimension, and some may be able to open temporary weak dimensional Portals, but a demon who claims to have power over the spaces between worlds is almost certainly lying to you.

Warlocks who can perform dimensional magic are even rarer, although they do exist and are frequently able to charge exorbitant fees for their services. The most dangerous dimensional magic that warlocks may possess is the ability to create dimensional "pockets"—small spaces between dimensions, where objects or people may be hidden and kept concealed from tracking magic.

NECROMANCY

For as long as there have been warlocks, there have been tales of supposed necromancers, magic users who were capable of returning the dead to life. Do not be fooled by these tales: There is no way for the magic of Hell to return the dead to the world of the living. That is magic that is reserved for Heaven and its servants— not the Nephilim, for we are but the servants of servants, but the denizens of Heaven itself.

Necromantic rituals do exist in some more obscure and forbidden texts of magic; these, variants on the classic mundane folkloric "bell, book, and candle" method of summoning the dead, produce a semblance of life but not a living creature. These revived beings, in theory, can range from a mindless, shambling revenant to a corpse able to repeat its soul's last living words, but in practice such things are rarely, if ever, seen. Necromancy is among the darkest of dark magic. It is punishable by death, but most warlocks are never punished by the Clave, as they almost never survive their attempts.

HELLMIST

Hellmist, or hellsmoke, is a weapon sometimes used by demons, and occasionally by powerful and evil warlocks, to aid their attacks. It is very dangerous for the unprepared Shadowhunter. It is a kind of conjured demonic fog that mutes the effects of magic. Hellsmoke is able to mute both the angelic magic that Shadowhunters use with our Marks and also other demonic magic. Luckily, few kinds of demons can produce it easily, and those that do will make use of it only rarely, since demons are often dependent on demonic magic to grant them power in our world. For instance, a demon with no eyes who needed magic to see their foe would work against themselves in releasing hellmist.

Hellmist becomes much more dangerous when used to cloak a physical attack, but demons rarely engage in even such simple tactical planning. A coordinated attack of that kind would almost without fail suggest the involvement of a Greater Demon or a powerful dark magician. *And ... what should you do about that?*

When the Codex doesn't give you a thing to do, assume its advice is, "Run!"

CONJURING OBJECTS FROM NOWHERE

This is not possible. Something cannot be created out of nothing. Warlocks who claim to be able to produce new objects from nowhere, or who appear to do so, are in fact merely teleporting the objects from some location known to them. This is still powerful magic and potentially dangerous, and it may well represent a violation of Law. Warlocks, for all their power, may enjoy fooling mundanes and more credulous young Shadowhunters by claiming more abilities than they have. Do not be deceived.

THE SUMMONING OF DEMONS

While the practice of dark magic by warlocks is an unfortunate reminder of the continued threat demons pose to our own home dimension, and is generally forbidden, such magic is permitted in the course of assisting a Shadowhunter investigation—for instance, when a specific demon must be located or interrogated. In those cases generally a friendly warlock is employed; this has become much more common since the Accords eased the formerly tense relationship between Nephilim and warlocks. *Read this to*

The demon-summoning rituals vary somewhat, *Magnus, he says* depending on the demon and the warlock involved, but *"ha!"* generally speaking they take the following steps:

- A pentagram or similar summoning circle is drawn on the surface on which the demon is to be summoned.
- Demonic runes of various kinds are drawn on the summoning circle, often at the points of the pentagram or by some other design specified in warlock magical lore.
- An invocation is made by the warlock.
- Often a sacrifice of blood is demanded, usually provided by the warlock performing the ceremony. (Beware any warlock who claims that he will need *your* blood to complete his summoning!)
- If possible, a piece of the demon itself, such as a tuft of its fur or some scales or a tooth, is put into the pentagram. *Mmmm ... PIECE OF A DEMON.*

At that point, if the warlock is competent, the demon should be summoned and bound. Be sure to consult the warlock ahead of time for any time limits, restrictions, or forbidden words or hand gestures that might be relevant in that particular summoning. *Wait, how do you get a piece of a demon to use to summon a demon if you don't already have*

THE PORTAL *a summoned demon to get a piece of demon from?*

New Shadowhunters usually don't have trouble *... What?* understanding how a Portal works. It transports you *That was a real* instantly from one place to another by means of your *question!* passing through it. It is usually set up by a warlock (see below for the reasons why), and it requires no skill to use. We include it here, however, because the invention of the

Portal stands as one of the great moments of collaboration between Downworlders and Shadowhunters in the modern age, a powerful demonstration of the creativity and discovery that the Accords make possible. This invention also represents one of the rare occasions when the Nephilim have been able to advance the knowledge of magic in the human world, despite our pious devotion to the boundaries marked out by the Gray Book.

Oh no it's another history lesson secretly

Today Shadowhunters depend heavily on Portals as a means for rapid travel all over the world. It would be easy to conclude from this that the Portal is an old and well-established Nephilim tool, but in truth it is a modern invention, dating back to the period between the First and Second Accords. The first successful Portal was created in 1878, a collaboration between Henry Branwell, then head of the London Institute, and a warlock whose name history, unfortunately, does not record. Branwell was at the time only the most recent in a long string of Shadowhunters (mostly Silent Brothers) and warlocks to seek a reliable, safe means of instantaneous travel. Dimensional magic of course has been in existence for as long as there has been magic in our world; the means by which demons are able to slip from their own world to ours is itself magic in the same family as the Portal. There were two major requirements in creating a workable Portal for Shadowhunter use—keeping it stable and safely open for the necessary amount of time and safely closed when no longer needed, and accurately controlling the destination that a Portal would open onto.

Working on his own, Branwell had designed a Portal that had solved the first of these problems; it could be opened and closed, but he could find no way to direct its destination, and so it could not be tested. A Portal opened to an arbitrary location could send a hapless Shadowhunter to any location in our world, to a different world entirely, even to the Void.

The difficulty here turns out to lie in our restriction to Gray Book Marks. We cannot arbitrarily describe a destination using the runic language we are permitted to use. The solution was discovered by Branwell and his anonymous warlock collaborator, and it is an ingenious merging of two runic systems and the magic inherent in the mind of the one traveling through the Portal. First, a "frame" of Marks (which have analogues in both seraphic and demonic runic systems) is created, and inscribed within and around this frame is a set of demonic runes that are drawn in an unstable, unfinished state.

These runes, however, only specify the destination

in vague terms. To "tune" the Portal to the exact location desired, the user of the Portal must picture clearly in their mind the destination they are traveling to. The Portal detects these details and modifies the demonic destination runes on the fly, to exactly describe the far end of the Portal.

This kind of runic manipulation isn't available to Shadowhunters, and so to this day Portals must be created by warlocks. To get around this, a large number of permanent Portals have been established to transport Nephilim to and from Idris, for instance, without having to hire warlocks for every trip. Even so, today Portal construction makes up the vast majority of jobs for warlocks hired by Shadowhunters.

Originally Portals had to be closed manually by their creator once they were no longer needed, but in recent years warlocks have been able to create Portals that close automatically after a certain amount of time has passed. This kind of Portal is what is usually used today, for purposes of safety.

But none of this is relevant to you because you can make new runes, so you can make Portals yourself. Without bothering a warlock.

I know how much those warlocks hate to be bothered.

Did you know you're related to Henry Branwell, at least by marriage? He was married to a Fairchild.

I did not know that. It is sort of weird that you do know that.

I had to memorize a lot of Shadowhunter genealogies at one point.

I can't believe Simon hasn't said anything terrible here yet.

His absence is almost eerie.

DISCUSSION QUESTIONS AND THINGS TO TRY

1. Learn a new rune you haven't ever used before. Practice it here on the page and try applying it in the field.

   I draw enough runes, thanks. Here is a drawing of Chairman Meow instead.

1A. WHO IS A WOOBUMS? IS IT CHAIRMAN MEOW? IS IT? *Yes it is!*

   THAT IS CORRECT!

2. If possible, witness some (safe and legal!) demonic magic being performed near your home Institute. Discuss with your fellow local Shadowhunters. What magic is taking place in your part of the world?

   It's New York, so … all magic? Is there anything we don't have? I'm pretty sure we've got all of it.

3. It can be very useful to learn to make your own magical wards. Find instructions and place a ward on something small, like a jewelry box. Practice removing and resetting the ward, then move on to something a little more complex. And so on.

   Do not do this. Seriously, wards are a big pain. And you almost never have to make your own unless you're replacing a broken one. No one reading the Codex as a new Shadowhunter should jump into making wards. They'll end up warding their own foot or something.

   Note to self: Do not ward own foot. Check.

CHAPTER SEVEN

"SED LEX, DURA LEX"

"THE LAW IS HARD, BUT IT IS THE LAW."

You have been immersed, quickly, in a whole world that is still beyond your reckoning. You've learned not just that there are intelligent magical creatures on Earth who are not purely human, but that there are many of them, and many who wear a human face. These people wield powerful magic and engage in powerful, sometimes violent feuds. You know of the Shadow World and what you will find there. Now we take up the question of how you should act there. *In the most pompous way possible.*

We Nephilim are, primarily in the Shadow World, the keepers of peace, and thus the keepers of the Law. The Law—our Covenant with Raziel—tells us what does and does not fall under our jurisdiction, how we may punish violations of the Law, and what rules we ourselves must obey in our interactions with mundanes, with Downworlders, and with one another.

The Law of the Nephilim is not a full code of conduct for Shadowhunters in all realms of their lives. First and foremost comes the injunction attributed to Jonathan Shadowhunter himself: "You are Man; serve Man; live among Man." Though Idris may come with its own body of general laws, the Shadowhunters assigned all over the world are expected to live among the basic moral codes of their civilization. Our own Law is foremost in importance, but mundane law must be observed as well. *Really? The Covenant says that? Note: Ask Jace.*

Yes we are supposed to follow mundane laws.

... Really?

Some of us are more careful than others.

HOW THE LAW AFFECTS: YOU

- You must investigate **any known instances** of Covenant Law being **violated**. In fact, you are required to consider even **rumors**, **urban legends**, and **folktales**, to assess their credibility.
- You **cannot reveal the Shadow World** to mundanes. In fact, Raziel's guidance is that as we protect and save mundanes they must not know they are being saved.

What about mundane governments?

Mundanes who already know are ok but...?

- Whenever possible, you must **obey the mundane laws** in the place where you live. *"Whenever possible,"*
- You must **never commit a crime against another Shadowhunter**. These violations are punished much more harshly by the Clave than crimes against mundanes or Downworlders. This is not because of moral superiority, or because a Shadowhunter is a more valuable person than a non-Shadowhunter, but rather because we Nephilim are few and our lives short. To cause another Shadowhunter to come to harm is to benefit the demons who seek to destroy us.

nudge nudge

I AM SHOCKED! SHOCKED!

Oh, stop.

See?!

- **Collaboration or collusion** with the demons who seek to destroy us **is considered treason** and is usually a capital crime. Colluding with demons to bring direct harm to Shadowhunters would bring down the Clave's harshest possible punishment, the end of that family's existence among the Nephilim. The perpetrator's Marks would be stripped and he would be made Forsaken, left to go insane and die. The rest of his family would merely have their Marks removed and be made mundane, removed from our ranks entirely.

Okay okay fine

176

Do a lot of new Shadowhunters need to be warned not to collude with demons and not to kill each other?

I guess the Clave wants you to know they mean busines

HOW THE LAW AFFECTS: DOWNWORLDERS

Since the Accords, Downworlders have been subject to the Law of the Covenant, with their consent. Downworlders are meant to police themselves, with Shadowhunters interfering only in cases where problems are too severe, or where issues affect other parts of Downworld or the mundane world. Downworlders also have the right to conduct their internal business privately, without the interference or oversight of the Nephilim. For instance, we allow werewolves to fight to the death for control of their packs. We cannot protect these werewolves from possible interference from mundane law enforcement, but we also don't consider these deaths to be murder under the Law.

A special exception here is the case of dark magic (see the Grimoire, Chapter 6). The practice of dark magic—necromancy, demon-summoning, magical torture, and so on—is strictly forbidden, and neither warlocks nor faeries are permitted to practice it. Exceptions are sometimes made for specific rituals done as part of a Shadowhunter investigation, but they are very rare.

REPARATIONS

Downworlders have the right under the Law to appeal to the Clave if they believe they have been mistreated by Shadowhunters, or believe that Shadowhunters have broken the Law in their dealings with them. They may request Reparations, monetary compensation for the harm brought to them. They may also call a trial, which will be administered by representatives of the Clave, and Reparations will be paid if the Downworlder can prove their case.

Mundanes also have the right to petition for Reparations, but obviously this comes up infrequently; only a few cases have been seen of mundane Reparations in the entire history of the Nephilim.

The Accords greatly improved the rights of Downworlders under the Law, and so the nature of Reparations changed significantly. Prior to the Accords, Downworlders had essentially no recourse or specific protection under Shadowhunter law; a Shadowhunter could kill a Downworlder under only the suspicion of wrongdoing, and all that could be done would be for a next of kin to file for Reparations. In the last hundred years claims for Reparations have decreased, now that Nephilim can be held legally responsible for abusing Downworlders whether or not someone comes forth to demand Reparations.

SPOILS

The term "spoils" refers to the taking of the possessions and wealth of a Downworlder as part of the punishment for a crime. Typically these spoils are forfeited to the Shadowhunter who has been wronged by the Downworlder. Or the spoils are forfeited to the Clave's treasury if no specific Shadowhunter seems the proper recipient. In practice, however, Downworlders' spoils have almost always ended up in the hands of individual Shadowhunter families. In fact, for many old wealthy Shadowhunter families, a goodly portion of their prosperity originates in spoils granted by the Clave.

The practice of taking spoils probably began very early in Nephilim history, but in isolated and informal ways. Spoils are first mentioned in official Clave Law around 1400, but records indicate that the Clave had been officially granting spoils in trials for years already. The awarding of spoils was no more or less popular than other forms of punishment, until the Hunts and the Schism of the sixteenth and seventeenth centuries made the awarding of spoils the most common punishment doled out by the Clave. There were two reasons for this. The first was to legitimize and place some limits on the pillaging of Downworlder property that was happening regardless of Clave involvement; the second, which may seem counterintuitive, was to save Downworlder lives. In the existing frenzy of Downworlder persecution, which could easily have involved widespread murder, it was hoped that the promise of spoils would stay the Shadowhunters' weapons in favor of the larger benefit to them of spoils. *See, we had to steal their stuff to help them.*

The practice of granting spoils lost some of its popularity with the end of the Hunts, but it was still the most common punishment for Downworlder offenses until the First Accords. For all of the language of philosophy and Law thrown about, much of the Shadowhunter opposition to the First Accords came down to economics. Those families strongly dependent on spoils for their wealth stood to lose quite a lot. They argued that the rules restricting spoils would harm the Clave directly. Although spoils were not technically taxed, it was considered virtuous for Shadowhunters, especially the wealthier families, to tithe a percentage of them to the Clave. The First Accords created the beginnings of complex legal language that did not eliminate spoils but strongly restricted the severity of the punishment, and also provided that the punishment of taking spoils from Downworlders could be executed only as part of an official sentence at a trial performed by the Clave. Many spoils have been returned in the past hundred years. Although, in cases where the family of the original owner could not be located, many other spoils have been placed on display in various Institutes, as historical curiosities.

Nice motorcycle, by the way, Jace.
That's not spoils. That was illegal. I was impounding it.

Mom suggested that I talk to Luke about spoils. I did. He went off on a lecture again. Here are the notes.

HOW THE LAW AFFECTS: MUNDANES

Luke says:
• No limits on spoils during werewolf hunts. All that in the Codex ridiculous:
just made pillaging nice and legal.

Mundanes are not subject to Covenant Law. They are not signers of the Accords, and only a few in the world know of the existence of Shadowhunters or the Shadow World. Even mundane members

• Returned some spoils after Accords, but not much—couldn't find families.
• Didn't even try to return money taken. That would be impossible.
• Apparently in Germany there's an Institute that was taken as a spoil from some vampires. They're still fighting about it.

179

of demonic cults cannot be prosecuted under the Law, since they are meddling with forces beyond their ken. (**Tip!** Demonic cults can be most easily neutralized by going after the demon being worshipped, who *can* be prosecuted and indeed killed under the Law.) *Well, thank goodness.*

This is one of the most controversial parts of the Law. Every Accords proceeding has featured strident demands from both Shadowhunters and Downworlders that mundanes be held accountable for their behavior. These demands are always declined, for the simple reason that our charge to keep our world hidden from mundanes must be paramount.

THE INQUISITOR

The Inquisitor is the Shadowhunter responsible for investigating breaches of the Law by Nephilim. Not even the Consul can refuse to cooperate with her investigations. When Nephilim are put on trial before the Council, the Inquisitor typically serves as the prosecuting attorney, and recommends or requests specific sentences for guilty parties. (These recommendations must then be ratified by the Council.)

The Inquisitor stands outside the rest of Shadowhunter government of Clave and Council. She is typically disliked by the Nephilim at large, because of the authority she wields. It is an infamously thankless job. But our history is full of the stories of heroic Inquisitors who have kept our society from falling into corruption, by rooting out Lawbreakers and seeing that they are punished.

2002 ADDENDUM

The Inquisitor's most recent high-profile task was the investigation of the Circle, Valentine Morgenstern's band of dissident Shadowhunters, after the failure of his Uprising against the Clave. The Inquisitor had to perform a complex task of separating out those who had been made to follow Morgenstern, those who had done so of their own free will, those who had recanted his beliefs but had been unable to leave out of fear for their lives, those who still believed in his apocalyptic vision, and so on. Most Circle members' lives were spared, and the punishments of the guilty varied widely, from compulsory tithes, to incarceration, to the loss of administrative duties, to exile from Idris. Thus is the Inquisitor's job a difficult one, and her role in meting out justice complex and imperfect.

—— THE LIFE OF A SHADOWHUNTER ——

Though Shadowhunters come from all corners of our world, we are Shadowhunters first, and citizens of our own ancestral homelands second. In the thousand years that we have existed, we have lived apart from mundanes, and the life of a Shadowhunter includes many features unique to us and our history. These are outlined here so that they may be recognized, and so that you may behave appropriately at times of celebration, struggle, and grief. *I had a book like this section for Judaism when I was little.*

BIRTH

The birth of a new Shadowhunter is an occasion for great celebration. We are not a numerous people, and we tend to die young; therefore any new young Shadowhunter is a cause for joy and delight. Births are normally presided over by Silent Brothers, who are able to use both their Marks and their knowledge of medicine to keep mother and child safe and healthy. As a result, we have always enjoyed a much higher rate of survival and healthiness in births than the mundane population.

When a Shadowhunter is born, it is traditional for a number of protective spells to be placed on the infant by an Iron Sister and a Silent Brother, representatives of their orders. (Usually the Silent Brother is the same person to have presided over the birth.) These are meant to strengthen the child, both physically and spiritually, in preparation for her first Marks later in life, and also to protect her from demonic influence and possession.

Note: ask Mom about this, me?!

TRAINING

Most new Shadowhunters want to know where they, or their children, will go to school. There is no such thing as a Shadowhunter school in the way mundanes use the term. Instead young Nephilim are tutored, either in their family homes or in small groups at their local Institutes. The training of new Shadowhunters is one of the responsibilities of all adult Shadowhunters, who are meant to share teaching duties, each from his own expertise. Parents are meant to lead the project of training their own children; orphaned Shadowhunters under the age of eighteen are the responsibility of the Clave, and will usually be sent to be raised and trained in their local Institute.

Shadowhunters (other than Silent Brothers) do not typically do scholarly work when young. What mundanes would think of as "higher education" is the kind of learning that we do in our older years, when we are no longer able to fight effectively or safely and we turn our minds to intensive, focused research and study.

MEN AND WOMEN IN TRAINING

Male and female Shadowhunter children receive identical training today, and are expected to reach the same standard of achievement in their educations. It has always been true that the Nephilim have included both men and women, but it is only recently that all women have been given full training as warriors. There have always been women warriors among us, but prior to 150 years ago or so, they were quite rare. Women were mostly, prior to that, keepers of Institutes, teachers, healers, and the like. Although the Laws officially preventing most women from becoming full Shadowhunter fighters were revoked in the mid-nineteenth century, it wasn't until the mid-twentieth century that Clave women were given combat training as a matter of course from childhood, as Clave men always had been.

The women warriors of Nephilim past took Boadicea, the great warrior who led her people in revolt against imperial Rome, as their patron and model, and that tradition has continued to this day. *Wooooo ladies rule*

YOUR FIRST MARK

Most Shadowhunters get their first Marks at twelve years of age. Since you, the reader, are likely to have entered the Nephilim from the mundane world, rather than being born into a Nephilim family, you may well be significantly older. This carries with it some inherent risks. It is usually considered ideal to get your first Marks when you are no younger than twelve, and no older than twenty, though there are exceptions. The older the person receiving the Mark, the greater the chance of a bad reaction.

Some things to keep in mind when receiving your first Mark:
- If there is going to be a problem, it is not going to happen immediately. If you react poorly to the influx of angelic power, Shadowhunters will be standing by ready to

cut the skin, which will disrupt the Mark and stop the effect short. You'll then receive full medical and magical attention.

- The act of inscribing Marks on skin creates a sensation that most describe as like an "icy burn." This sensation will fade with time as your body grows accustomed to being Marked. The inscription of Marks also creates a scent in the air of something faintly burned. This scent will *not* fade with time. Do not be alarmed.

- Sometimes the newly Marked go into shock. The good news is, if this happens to you, you are unlikely to notice, because you will be in shock. Shadowhunters are trained to recognize shock along with other bad reactions to Marks and will treat you accordingly.

- In the next few days, especially if you are at high risk for side effects, you may experience such symptoms as screaming nightmares, night terrors, fear-driven bed-wetting, stark perceptions of the bottomless abyss of existence, restless arm syndrome, apocalyptic visions, acute illusory stigmata, and/or the ability to temporarily speak with animals. These reactions are normal and only temporary. *"acute illusory stigmata?"* **Barely ever happens. I think.**

- If you are not absolutely sure that you are not a warlock, we implore you to be tested before being Marked. Families with the vagaries of faerie blood, or even with known werewolves in the lineage, should be fine, since the Nephilim power will overwhelm these.

So this is more a "do as the Codex says, not as Jace does" situation, I guess. Since he just Marks any

AFTER YOUR FIRST MARK *girl he likes, apparently.* **When she is dying, ye**

Congratulations! You have survived your first Mark. We can promise that each successive Mark is easier than the previous. Your eagerness to learn by returning to the Codex is commendable, but before you return to your studies, you should make sure that the Shadowhunter inscribing you confirms you are capable of work. You may find a need to sleep extensively; this too is normal.

The Codex sure does congratulate you a lot.

GAINING THE SIGHT

Congratulations!
Don't second-guess this decision!

Unless you are among those rare mundanes born with the Sight (see the Grimoire for details), you will need to learn to see through glamours. You may have started this process already. Usually, new adult Shadowhunters first receive a Voyance Mark, and several other temporary Marks that enhance magical vision. (We do not keep these Marks, because in the long term they impair normal vision.) You will then be shown glamours of various kinds and will be trained in seeing through them.

"BLIND" NEPHILIM

Most Shadowhunters have the Sight from birth, and those who do not mostly gain it in the first two or three years of life. Some, however, are born "blind" and must be trained to see. Usually it is sufficient to deliberately show children glamours and their revealed true shapes; this produces full Sight in almost all Shadowhunter children by the time they are beginning their training in earnest, at five or six years of age. It is only as humans grow older that we need the assistance of Marks to initially develop the skill.

How could I possibly have already known this, Codex?

Did you know?

Before it was made illegal, it was traditional in some parts of the world to "jump-start" a Nephilim child's Sight by inscribing a deliberately weak Voyance Mark on the child, at a much younger age than we would today consider safe. (In some cultures the Mark was

185

inscribed and then the skin under it was purposefully wounded to disrupt its effectiveness.) When the Marking was successful, some haphazard level of Sight occurred at times for the child, and at least sometimes this successfully caused the child to have the Sight permanently even after the Mark was removed. Unfortunately, this process also occasionally caused children to die of shock, from the simultaneous effect of a too-early Mark and the abrupt appearance of Sight. The practice is still done in a few places, but thankfully it has mostly disappeared in the modern age.

MARRIAGE

If you are already married, your spouse is very likely also becoming a Shadowhunter alongside you. If you are not married, when you someday do marry, you will do so as a Shadowhunter. Marriage is considered one of the sacred tasks of the Nephilim, both because the union strengthens the community and because it brings about more Nephilim.

Many hundreds of years ago aristocratic Shadowhunter families typically arranged marriages for their children in order to strengthen and mix family lines; in the modern age this practice is mostly extinct, and Shadowhunters choose their partners based on their own feelings of love and affection, as most mundane cultures today do.

Shadowhunters have always exchanged trinkets and tokens to mark marriages, to signify love and connection between the bride and the groom, mostly borrowing these customs from their cultures of origin or their current cultures. Among Nephilim, marriage is consecrated officially by the exchange of Marks. On each participant a Mark is placed on the arm, and another over the heart. This tradition is believed to come from the Hebrew Bible, whose Song of Solomon reads:

Set me as a seal upon thine heart, as a seal upon thine arm: for love is strong as death; jealousy is cruel as the grave.

INTERMARRIAGE

Shadowhunters are permitted to marry other Shadowhunters and, in most cases, Downworlders. (Since the Clave's primary concern is the ability to birth more Shadowhunters, it is somewhat frowned upon to marry a warlock or a vampire, since they will have no children, but it is allowed.) Shadowhunters are *not* permitted to marry mundanes. They are, however, allowed to petition the Clave and ask that the mundane they wish to marry be allowed to become a Shadowhunter, in a process known as Ascension. (You may even be reading this Codex because you are yourself an Ascender!)

The Shadowhunter who wishes to marry a mundane applies for Ascension on behalf of his partner. For three months the Clave considers the petition, examining the history of the Shadowhunter who has applied, and his family, in addition to the background and nature of the possible Ascender. Of necessity this is all done without the knowledge of the Ascender; prior to the Clave's decision in the affirmative, it remains illegal to tell the mundane applicant any details of the ways of the Nephilim. Once the Clave has granted the petition, the Ascender is told about her situation, and she embarks on three months' study of Shadowhunter Law and culture. At the end of these three months, the Ascender is given to drink from the Mortal Cup and made a Nephilim; provided she survives this process, she is rendered a full Shadowhunter, with all the protections and rights of the Law that any Shadowhunter would have.

"provided she survives"?!

ASCENSION OF CHILDREN

Though it is very rare, Shadowhunters in the position of adopting a mundane child may petition the Clave for the Ascension of that child. In almost all cases this Ascension is granted, especially inasmuch as the child is entering an existing Shadowhunter family and will take an existing Shadowhunter family name. The three-month waiting period still applies, but after Ascension the child is typically brought up and educated in the way of any other young Shadowhunter.

What about same-sex marriage?

A BRIEF HISTORY OF SHADOWHUNTER INTERMARRIAGE

In the earliest days of the Nephilim, our highest priority was recruitment. Marrying mundanes was not only legal, it was encouraged. Shadowhunters were taught to view their search for a spouse as a kind of recruitment, and Shadowhunter families boasted about the quality of mundanes they had brought into the Nephilim by their children's marriages.

The practice grew much less common as the population of Shadowhunters became fairly stable and recruitment became a lower priority. In the 1400s the Council officially revoked Institute heads' ability to create new Shadowhunters without Clave approval. The Clave representatives in Idris had no mechanism for evaluating a possible marriage, and began refusing almost all requests for intermarriages with mundanes. In 1599 the Council outlawed all Shadowhunter-mundane intermarriages of any kind.

One would expect outrage from Shadowhunter families, but in fact the new Law appeared during the height of the Schism and the Hunts (see Appendix A). These events made

Okay, I went and asked Jace about same-sex marriage, and he looked at me strangely, and I told him I'd have to research it in the library, because he is cruel and heartless. Actually I think he didn't know the answer and was covering it up.

This sidebar is very long and is full of dates. It can be safely ignored. Your service as a Shadowhunter will never depend on knowing how intermarriage worked five hundred years ago. I promise.

Answer: Same-sex marriage recognized in Idris, legal for Shadowhunters in countries where it is allowed. There has never been an Ascension of same-sex partners, but Ascension very rare now so could happen in future anytime.

the Shadowhunters a much more isolated, militaristic, and monastic organization for a time. Nephilim stopped living among mundanes, as they had done in European villages for hundreds of years, and reorganized their Institutes as barracks. Even after the end of the Schism, this isolationism remained for many generations. To some extent the principles of isolation established in the Schism still guide the relationship of the Nephilim with mundanes today.

The fact of the modern world, however, is that Nephilim, especially in large cities and other populous areas, cannot help but encounter mundanes in their day-to-day lives, and no one today would consider it reasonable to forbid Shadowhunters to interact with mundanes at all. Thus in 1804 the Law prohibiting intermarriage was revoked and the method of Ascension developed. Ascension has always been, and remains, rare, but it is a crucial tool for keeping Shadowhunter populations thriving, happy, and dynamic.

BATTLE

There are many seasons of a Shadowhunter's life, and many turns that life may take, but the core occupation of the Shadowhunter is, so to speak, the hunting of shadows. We are warriors, holy soldiers in a ceaseless battle, and while our adult lives include the same joys and sorrows as any mundane's, the defining characteristic of our lives is that of fighting, of seeking demons invading our world and sending them, broken, back to theirs. It is the greatest honor for a Nephilim to die in combat with demons. Thus we say: Do not shirk from battle. Have faith, seek courage. A Shadowhunter who does not fight is not a complete

189

Shadowhunter. (Unless that Shadowhunter is a Silent Brother or Iron Sister, of course.)

It is true, however, that many Shadowhunters put aside their weapons as they grow older, and seek a quieter life of study or research. But we do not do this until we have lived a full warrior's life and are ready to put it aside with a feeling of completion.

Did You Know?

It is considered bad luck to say "good-bye" or "good luck" to a Shadowhunter who is going off to battle. One must behave with confidence, as though victory is assured and return is certain, not a matter of chance. *I actually did know that!*

Even I knew that. Come on, Codex.

THOSE WHO LEAVE *Everyone knows THAT.* *Why do I keep letting you write in this thing?*

Rarely, a Shadowhunter will choose to leave the Clave and enter the mundane world. There may be many reasons for this, but the Nephilim do not often look kindly on those who choose this path, whatever their reason. We are too few as it is, and we are meant to regard our status as Nephilim as a gift from Heaven and a divine calling, not as an accident of birth or a career path to be chosen or declined.

As such the Law is clear on the responsibilities of those who leave the Clave:

- They must sever all contact with Shadowhunters, even those of their own family who remain in the Clave. They must never so much as speak to Nephilim or be spoken to by them.
- In renouncing the Clave they also renounce the Clave's obligation to offer them assistance in case of danger. They are not even afforded the protections given by Law to mundanes.

- Their children, even future children, remain Shadowhunters by blood and may be claimed by the Clave. Shadowhunter blood breeds true, and the children of Shadowhunters will be Shadowhunters, even if their parents have left, even if their Marks have been stripped.
- Every six years a representative of the Clave is sent to ask those children of ex-Shadowhunters if the children would like to leave their family and be raised among Shadowhunters in an Institute, as if they were orphans. Only when the child has turned eighteen does this practice end. (Those who reject the Nephilim into adulthood are not treated with the stigma of ex-Shadowhunters but have the same rights of protection as any mundane. The Clave has no wish to punish children for the crimes of their parents.)
- A Shadowhunter who has been turned into a Downworlder can no longer be Nephilim but should not be punished in the manner of those who chose to leave. In these cases the person gives up the protection owed him by the Clave for being a Shadowhunter but becomes newly entitled to the protection granted to Downworlders.

DEATH

Most Shadowhunters die as Shadowhunters. And most die in battle with demons. *Major buzzkill, Codex.*

We Nephilim burn our dead, discarding the fragile physical body that has trapped us and restricted us for our short human lives. Our remains are then interred. Those who die in Idris are

191

traditionally entombed in its necropolis, outside Alicante's walls. Those who die outside Idris are entombed in the Silent City. The Silent Brothers have responsibility over the dead in both locations. Most Shadowhunter families are old families and as a result have not merely grave plots but large family tombs and mausoleums, often one in each of the two necropolises.

Before being set on the funeral pyre, the Shadowhunter's body is presented so that words of mourning can be spoken and those left behind can pay their last respects. Those in mourning traditionally wear white, and Mark themselves in red. The eyes of the dead Shadowhunter are bound with white silk, and he is laid to rest with his arms crossed over his chest, a seraph blade clutched in the right hand and resting over his heart. Funeral rites vary depending on the part of the world the Shadowhunter is from but traditionally conclude with a sentence from *The Odes of Horace*: *Pulvis et umbra sumus*. "We are dust and shadows."

Hoo boy, I can't read this right now. No no no. Too much.

Yeah, for me too. We've had a little too much dust and shadows lately.

SILENT BROTHERS AND IRON SISTERS

THE SILENT BROTHERS

Our Unnerving Allies

And Jonathan took his stele, the first stele, and slowly he drew a V, then another, then another, in a continuous line, VVVVV, from David's upper lip to his bottom lip and back again. The stele was warm in his hand and left a fine indentation of crosshatch that remained even after the stele's point was withdrawn.

Jonathan drew back, finished, and cocked his head at David, not sure if the Mark had taken.

David began to open his mouth to speak, and as he did, the lines on his mouth burned gold, and his lips caught just slightly open, held together by black threads, thin but strong. Jonathan stepped back and lifted the stele without thought, unsure. But the corners of David's mouth turned up slightly in what he was now able to produce in lieu of a smile.

"Sir?" Jonathan said, his voice wavering.

It is good, Shadowhunter, David said abruptly in Jonathan's mind. His voice was strong and calm and echoed in Jonathan's head much more loudly than Jonathan would have expected. *Now,* David went on, lifting two fingers to his own face like a gesture of blessing. *Now the eyes.*

—From *Jonathan and David in Idris,* by Arnold
    Featherstone, 1970

The Silent Brothers are indeed our brothers—brothers to all
Nephilim. Do not be frightened of them. Their appearance may be *No
sudden moves,
though*
disconcerting, or even sickening, to you on first glance, but they
are Nephilim, like you, and you fight on the same side, toward
the same goals. (Most Shadowhunters get over their fear of Silent
Brothers the first time they are injured in battle and the Brothers
nurse them back to health.) It is worth noting that many Silent
Brothers enjoy unsettling their fellow Nephilim, and deliberately
play up their spookier features. This is a kind of hazing and should
be taken as the good fun it is intended to be.

It is easy for new Nephilim to look upon the Silent Brothers
as somehow more holy or angelic or powerful than the rest
of us, but this is not in fact the case. The Silent Brothers rarely
fight and lack any of the many combat runes that you will
likely receive to enhance your physical and mental abilities.
Instead they have taken Marks upon themselves that grant them
access to the more esoteric corners of the Gray Book. They are our
doctors, our scholars, our archivists. To them is given jurisdiction
over the Nephilim dead. This of course includes those who rest in
the Silent City, but the cemetery of Idris, too, is the Silent Brothers'
domain.

The Marks that the Silent Brothers use in their work are not so
much forbidden to other Nephilim as hidden from our sight. In
essence, parts of the Gray Book are locked and invisible to us, and
the Marks the Brothers are inscribed with are the key. The Silent
Brothers therefore have access to strange magic that you will not
see performed by other Nephilim. In exchange for their special
abilities, they have given up some of their humanity, moving
farther from the Earth and closer to Heaven than the rest of us.
They are still human, but their extraordinary nature makes them
often disconcerting to us: They leave no footprints, do not cast
shadows, do not move their mouths to speak, and do not sleep.

Their bodies are tugged upward by Heaven, just as vampires' bodies are tugged downward by Hell.

Befitting their seraphic alliance, the Silent Brothers are sometimes called the Grigori. The term refers to the Watchers, one of the higher orders of angels (the Watchers are the angels who are present in the trial of Nebuchadnezzar in the Hebrew Bible, for example), and is applied to the Silent Brothers not to claim their status as more heavenly than other Nephilim, but rather as a reference to their role among the Shadowhunters: watchers rather than fighters. The term has gone out of fashion and is considered archaic but can be found in many older Nephilim writings.

The official habit of the Silent Brothers is a parchment-colored, hooded robe, belted at the waist. Novice Silent Brothers will usually have plain robes, while those who have advanced to full Brotherhood will have decorative Marks circling the cuffs and hems of their robes, in bloodred ink. High-ranking Brothers are sometimes known to carry scepters; these scepters are usually pure silver and are also decorated with Marks, with the head carved in a figurative symbolic shape, such as an angel with outstretched wings, a chalice, or the hilt of a sword. Silent Brothers cast no shadows on the rare occasions they are found in the sun; this is widely believed to be an affectation, like the robe, rather than having some actual purpose.

The Silent Brothers must, by Law, have both their eyes and mouths shut with Marks. There are several different Marks that accomplish this, and the different processes vary, from magically stitching the eyes and mouth shut; to merely keeping the eyes and mouth permanently closed with the Mark of Fettering; to cleanly removing the eyes and/or mouth entirely, leaving blank spaces of flesh where they once were. The latter is, obviously, the most permanent and irreversible of these and is considered the most devout means of Marking oneself as a Silent Brother.

THE IRON SISTERS

The Iron Sisters are a monastic order, like the Silent Brothers, the members of which have taken Marks upon themselves for a specific purpose that requires them to become more than merely human. In the case of the Sisters, however, they have taken upon themselves the ability to work the angelic stone *adamas*, and craft it and whatever other mundane materials are needed into the arms, armor, and tools that keep the Nephilim alive and protected. The Sisters are the only Nephilim permitted to handle *adamas pur*, unworked *adamas*.

Like the Brothers, the Iron Sisters must join the order by taking Marks upon themselves that act as keys to unlocking normally hidden sections of the Gray Book. These Marks also serve to distance them from the rest of humanity. (The Marks are different between the two orders, and being Marked as a Silent Brother does not give you access to the Iron Sisters' Marks, nor vice versa.) Also like the Silent Brothers, the Iron Sisters are not fighters, do not marry, and do not normally attend Council meetings or venture outside of their usual domain.

Iron Sisters are rarely encountered by most Nephilim, but when they are, they are significantly less unsettling in appearance than the Silent Brothers. Their eyes and mouths are not magically closed, and they can neither read minds nor speak telepathically. They wear simple clothes, long white gowns bound tightly at the wrists and waist by demon-wire, to protect their clothes from the holy fires in which their materials are worked. Apart from an appearance of agelessness, their only odd physical feature is their eyes, which typically glow with the colors of flames. It is said that the fires of their great forges burn behind their eyes.

Despite their somewhat more familiar mien, the Iron Sisters are even more private and removed from Nephilim society than the Silent Brothers. They live in solitude in their great Adamant Citadel—whose location on the Earth is unknown to any other Nephilim—and rarely venture outside their fortress. They do not like to be bothered and prefer to work in isolation. A Shadowhunter may live many years without seeing even one Iron Sister in the flesh.

The first Iron Sister, Abigail Shadowhunter, was concerned that despite the gender neutrality of the Shadowhunters, the Sisters would need to be protected from unwanted interference from male Shadowhunters, and so the Adamant Citadel was built to be, and has always been, open only to female Shadowhunters. Indeed, only women are permitted to speak to Iron Sisters.

DISCUSSION QUESTIONS AND THINGS TO TRY

1. Why do you think the Nephilim live under such a strict code of Law? How does it benefit our overall mission?

    SHEER UNBRIDLED CUSSEDNESS. BEING THE BADDEST HOMBRES IN TOWN. I wouldn't have put it that way, but that's pretty much the answer the Codex is looking for.

    Law and order good! Chaos and anarchy bad! Chaos and anarchy also part of our tools, but the Codex doesn't like to admit it.

2. Have you been Marked? Describe the experience here. Did you have a bad reaction to it? Did you notice it working immediately? How have any Marks since the first Mark felt different?

    The Codex actually sounds kind of creepy here. "Yeeees, tell me eeeeverything." I was Marked by a very cute boy with terrible impulse control. I don't remember because I was basically unconscious but everyone was mad at him when I woke up. The end. love Clary.

    OH MY GOD, YOUR LOVE IS SO EPIC.

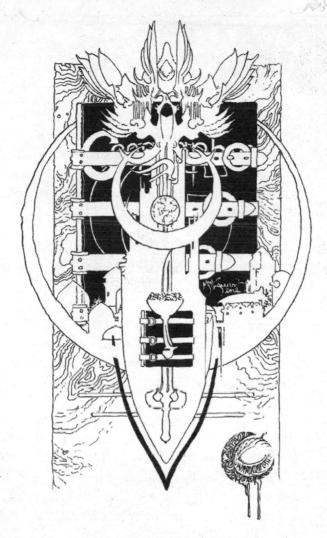

CHAPTER EIGHT

GEOGRAPHIE

IDRIS,
THE NEPHILIM HOMELAND

Idris is our country, our land of sanctuary and safety. If you, soon-to-be Shadowhunter, have not yet traveled there, you will likely do so in order to drink from the Cup and receive your first Marks, and there you will see the beauty and tranquility that have made it the best-loved of all Shadowhunter places. Angelic enchantment appears in each leaf, each river stone, each dwelling. The land stands presided over by the soaring fingers of *adamas* that form the towers protecting its capital, Alicante. These towers surround us with angelic light and shield the city and its people from demonkind. Usually.

WHERE IS IDRIS? WHAT IS IT LIKE?

The country of Idris is small, barely visible on a map of Europe. It is in fact little more than the city of Alicante, the plains that gently unroll beneath its walls, and the surrounding mountain range that protects it. Alicante is the only city—indeed, the only major settled area—in the country. This makes much of Idris difficult to traverse, even for Shadowhunters; its mountains are impassable except in high summer, due to heavy snows, and its woods, especially Brocelind Forest, are dense and unmarked by trails. Idris is, nonetheless, very beautiful country: low Alpine, stacked with sheaves of pine trees, among which meander countless rivulets and brooks. Though the land is different from any of its mundane neighbors—Germany, France, Switzerland—it evokes the same beauty as the landscapes of those countries.

Idris was not, as is commonly believed, made from land "stolen" from its bordering countries. Instead Raziel created an entirely new country, like blowing a bubble, in the middle of Europe. It is land made for no purpose other than to be a home for the Nephilim.

HOW TO GET TO IDRIS

Practice, practice, practice.

In order to reach Idris by air, one must fly to one of the airports in a neighboring country and travel overland across its border. Those who are used to the delights of mundane transportation technology may find this somewhat retrogressive, but we invite you to think of it instead as charmingly quaint. Of course, until the beginning of the twentieth century, the only means of reaching Idris at all was overland travel. The travel problem caused by Idris's landlocked status was eventually solved by the invention of the Portal, now the most common means of getting there and back.

THE WARDS OF IDRIS

Come visit the wards! You can't see them!

The wards around Idris are unique, and have proved impossible to comprehend or duplicate despite all our years of study. Humans are able to create wards that divert certain individuals away from a place or an object; they do this sometimes by illusion and sometimes by distraction. This is true of both Gray Book Marks and warlock magic. If a mundane passes through the Idris wards, however, he will be transported instantly to the corresponding location on the opposite border. This happens without any side effects or signs, so a mundane will have no awareness that he has passed instantly through an entire country. From the perspective of mundanes, it is as if Europe exists with no Idris in it at all, and indeed, this is how mundane maps depict things.

The wards of Idris were created by Raziel himself, as part of the initial set of gifts that he presented to Jonathan Shadowhunter. Their magic was not, apparently, magic that Raziel decided to share with his creations the Nephilim, and so we are unable to duplicate elsewhere, or at all modify, the wards of the Idris borders. Over the years Nephilim have argued endlessly about why the Idris wards allow the free passage of Downworlders and even demons themselves into Idris. In other words the wards prevent the discovery of Idris by the mundane world, but all members of the Shadow World may pass in and out freely. Many Shadowhunters have argued that Raziel's purpose in warding Idris was to prevent the Nephilim from ever becoming involved in land conflicts with its neighbors. Idris is meant as a hidden sanctuary from the mundane, and as a home, not as a political entity among the nations of the world, and as such, its borders can never be altered.

IDRIS AND THE MODERN WORLD

Idris's unspoiled nature is maintained in part by its wards, but strict Law also prevents the country from becoming modernized. This is partly because such improvements would be unworkable: magic easily disrupts modern technology. The wards that prevent mundanes from being able to enter or even detect Idris cause the whole country to exist in a "magical cage" that prevents machinery from working reliably within its borders. (This is similar to the disruption that prevents Marked firearms from functioning, and indeed, no firearm can be successfully fired within Idris.) As such,

Alicante is lit and powered primarily by witchlight, as are those rare roads that have been illuminated.

IDRIS AND DOWNWORLDERS

Idris is home to a number of Downworlder groups—faerie courts, werewolf packs in the forests, vampire clans in caves or in dark rocky valleys. For these Downworlders, Idris provides a space where they can live freely without having to disguise their identities, and where they can have land of their own, under their control. Those who live in Idris tend to be among the wildest of Downworlders, since they are the ones most willing to renounce the human world and live entirely away from mundanes. (This is even true for faeries, who, despite their prickliness, have a real affinity for humans and usually prefer to live among them.)

On the rare occasion when it has been necessary to bring an individual mundane into Idris for a moment of collaboration, or as part of Ascension proceedings, a Portal has proved the only method of circumventing the wards.

LAKE LYN

Other than Alicante the most sacred site for Shadowhunters in Idris is Lake Lyn, sometimes called the Lake of Dreams. It is the location where the Angel Raziel first appeared to Jonathan Shadowhunter, rising out of the waters and bearing the Cup, Sword, and Mirror that birthed our warrior race. Though the lake is sacred, its waters are in some way cursed: While Downworlders can drink from it safely, Shadowhunters who do so will suffer fevers, hallucinations, and sometimes, in severe cases, permanent madness. A Shadowhunter who has drunk from Lake Lyn can be healed with the use of healing Marks and other interventions, but they must be treated quickly, before the water has been absorbed fully into the system and cannot be drawn out again.

The shores of Lake Lyn give way to Brocelind Plain, a flat terrain of high grasses, which leads, as one heads toward Alicante, to Brocelind Forest. Writings tell us that the forest used to be much larger and covered the majority of the lowlands of Idris. Much of it was cleared as Alicante grew from being a small settlement in the center of a ring of demon towers to a large, bustling city. More of the forest was cleared to keep an easily patrolled border of open land around the city; Brocelind Forest has for hundreds of years been a favorite hiding place for vampire nests and werewolf packs. *ITS THE MIRROR. EVERYONE. Seriously, how did it take hundreds of years to figure this out?*

Never came up.

ALICANTE

Alicante, the Glass City. The holy city of the Nephilim. For Shadowhunters, Alicante is Jerusalem and Rome and Mecca and Shamballa and Bodh Gaya all in one. This must never be forgotten: While daily life goes on in the city as in any other, full of routine human needs and exchanges, it is the Forbidden City, the place given only to Nephilim as our base of operations and our haven on Earth.

To that end its towers protect it from demons, who cannot pass through the wards. Downworlders are able to pass through the wards without difficulty (a common argument for many years in favor of Downworlders' status as humans with souls, rather than demons), but they may not enter Alicante without permission. They are allowed to enter only as an invited guest of a Shadowhunter, and must either be accompanied by the Shadowhunter or carry with them the appropriate enchanted signed paperwork. (It is possible that you yourself have been through this process, if you were lucky enough to visit Alicante prior to your Ascension.) By tradition Downworlders are permitted to enter the city only through its north gate, which is guarded night and day.

In addition, for security reasons new Portals may not be opened directly into Alicante. Despite the partially demonic origin of the Portal, Shadowhunters have grown used to its convenience, and so typically Portals are opened to the outskirts of Alicante, outside the walls. The only exception is the permanent Portal in the Gard (see page 208). Shadowhunters often grumble about it, but the prohibition remains: Portals are created by warlocks, and while we are allied with warlocks as a group, we could not leave a hole in our defenses that would allow any possible rogue to open a Portal directly into our sanctum sanctorum.

FEATURES OF ALICANTE

The city is found in a shallow valley and divided by its river. The construction is mostly in gold- and honey-colored stone, with red tile roofs. Alicante rises up the side of a steep hill on one side, and its houses pile atop one another. From the river, canals have been dug, of which the largest is Princewater Canal. The new Shadowhunter is encouraged to stroll down Princewater Street and stand upon Oldcastle Bridge, from which the sound of the lapping water of the canal will accompany your excellent view of both the Gard and the Great Hall.

Apart from its unusual demon towers, Alicante is a city of canals. Since wells must be kept shallow to avoid piercing the *adamas* veins below the city, and the *adamas* provides a similar problem for Roman-style aqueducts, for many hundreds of years most fresh water was brought into the city by a series of artificial canals, crossed by Alicante's distinctive arched stone bridges. Today a network of underground pipes allows for running water in most Alicante homes, and its canals remain as reminders of an older age and as a charming feature of the city.

THE DEMON TOWERS

The demon towers of Alicante are Idris's most dramatic physical feature, a true wonder of the world. With the towers soaring into the sky like the finials of a heavenly crown, formed of pure *adamas*, it seems impossible that they could have been made by human hands. And in fact our history teaches us that they were not: The accounts of Jonathan Shadowhunter that have come down to us suggest that they were brought into being by Raziel, and that they grow out of a thick vein of *adamas* placed by Raziel under the earth to be mined for our Nephilim weapons and tools.

Raziel's words to Jonathan Shadowhunter include, in addition to the discussion of the Mortal Instruments, a mention of "a gift I bring to you upon the Earth." It's been often thought that this refers to the carving (and warding) of Idris out of the wilderness in the southern part of the Holy Roman Empire, but others have argued that it refers to the demon towers.

All Shadowhunters should look to the demon towers to remind themselves of their appointed station. These warded spires are a constant reminder that we are chosen and protected by the Angel, and that we are not entirely alone in our mission.

The demon towers have stood unchanged since the time of the very first Shadowhunters. Unlike with all other examples of worked *adamas*, their glow does not diminish with use, and their power has no need of being refreshed. Scholars have worked to determine why this might be, and whether the towers behave like normal *adamas* in other ways—whether they could be disabled by a dark ritual, whether they could be Marked, and so on. The towers remain the greatest lasting mystery of Raziel, and one that those in Alicante will find themselves contemplating as they pass under the towers' shadows. *Next Codex revision—demon towers less majestic and mysterious. More reminder of bad stuff.*

Yeah, this part seems a little naive now.

THE GARD

The Gard is the official meeting place of the Clave. It is the home of the Consul and Inquisitor and their families, and it is where the Law is made and debated. When the Clave is officially in session, only adult Shadowhunters are allowed onto its grounds.

The building is of dark stone and is basic in its architecture— a simple fortress, built for safety and supported on all sides by undecorated pillars. (Undecorated by architectural features, that is; the pillars are of course extensively inscribed with protective Marks.) Four demon towers, smaller than the ones that guard the city, rise from the four cardinal points of the building. Legend tells us that it was to the center of these demon towers that Raziel brought Jonathan Shadowhunter before telling him, "This is where your work shall begin." The Gard is thus believed to be on the site of the original small settlement that became Alicante, although the original structures are long gone; earlier generations did not have the reverence for history that we do now.

The gates of the Gard are among its most dramatic features; several times taller than a man, they are wrought from a combination of silver and cold iron, and are covered in calligraphic interpretations of Marks. On either side of the gates stand the stone statues, known colloquially as the Guardians. Each is a warrior-angel holding a carved sword and standing above a dying creature meant to represent the demonic enemies of the Nephilim—a reminder that angels are beautiful, but also terrible, and that just as we are in part angel, so are we warriors.

There is only one Portal open in Alicante, and it is in the Gard, for the use of the Clave in times of emergency. The potential danger of this "back door" is mitigated by this Portal's being "reverse-warded" in the manner of an Institute's Sanctuary. That is, Marks block it off as a place outside the protection of wards. The demonic magic involved in Portal construction can function inside this one room of the Gard, much as a vampire could stand safely in the Sanctuary of an Institute. This of course represents a large potential security risk, and so the exact location of the Portal is a closely guarded secret.

ANGEL SQUARE AND THE GREAT HALL

One of Alicante's most picturesque and historically relevant spots is the plaza located at the city's center, Angel Square, known for the bronze statue of the Angel Raziel that stands at the heart of the square. It is the largest statue of Raziel in the world, although one can find many smaller copies of it in Institutes around the globe. (Many of these claim to be recasts of the original sculpture, and some are, but others are definitely not; this distinction is, however, of interest only to historians of Shadowhunter art and thus will not be addressed in detail here.)

At the northern end of the square stands the Great Hall of the Angel, built in the eighteenth century as a general meeting hall for all Shadowhunters. This neoclassical edifice, with its long marble staircase and its magnificent pillared arcade, is a symbol of the enduring strength and integrity of the Nephilim.

In 1872 the Great Hall was used as the location for the historic signing of the First Accords, since Downworlders are not being permitted to enter the Gard. This signing marked the first occasion when Downworlders were permitted into Alicante in large groups; they entered the city through the north gate as is traditional. Since the signing, the building has been commonly referred to as the Accords Hall, and it continues to be used every fifteen years for the revising and signing of the Accords. In other times it is the site of celebrations, ceremonies, weddings, and festivals.

The majority of the interior of the Hall is taken up by a single large room, the site of these ceremonies; its walls are pale white and its ceiling high, with a large glass skylight that allows natural sunlight in. In the center of the room stands a large fountain in the shape of a mermaid, commissioned and sculpted in 1902 to celebrate the Third Accords, the first of the new century.

THE ARMORY

The Armory is an imposing stone stronghold on the eastern side of Alicante, part storehouse, part museum, part research center. It represents the only presence of the Iron Sisters within Idris proper, although visitors rarely see them, since the Sisters spend most of their time below ground level, working on new weapon designs, performing repairs, and the like. The Armory serves the same function for Alicante as the weapons room does for an Institute. The Clave has the authority to take whatever weaponry they need from it to outfit Shadowhunters for conflict within Idris. Those who are not Clave members are restricted to the south wing, which serves as a museum of antiquated weapons no longer in use, and showcases a small collection of weapons made famous in Shadowhunter legend.

The building was constructed in a medieval style, echoing fortress imagery, with its high stone walls lined in turrets. However, it dates only from the early 1800s and was built in a self-consciously antiquated style. The interior is not at all laid out like a fortress, and the impression that it gives of being able to withstand artillery fire is mostly a surface affectation. The Iron Sisters are protected instead by doing their work in its extensive and labyrinthine basement levels. A passage somewhere in those basement levels is said to lead directly to the Adamant Citadel.

—— THE SILENT CITY ——

For many Shadowhunters the Silent City is something taken for granted, a home for the Silent Brothers and a complex city of levels and chambers that has always been there, that has been inhabited for eternity. In truth the Silent City constitutes one of the great engineering feats of its millennium, on par with the building of the greatest of mundane cathedrals and temples.

THE BUILDING OF THE SILENT CITY

The actual construction of the Silent City was undertaken by the Silent Brothers, and it took roughly four hundred years for the City to attain its current size and reach. It began as a cavern of worked stone in the mysterious non-geographical space beneath Idris, no more than a small council chamber, a small area used as living quarters, and the earliest Shadowhunter graveyard. That is how David the Silent described it. At that point, of course, it would not have been described as a city. It became known to Shadowhunters as the Silent Cloister and was slowly expanded over the first hundred years or so of the Shadowhunters. Although it had become much larger than its original state, it was still more like a great underground manor house than like a city. Residences for the earliest Silent Brothers had been moved to a separate level; the area for gravesites had been, inevitably, expanded; and the Sword-Chamber, as it was then known, was larger and more imposing.

THE CITY EXPANDS

In roughly 1300 the first two entrances to the Silent Cloister were built outside Idris: one in what is now the city of Bangalore, in southern India, and one in the city of Heidelberg, in what is now southern Germany. Both were created to allow Silent Brothers much easier access to the extensive research materials those cities contained; the Silent Brothers also began to recruit for their ranks among the mundane monks and scholars who either lived in or traveled to those cities for wisdom.

At this point construction and expansion of the Silent Cloisters accelerated rapidly. Already by 1402, Council records referred to "That Great City, whose levels we know not and whose secrets the Brothers keep in Silence." The means by which the Silent Brothers were excavating their city, and even the location on Earth where this extensive city resided, was a closely guarded secret. It remains one of the mysteries that only Silent Brothers are permitted to know. (It's widely believed that the Iron Sisters assisted in the construction presumably by building devices for digging and construction. The Iron Sisters, however, keep their secrets just as faultlessly as the Silent Brothers.) Specific historical details are few, but we do know that the prisons of the Nephilim were moved from an outbuilding of the Gard in Alicante (now long demolished) to the deepest levels of the City in 1471, and that the council chamber that most Shadowhunters who have visited the City have seen was completed and opened to Shadowhunters in 1536. Construction and expansion continued after that, however. In fact, we cannot say for sure that the Silent Brothers are not *still* expanding, building their City ever larger; we have no proof either way.

VISITING THE SILENT CITY

Most Shadowhunters only ever see the two upper levels of the City—its archives, and its council chamber, where the Soul-Sword resides. There are, however, levels upon levels, plunging deep into the earth. The vast majority of these levels are off-limits to anyone who is not a Silent Brother, and the details of the Silent Brothers' living quarters, sustenance, laboratories, etc., remain a closely guarded secret. The exceptions are at the lowest depths of the city, where a series of levels holds the necropolis of the Shadowhunters and thousands and thousands of our people are laid to rest. And below these, on the very lowest levels, are the prisons.

The prisons of the Silent City can hold the living, the undead, and the dead; they are designed to constrain all creatures, however magical. (The exceptions here are demons, who may be powerful enough to break out of even the strongest cells.) Where those guilty of lesser violations may be incarcerated in Alicante, or in the keeps of Institutes, the cells of the Silent City are reserved only for the worst of Lawbreakers and the most dangerous of wrongdoers. Pray that you never need see them yourself.

SILENT CITY: NOT A TRANSIT HUB!

Since there are entrances to the Silent City all over the globe, one might reasonably ask whether the city provides Shadowhunters with a convenient route for travel. One could presumably travel quickly between distant places by, say, entering the Silent City in New York City and exiting in Tokyo. Indeed, Silent Brothers do use the Silent City's entrances in this fashion, so that they can be rapidly deployed where they are needed. Iron Sisters, too, are permitted to use the City this way, although they are rarely seen outside their Citadel. Regular Shadowhunters are not permitted, by tradition and Law, to use the City as a glorified train station. The general consensus is that this would not be a good idea, as it would likely involve passing through parts of the Silent City that the Nephilim who are not Brothers would find too horrifying to experience without losing their minds. This may or may not be true, but the Silent Brothers have done nothing to deny the rumors.

THE ADAMANT CITADEL

As the Silent Brothers carefully keep the secrets of their City, most Shadowhunters know even less about the Adamant Citadel, the home of the Iron Sisters. In many ways it is simpler, of course, since it is a single fortress rather than an entire city. On the other hand its mysteries are such that, for all we know, it could extend as extensively and as deeply as the Silent City; its inner chambers may be walked by only the Sisters themselves.

The Adamant Citadel stands on a volcanic plain, a stretch of dried lava beds, black and forbidding; a narrow river of molten lava rings it like a moat. It is reached—like the Silent City—through one of a number of entrances scattered around the world, the oldest of which resides on the lowest floor of the Armory in Alicante. The volcanic activity serves as a convenient defense for the Citadel, of course, but the location was probably selected to provide the Sisters with the extreme heat that they require for their forges.

The Portals that lead to the Citadel will not take you directly into the fortress, but rather to the volcanic plain, outside the walls. A ring of smooth, unbroken *adamas*, many times taller than a person, surrounds the Citadel; this ring, which appears to be a single continuous band of *adamas*, with no signs of mortaring or structural engineering, is an imposing sight, a reminder that the Iron Sisters are not simple blacksmiths but rather are working with seraphic forces that we can barely comprehend. In the walls is set one gate, formed of two gigantic blades that cross each other to form a pointed arch. This gate is normally left open but can be closed and sealed in times of emergency.

Through the gate, however, the fortress is still well protected. The actual Citadel building can be reached only by crossing a drawbridge, which can be lowered only by a small sacrifice of blood from a female Shadowhunter. The bridge is strewn with knives, embedded blade-upward, which must be carefully avoided. It is therefore not possible to approach the Adamant Citadel in haste; its gates cannot be stormed and its walls cannot be laid siege to.

The fortress is a dramatic structure, soaring into the gray skies above the lava plain, with a ring of towers around it that call to mind the demon towers of Alicante, though these are more regular and less graceful, having been constructed by the hands of humans. The towers are tipped with glittering electrum, but otherwise the whole structure is of *adamas*, glowing gently with white-silver light.

Once in the fortress a visitor would find herself in the antechamber—and this is all of the Adamant Citadel that those other than Iron Sisters are permitted to see. The antechamber is a simple room; the walls glow with *adamas*, as does the floor and the ceiling far above. In the floor is a black circle in which is carved the sigil of the Iron Sisters: a heart pierced by a blade. There are no furnishings or comforts; the Iron Sisters do not appreciate visitors and will endeavor to complete their business as rapidly as possible.

The walls of the Adamant Citadel are like the lives of the Iron Sisters themselves: hard, unyielding, and strong. Their motto, and the motto of the Citadel, makes this clear: *ignis aurum probat.* "Fire tests gold."

The Iron Sisters seem pretty awesome.

If by "awesome" you mean "completely terrifying," then yes, agreed.

— INSTITUTES OF THE CLAVE —

At first, there was no need for Institutes. For a few dozen years after the birth of the Nephilim, all the Shadowhunters in the world could reach the gates of Alicante in, at most, two or three days' ride. But we were created to be a global organization, and it quickly became necessary for outposts to be built, places of angelic power where Shadowhunters could organize and remain safe. And so were created the Institutes, the local power bases of the Nephilim.

Institutes function like the embassies of mundane governments. They are Nephilim homes, as much as Idris itself is. Crossing the threshold into an Institute, you are no longer in the country or state or city that the Institute's building stands in, but are rather in Nephilim land, where our Law is predominant.

The corollary to this is that Institutes are the responsibility of all Shadowhunters, not just the Shadowhunters who are stationed at a particular Institute or who are a part of the Conclave of that Institute's region. The oaths we take to protect our lands extend to all Institutes, around the world.

There are some features common to all Institutes. They are built on hallowed ground and are heavily warded. They are constructed to repel demons and to prevent the unhallowed from entering. Their doors remain locked to anyone lacking Nephilim blood. (The reverse is also true: The doors are open to anyone possessing Nephilim blood.) The mortar for the buildings' stones are mixed with the blood of Shadowhunters, the wooden beams are of rowan, and the nails are of silver, iron, or electrum.

Never has the invention of the regional office been treated so melodramatically.

Mmm delicious blood I eat your Institute nom nom nom

Very mature, Lewis. 217

Aside from these commonalities, one can find Institutes of all shapes and sizes, from the single-story sprawling villa of the Mexico City *Instituto* to the Eastern Carpathian Mountains fortress *Institut* high above Cluj in Romania. Each continent has an Institute that contains the Great Library for that region of the world; each of these is the largest Institute on its respective continent. These are: London, in Europe; Shanghai, in Asia; Manila, in Oceania (which region encompasses Australia and the Pacific Rim); Cairo, in Africa; São Paulo, in South America; and Los Angeles, in North America. Each of these larger Institutes has the capacity to house hundreds of Shadowhunters, although most Shadowhunters do not permanently live in an Institute. Normally, even the largest of Institutes has only a small number of permanent residents, who are responsible for maintaining the premises and equipment.

All local Shadowhunters will be called to their Institute for Enclave meetings, to discuss local affairs that need not involve the Clave or Council. In some parts of the world, the head of the local Enclave is always the head of the largest local Institute; in some places they are different persons. Local traditions and history dominate; the only requirement is that the region be adequately represented in the Clave, however the local organization is structured.

THE CONSTRUCTION OF INSTITUTES

Shadowhunter Institutes are built to serve as symbols of the power and sanctity of the Nephilim; they should stand as monuments to the Angel and glorifications of our mission. Often they include architectural elements meant to evoke well-known buildings in Alicante. There are many smaller copies of the Gard's Council Hall wooden doors, for instance.

Typically, and especially in well-populated areas, Institutes are glamoured to blend in with their surroundings. This glamour is usually chosen to make the Institute look not only ordinary but unappealing to visitors. For instance, the Institute of New York City, though in truth a magnificent Gothic-style cathedral, is glamoured to appear as a broken-down, boarded-up church, a derelict awaiting demolition.

Although the wards of the demon towers of Alicante prevent electricity and similar power sources from working reliably inside its borders, the weaker wards of Institutes typically do not cause this problem. Most Institutes today are wired for electricity, or at worst gaslight, although witchlight is often used for atmospheric effect or as a backup in places where electrical supply may be unreliable. There are exceptions, of course—a few of the Institutes in more historically besieged areas, or more remote locations, are either too warded or too far from mundane civilization to use modern power sources.

Institutes do not have keyed locks, except out of historical preservation. Instead any Shadowhunter may gain entrance to any Institute by putting her hand to the door and requesting entrance in the name of the Clave and the Angel Raziel.

SANCTUARIES

Most Institutes built before the 1960s contain Sanctuaries. Sanctuaries are meant to solve an obvious problem with the Nephilim practice of building Institutes on sanctified ground. While doing so prevents demons from entering an Institute, it also prevents all Downworlders from entering. There was a time when this policy was a wise one, but it creates the problem of preventing Institutes from holding a Downworlder temporarily—for example when there's a need to interrogate one, and incarceration in the Silent City would be more complicated than the situation warranted. Then too, in this modern age the Nephilim maintain cordial relations with many Downworlders, who assist us with information. To solve this problem Sanctuaries— unsanctified spaces that connect directly to the sanctified spaces of Institutes—were attached to most Institutes. Here Downworlders may be held or, as the case may be, hosted. Sanctuaries are typically well-protected and warded, typically by mundane key and by Mark as well.

Projection magic was invented by an unnamed warlock (or team of warlocks, possibly) on the Indian subcontinent in 1958, and spread quickly through the world, mostly obviating the need for Sanctuaries. Most Institutes, however, predate that year, and their Sanctuaries have been maintained as contingencies and out of historical interest.

NYC Institute has one. I'll show you sometime if you want.

It's a date.

It is maybe the least romantic spot in the Institute, by the way.

You'll make up for that, I'm sure.

JEEZ, GET A LOCKED ROOM ON UNSANCTIFIED GROUND, YOU TWO.

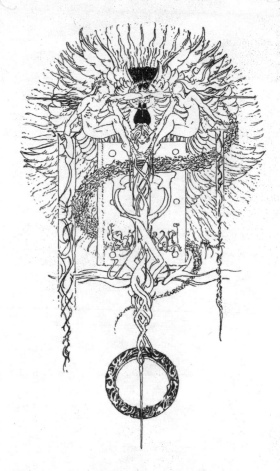

APPENDIX A

EXCERPTS FROM
A HISTORY OF
THE NEPHILIM

BEFORE THE NEPHILIM

We cannot say much about the origin of demons. All we can say for sure is that they were in our world well before humans came to be.

In the beginning was the world, and light, and humanity, and goodness, but in the beginning too were the demons, Sammael and Lilith, mother and father of evil to come, the paragons of corruption and sin. They were created when the world was created, and roamed freely, creating other, lesser demons, sowing chaos. They mated with humans and created warlocks. Their kind mated with angels, who in those times could be found on Earth, and created faeries. Sammael took the form of a great Serpent and tempted humanity into iniquity. Lilith, first wife of Adam, rejected the ways of mortals and cursed their children to torment. Or so say the oldest texts of the Nephilim. *The newer ones say they were a song-and-dance team. We get it.*

The history of demons is murky and mythological in nature. *you don't have a clue.* Within the Jewish, Christian, and Muslim traditions there are dozens of variations on the story of these two ur-demons and their offspring, and in other major religious traditions there are tales that may or may not be discussing the same entities. All religions, after all, have a tradition of demonology. We can say only that at some time around the very beginnings of humanity, the demons grew too strong and too many, and Heaven declared war on them. Heaven won the war, but the angels were unable to eradicate demons from the world. They had to be satisfied with banishing demonkind to the Void, and they modified our world in some subtle way unknown to us, which made it dangerously toxic to demons, preventing their return.

Nephilimic folklore tells us that this war between Heaven and the demons decimated Earth, and that the mythological objects of human religion—the Tower of Babel, the Garden of Eden, the World-Tree, the original pyramids—were wiped away by the destruction. So too were the supernatural animals of mythology, the unicorn and the dragon among them. We cannot know, of course, the truth of it. All we can say for sure is that the faeries survived.

Time passed. Stability came to Earth, and human history as we know it began. Demons were mostly kept out of our world, since they could not survive its poisonous effect on their bodies for long. Some of the more powerful demons could remain for a matter of hours or even days. Eventually, however, they would fall apart as their energies were snapped back to the Void. Humanity cursed what evil it found, not knowing the peace they luxuriated in.

WARLOCKS AND FEY: THE EARLIEST DOWNWORLDERS

The fey are the oldest race of Downworlders in existence; they are known, in fact, to precede humans by eons, although it is assumed that they were very different in those early days. Warlocks are almost as old a group. They were very few in number, but some individual demons were able to survive in our world long enough to create warlocks. Only through these warlocks did humans know anything of demonic magic.

WARLOCKS BEFORE THE NEPHILIM
It was a warlock who was the first Downworlder that Jonathan Shadowhunter directly interacted with—Elphas the Unsteady. Elphas wrote the earliest known "Nephilim-approved" demonology, compiling data from his and the

first-generation Shadowhunters' personal experiences and offering extensive commentary on other earlier demonologies, since new Shadowhunters often would possess some "foreknowledge of Downworld" that turned out to be entirely false and based on popular, incorrect texts.

There are today eight warlocks living who claim to have been born earlier than Jonathan Shadowhunter. Of these, scholars believe that five are probably credible, and of those, two have enough corroborating evidence to indicate that they're telling the truth. One of these, Baba Agnieszka, is known to be the elder sister of Elphas the Unsteady and has lived quietly in Idris since 1452, in a cottage built and maintained for her by the Nephilim in honor of her family connection. She is unfriendly to visitors and appears to prefer to be left alone. Recent reports from those who have visited her have described her as mad and doddering, which is not normally something that happens to warlocks.  Agnieszka appears to have deteriorated mentally not as a result of physical aging but rather due to a slow decay caused by eccentricity and isolation. She is something of a relic, but to the Nephilim she is a holy relic.

The other verified ancient living warlock is far older than Agnieszka. Isaac Laquedem's birth has been traced to what is now southwestern France, in the early part of the seventh century. He became known widely for his warlock mark, a large and impressive set of stag's antlers. The

legends of a man with antlers who rode on a hunt across France, never resting in one place, are likely to originate with him. Early French Shadowhunters, who were sure that the Wandering Hunter was a myth or at best a composite of a number of different figures, were astonished to meet Laquedem and discover not only that he was real but that the stories about him were almost entirely true.

Laquedem's hunting days have come to an end, and he chooses to live out his eternity on a farm not far from Bergerac in France. Despite his age Laquedem is useless as a source of historical knowledge on any topic except the forests of France, about which he knows an enormous amount. The rest of history has largely passed Laquedem by.

We must go hang out with that guy!

No!

He's actually pretty boring. Also hope you like eating a lot of venison.

THE INCURSION

Always have to one-up me, don't you. You magnificent bastard.

The demon Incursion, their large-scale invasion of our world, began shortly after the first Christian Millennium (that is, AD 1000) and has not yet ceased.

After what seemed like thousands of years of dormancy, Lilith and Sammael awoke and—so the story goes—performed a demonic ritual, of enormous power, that could be performed only once and never again. The ritual affected the whole of the

demon city Pandemonium, and with this act they massively strengthened all of demonkind's resistance to the toxicity of our world. After the ritual, demons were still poisoned by our world, but to a much lesser degree, and demons began to enter our world and remain here for long periods of time, drinking the life from it and bringing with them ruination and rot. They invaded, and humanity suffered.

CRUSADES AND CULTS

The Incursion was disastrous for humanity, in more ways than one. The most obvious consequence was the sheer physical damage, of course—demons wiped out whole villages, burned crops, turned brothers against one another.

But the more extensive damage lay in humanity's response to the threat. The presence of demons gave rise to apocalyptic cults that disrupted the normal structures of life and religion. Some cults were demon-worshippers, hoping to be spared by their conquerors. Other cults tried to band together to fight the demons, usually bringing destruction upon themselves and anyone unlucky enough to be close by. These cults spread fear and chaos where they went.

Worse, perhaps, than isolated apocalyptic cults was the larger political response. Christian Europe decided that the demons were spreading over their lands because their Holy Land of Jerusalem was not in Christian hands, and declared the first Crusades in order to get it back. Thus, rather than turning their attention to the immediate demonic threat, the Islamic Near East and the Christian West entered a long series of bloody wars and recriminations that, if anything, only helped the demons spread mayhem and death.

JONATHAN SHADOWHUNTER

The Crusades soon became a popular career path for young men of Europe seeking their fortune and name in battle. It was an opportunity for renown. Some, like Jonathan Shadowhunter, were younger sons of nobles and would not inherit their family's fortune. Jonathan felt pulled to battle because of honor and duty, surely, but the Crusades also were one of the few avenues available to him.

Unfortunately, the man Jonathan is something of an enigma to us today. We know little of his life before the Nephilim and even less of his childhood or family of origin. (A medieval tradition tells us that he was the seventh son of a seventh son, but no evidence of this exists.) We know that his family were wealthy landowners but he would inherit nothing from them.

Of the fateful trip that changed his life and our whole world, we know that Jonathan was on his way to Constantinople to join the European forces mustering there. He traveled not alone but with two companions: David, his closest friend, who hoped to join the Crusade not as a soldier but as a medic; and Abigail, Jonathan's elder sister, bound too for Constantinople, not to fight but to join the man to whom she was betrothed. (Of this doomed fiancé no knowledge remains, except that Jonathan was unhappy with the match and often spoke about his pleasure at Abigail remaining with him rather than wasting away "in some tiny hamlet on the Black Sea.")

A NOTE ON JONATHAN SHADOWHUNTER'S ORIGINS

While the story of the creation of the Nephilim is one that has been told and retold continually since that creation, there are several key details of Jonathan Shadowhunter himself that are, frustratingly, lost to history. His home prior to his encounter with Raziel is known only to be somewhere in central, northern, or western Europe, because at the time his journey was interrupted. David reports that their party was traveling east. Over the course of history almost every nation has made a claim as the home of Jonathan Shadowhunter; there was a powerful faction in the eighteenth century that believed him to have been a massive Icelandic warrior, for instance, though we now believe that theory is somewhat far-fetched.

A DREAM OF SHADOWS

Our only direct report from the group that beheld Raziel comes from translations of accounts supposedly written by David. It's not known whether he wrote these accounts as they were happening or wrote them as memoirs later in his life. They are, however, the closest we can come to the truth.

In his notes David relates a conversation that, he says, took place the night before the creation of the Nephilim. The three travelers were camped in the forest. Several days before, they had met and fought a small lone demon on the road. They did manage to chase it off, but not without Jonathan suffering a deep, dangerous wound in his right arm. The wound was thickly bandaged, and Jonathan held his arm immobilized in a sling, but then, by the light of a small, almost smokeless fire, he unwrapped the bandages from his arm, and he said to his companions, "This cut is deep and long. The demons have put such a wound into the flesh of the world itself, which can be bandaged, but under the bandages it will not heal."

Abigail agreed that this was true, but that the three of them, young and inexperienced, had little power to help. David remained silent, as was his preference, staring into the fire and considering.

Jonathan continued, "It does not work simply to kill demons. They damage the world by their very presence. They must be eliminated, the wound of the world bound and dressed so that it might begin to heal."

He told them of a dream: "On the night that I pledged my sword to the Crusades," he said, "I dreamed I stood in blazing sunlight, golden like the light of heaven, and my sword shone so that I myself was blinded. On the night my arm suffered this scratch, I dreamed differently. I had realized that the demons I sought would not come to me, in the light. They remained safe in darkness, and their power lay in keeping their secrets.

"In this dream I still held my sword, but it did not shine. Instead I crept through the shadows, which embraced me like a child. The shadows became not the demons' ally but mine. When I struck with my sword, it was with silence and speed, and none but myself and the demon knew what had transpired."

We cannot know whether the events that led to the creation of the Nephilim were destined, or were manipulated into place by Heaven, or just arose by chance. Whether the world would have been destroyed without Jonathan Shadowhunter, or whether some other leader would have arisen, is a matter for speculation. The fact is that in the hour of greatest need, Jonathan Shadowhunter did rise up and become that leader.

LAKE LYN

The next day (according to David), the party's travels took them to Lake Lyn, in the mountains of Central Europe. The lake was not the glittering blue of today but a black roiling tear in the fabric of the world through which demons passed back and forth freely. Jonathan, David, and Abigail were attacked there by a swarm of demons, of some species we can't now identify. (There are a few possibilities supported by different scholars, but all we have is David's description—"very large, like a bat and a shadow, an eagle and a serpent, that towered over us like a thunderstorm." *Idiots.* *Obviously it was a swarm of serpent-eagle Thundershadowbats.*

The party fought the demons back as best they could, but Jonathan was already wounded, and neither Abigail nor David possessed great physical strength. David tells us that Jonathan threw off his sling and bandages and fought valiantly through the pain. They held the demons off from killing them, but were overwhelmed. Finally the demons took all three into the lake, to drown them.

Fighting against his fate, Jonathan used what little breath he had to ask a blessing on the lake, to sanctify it as a place where things of evil, such as these demons, would not be welcome. He prayed, and his prayer was answered.

Summmmmmre

RAZIEL AND THE MORTAL INSTRUMENTS

And Raziel rose from the lake, bearing with him the Mortal Instruments. All action ceased. Even the demonic energies of the tear in the world seemed to stop. In the forests surrounding them, birds quit their singing.

Raziel spoke, saying, *Be not afraid.*

I am an angel of the Lord come unto you, Jonathan. You have called me and I have come.

Jonathan said, "Please, save my friends."

We cannot blame Jonathan for not asking Raziel for a greater gift; indeed it is admirable that in such a moment he would think first of the lives of his companions.

Raziel lifted Jonathan, David, and Abigail from the lake and placed them on the shore. The Angel's figure was human, but so large that he could cradle the three mortals easily in his palms.

Then he lifted his arms, and with a single great motion he flung the remaining demons high into the air. Jonathan watched them rise and rise, eventually fading to pinpricks that vanished against the stars. Then Raziel turned his gaze back to Jonathan. *I know your dream,* he said. RAZIEL THREW THEM INTO SPACE. AWESOME.

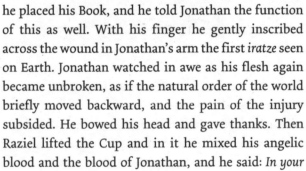

Jonathan was struck silent. He looked to his friends, and saw that they were not conscious but were breathing.

On the banks of the lake, Raziel placed the Cup, the Sword, and the Mirror, and told Jonathan each of their functions. Beside them he placed his Book, and he told Jonathan the function of this as well. With his finger he gently inscribed across the wound in Jonathan's arm the first *iratze* seen on Earth. Jonathan watched in awe as his flesh again became unbroken, as if the natural order of the world briefly moved backward, and the pain of the injury subsided. He bowed his head and gave thanks. Then Raziel lifted the Cup and in it he mixed his angelic blood and the blood of Jonathan, and he said: *In your dream you saw a great truth—that to destroy the things of darkness, it is sometimes necessary to descend into the shadows to join them. You shall bring men and women into the darkness with you, and you will master the shadows, and you will hunt.*

> *From now until the end of the world,*
> *You shall be called Jonathan Shadowhunter*
> *For you and your kin will drive the shadows of the world away*
> *And you will make light in dark places*
> *And you will be called Nephilim, as it says in the*
> book of Genesis:

"The Nephilim were in the earth in those days, and also after that, when the sons of God came unto the daughters of men, and they bore children to them: the same were the mighty men that were of old, the men of renown."

For you will be of men and yet you will be of angels; both in one.

Raziel seemed less annoyed with everybody back then.

Dealing with humans for the last thousand years probably hasn't helped his mood.

IDRIS

The Angel Raziel, in his generosity, had two more gifts for Jonathan Shadowhunter.

The first was the gift of *adamas*, the heavenly crystal that glowed with heavenly fire, that could not be cut or carved by mundane means, and the secrets of whose working could be found only in the Gray Book. *Demons will recoil from its power*, said Raziel. *It shall be the metal of the Nephilim forevermore, however much is needed.* And he presented to Jonathan a polished branch of *adamas*, the first stele. *With this will you draw the sigils of Heaven.*

Then he raised his hands, and from the ground came spires and towers, many times the height of a man, spiked and yearning toward the sky. From many places on the plain they came, and when they had all grown, Raziel led these first Nephilim to a spot in the midst of the towers, where four smaller towers stood describing a diamond, and there he gave them the second gift, the gift of Idris.

This shall be your country, he said. *A haven for all the Nephilim and those who beat against the shadows of this world.* He described the wards he had created, and the safety they promised. And then he began to rise back toward Heaven. *Now never contact me again, he said.*

Legend tells us that then Jonathan Shadowhunter cried out in a moment of human weakness, asking Raziel how he could be called if the need became too great for mortals to bear. And Raziel answered him that he had given all he could, the many gifts of Heaven: the Cup, the Sword, the Mirror, the Gray Book, the *adamas*, the land of Idris. He could give no more. This mission, he said, must be the mission of men. But then he relented, and his sternness briefly faded, and he said, *If you again find yourself in true need—true need—of me, take the Cup, the Sword, the Mirror—these Mortal Instruments—and summon me by the shores of the lake.*

And then he departed. *But seriously, never call me.*

THE RISE OF THE NEPHILIM IN THE WORLD

We owe a great debt to the earliest Nephilim, Jonathan, David, and Abigail (for Jonathan's first task once Raziel had left was to nurse his friend and his sister back to health, and to have them drink water from the Mortal Cup to transform them, too, into Nephilim like himself). On their own, recruiting as they could from among locals and trusted associates, they laid the stones upon which all of Shadowhunter society was built.

Abigail Shadowhunter set the precedent for Shadowhunters comprising both men and women, a guiding principle that has continued to this day. With the intensity of a new Boadicea, she established that the female Shadowhunters were no less fierce and resolute than the men organized under Jonathan's banner. When she grew older, and could no longer wage war against demonkind as she once had, she turned to the esoteric knowledge of the Gray

Book and the beating angelic heart of *adamas* beneath Idris to become the first Iron Sister. Along with six other Nephilim she constructed the first *adamas* forge, and the earliest incarnation of the Adamant Citadel upon its volcanic plain.

David, by contrast, was never a warrior and always a scholar and medic. Early in his time among the Nephilim, he witnessed a ritual sacrifice performed by a Greater Demon in an anonymous cave in Idris, and the horror of what he saw caused him to take a permanent vow of silence. This sent him, too, to the farthest depths of the Gray Book, into deep research. Over time he and his followers grew away from the world, remaining Nephilim but sacrificing some of their humanity for more angelic power. David became the founder of the Silent Brothers, and with the help of the Iron Sisters, he exorcised the cave of his nightmares and created the beginnings of the Silent City.

Meanwhile, Jonathan and his followers went out into the world to recruit more worthy men and women to become Shadowhunters. When possible they recruited whole families, bringing them wholesale into the Nephilim and granting them new names, in the compound model of the Shadowhunters. There is, of course, scarce space in these pages to tell the stories of those early Shadowhunters, blazing their warrior's trails across Earth, but we encourage the interested Shadowhunter to seek out some of the more interesting tales in the library of their local Institute:

- The tale of the first Institute on the British Isles, in Cornwall, where the first Nephilim arriving with the Cup were believed to be wielding the Holy Grail, and whose tales of bravery and vigor have become mixed up with the mundane folklore of the isles.

- The earliest European Nephilim to arrive in the New World, and their struggles to survive the harsh winters and totally unfamiliar demons. Many were slaughtered, and if not for the assistance of the first peoples of that continent and a small number of helpful warlocks among them, they would surely have perished.

- The massacres of the 1450s, when the Institute at Cluj in Transylvania changed from a small mountain backwater to the busiest and most treacherous Nephilim posting in the world.

- Patrick of Cumbria, who united faeries, Shadowhunters, and mundane earls across Ireland in 1199 to drive the demons out (and whose work was unfortunately undone by Henry VIII, who ended several hundred years of demonlessness in Ireland when he began to reassert English control over the kingdom of Ireland beginning in the 1530s).

- The great Scorpion-Riders of the Australian backcountry, in the mid-1600s.

- The doomed Dazzling Charge of 1732, when a crack squad of Nephilim warriors in central France discovered, to their horror, the ineffectiveness of firearms in fighting demons.

- The lost Ethiopian Nephilim, separated from the entire Clave and Idris for hundreds of years beginning in the 1300s, but who kept up the ways of the Shadowhunters, the knowledge of Marks, and the use of the seraph blades independently, until they rejoined the world body in the 1850s.

Oh, come on, these sound great. Codex gives fifty pages of demon history but not this interesting stuff?

So go find stuff in the library! That's what it's for.

CLARY, I HEREBY ORDER YOU TO GO READ ABOUT SCORPION-RIDERS, WHATEVER THEY ARE. SCORPION-RIDERS. THEY RIDE SCORPIONS. I ASSUME.

MUNDANE RELIGION AND THE NEPHILIM

In the earliest days of the Nephilim, their greatest worry was the possible negative response by the dominant religious-political powers in Europe at the time, the Catholic and the Eastern Orthodox churches. Both churches were very watchful through the Middle Ages for what they would consider heretical positions, and while many of their interests were aligned with the Nephilim's, we could not be said to in any way be in line with church orthodoxy. While local skirmishes sometimes broke out, the leadership of the churches and the Clave prevented any all-out battle.

It was, in fact, a difficult moment in history to recruit for a secret confraternity. There was a tremendous amount of competition, in the form of the various orders of religious knights that were appearing then in the world in the wake of the Crusades. The Knights Hospitaller were founded around the same time as the Nephilim; the Knights Templar in 1130; even the famed Assassins came about only in the 1090s. The Nephilim had to be very selective and chose to recruit only superlative candidates, "allowing" those they rejected to take vows in a military order. On the other hand, disappearing into the ranks of the Nephilim was not as difficult as it would be today, since such life-changing vows were fairly common.

In the course of the first several hundred years of the Nephilim, contacts were made between us and the more mystical orders of the world's major religions. A very small but well-chosen collection of religious leaders signed secret treaties to provide havens and weapons for Shadowhunters in exchange for protection.

I bet the church excommunicated the heck out of Jonathan, though.

Nope, they'd have had to make a public statement, officially they'd never heard of JS.

Warning: If you don't already know about this, it is some bad stuff.

—— THE HUNTS AND THE SCHISM ——

Many are the stories of noble Nephilim, stouthearted and powerful men and women who can inspire us today with the tales of their courage and valor. History is, however, not a storybook, and we would fail in our duty of instructing the new Shadowhunter if we ignored the more shameful and contemptible actions of our forebears. The Nephilim have always acted with morally upright objectives and out of a desire to do good in the world, but with our modern sensibilities we must mention, and condemn, those occasions when from those ambitions came behaviors that we would now consider to be evil.

The sixteenth and seventeenth centuries saw a tragic fad sweep through Europe: witch-hunting. It arose for a number of historical reasons—among them, religious fervor coinciding with the Protestant Reformation and a renewed interest on the part of the Catholic Church in condemning "devil-worship." What began as the lynching of innocent and mostly mundane women (and some men) as "witches" expanded quickly, to become official mundane law. England, for instance, passed the first version of its Witchcraft Act in 1542, which made it illegal to:

> ... use devise practise or exercise, or cause to be used
> devysed practised or exercised, any Invocacons or
> conjuracons of Sprites wichecraftes enchauntmentes
> or sorceries, to thentent to get or fynde money or
> treasure, or to waste consume or destroy any persone
> in his bodie membres or goodes, or to pvoke [provoke]

any persone to unlawfull love, or for any other unlawfull intente or purpose ... or for dispite of Cryste, or for lucre of money, dygge up or pull downe any Crosse or Crosses, or by suche Invocacons or conjuracons of Sprites wichecraftes enchauntementes or sorcerie or any of them take upon them to tell or declare where goodes stollen or lost shall become ... *

Many Shadowhunters attempted to calm their local mundanes and direct their attention to less violent concerns; however, historical accuracy demands that we admit that many

Shadowhunters took upon themselves the people's fervor for witch-burning and helped them pursue it. Some Shadowhunters thought that this new enthusiasm for stamping out demons could be directed usefully, that mundanes might become aware of and able to deal with demons on their own. Instead the Enlightenment happened, mundanes developed modern science and began to build modern technology, and belief in witchcraft became something an educated mundane would consider a silly superstition. By the end of the 1700s, across all of Europe witch-hunting had died out, and maintenance of Downworld had reverted fully to the Nephilim.

In those two-hundred-odd years, however, Downworld suffered badly from these Hunts. Warlocks, especially those with

---

*Gibson, Marion, *Witchcraft and Society in England and America*, 1550–1750 (London: Continuum International Publishing Group, 1976), 1–9.

I did not know about this. It is pretty bad, yeah.

It's not like your country or your religion behaved way bett

marks that could not be easily disguised or hidden, were especially in danger. Such "disfigurements" were seen as clear evidence of witchcraft among mundanes. Luckily, most warlocks were living among mundanes already and were used to either hiding or explaining away their warlock mark, and most were able to avoid accusation. *I know about this, we read* <u>The Crucible</u> *in English class.*

In fact the Downworlders who suffered most directly from the Hunts were the werewolves. Recall that the mundanes' zeal for witch-hunting was based on a belief that witchcraft represented dalliance with "satanic forces." Just as the towns and cities were cleared of their witches, the forests of Central Europe had their werewolf populations decimated by mobs that swept through them, often with bands of hunting dogs, seeking to kill the "half-men who dally with the devil in the guise of a terrible wolf." Unlike "witches," who were regular people who had committed terrible crimes, werewolves were considered less than human and thus did not merit a trial before the death sentence was passed. Shamefully, the Council in 1612 declared its support for werewolf-hunting, arguing that those werewolves who lived in the forests rather than towns had become out of control, like wild animals, and could be put down like animals. The forests, the Clave said, contained only "savage werewolves" rather than "those respectable lycanthropes who are in control of their unusual Trait and integrated into the mundane town and city." The Council, however, knew well that the forests being hunted were full of werewolf collectives who had gone to live under a more lupine social order in places where they would not be persecuted for it; these very human werewolves were given up by the Clave and were allowed to be destroyed. Werewolves died by the hundreds, possibly the thousands.

While warlocks suffered less from the mob violence that decimated European werewolves, a different kind of damage was

Not sure I even want to ask Luke about this.

done to them by this anti-"satanic" fervor. Prior to this time, war-locks and Nephilim had been mostly allied, and often were close collaborators in pursuing demonic activity. We Shadowhunters possessed the tools most effective in killing demons, while the warlocks had access to magic and magical research that were of great help to us but that we could not perform ourselves (most obviously, demon-summoning). Jonathan Shadowhunter's friendship with the warlock Elphas the Unsteady set a precedent that lasted more than four hundred years.

In the wake of the witch hunts, however, a great Schism came to pass between Nephilim and warlocks. Many Shadowhunters, caught up in the fervor of the Hunts, declared warlocks to be "by nature Demonick" and fully evil. In 1640 the Clave forbade the hiring of warlocks to assist in Shadowhunter business. In some parts of the world warlocks were rounded up, or were required to make evident at all times their warlock mark (thus instantly making criminals of all those warlocks whose marks were usually hidden by clothes and the like). In other parts of the world, warlocks went into hiding, sometimes banding together for safety but more often making their way alone. These actions by the Clave worked against the interests of Shadowhunters, making it significantly more difficult for them to hunt demons. They also antagonized and dehumanized those other members of Downworld most likely to be willing partners of the Shadowhunters.

In 1688 Consul Thomas Tefereel brought about his set of well-known Reforms, which officially declared that being a werewolf and living outside mundane habitations was not in itself a capital crime. The Reforms also required Nephilim to "be careful and clear" in judging werewolves and warlocks, such that these Downworlders would be persecuted only if they were actually breaking the Law. It was not, however, until the notorious trial in 1721 of Harold and Robert Grunwald—Shadowhunter brothers

who had set fire to a local tavern house in which had been gathered the entire local werewolf clan—that the werewolf hunts died away for good. The Clave was horrified by the Grunwalds' actions and, unusually, turned over the brothers to mundane authorities, who hanged them. The proactive persecution of warlocks continued in pockets around the world and dwindled only in the early nineteenth century. Warlock persecution was officially made illegal, and the laws against Shadowhunter-warlock collaboration revoked, in the First Accords in 1872. *Okay, went and asked Luke anyway.*
He didn't have much to say:
• Yes, the Hunts were bad. • No, the Clave hasn't ever really made up for it, except for making it illegal now. • There are still Shadowhunters

----

THE ACCORDS

who think it should be illegal to "collaborate" with warlocks.

THE FIRST ACCORDS, 1872

• Easy for the Clave to take blame for something that ended three hundred years ago; think they're so great. You get the idea, I think.

A group of serious-looking men and a few women stand around a table rough with years, and examine the twenty-eighth draft of what, since the twenty-first draft, has become known as the Accords. This is Consul Josiah Wayland's high Victorian Council Hall; he runs things with the discipline and rigidity of a German schoolmaster. Across the table from the Council members are the various Downworlder representatives. They feel the rights of Downworlders in Reparations trials are not sufficiently spelled out. *WAYLAND,* Wayland suspects them of trying to build loopholes into the Law.
YOU FIEND!
It is the hottest summer in fifty years in Alicante. Temperatures remain above ninety degrees for weeks at a time; moist hot air drapes itself over the Accords deliberations like a robe, shortening everyone's patience and goodwill. Tempers flare. A constant argument occurs about whether the windows should remain open or closed. When open they allow at least the slight relief of a cross breeze, but they also let in a population of black flies that must

248

be waved off with flyswatters. Everyone is constantly physically uncomfortable, except for the faerie and vampire representatives, who take the experience in stride, thus irritating the rest of the assembly all the more.

That Wayland would preside over what is almost certainly the most important event in modern Shadowhunter history is an interesting accident of timing. Wayland was not much loved as a Consul, and has not been remembered fondly for either his personality or his wisdom. In truth the groundwork for the Accords had been laid across the entire nineteenth century, beginning with the historic European Downworlder Treaty that was signed at the end of the Napoleonic Wars in 1815 and marked the first time an official document promised any protection under the Law for Downworlders. Most of the credit for the ideas that led to the Accords should be given to the Consul at that treaty of 1815, Shimizu-Tokugawa Katsugoro. It is a testament to Shimizu-Tokugawa's ideas and drive that even after his death in 1858, the work that led to the Accords continued until they were finally signed in 1872.

The other great hero of these First Accords was the head of the London Institute at the time, Granville Fairchild, who acted as a great peacekeeper throughout the long hot summer and constantly smoothed over relationships between the delegations at times when their clashing interests led to offense and resentment. He possessed a preternatural ability both to make the Council understand and appreciate the wishes of the Downworlder delegation, and to help the Downworlders understand and appreciate the wishes of the Nephilim. Sadly, Fairchild did not live to ratify the Accords he himself had worked so hard to complete. As negotiations were concluding, he traveled to the island of Cyprus to offer his expertise in demonology to the Institute there. The Cypriot Nephilim were fighting the Greater Demon

Stheno, who was ravaging the countryside. There Fairchild died, as befits a Shadowhunter, in battle with Stheno. Though they were drastically different men, Fairchild and Consul Wayland had a great friendship, and Wayland dedicated the signing of the Accords to Fairchild's memory.

(In an unusual end to the story, Stheno was eventually dispatched back to the Void in Scotland in 1894 by a team of English Shadowhunters; though Stheno was in disguise, he was recognized because he was wearing Granville Fairchild's favorite Ukrainian fur hat, which had been a gift from Wayland.) *Ha!*

These First Accords were opposed heavily by some Shadowhunters, mostly those who stood to lose significant income as a result of the proposed Reforms. (See "Spoils," page 178.) Luckily, compromises were found that allowed the Accords to be ratified and signed. The final draft, the thirty-third, was agreed upon near the end of the summer of 1872. Fifty signers were present to ratify it: ten vampires, ten werewolves, ten warlocks, ten faeries, and ten Nephilim. Vampire representative Aron Benedek famously described the final document as a "compromise of compromises," but in truth the skeleton of the subsequent Accords was fully in place with this first agreement. The Accords that have followed have hewn to its model more often than not.

Among the landmark resolutions adopted as part of these First Accords were:

- The declaration of Downworlders as beings with souls, and thus entitled to the protections due to humans.
- The revoking of Laws making it illegal for Downworlders to adopt mundane children.
- The granting to Downworlders of the right to a court trial when accused of breaking the Law; no longer could Shadowhunters adjudge them guilty of crimes and punish them immediately.

- Legal language restricting the penalties that could be placed on Downworlders, to prevent punishment out of proportion to the crime.
- The granting of Downworlders' right to their own internal organizational schemes—vampire clans, wolf packs, faerie courts, et cetera—without interference from the Clave. In fact, the Accords made membership in one of these internal organizations a requirement for Downworlders; "unaffiliated" vampires or werewolves were considered rogue and were not afforded the same protections under the Law.
- Acknowledgment of the Nephilim as the official law-keeping force of Downworld, and agreement by the Downworlders to abide by Covenant Law. Acknowledgment of the theoretical body of Heaven, through its representative Raziel, as the ultimate authority over our world.

It is interesting to examine the updates in the Accords over the years, and how the Accords today differ from the original document signed those many years ago. The major differences include:

- Increasingly detailed and specific language about the rights of Downworlders in criminal trials. The need for more and more legalism in the Accords came about as Consuls and Inquisitors varied wildly in how they interpreted things, sometimes adopting draconian rules against Downworlder groups, who had little recourse but to try to get the rules made more specific in the next Accords. Interestingly, the criminal law section of the Accords is now treated as a separate document and is framed by a different group of representatives—ones with legal expertise—from those who write the rest of the

Accords. This is in part because the criminal law section of the Accords is now significantly longer than the entire rest of the Accords put together. This separate document is, however, the only place where a Downworlder's right to trial is officially recognized by the Nephilim, and so the document has grown in importance with each successive Accords.

- A much stronger declaration of the rights of mundanes to live their lives unimpeded by the vicissitudes of Downworlders. It was at the Seventh Accords, for instance, that it first became illegal for vampires to keep subjugates.

- During the time of the first three Accords, warlocks were habitually summoning demons at the request of Nephilim. Technically this was illegal. The Fourth Accords specifically made it legal for warlocks to do whatever magic was deemed necessary in the course of a Nephilim investigation.

These and other such social reforms teach us that the spirit of the Accords is alive in Idris, and that we continue to refine and ever improve relations between Idris and Downworld.

So progressive, we couldn't murder Downworlder in the street anymore.

Big change, though—from "Downworlders are basically demons" to "Downworlders are basically humans."

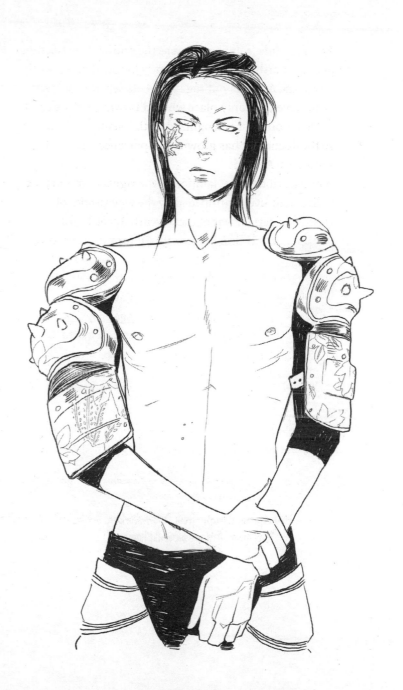

APPENDIX B

THE NINTH ACCORDS, 1992

Addendum to the *Shadowhunter's Codex*, 27th edition, added 2002
By Christopher Makepeace, Institute Head, Melbourne, Australia

I hereby render unconditional obedience to the Circle and its principles... I will be ready to risk my life at any time for the Circle, in order to preserve the purity of the bloodlines of Idris, and for the mortal world with whose safety we are charged.

—Loyalty oath of the Circle

The Accords have never had the unanimous support of the Clave. Almost every Accords negotiation has drawn protests, objections, internal squabbles from among the Nephilim. Those in far-flung territories, especially, with sparser populations, have often argued that Downworlder relations in such "wilds" require a looser hand, that the restrictions on Shadowhunter behavior in the Accords severely limit their ability to do their jobs.

These arguments have been heated and impassioned. Tempers have flared. Respected members of the Clave have stormed out of the Accords Hall in fury. Certain Downworlders and certain Shadowhunters have had to be carefully seated far from one another in the negotiation chambers.

At heart, though, the Nephilim's and the Downworlders' aims have aligned. We have all wanted peace. Everyone has, at root, wanted peace. Until the Circle.

Valentine Morgenstern, the only living son of a widely respected and long-standing Nephilim family, and his followers, disrupted the Accords. Not disrupted—invaded. I was there. Some have, in the years following, downplayed the horror and the violence of that day, to paint Morgenstern and his followers as noble dissidents, protestors using dramatic actions to make their point. But I was there.

Let us not mince words. The Circle despised Downworlders. They believed in the purity of humans and the impurity of Downworld, believed that Downworlders were at their root demons, and believed that Downworlders should be slaughtered to keep the world pure for humans. They viewed those Shadowhunters who disagreed with them as complicit in the profanity they believed Downworlders brought to our world. The Circle members were not protestors; they were violent fanatics.

(It is worth noting, in fairness to certain families, that many of the original members of the Circle, and many of the closest of Morgenstern's original followers, had before the Accords fled from him because of the extremity of his views and the brutality of his plan, and were not present for the events in the Accords Hall. Not all of Valentine's followers went along forever with his heinous crimes.)

Like so many other Shadowhunters, the Circle were in the Accords Hall that day, among the vast audience of Nephilim and Downworlders in the gallery awaiting the signing of these Ninth Accords. Unbeknownst to anyone else present, they had smuggled demonic weapons into the Hall—their fanaticism was such that they would use the tools of the explicitly demonic if they believed it would satisfy their supposedly noble ends. At the moment when the Accords were presented for signing, the Circle, as one body, rose and bared their weapons. Panic broke instantly over the Hall like a wave in a storm.

Amid the tumult it became clear that a number of Downworlder groups had been aware of the Circle's plans and had laid in wait outside the Hall in secret to fight them. At the explosion of chaos these groups burst into the Hall and joined the battle. In truth this was not the shock it might have been. Valentine had been vocal in his protests for many months, and many expected some demonstration from him and his followers during the Accords— but nothing like the melee that occurred.

To attempt to describe the disarray and carnage of battle calls to my mind age-old clichés that cannot convey the power of the moment: *It was horrible. It will stay with me forever. It was worse than your imagining.* But all of these things are true. Good men and women were cut down in front of me, for no better reason than that the blood spattering their Accords robes would highlight the message of the Circle's attack. Downworlders whose only crime was a demonic parent, or a demonic disease beyond their control, were murdered for having the misfortune of being present. Council members and Downworlder representatives alike shouted themselves hoarse, trying to restore order, unable to be heard over the din of metal smashing against metal and into human bodies.

I can close my eyes today, ten years later, as I write these words in my quiet office atop the tall crystal towers of the Melbourne Institute, and the smell of blood and the sound of slaughter come back to me as if I were still there. I think that probably the memory will never depart the dark places behind my eyes.

Worst harmed in the battle were the Shadowhunters unaffiliated with the Circle. They were killed, often indiscriminately, both purposefully by the Circle and accidentally by Downworlders who believed them to be among the enemy. Nevertheless, with the help of the Downworlder armies, the Circle was beaten back, and fled. They were only barely defeated. Valentine Morgenstern fled the Hall and retreated to his own house on the outskirts of Alicante, where he set a great fire and burned himself to death, along with his wife and his young child. Defeated, Valentine must have known that his life was forfeit; he was guilty of the greatest of Nephilim crimes, the murder of Nephilim. It is only fitting that he dispatched two last innocent victims, his own family, as his final act in the world.

ACE ✣ CUPS.

. . .

The Uprising ended in failure. The Nephilim and the Downworlders treated their wounded and saw to their dead. A great funeral was held in Angel Square in Alicante to honor the memory of those lost. Many surviving members of the Circle threw themselves upon the mercy of the Clave, and cooperated with the investigations into the whereabouts of those still loyal to Valentine. There was much speculation that the Accords had fallen apart, that peace between Idris and Downworld was impossible.

But the Ninth Accords were signed. In a stroke of irony Valentine's terrible acts helped to uphold the Shadow World's commitment to the Accords' passage. It had been a difficult negotiation that year, full of clashing personalities and strong opinions, but after the Uprising a great sense of fraternity was felt by Downworlder and Shadowhunter representatives alike, united against their common foe, and they were able to ratify the Accords only a few weeks later.

The Tenth Accords (2007), just terrible for everyone.

THINGS TURNED OUT OKAY, THOUGH, RIGHT? GUYS?

The Great and Tragic Love
of Jonathan Shadowhunter
and David the Silent, by
~~Clary Fray, Aged 17~~
SIMON IT WAS BY SIMON NOT ME

JONATHAN SHADOWHUNTER:
I am Jonathan Shadowhunter, and I am about to form a holy order of warriors to defend Earth from demons! I am louche and aristocratic and callow!

DAVID: I am David and I witnessed something truly horrific in a cave and as a result I have taken a vow of silence and sworn myself to killing demons. I am only thinking these things, rather than saying them out loud, because I have taken a vow of silence.

JONATHAN: I throw myself at demons indiscriminately!

DAVID: Verily, you shall be killed if you keep doing that. You need an influence of calm and meditative spirit in this mission. It is not just a war; it is a holy war. Meditate with me.

JONATHAN: This meditating business is very nice, and I feel more balanced and together than ever before, but have you noticed that we are supposed to be demon hunters but in fact neither of us has actually killed a demon in many moons?

DAVID: Are you suggesting that only the combination of both your rash bravery and my levelheaded thinkiness can hope to defeat the darkness, rather than either alone?

JONATHAN: ... No, but that's much better than what I was suggesting, so let's go with that!

DAVID: We kill demons awesomely now! We go on adventures and repeatedly save each other's lives!

JONATHAN: Oh, David, I would trust you with my life!

DAVID: Oh, Jonathan, I would sacrifice my own life for your holy mission!
[He almost does.]
I regret nothing.

JONATHAN: (weeping) David, you must return to me! I need you! I cannot do this thing without you!

DAVID: Lo, I return!

JONATHAN: ~~Zounds! I feel a great stirring in my pantaloons.~~

DAVID: ~~What doth thy pantalo~~
SIMON I WILL KILL YOU

DISCUSSION QUESTIONS AND THINGS TO TRY

---

1. With which of the founders of the Nephilim—Jonathan, David, or Abigail—do you feel a bond? Why? What about their lives can inform the way you live your own?

Um, I guess Abigail because she's the only girl, Codex. I mean, really? At least boys get two different people to choose from. Abigail's defining feature is she's female.

Some would say Abigail's defining feature was that she learned how to work the very material of Heaven on a forge, and then she built a gigantic fortress and never came out again. *I don't see that as a reason not to feel a bond with her.*

Where do you want to get lunch?

MY PSYCHIC VAMPIRE POWERS SAY YOU WANT NOODLES.

I always want noodles.

YOUR PSYCHIC NOODLE POWERS DEPEND ON THEM. *True.*

What are you guys, twelve? Stop passing the thing back and forth.

HISTORY OF THE CODEX

Did You Know? *How could you possibly care?*
The first edition of *The Shadowhunter's Codex* is a hand-illuminated book written in Vulgar Latin, on pages of vellum. It can be seen in a carefully preserved display among the treasures of Alicante. For many years this first edition was believed to have been written by Jonathan Shadowhunter, in his own hand, and thus was dated to the late eleventh century. Modern research and dating techniques have, unfortunately, revealed that this date is not correct, and the first edition instead dates to the early

thirteenth century, almost a hundred years after Jonathan Shadowhunter's believed date of death. Its author and its illuminator, whether the same person or different, remain unknown. Many different Enclaves of Shadowhunters in Europe have laid claim to being the rightful inheritors of the original *Codex*, but no evidence has ever arisen to allow a definitive claim. In any event it is logical to understand the *Codex* as a document dating from after the deaths of the first Shadowhunters, when the Nephilim of Idris were actively working to find recruits to their mission and to drastically expand their numbers and their geographical reach. The *Codex* would have provided an expeditious method of teaching the literate, at the very least, about the Shadow World and its denizens.

The first edition of the *Codex* produced on a printing press is not nearly as mysterious. The *Codex* was first printed, in German, on the presses of the Institute at Frankfurt-am-Main in what was then the Holy Roman Empire. It was brought to that Institute from Heidelberg, where a group of Nephilim had been studying demonology in collaboration with scholars of the university there. It is unknown how many copies were made, but of them, forty-eight survive. Of these, several can be found in Alicante, and at least one can be found at each Great Library. The rest are spread among smaller Institutes, mostly in Central Europe, and a small number of Shadowhunter private collections.

This edition of the *Codex* is a minor revision of the twenty-seventh edition, first published in 1990. Only material related to the Ninth Accords has been added. *I care.*

Don't you quote Star Wars at me, Lewis.

NOTES:
DO NOT DOODLE IN THIS SPACE

NOTES AREA

Please use this blank space provided to practice Marks. Note: Please practice your Marks with a waster and not with a real stele. Paper is too fragile to withstand the force of heavenly fire.

ARTIST ACKNOWLEDGMENTS

Rebecca Guay provided us with the frontispiece, a study of the primary players from the Mortal Instruments books.

Charles Vess supplied the endpiece, a similar study of the characters of the Infernal Devices. (That's the London Institute they're frolicking upon.)

Michael Wm. Kaluta produced the chapter headings, and understood what we meant when we said, "Do it like an old-school gaming manual."

John Dollar illustrated the history of the Nephilim, choosing what to illustrate from the text himself, rather than being given a specific list of requested subjects.

Theo Black was commissioned to do two pieces of faerie-themed art and then sent us five. We used all five.

Elisabeth Alba's quickly dashed-off practice sketches were good enough to print, but we were glad we waited for the actual finished pieces. She contributed beautiful, mostly pencil-based work across the whole Codex.

Jim Nelson also contributed beautiful work across the whole Codex, but most important, he added three new demons to the Shadowhunter universe. They are wonderfully disgusting and we are proud to have them.

Cassandra Jean as Clary Fray. Cassandra Jean drew all over this thing, and filled the back of it with portraits.

Michael McCartney at Simon & Schuster designed the book, placed the art, and was very, very patient with our many detail-oriented requests.

And of course, thanks to **Valerie Freire** for her rune designs and her inspiration.

ZEN PHYSICS

OTHER BOOKS BY DAVID DARLING

Soul Search

Equations of Eternity

Deep Time

ZEN PHYSICS

The Science of Death, the Logic of Reincarnation

DAVID DARLING

HarperCollinsPublishers

HarperCollins books may be purchased for educational, business, or sales promotional use. For information please write: Special Markets Department, HarperCollins Publishers, Inc., 10 East 53rd Street, New York, NY 10022.

FIRST EDITION

Designed by Nina Gaskin

Library of Congress Cataloging-in-Publication Data

Darling, David J.
    Zen physics: the science of death, the logic of reincarnation/David Darling.
        p. cm.
    ISBN 0-06-017352-1
    Includes bibliographical references and index.
    1. Reincarnation (Buddhism) 2. Zen Buddhism and science.   3. Death—Religious aspects—Zen Buddhism. I. Title.
BQ4485.D37 1996
294.3'4237—dc20   95-51829

96 97 98 99 00 ❖/HC 10 9 8 7 6 5 4 3 2 1

I believe that there is some incredible mystery about it. What does this life mean: firstly coming-to-be, then finally ceasing-to-be? We find ourselves here in this wonderful rich and vivid conscious experience and it goes on through life, but is that the end? . . . Is this present life all to finish in death or can we have hope that there will be a further meaning to be discovered?

—*Karl Popper*

Men fear Death as children fear to go in the dark; and as that natural fear in children is increased with tales, so is the other.

—*Francis Bacon*

Human kind cannot bear very much reality.

—*T. S. Eliot*

ACKNOWLEDGMENTS

I am very grateful to the many people across five continents who, having read my earlier books, have taken the trouble to write to me over the past few years with a wealth of fascinating ideas, comments, and suggestions. Most of all, I would like to thank those individuals who have shared freely with me accounts of remarkable personal experiences that have helped clarify and confirm my own opinions on the nature of life, death, self, and consciousness, as expressed in this book. Writing is generally a solitary business but is made to seem less so by such frequent and heart-warming contact.

I am also deeply indebted to my editor at HarperCollins, Eamon Dolan, for helping transform a spaghetti of a manuscript into a balanced two-course meal of a book. And, as always, my thanks go to my friend and wonderful agent Patricia Van der Leun for making sure that my work remains on the menu.

Finally, I want to thank those who help least with my books but most with the rest of my life—my dear family.

CONTENTS

INTRODUCTION

Truth sits on the lips of dying men.

—*Matthew Arnold*

It may happen in five minutes or in fifty years, but at some point you *will* die. There is no escaping it. And then what? Will it be the end? Is death a void, a nothingness that goes on forever? Or is it merely a phase transition—the start of a new kind of existence, beyond our old bodies and brains? This is the ultimate question a human being can ask: the question of his or her own destiny. Yet to most people it must seem frustratingly unyielding, an impenetrable problem to which only death itself will bring a solution. Try as we might, we seem never to come any nearer to understanding what our final fate will be. So we look around in every direction for guidance, but what we are asked to believe depends on whom we listen to. When we are young, we quiz our parents, teachers, and friends about what happens when we die, but for the most part we are treated to platitudes, folk tales, or embarrassed hesitations. Later, perhaps less bright-eyed and more pragmatic, we may simply give up asking, having reached the unsatisfying conclusion that no one from the pope on down really has a better insight into the problem of death than we do. The priest, the physicist, the mystic, the brain physiologist, the fellow standing next to us in the bar—all may have something worthwhile to say, providing they are willing to break one of society's greatest taboos and talk freely about death. But their opinions are discouragingly diverse.

Still we cannot help wondering: Do we have a soul? Or are we nothing more than biological machines whose consciousness ends forever at the instant our organic works break down? If it turns out that there is nothing supernatural in the world—no spirits, no heaven, no God in the customary sense—does this also rule out the possibility of survival beyond the grave?

There are many profound, unresolved mysteries in the universe, but none that touches us so deeply and intimately as the mystery of death. It can be unnerving to realize that every breath we take may be our last, that we stand each moment on the brink of . . . what? Everlasting life? Or eternal nonexistence?

The past two decades or so have seen a dramatic upsurge of popular interest in the possibility of an afterlife, similar to that around the turn of the last century when spiritualism created such a stir and was eagerly espoused by many as offering a possible portal on the world to come. Today's excitement stems mainly from numerous well-publicized stories of near-death experiences (NDEs). However, research into the phenomenon of NDEs, fascinating as it is, represents only one of many current lines of inquiry which can be used to deepen our understanding of what happens when we die. As I hope to show, enough is already known to begin a preliminary mapping of the terra incognita that lies on the other side of death—a mapping based not on faith or travelers' tales of worlds beyond (however valid these may be), but on direct logical and scientific inference.

Science has an outstanding track record. We have been able to apply it successfully to probing the origin of the universe, the composition of stars, the structure of atoms, the evolution of life, and a great range of other problems that might at one time have seemed well outside our scope. So there is no reason to suppose in advance that the problem of death should be scientifically intractable. On the contrary, we can start out with every hope of reasoning our way to a deep understanding of the process, meaning, and consequences of death.

At the same time, in tackling an issue like this, we need to recognize that it has both important objective and subjective elements. And, in fact, it is questions such as "What does death *feel* like?" and "What will death mean for *me*?" that interest us most on a personal level. The future of each of us as individuals and the threat that death poses to our identity, our very being, is what fascinates us above all else. Therefore, it would be missing the point to approach death in a too rigidly objective or reductionist frame of mind. We need the analytical tools of the physicist, yes. Rationality has to prevail if we are to make any progress at all. But it must be rationality tempered by a tolerant, human-centered outlook that allows into its inquiry not merely quantitative data but also the sincerely reported feelings and experiences of people who have encountered situations that are relevant in the context of death. Such an approach is more characteristic of Eastern modes of thought. Hence, *Zen Physics: Zen* for the subjective, *Physics* for the objective. But there is another, deeper reason for this choice of name, which, it will emerge, relates to the underlying nature of self and consciousness. We need, I believe, a whole-brain approach during life to appreciate what losing our brain at the point of death implies.

When I first began thinking seriously about the problem of death, some fifteen years ago, I held no firm beliefs about such things as the soul or the afterlife. If pressed, I would have said it was most likely that death was simply the end of us. But I have been surprised and profoundly influenced by what I have found.

Two main conclusions will be presented, both of which are remarkable and both of which, were it not for the force of evidence supporting them, might seem entirely beyond belief. The first is that *a form of reincarnation is logically inescapable*. There *must* be life after death. And there must, moreover, be a continuity of consciousness, so that no sooner have you died in this life than you begin again in some other. The second and even more significant conclusion is that *far from giving rise to consciousness, the brain actually restricts it*. Mind, it will become clear, is a fundamental and all-pervasive property of the universe.

Too often, science is seen as a potential destroyer of man's last hope of survival in a greater world. But this need not be so. Science after all means simply "knowledge." And you may find, as I have, that something akin to a spiritual—or at least a deep psychological—transformation can be achieved through logic and thought alone. Science, no less than mysticism and religion, offers a genuinely hopeful path to the future.

Part I

YOU AND OTHER STORIES

I am not afraid to die . . . I just don't want to bc
there when it happens.

—*Woody Allen*

1

OUR GREATEST FEAR

A wise man thinks of nothing less than death.

—*Spinoza*

Soon, very soon, thou wilt be ashes, or a
skeleton. . . .

—*Marcus Aurelius*

When life is full and we are young, a bright world surrounds us, open
to our inquiry. Only in the far distance is there a speck of darkness, a
missing point of the picture. But as we age, this speck grows larger.
As our lives draw to a close, this region of darkness fills the ground
before us like the opening of a forbidding cave. Others have entered
that cave before us—billions of others, including our relatives and
friends—and it is claimed even that some have returned from a brief
sortie across its threshold during so-called near-death experiences
(NDEs) or, less convincingly, as ghosts. Yet, despite what comfort we
may choose to draw from accounts of NDEs, tales of spiritual manifestations, or the reassurances of various religions, most of us remain
deeply uncertain, and afraid, as to what lies ahead. Death is the great
question mark at the end of life, the mystery we long to solve but
seem unable to. And yet it is an event, a transition, a portal, we must

each go through sooner or later. It is a question that, in the end, holds an answer for every one of us.

Your death became a future fact at the moment a particular sperm cell from your father united with a particular ovum inside your mother. At that instant your personal hourglass was upturned and the sands of your life began to fall. Now no matter how hard you try to stay vigorous in body and mind, it will not affect the final outcome. No amount of progress to combat the effects of aging, through drugs, surgery, or other means, can do more than briefly postpone the inevitable. Your body is destined progressively to wear out and ultimately to fail. And then?

As soon as a person's heart stops beating, gravity takes hold. Within minutes a purple-red stain starts to appear on the lowermost parts of the body, where blood quickly settles. The skin and muscles sag, the body cools, and within two to six hours rigor mortis sets in. Beginning with a stiffening of the eyelids, the rigidity extends inexorably to all parts of the body and may last for between one and four days before the muscles finally relax.

Two or three days after death, a greenish discoloration of the skin on the right side of the lower abdomen above the cecum (the part of the large intestine nearest the surface) provides the first visible sign of decay. This gradually spreads over the whole abdomen and then onto the chest and upper thighs, the color being simply a result of sulfur-containing gases from the intestines reacting with hemoglobin liberated from the blood in the vessels of the abdominal wall. By the end of the first week, most of the body is tinged green, a green that steadily darkens and changes to purple and finally to black. Blood-colored blisters, two to three inches across, develop on the skin, the merest touch being sufficient to cause their top layer to slide off.

By the end of the second week the abdomen is bloated. The lungs rupture because of bacterial attack in the air passages, and the resulting release of gas pressure from within the body forces a blood-stained fluid from the nose and mouth—a startling effect that helped to spawn many a vampire legend among peasants who had witnessed exhumations in medieval Europe. The eyes bulge and the tongue swells to fill the mouth and protrude beyond the teeth. After three to four weeks, the hair, nails, and teeth loosen, and the internal organs disintegrate before turning to liquid.

On average, it takes ten to twelve years for an unembalmed adult body buried six feet deep in ordinary soil without a coffin to be completely reduced to a skeleton. This period may shrink drastically to between a few months and a year if the grave is shallow, since the body is then more accessible to maggots and worms. However, soil chemistry, humidity, and other ambient factors have a powerful effect on the rate of decomposition. Acid water and the almost complete absence of oxygen in peat, for instance, make it an outstanding preservative. From Danish peat bogs alone, more than 150 well-kept bodies up to five thousand years old have been recovered in the last two centuries. And likewise, astonishingly fresh after five millennia was "Otzi the Iceman," found in 1991, complete with skin tattoos and Bronze Age tool kit, trapped in a glacier in the Ötztal Alps on the Austro-Italian border.

Accidental preservations aside, people throughout the ages have frequently gone to surprising lengths to ensure that their corpses remained in good shape. Most famously, the ancient Egyptians were obsessed by corporeal preservation, to the extent of mummifying not just themselves but also many kinds of animals which they held to be sacred. The underground labyrinths of Tuna-el-Gebel, for instance, are eerily crowded with the mummies of baboons and ibis. Incredibly, at least four million of the latter went through the elaborate embalming process—a process that made copious use of the dehydrating salt natron, excavated from around the Nile and parched desert lakes.

All mummies preserved by the old Egyptian method are very long dead—with one bizarre exception. In 1995, the Egyptologist and philosopher Robert Brier of Long Island University completed the first mummification in this traditional style in more than 2,000 years. His subject was a seventy-six-year-old American who had given his body to science. Brier went to great pains to follow the old methods, traveling to Egypt to harvest his natron (principally a mixture of sodium carbonate and bicarbonate) from the dry shores of Wadi Natrun, and using authentic replicas of embalming tools from the first millennium B.C. Just as the mortician-priests of the pharaonic tombs would have done, Brier drew out the man's brain* by way of the nostrils, extracted the major organs before storing them individually in canopic jars, and finally left the body for several weeks to completely dehydrate, swaddled and packed in the special salt. Only the subject's feet were visible, wrapped in blue surgical booties. Rejecting criticisms that his research was in poor taste, Brier claimed the experiment had shown beyond doubt that it is the action of natron, more than any other factor, that affords mummies their well-kept look.

The Romans, too, were familiar with the drying and preservative properties of certain chemicals. So-called plaster burials, in which lime or chalk (both drying agents) or gypsum (a natural antiseptic) was packed around the body in the coffin, have turned up in Roman cemeteries in Britain and North Africa.

More recently, wealthy Victorians went to enormous trouble to carefully dispose of their corpses. Burial in crypts and catacombs came into fashion—and not only because it gave the well-heeled, through the ostentatious grandeur of family vaults, a way to display their social standing. There were more sinister reasons to try to ensure a safe place for burial. Locked doors were a deterrent to body snatchers who might otherwise hawk your remains for illegal medical dissection or, worse, pry out your teeth for use in making dentures. Also, the Victorians had an acute fear of being buried alive—better, they reasoned, to revive in a room with some chance of escape than in a horribly cramped coffin piled over with earth.

It is no coincidence that the average interval between death and burial in Britain lengthened from about five days in the late eighteenth century to eight days in the early nineteenth century. The object was to allow plenty of time for obvious signs of decay to develop, which would serve a dual purpose: to reassure relatives that their loved one was indeed dead and also to render the body less desirable to thieves.

People at this time often included in their wills bizarre requests

---

*The Egyptians discarded the brain because they drew no connection between it and the person's mind or soul. Mental life, they believed, was concentrated in the heart. To us this seems odd since it "feels" as if thought takes place inside our heads. If we concentrate hard for too long our head aches. Did the Egyptians experience "heartache" instead?

concerning the disposal of their bodies. They would ask, for instance, that bells be attached to their corpse or that a razor be used to cut into the flesh of their foot to make absolutely sure they were not still alive before being interred. And in Imperial Russia perhaps the most wonderfully eccentric precaution of all was dreamed up to counter the possibility of premature burial. In 1897, having witnessed the remarkable revival of a young girl during her funeral, Count Karnice-Karnicki, chamberlain to the czar, patented his "life-signaling coffin." The slightest movement of the occupant's chest would trigger a spring-loaded ball, causing a box on the surface connected to the spring by a tube to open, thereby letting light and air into the coffin. The spring was also designed to release a flag on the surface, a bell that would ring for half an hour, and a lamp that would burn after sunset. Alas, history does not record if the count's ingenious invention ever left the drawing board.

Our choice of whether to be buried or not may be made on purely aesthetic grounds. We may be somewhat comforted by the idea of our bodies returning to nature as part of the grand recycling process. Alternatively, we may find the thought of being consumed by insects and bacteria too revolting to contemplate and, as a result, opt for a less organic mode of disposal. But, for some people, burial after death is important for religious reasons. Most obviously, according to Christian doctrine, there will be a resurrection of the dead on the Last Day of Judgment. The graves will be opened, say the scriptures, and saints and sinners will stand before the Son of God and be judged. Interpreted literally, this might suggest we should do our best to try to preserve whatever we can of our erstwhile selves so that there is at least something left of us *to* resurrect. And yet, in all honesty, it is hardly a realistic ambition. Whatever precautions we take to have our remains securely interred, nothing of our bodies—not even our bones—will survive the many millions of years that lie ahead in the Earth's future.

By contrast with burial, today's most common mode of disposal, cremation, annihilates a corpse at tremendous speed. In less than an hour, in a gas fire at temperatures of between 1100 and 1750 degrees Fahrenheit, the body reduces to just a few pounds of white ash, which can then be stored or dispersed according to whim—scattered over a favorite hillside perhaps, or, in the most exotic way imaginable, jettisoned into space from the shuttle to boldly go where Gene Roddenberry, creator of *Star Trek,* has gone before.

Alternatively, organs of the body may be bequeathed so that they go on serving a useful function, other than as fertilizer, inside someone still alive. Yet another option was that chosen, in pretransplant days, by the British geneticist and writer J. B. S. Haldane:

> When I am dead I propose to be dissected; in fact, a distinguished anatomist has already been promised my head should he survive me. I hope that I have been of some use to my fellow creatures while alive, and I see no reason why I should not continue to be so when dead. I admit, however, that if funerals gave as much pleasure to the living in England as they do in Scotland I might change my mind.

Tragedy and dark comedy often seem to be companions in death. We take ourselves so seriously, invest such effort in our public image, work so hard at building a secure and comfortable niche for ourselves—and then what? All the pretense of modern life is stripped away and we end up desiccated, dissected, or decomposed.

Or do we? Our organic forms are obviously doomed. But are we more than just our living bodies and brains? Does some part of us— an inner essence, a soul or spirit—escape the dissolution of flesh?

Haldane put the case for the prosecution:

> [S]hall I be there to attend my dissection or to haunt my next-of-kin if he or she forbids it? Indeed will anything of me but my body, other men's memory of me, and the results of my life, survive my death? Certainly I cannot deny the possibility; but at no period in my life has my personal survival seemed at all a likely contingency.
>
> If I die as most people die, I shall gradually

lose my intellectual faculties, my senses will
fail, and I shall become unconscious. And then
I am asked to believe that I shall suddenly
wake up to a vivid consciousness in hell,
heaven, purgatory, or some other state of existence.

Now, I have lost consciousness both from
blows on the head, from fever, anesthetics,
want of oxygen, and other causes; and therefore I know that my consciousness depends on
the physical and chemical condition of my
brain, and that very small changes in that organ
will modify or destroy it.

But I am asked to believe that my mind will
continue without a brain, or will be miraculously provided with a new one.

The basic materialist view of death, now widely held by scientists
and layfolk alike, seems, on the face of it, bleak beyond despair.
"We"—our minds—appear to be nothing more than outgrowths of our
living brains, so that inevitably we must expire at the moment our
neural support structures collapse. Death, from this perspective,
amounts to a total, permanent cessation of consciousness and feeling—the end of the individual. Considering how anxious most of us
are at the thought of losing merely our jobs or possessions, it is hardly
surprising that, in an increasingly secular society, the fear of death—
of losing *everything,* including ourselves—has become so deep and
widespread. Yet exactly what are we afraid of?

Epicurus pointed out the irrationality of fearing the end of consciousness in his *Letter to Menoeceus:*

Become accustomed to the belief that death is
nothing to us. For all good and evil consists in
sensation, but death is deprivation of sensation.
And therefore a right understanding that death
is nothing to us makes the mortality of life
enjoyable, not because it takes away the crav-

ing for immortality. For there is nothing terrible
in life for the man who has truly comprehended
that there is nothing terrible in not living.

Others have echoed this view, including Ludwig Wittgenstein: "We do not experience death," he insisted; "Our life has no end in just the way in which our visual field has no limit." To use a mathematical analogy, just as an asymptotic curve comes closer and closer to a line but never actually touches it, so we move ever closer toward death throughout life but never actually reach death in experience (if by death we mean the end of an individual's consciousness).

Ironically, one of the possibilities we tend to dread the most—that death represents a one-way trip to oblivion—turns out to be something we need have no fear of at all. Socrates even enjoined us to look forward to it. In his *Apology* he explained:

Death is one of two things. Either it is an anni-
hilation, and the dead have no consciousness of
anything, or . . . it is really a change—a migration of the soul from this place to another. Now
if there is no consciousness but only a dreamless sleep, death must be a marvelous gain . . .
because the whole of time . . . can be regarded
as no more than a single night.

We can put it even more dramatically than this. If death marks a permanent end of your consciousness, then *from your point of view* when you die, the entire future of the universe (running into tens of billions of years or more) must telescope down not just into a night, as Socrates described, but into a fleeting instant. Even if the universe were to go through other cycles of expansion and contraction, then all of these cycles as far as you are concerned would happen in zero time. What conceivable basis for fear could there be in such an absence of experience? We may as well be afraid of the gap between one thought and the next.

Marcus Aurelius was among those who offered another way to come to grips with the prospect of nonbeing: the period after death, he pointed out, is like the period before birth. You didn't spend the billions of years before you were born in a state of anxiety and apprehension, because there was no "you" to be aware of anything. Looking back now, it doesn't seem frightening that there was once a time when you were not conscious. Why then should you be concerned about returning to that nonexistent, nonconscious state when you die?

On a purely academic level, we can follow these arguments and appreciate the logic in them. And yet, for most of us, they ring hollow. They fail utterly to dispel the visceral dread we have of plunging into the terminal darkness, alone. The fear of death, *timor mortis*, the horror of the ultimate abyss that waits to claim us all, is far too deeply ingrained in our nature to be alleviated by mere rhetoric. Indeed, it is a fear whose origins go back to the very dawn of our planet.

On Earth, at least, life began as molecules of increasing complexity came together purely by chance in the primitive terrestrial ocean. A rich chemical broth activated by unshielded high-energy radiation from the sun and powerful lightning strikes gave rise to the first molecules that could make copies of themselves—the precursors of today's DNA. There is no mystery about this. Any assortment of objects, especially "sticky" objects like molecules, randomly stirred for long enough will give rise to every conceivable possible combination. Over millions and millions of years, the simple atomic and molecular units bumping into one another, under energetically favorable conditions, must have come together in all sorts of different ways. Most of these complicated associations would have been unstable. And even if they had been stable under normal conditions, a hard enough collision with some other particle or a well-aimed ultraviolet ray would have broken them apart. Eventually, however, a certain formation of molecular units combined to give a supermolecule that, by chance, could act as the template and docking station for making precise copies of itself. No sooner did this happen than the supermolecule spread rapidly throughout the waters of the young Earth. Possibly there were several variants of such self-replicating substances which competed for resources. Not that there was any thought of competition at the time; there was as yet no substrate for thought at all. But in the chance emergence of self-copying molecules we can discern, from our future vantage point, the first stirrings of life, the beginnings of the struggle to survive in a potentially hostile world—and the origins of self.

Nature lays down no boundaries between life and nonlife. What we choose to call living is our own affair. Is an intricate self-replicating molecule alive? What if that molecule, through natural selection, acquires a kind of protective skin? The point at which we want to say that life has developed from nonlife is open to interpretation and debate since it is purely a human issue—a question of labels.

In reality, self-copying materials just became progressively more effective at surviving, more elaborate, and more capable through a process of blind, natural competition. Having internalized, as it were, their own blueprint, they became subject to random mutation. Struck by a penetrating photon from the sun or possibly a cosmic ray, a self-replicator risked its internal code being minutely altered. And, if this happened, then in the next generation an individual built according to a slightly different design would be created (providing the change had not altogether impaired the assembly mechanism). Most commonly such a mutant would prove less effective than its parent at staying in one piece long enough to have offspring of its own. But very occasionally a mutant would be born with an advantage over its parent and peers—the ability, for instance, to make copies of itself more rapidly, or to better resist attack from competitors.

In general terms, then, there is no problem in understanding how a variety of competing life-forms—primitive but steadily evolving toward greater sophistication—appeared on Earth long ago. None of these early creatures was anything more than a bundle of biochemicals wrapped up in a membrane bag. Even so, in their makeup and activity, we can recognize the inception of a new quality in the universe. These ancient gelatinous specks of matter showed the beginnings of self-interest and purpose. They had established barriers, definite, sustainable boundaries, between themselves and the outside world. And although the heady heights of human intellect and introspection lay almost four billion years away, even the most elementary of life-forms harbored information at some level about what was part of their own constitution and what was not. They were, at least chemically, self-aware. Thus, the foundations for dualism—the belief in the separation of self and the rest of the world—were laid.

What we see from our biased viewpoint to be the most significant advance in evolution is the movement toward increased cerebration—the development of bigger, more elaborate brains and nervous systems. The ability of a creature to retain within itself a sophisticated representation of the world outside is held by us in high regard. But the greatest accolade of all we reserve for ourselves and the capacity we alone seem to have to be conscious of ourselves as free agents in a world amenable to our control.

Natural selection gives no vector of progress. There was never any master plan to build bigger, better brains. But with hindsight, it seems almost inevitable that once life had become established it would develop in the direction of increased self-awareness. To be aware of yourself is to have an effective knowledge of where you end and the rest of the universe begins, so you know precisely on which battle line to fight. And being an individual in the wild *is* a battle, a continual, desperate struggle to stay alive. Any number of events can destroy you. A terrifying array of predators are out there trying to make you their next meal. Or, if you are not sufficiently aware of what is going on around you, you may fall victim to some other unfortunate accident. Or you may simply not find enough to eat. And no one is going to help you. On the contrary, your equally determined adversaries will take full advantage of any sign of weakness that you display. Given such perilous circumstances, the stronger your sense and skills of self-preservation, the better it is for you. Indeed, being and remaining an individual *necessitates* that you be uncompromisingly selfish.

We sometimes wonder how humans can be so cruel and ruthless, how they can lay waste to the planet with impunity, how they can exterminate other species and kill one another in alarming numbers. But such acts are not difficult after four billion years' practice. To stay alive at any cost, at anyone else's expense, is in our nature. It is the prime directive of our genes.

We are driven relentlessly to survive. And to aid us in this quest we have become equipped with the most remarkable survival organ in the known universe—the human brain. Such is the brain's power that it can construct and maintain a vivid sense of its own identity, its own unique selfhood. And yet it can also, with equal ease, cast its thoughts into the future and see its own inevitable demise.

Here, then, is the source of our greatest fear. We know full well that the brain and body will eventually break down. Yet such is our urge to carry on living that we cannot come to grips with the notion that the self presently associated with this doomed receptacle may similarly come to an abrupt end. The world and other selves will survive our personal death, we know. But this seems like small consolation if the particular selves that are you and I cannot, at least in some recognizable form, continue indefinitely.

Perhaps it was bound to happen that our race would go through this stage of uncertainty in its development. Maybe all creatures in the universe who become self-aware pass through a lengthy phase when they wrestle with the potentially devastating contradiction of a self-conscious survival machine that knows beyond all doubt that it *cannot* survive. But our combined intellect is formidable, capable of revealing deep, unexpected truths about the origin and nature of the cosmos. And there are no grounds a priori to suppose that it cannot also penetrate the more personal mysteries of the human self and mortality. Considering the importance of these issues to us, the time is surely ripe to embark upon such an investigation. And, providing we are prepared to take a broad-minded scientific approach, we can expect after millennia of doubt to shed real light on the problems of who we are and what happens to us when we die.

2

THE SOUL IS DEAD, LONG
LIVE THE SELF

And we, who are we anyway?

—Plotinus

Throughout history, people have countered the threat of death by believing in the existence of an immortal human spirit or soul. This soul, which is supposed to encapsulate all that is important about a person, is generally thought of as being like a pilot who, during life, works the controls of the body and brain. At death, as the physical body plunges to its doom, the ghostly pilot ejects in the nick of time (or is rescued by divine intervention) and hence survives to live on in some hereafter. Or so the hope goes. It is an attractive and comforting idea. And there is no doubt that most of us do need some notion of this sort to hold on to, if only to imbue our lives and the lives of our loved ones with more meaning.

It would be immensely reassuring, for instance, if a theory like that of the seventeenth-century French philosopher René Descartes were to be scientifically vindicated. Descartes believed strongly in the separate existence of the body and the soul. And he went so far as to identify the seat of the soul as the pineal gland, a neurological structure he chose because it was both centrally located and the only bit of the brain he could find that was not duplicated in the two cerebral hemispheres. The tiny pineal gland, in Descartes's view, served as the meeting place, or interface, between the material brain and the immaterial soul, which he equated with the mind or ego.

At first sight, it seems a reasonable enough conjecture (even though we might dispute the choice of the pineal). But the problems for any seat-of-the-soul hypothesis start as soon as we focus on the exact means by which the brain and the soul might interact. The brain is demonstrably built of ordinary matter, whereas the soul is presumed to consist of something else entirely—"mind stuff," or *res cogitans,* as Descartes called it. Crucially, the soul is held to be not merely tenuous, with an elusive nature similar to that of photons (light quanta) or neutrinos (particles capable of passing straight through the Earth without being absorbed), but actually *nonphysical.* In its very conception the soul stands outside the normal scheme of physics. And so, from the outset, we are at a loss to understand how it could possibly influence or be influenced by material objects, including the brain.

By the same token, the soul could not be expected to leave any trace on a detector or measuring device—a point, however, that has failed to deter some researchers. Sporadic efforts have been made over the past century or so to disclose the departure of the soul by weighing people shortly before and after death, but with negative results. The intriguing electric fields that surround living things and that can be visualized through the technique of Kirlian photography have also been posited, unconvincingly, as evidence for a spiritual life force. And, most recently, advanced scanning methods have been employed, notably by the American neurologist Richard Restak, to search the inner recesses of the brain for a soul in hiding, but to no avail. The fact is, the soul as it is normally presented is not a phenomenon open to scientific investigation. Nor is there any logic in claiming, on the one hand, that the soul is nonphysical or supernatural and, on the other, that it can have physical effects. Science will never be able to *dis*prove the existence of the soul, any more than it can disprove the existence of fairies or fire-breathing dragons. The gaps between what we know can always be filled with whatever people choose to dream up. But any rational inquiry into death must start from the evidence at hand.

We also need to be cautious before jumping to conclusions about the soul when there is such a clear and powerful motive for us to *want* to believe in it.* Potentially, the soul is a lifeline, a way of avoiding the terrifying finality of death. Imagine what a difference it would make to us psychologically if we knew, as certainly as we know we have a brain, that there is part of us that cannot die. We have a vested interest in the soul hypothesis being correct. And *this fact alone* is sufficient (whatever other elements may be involved) to account for the global, intercultural, long-standing belief in souls and an after-life—a belief that has flourished in spite of a conspicuous lack of evidence.

Clearly, there is something very different between a lifeless corpse and a living, breathing, sentient person. But *what* is different? During life, is there an aspect of us that is above and beyond the mere workings of a biological machine? Or are we, after all, nothing more than a temporary aggregation of chemicals and cells?

We have a strong tendency to feel as if we are something extra beyond our bodies and brains—that we are, in effect, an intelligent life force dwelling within an organic shell. This makes it easy to go along with the suggestion of dualists such as Descartes, that the mind is not just an upshot of the functioning brain but, on the contrary, is a deeper and further fact. In the dualist's scheme, each of us has—or is—a "Cartesian ego" that inhabits the material brain. And from this position, in which the mind is held to be distinct from the living brain, it is a short (though not inevitable) step to the assertion that the mind is capable of an entirely independent existence, as a disembodied soul.

Dualism is simple and desirable to believe in. But then, from a child's point of view, so is the Easter Bunny. In time, we come to appreciate (often with regret) that an extremely large, beneficent rabbit is not essential to explaining the origin of a surfeit of concealed eggs at Easter. Similarly, most neurologists have now reached the conclusion that a Cartesian ego or soul is not needed to account for the existence of the self.

---

*The same argument applies to other marginal phenomena, such as ghosts, telepathy, and UFOs, all of which appeal to our need for a "higher" truth.

It is a consensus fast approaching unanimity in scientific circles that "we" (our selves) are no more than the consequences of our brains at work. In the modern view, we are mere epiphenomena or, more charitably perhaps, culminations, of the greatest concentration of orchestrated molecular activity in the known cosmos. And although it is true we don't yet know exactly how the trick is done—these are still frontier days in the brain sciences—it is widely held to be only a matter of time before those who are teasing apart the circuitry of the human cortex lay bare the hidden props of the illusion. The situation is as brutally materialistic as that. There is not the slightest bit of credible evidence to suggest there is more to your self, to the feeling of being you, than a stunningly complex pattern of chemical and electrical activity among your neurons. No soul, no astral spirit, no ghost in the machine, no disembodied intelligence that can conveniently bail out when the brain finally crashes to its doom. If science is right, then you and I are just the transitory mental states of our brains.

We think of ourselves as being definite people, unique individuals. But, at birth, within the constraints of our genetic makeup, *we are capable of becoming anyone.* For the first year or two of life outside the womb, our brains are in the most pliable, impressionable, and receptive state they will ever be in. At the neural level this is apparent in the fact that we are all born with massively overwired brains that contain many more embryonic intercellular links than any one individual ever needs. Such was the surprising finding of the first extensive electron microscope study of human neural synapses (brain cell connections) by pediatric neurologist Peter Huttenlocher of Chicago's Pritzker Medical School in 1979. By staining and examining tissues from the frontal cortex, Huttenlocher found that the infant brain has, on average, about 50 percent more synaptic connections than has an adult brain, though the immature synapses are different in shape and much less well defined. It is as if a wide selection of the potentialities of the human race, acquired over millions of years, are made available to each of us at birth.

During the first twelve months of life, a remarkable 60 percent of a baby's energy intake goes toward fueling the development of its brain. In this critical period, huge numbers of embryonic connections between neurons are lost (through lack of use) while others are reinforced and developed (through repeated use). From being an incredibly sensitive, information absorbent, but otherwise useless lump of flesh, the brain rapidly acquires a highly patterned infrastructure that encodes a particular set of memories and beliefs about the world. Each brain loses the potential to become anyone, but gains, instead, the much more useful ability to conceive of itself as being a certain someone.

This transformation might seem almost magical if it weren't for the fact that we know, at least in general terms, how and why it comes about. A brain that was simply passive, naively experiencing its environment, reflecting everything but interpreting nothing, like a grinning Buddha, would quickly end up as a juicy morsel inside someone else's stomach. And so it would die, in blissful ignorance, before it could pass on its genes. And so there would be less grinning Buddhas in the future, but plenty more non-Buddha Buddha-eaters.

A real human brain starts out like a Buddha, all-receptive. But four billion years of ultrapragmatic live-and-let-die evolution have ensured that it immediately, under preprogrammed genetic control, gets down to the business of metamorphosing into a tough, practical survival machine. Its onboard genetic commands swiftly guide it in the process of condensing from a sort of gaseous state of total, nondiscriminating naïveté to a sharp, crystalline state of effective self-centeredness with the wits and street savvy needed to stay alive.

Unfortunately, we are absolutely, pathetically helpless throughout the period that this momentous development takes place, which is why a lengthy, protective, nurturing environment is so essential to humans (and other brainy animals). Simpleminded creatures, like amoebae, ants, and even alligators, come into the world "knowing" as much about their self-boundaries as they will ever know, albeit this knowledge is based purely on dumb reflexes and instinct. But our self-knowledge is a much more elaborate affair. Survival in the *Homo* niche demands being able to experience the self as an *agent* in the world, as an individual with the power to plan and predict and decide among alternative courses of action. Such knowledge can only be garnered through individual experience, by watching and learning from others who are already proficient at being the most ruthlessly effective survival machines in the known universe—men and women.

A crucial part of the development of our self-image involves the brain latching onto the game rules by which the individuals around it play. During infancy, and continuing into childhood and adolescence, the brain organizes itself around the prevalent attitudes and beliefs to which it is exposed. But it goes beyond building a general sociocultural belief system; otherwise everyone within a given race or clan would turn out pretty much the same. The brain *personalizes* its belief system by consolidating numerous, often highly subtle impressions it picks up from others about its particular character, intelligence, and status; its bodily appearance, gender role, and capabilities. Whether these impressions, received from parents, siblings, friends, and other people who are most influential during childhood are, in any absolute sense, "right" or "wrong" is not the issue. The brain will take them onboard whatever their merits, because they have come from the only authorities it recognizes and has access to. As these specific, private details are absorbed and assimilated, they begin to form the personal dimension of the brain's emerging worldview. Consequently, the brain starts to think of itself not just as being in a particular world, but as being a particular someone in that world—a person, an agent with powers of its own, with qualities, both good and bad, desirable and undesirable, by which it is uniquely distinguished from all others.

With the rudiments of a belief system in place, the brain starts to *interpret* and *evaluate* everything that comes to its attention in terms of this resident catechism of received wisdom. Every sensation and perception, every incident and event, every word, gesture, and action of other people, is construed within the context of what the brain understands the world and itself to be like. Thus the brain steadily becomes more and more dogmatic, opinionated, and biased in its thinking. It tends to hold on to—that is, to remember—experiences that comply with and support its acquired worldview, while at the same time it tends to reject or deny anything that seems incongruous with its system of beliefs. So, the emerging belief system is further strengthened and validated. And in this way the brain builds for itself an island of stability, a rock of predictability, in the midst of a vast ocean of potentially fatal chaos and inexplicable change.

We are inventions of our genes, our culture, our society, our particular upbringing, but oddly enough we're not aware of being so utterly contrived. We recognize that other people in other places and times may hold views different from our own. But we tend greatly to underestimate the extent to which we ourselves are caught up, constrained, and molded by the paradigms imposed upon us. Our indoctrination begins at such an early age and is so all-pervasive that the rules and theories we acquire become hard-wired into our brains. In particular, the power of our closest caretakers to shape us is awesome. Our parents or guardians reflect back at us, with approval, those sounds and actions we make as infants which are considered most desirable and appropriate in progressing toward the people they want us to become (just as they, too, were once similarly shaped). Subsequently, we fail to recognize that the beliefs about the world and about ourselves which we carry around with us like sacred relics are tentative, and possibly completely wrong. Instead we go through life fully convinced that they are true. We come to share and accept with unquestioning obedience the concepts of normality held by those around us, because these concepts are literally part of ourselves: we are their embodiment.

Our early environment and interpersonal relationships determine the precise neural circuitry of our brains, and this circuitry in turn determines who we are. Having encoded a particular model of reality, the brain, without "us" even realizing it, gives a spin to every sight, sound, smell, taste, and touch that enters through the senses. In fact, the conditioning begins even before the conscious brain goes into action. Evolution has furnished us with a range of sensory repression systems that save us from having to be aware of and thereby hopelessly overloaded and distracted by every minutia of our surroundings. So, just as the president has a team of minions to deal with all but the most crucial, relevant paperwork, the brain is able to deploy its attention, its executive power, where most needed by having the bulk of sensory input weeded out at a lower level.

Human vision, for instance, is an active process in which signals and perceptions are highly filtered, screened, and manipulated before they ever reach the higher centers of the cortex. We may feel as if we are directly and immediately aware of whatever images fall upon our retinas, but we are mistaken. Most of the handling of data from our eyes takes place at a subconscious level through a variety of largely independent specialized subsystems. And, strange though it may seem, some of the visual subsystems in our brains produce an output that "we" cannot see. They contribute to brain function and even to our awareness of the world, but no amount of introspection can make us aware of the subsystems themselves. One of the ways this is made most strikingly clear is by the strange neurological condition known as blind sight. Following some kinds of injury to the visual cortex, people may become blind in one half of their visual field. But although they claim an inability to see anything in their blind half, they sometimes seem capable of absorbing information from that half. For example, if asked to point to a spot of light on a screen on their blind side they will say they cannot see it at all and that they are just guessing its position. Yet they are able to point to it correctly far more often than would be expected by chance alone. Many other investigations, too, over the years have shown that much of what is actually registered by our eyes and brain escapes our conscious attention.

Survival for our ancestors would have been impossible if every datum of sensory input had been allowed to gain access to the inner sanctum of consciousness. By various means, then, we are shielded from the endless flux, the seething, ceaseless commotion both outside and among our neurons, the *fact* that neither we nor the world are ever the same from one moment to the next. Only when the integration is complete, and the flux has been smoothed and transformed into stability, does a final, coherent picture appear in our awareness.

All human beings are subject to similar biological and genetic conditioning. A Pygmy's eye works in the same way as a Parisian's; a neurologist would be at a loss to distinguish between the brain of a Japanese and that of a Scot. But the impact of different societies and cultures upon the developing self is much more diverse. We tend to underestimate this impact and so assume that people have always held their individuality and mortality clearly in mind, as we Westerners do today. However, looking at the history of death, and of how death was dealt with by people in the past, gives some clues to a possible evolution of self-awareness even over the past few hundred years. This is not to say that our relatively recent ancestors had no concept at all of themselves as unique individuals; to believe that humans have not always been self-aware to some degree is radical in the extreme.* But it does seem as if there was a trend toward a more intensely focused awareness of self, especially during the early modern period.

In medieval Europe, society was rigidly structured. Everyone knew their place in the scheme of things—a scheme based on lineage, gender, and social class. There was virtually no chance of escaping one's birthright, whether as a peasant or a feudal lord, no scope for social mobility. To appreciate more readily the mentality of this time we have to recognize that our modern emphasis on the fundamental, overriding importance of the individual is not universal. Medieval attitudes lacked this emphasis, in large measure because of the overarching influence of the Church of Rome. The medieval faith in Catholicism was absolute. But what mattered in this faith was not the individual's role but the broad cosmic sweep of holy law and salvation. Personalities, individual differences and opinions, were considered irrelevant and undesirable in the face of such totalitarian religious belief. And this downplaying of the personal is reflected in the fact that medieval times produced virtually no autobiographies and very few biographies—and then only inaccurate, stereotypical lives of saints. In these writings, the psychology of the person makes no appearance; all that comes across is a cardboard cutout of a man or woman, an anodyne approximation to the Christian ideal, unashamedly embellished with archetypal miracle tales.

By the end of the Middle Ages, however, a change was evident. Instrumental in this was the rise of Protestantism, particularly in its most extreme form—Puritanism. John Calvin preached that some, "the Elect," were *predestined* to enter heaven, while most were doomed to spend eternity in hell. Absurd and intellectually offensive though this idea may appear now, it had the effect at the time of casting the individual into sharp relief, of differentiating between one person and another. And, in general, Protestantism of every kind argued

---

*Just such a view is expressed by Julian Jaynes in his book *The Origin of Consciousness in the Bicameral Mind*. Jaynes, an American psychologist, has suggested that human self-awareness originated within the last two thousand years.

for the private nature of religion. Catholics did not need, and were not expected, to face God alone. Priests, nuns, saints, the Virgin Mary, and all manner of rituals were on hand to intercede for the masses, so that the masses didn't have to think too hard or deeply for themselves, didn't have to become too involved as individuals or worry too much about the implications to themselves of the great issues of life, death, and redemption. Protestantism, by contrast, sought to diminish the gap between layperson and God, while Puritanism sought to close it completely. The Puritan faced God alone—in the privacy of the individual mind.

And there were soon to be other factors at work in the West, helping to turn the spotlight even more fully on each man and woman, forcing the self out of hiding. Not the least of these was the Industrial Revolution and, at its heart, that great engine—literally and figuratively—for change. Suddenly, the old agricultural lifestyle in which son did like father, and daughter like mother, generation after generation, and in which it was frowned upon and futile for the individual to act any differently from the rest, was swept away. And in its place was development (often for the worse for those who lived in the new slums) and technological progress, the rise of personal ambition, of the entrepreneur, the winner and loser, and a new emphasis on individuality and concern for one's own welfare. Suddenly, it was good and potentially profitable to be an individual, to go one's own way, to be different from the crowd. And that attitude has not altered to this day.

In the modern West, we revere the self, we set it up on a pedestal. There has never before been a culture, a time, in which people focused so obsessively on the well-being and elevation of their egos. And what do these egos turn out to be? Nothing, says science, but artifacts of the brain. We—our feelings of being someone in the world—survive as long as the brain lives. And when the brain dies . . .

Our prospects look bleak. The very mode of inquiry that has helped shape the modern world and that we have come to rely upon so much informs us that, in effect, we are the dreams of carbon machines. There is no real substance to us, no deeper, further fact to being a person than just one feeling after another after another.

Impressions, sensations, thoughts, emotions, continually well up into awareness and the sequence of these experiences, bound together by that fragile thing called memory, is projected by the brain as you and me.

Our choice of how to respond seems simple. We can despair or we can deny. We can throw up our hands and acknowledge that we are nothing more than illusions that will be exposed as such at the instant our brains die. Or we can reject the tenets of reductionist science and insist, based on faith alone, that some form of immortal soul *does* exist.

But there is a third option—one that appeals both to the intellect and to the heart. And this is to recognize that although, at one level, selves may not be as substantial as they normally appear, at another level they are real and important objects of inquiry. The very same situation applies to atoms, because modern physics has revealed beyond reasonable doubt that atoms consist almost entirely of empty space. And even the supposedly tangible nuggets of matter inside atoms— quarks (which make up protons and neutrons) and electrons—give no sign whatever of having any extension. Knowing this, it might seem incredible that, in large numbers, atoms can give such a convincing impression of solidity. And yet, in the everyday world, solid they undeniably are. If you bang your head, it doesn't ease the pain to be lectured on the fundamental immateriality of matter. In the same way, it is totally unconvincing, in the light of what we experience every day of our lives, to be told that selves have no real existence. On one level, at least, they certainly *do* exist. And we are just as entitled to regard selves as entities in their own right as we are to credit an independent existence to anything, from germs to galaxies, that fundamentally is composed only of empty space and pointlike particles.

The soul—whether it exists or not—appears to lie outside the realm of scientific inquiry. But this is not true of the self. We can probe the self in many different ways and, as a result, hope to learn more about what it means to have a self—and to lose it.

3

HEADS AND TALES

There was a young man who said "Damn!

"It is borne upon me that I am

"An engine which moves

"In predestinate grooves

"I'm not even a bus, I'm a tram!"

—*Anonymous*

We would rightly regard someone who habitually spoke of himself as being a robot or a machine as being crazy. Yet this is precisely what science seems to be telling us about ourselves. The brain? An organic computer. Love? A process in those neurological systems that underpin mood. Anger? An activation of neural impulses in the amygdala-hypothalamus structures. And self-consciousness as a whole? A fairly recent, emergent phenomenon of matter.

All of this may be true. We may, in one sense, be awesomely complex machines. But such a description fails to do proper justice to the human condition, because we are not only objects in the world but also *objectifiers*—and both aspects of our nature, the outer and the inner, need to be encompassed by any credible worldview.

Other people see you objectively, from a spectator's standpoint, as a living human being with certain unique characteristics. They observe a body and, most importantly, on that body, a head. On that head they see a face—a face that in the subtleties of its ever-changing expressions projects a certain persona to the world. The eyes, in particular, have been called "the windows of the soul." But this pretty description does not allow for the fact that the face may be—and generally is—a kind of mask (the Latin *persona* refers to the mask worn by actors in ancient theater)* hiding our genuine feelings. The outward face we present for the benefit of others (and so, indirectly, of ourselves) more often than not is a pretense, a concealment or misrepresentation, of the true state of the mind.

There is, then, this exterior view of you as within the *dramatis personae*—an actor playing his or her part on the world's stage with the help of a convincing disguise. But there is also an interior view, to which you alone are privy. In mechanistic terms, as well as the appearance of the brain-body machine, there is the feeling of what it is like to be that machine—the subjective experience of being a certain someone. Consciousness, we might say, is the symmetry-breaking factor between the objective and the subjective.

To make this more clear, imagine that you are having your brain monitored by a superscanner. This scanner creates a detailed three-dimensional image highlighting the regions of the brain that are most active at any given time. Suddenly, a large screen in front of you, which had been dark, glows bright red. At the same instant, the scanner reveals a new region of activity in your brain—the physical correlate (presumably) of your perception of redness. Next, several other people have their brains scanned under exactly the same conditions. The result is a series of scans, including the one of your own brain, all of which are very similar. As far as you are concerned, the brain scans of the other people encapsulate all you can know of their reaction to the color red. In the language of physics, they represent complete "state-descriptions" of your companions' brains. But when it comes to the scan of your own brain, it is patently obvious that it falls well short of capturing everything about your experience of redness. For what it leaves out is nothing less than the conscious experience itself! A more precise definition of consciousness follows, then, as that prop-

---

per = "through," *sonus* = "sound"; hence, literally, the sound that comes through the mask.

erty which makes a detailed state-description of the observer's own brain seem incomplete when compared with equally detailed state-descriptions of the brains of other people. Another way of saying this is that no form of symbolic communication, verbal, graphical, or mathematical, can convey the essence of what it is like to be someone. Fortunately, each of us, being human, is already intimately familiar with what it is like to be one person. And since there is no reason to suppose there are any great differences between the subjective experiences of one person and those of any other, language is *in fact* a useful way of telling each other what we are feeling.

Still, you are you, and I am me. Alike we may be in many ways, but undeniably we have our differences. Indeed, to a large extent, we are *defined* by our differences. To be a self is to be different from anyone else and to know it. And to be different and to know it involves having a clear conception of where "you" end and the rest of reality begins—an awareness of one's boundaries.

At first sight, it may seem obvious that a person's boundary—their interface with the external world—is just the surface of their skin. As Sigmund Freud put it: "The I is first and foremost a bodily I." And it is certainly the simplest criterion of "I-ness" to apply. When we look at another human being, we have no trouble in deciding what is part of him or her and what is not. But the bodily I, by itself, is too simplistic a notion to capture all the possibilities of what we might consider ourselves to be. There is the question, for instance, of whether we *are* our bodies or whether we simply own them. The reductionist, the materialist, would claim the former, the Cartesian the latter.

In fact, the physical boundaries of self are nowhere near as fixed or well defined as we sometimes imagine them to be. If I lose an arm and have it replaced by a sophisticated prosthesis, does the artificial substitute become part of me or merely a new possession?

Today, implants, transplants, and prostheses can act as highly effective surrogates for so many bits of our original bodies that we are being forced to confront the issue of how much of a person can be replaced before a new individual is created. This dilemma will reach new proportions as partial transplants and prostheses for the brain become available. And in other ways, too, our physical bounds can appear to shift according to circumstances. Normally mild-mannered and soft-spoken individuals, for instance, can at times seem to mutate alarmingly into aggressive, raving monsters when behind the wheel of a car, while skilled drivers and pilots often feel their vehicles to be seamless extensions of themselves. Has the link between man and machine become so close that we can sometimes regard the combination as being effectively like a new individual? And if so, what will be the consequences of even more intimate relationships between ourselves and our technology in the future as developments such as virtual reality take hold?

If you are nothing more than your body (or extended body), then is your corpse still you—or yours—after you die? Semantic problems obscure an easy answer. But more to the point, we are not really interested in our corpse, or the issue of its ownership, any more than we care about the fate of our hair once it has been cut off. What really matters to us is not what happens to our bodies when we die, but what happens to *us*. The implication is clear: we instinctively consider ourselves to be something more, or at least something very different, than just the material contents of our bodies and brains. We are the "what it is like to be" experience that our bodies and brains give rise to. And it is the long-term future of this "what-it-is-like-to-be-ness" that concerns us above anything else.

William James wrote: "Each of us spontaneously considers that by 'I' he means something always the same." We know that our moods and attitudes alter from one day to the next. And we recognize, too, that great changes are associated with going through the various stages of life. Adolescence, in particular, is a time of dangerously rapid physical and psychological transformation—a time of enormous upheaval and insecurity. Yet, through it all, we believe that at root we remain one and the same person.

Two aspects of ourselves stand out as appearing to be of crucial importance. First: *personal identity*. You may not look or even think much like you did when you were five years old, yet in spite of this you believe that, in a deep, underlying sense, something about you— your identity—has remained uncompromised. This belief of yours is shared unquestioningly by the rest of society and has to some extent been cultivated in you by society's influence. How very different the world might be if this belief were not widely held. If people did not generally maintain that personal identity were an inviolable fact then it would bring into question, for instance, whether an individual could be held responsible for a crime that he or she was supposed to have committed some time ago. If a person could not be uniquely or conclusively identified with any past self, then that person could not be said to have existed at the time of a particular crime. By the same token, we would not be able to take credit for anything worthwhile we thought we had done, since the achievements would be considered by others to belong to someone else who was no longer alive. Conventions such as marriage, parental rights, nationality, and ownership or membership of any kind would lose their meaning.

The second aspect of ourselves we consider to be fundamentally important is *continuity*. Identity and continuity may be spoken of as different qualities, but clearly they are related. The former implies the latter. Your identity is rooted in the continuous existence of your body. You look more or less the same as you did last year. And last year you looked more or less the same as you did the year before that. The chronologically arranged photos in your family album testify to the smooth and steady development of your body and appearance from infancy to the present day. No one would seriously argue with this. And just as obviously there seems to be a continuity in your mental life because of the relationship between your awareness and your brain.

"A person," says philosopher Jonathan Glover, "is someone who can have I-thoughts." To be capable of I-thoughts seems to imply the existence of self-consciousness. And yet both are elusive concepts. You know that you have I-thoughts. You know you are self-conscious. But in others it is not obvious how to decide when self-consciousness shades into a less focused form of awareness and when this, in turn, merges into an almost unconscious state. With regard to nonhuman species, for instance, how can we judge if any other animals might qualify, in a limited or modified sense, as persons? Does the brain of a bonobo (a pygmy chimp, the creature most genetically similar to ourselves) or a dolphin integrate its experiences in a manner that enables something resembling I-thoughts to emerge? Or, are I-thoughts the exclusive privilege of life-forms that have evolved a language sophisticated enough to subtend a symbolic image of self? In considering such matters we need constantly to bear in mind that just because we have words such as "I," "self," and "person" in our vocabulary gives no guarantee that they correspond to anything real outside of our cultural context. How we choose to define and interpret the terms we have invented is entirely up to us, and nature is not compelled to follow suit.

Most people would be happy to agree that a jellyfish is not a person in that it almost certainly can't think of itself as an "I." To say that it can't think at all would be going too far—a jellyfish *can* process some kinds of information in ways that today's artificial intelligence researchers would be only too glad to be able to emulate in their machines. But a jellyfish cannot (as far as we know) generate thoughts such as "I'm happy," "I am being touched," or "I am stinging my lunch to death."

Children sometimes ask: "If you had to be a different kind of animal, what would it be?" Few people in their right minds* would choose to be a jellyfish—or an ant, a worm, or a grasshopper. To be any of these, most of us might imagine, would probably be not much better or worse than being nonexistent. On a wish list of alternative life-forms, creatures with small brains or no brains at all would tend to come near the bottom—for the simple reason that we use mental prowess (gauged roughly by brain-to-body-size ratio) when differentiating between lower or primitive animals and those considered to be further up the evolutionary ladder. If you couldn't be human, the chances are you'd choose to be an ape, a cetacean, or a relatively smart domesticated animal such as a dog or a horse. You would naturally opt for a species that seemed to have a relatively secure, pleasant life, and that also had the wits to appreciate it—a species, in other words, that was as nearly human as could be arranged.

We sometimes wonder what it would be like to be a different kind of creature. Yet, in a sense, we already know, because we have effectively *been* different kinds of creatures during our own development. The growth of an individual human parallels, or recapitulates at a

---

*Or, rather, in their left minds—see Chapter 6.

vastly accelerated rate, the general evolution of life on earth. We start out as a single-celled organism, like a bacterium or an amoeba. Then we progress through a simple, undifferentiated multicellular stage (a blastula) to become an embryo that, early on, is barely distinguishable from the embryos of many other animals, including reptiles and amphibians. For the first few weeks after conception we are truly a lower form of life ourselves, bathed in a warm amniotic sea. So, how *did* it feel to you? Can you recall? The problem seems to be that *you* were not really around at the time. And, consequently, it is difficult to imagine in what form any memories of this primal, pre-you phase of existence could be meaningful or capable of being experienced by you now. By the same token, our brief spell as primitive creatures in the womb strongly suggests that lower life-forms have no well-developed conscious sense of self.

It seems that what we really mean by ourselves—the *feeling* of being an "I"—is not an all-or-nothing affair. In other species it may exist in a guise unfamiliar to us. In humans, it develops and changes over time. What we call self-awareness surely emerges as our minds construct an increasingly sophisticated symbolic representation of the outside world—an internalized portrayal of reality that, at some point during early childhood, comes to include our own bodies. Almost certainly, the same process took place during the evolution of mankind as a whole.

Much of what we believe about ourselves derives from how others relate and react to us. And, for this reason, total isolation from society can prove devastating. In 1988, a French woman, Veronique Le Guen, spent a record-breaking 111 days alone underground, 250 feet below the surface at Valat-Nègre in southern France. Deprived of a clock, natural light, and any form of contact with others, Le Guen had only her diary for company. In one of the entries she described herself as being "psychologically completely out of phase, where I no longer know what my values are or what is my purpose in life." It was an experience from which she never properly recovered, and in January 1990, at the age of thirty-three, she committed suicide. Her husband said, "She had an emptiness inside her which she was unable to communicate."

Regular, close social interaction is vital to our self-definition, to bringing the fuzzy edges of our psychological bounds back into focus.* (This is strangely analogous—and I wonder if it may more than that—to the situation in quantum mechanics [see Chapter 10] where repeated observations of an atomic nucleus serve to prevent it from decaying.) We assimilate the responses of our fellow humans both to our appearance and our behavior. And this results in a feedback loop. Our appearance and behavior are subject to change according to the internal image we hold of ourselves. And any modifications in how we appear outwardly affect people's responses to us, which may result, again, in further alterations to our inner beliefs about ourselves. If people approve of how we look and act—if we conform to some positive, preconceived stereotype—then we will be praised and generally treated well, a response that will strengthen the already good self-image we hold. On the other hand, if we deviate much from the norm and act disreputably, the feedback we receive will serve to confirm our worst fears that we are among society's outcasts.

Experiments have been carried out in which people's usual personas and roles are temporarily and drastically altered. In one of these studies, a group of college students was arbitrarily divided into two groups—prison warders and prisoners. The students were cut off from the outside world and encouraged to act their respective parts as realistically as possible. The warders pretended to treat their charges as potentially dangerous and untrustworthy criminals, while the latter feigned to look upon the uniformed officers as hated oppressors. After a short time, however, the students found themselves completely taken over by their roles; they were no longer acting. The warders genuinely regarded the inmates as being inferior and often behaved toward them in a brutal and domineering way. The prisoners, on the other hand, became cowed and actually afraid.

It is remarkable how much and how easily our self-image can be changed by outside influences. Dress one day in torn jeans and unironed shirt, your hair unkempt, your attitude careless; then the next day go out to the same places in your best attire, immaculately groomed, acting confidently and assured. The difference in how oth-

---

*Mystics and ascetics often choose isolation for the very reason that it encourages a breakdown of conventional self-boundaries.

ers will treat you is staggering (I speak from experience!). Moreover, this dramatic shift in the attitude of others will have a powerful influence on how you feel about yourself. You will feel, literally, like a different person.

Of course, most of the time we don't go out of our way to fabricate a new image of ourselves every day. We wear a uniform, in the broadest sense—a stable overall persona—because in this way we ensure that the reactions of others to us are reasonably predictable. And so the world is rendered less threatening and stressful. Our efforts at conforming to some particular role, whether it be as a rebel or as a stalwart of society, and the subsequent stabilizing of others' reactions to us, results in the creation of what seems to us, on the inside, a fairly well-defined, consistent self. We recognize "ourselves" more and more easily as we age; our life patterns become more and more predictable. But this is not to say that the self is ever *really* solid or secure. The self, the inner "I," remains no more than whatever feeling we are having at the present moment—a feeling shaped by the memories our brains have laid down of past experiences.

You and I are different not because different things are happening to us right now, but because, throughout our lives, our brains have acquired different narratives and ways of responding to the world. We are the products of our life stories. Your story is different than mine. But what is crucial in defining and distinguishing between us is not so much the differences between the actual events and surroundings that you and I have encountered, as it is the different way in which our brains have interpreted and remembered what has happened to us. An essential part of being human involves trying to make sense of the world, seeking and finding meaning (whether it is there or not). We have to do this from one moment to the next, every second of our lives. So, inevitably, a lot of what we remember is not what *actually* happened—whatever this may mean—but rather a kind of myth or confabulation that helps us sustain the impression that we know what is going on. We tell ourselves white lies all the time to bridge the gaps in our understanding of an impossibly complex world. And not only do we fail to realize they are untruths (indeed this would undermine all our efforts) but we lay down these countless little fictions in our memories and subsequently treat them as if they were factual. We maintain a sense of continuity and so provide a basis for our feeling of personal identity at the cost of never knowing what is true. We are as much a myth as the stories we tell ourselves.

How then can we discover what is real—assuming there is such a thing? Stories we may be. The self, the "I," the ego, whatever we choose to name what we thought was our true essence, may be as insubstantial as a unicorn's fear of a dragon. But we cannot just leave it there. We *do* feel like someone, a being with inner depth. And we do want to know what it will feel like to die, and whether what follows death feels like anything at all.

4

REMEMBER ME?

You have to begin to lose your memory, if only
in bits and pieces, to realize that memory is
what makes our lives.

—*Luis Buñuel*

Almost everything you do and think is based on what your brain remembers has happened to it in the past. And everything you do and think in the future will serve to reinforce the patterns of behavior and response associated with the particular person that you, and others, think of yourself as being. All new experiences and perceptions from one moment to the next are interpreted in the context of your apparently central, abiding self. Memory is your link with the past and your basis for action in the future.

To be a person, one must have a memory—a unique, accessible set of recollections—because to be a person means to hold one's life story and be actively, intimately involved with it. We must be able to see who we are now in terms of who we have been at different, successive stages along our journey from early childhood. We must hold the script to the inner drama that is ourselves, to know our own narrative. For if we cannot do this, we are without an identity or self.

Fortunately, our memories are remarkably durable. They survive despite the never-ending metabolic turnover of particles in every cell of our bodies, a fact lyrically captured by Loren Eisley in *The Immense Journey*:

> I suppose that in the forty-five years of my
> existence, every atom, every molecule, that
> composes me has changed position or danced
> away and beyond to become part of other
> things. New molecules have come from the
> grass and the bodies of animals to be part of
> me a little while, yet in this spinning, light and
> airy as a midge swarm in a shaft of sunlight,
> my memories hold, and a loved face of twenty
> years is before me still.

Atom for atom and cell for cell substitution poses no threat whatever to the self, as experience clearly shows. In the case of people who recover fully after having been in a coma for several months there has been an almost complete replacement of their constituent atoms in the period during which they were unconscious. Yet, upon waking, they have no sensation of being any different or of any time having passed.

A far more extreme case of the "persistence of self" was imagined by H. G. Wells in *The Sleeper Awakes,* in which a young man falls into a trance that lasts two centuries. As the trance begins, Wells asks: "Where was the man? Where is any man when insensibility takes hold of him?" And two hundred years later:

> What a wonderfully complex thing! this simple
> seeming unity—the self! Who can trace its
> reintegration as morning after morning we
> awaken, the flux and confluence of its count-
> less factors interweaving, rebuilding . . . the
> growth and synthesis of the unconscious to the
> sub-conscious, the sub-conscious to the dawn-
> ing consciousness, until at last we recognize
> ourselves again. And as it happens to most of
> us after the night's sleep, so it was with
> Graham at the end of his vast slumber.

When he conceived this fantasy, Wells could hardly have imagined how close reality was to emulating his fiction. Between 1916 and

1927, there occurred a worldwide epidemic of *encephalitis lethargica,* or sleeping sickness. Nearly five million people contracted this devastating illness, one third of whom died shortly after as a result. But for others there followed a bizarre trancelike state—not unconsciousness but a conscious stasis—in which time seemed to stand still. It was for them as if the world, instead of giving the appearance of continuous change as in a movie, had instead become stuck in a single frame.

Then, as in Wells's story, came the awakening. More than forty years after they had been struck down, the victims were temporarily and almost miraculously freed from their frozen state by the administration of massive doses of the anti-Parkinson's drug L-dopamine. For those who had been most deeply affected, their last living memories were of the world as it had been shortly after World War I. More than four decades had elapsed during which all the substance of their bodies and brains had been replaced many times over. But upon resuming relatively normal consciousness, the patients were in no doubt as to who they were. It was for them as if there had been no vast temporal chasm. And for this very reason, they were confused, disoriented, by what they found—or did not find—in the new world into which they had been catapulted. One profoundly affected patient, for instance, upon being revived used strangely outmoded turns of phrase and spoke of Gershwin and other contemporaries as if they were still alive. She knew it was 1969, because during her trance she had absorbed news of current events such as the bombing of Pearl Harbor and the assassination of Kennedy, but she *felt* with overwhelming conviction that it was 1926.

In his remarkable account of such cases in his book *Awakenings,* the neurologist Oliver Sacks supports the argument, first expressed by Leibniz (*"Quis non agit non existit"*), that we must be active or we cease, in any ontological sense, to exist—that activity and actuality are one and the same. How else, he wondered, could the instantaneous return to normal movement and speech be explained in a person who had been totally inactive for more than forty years. Most of us stiffen up if we remain in the same position for a couple of hours. Six weeks with a broken leg in a cast and we need at least a few days to recoup the strength in our muscles and the flexibility in our joints. Yet some of the sleeping-sickness victims, having been virtually motionless for half a lifetime, were, within a few seconds of their "unfreezing," jumping up, walking about with great energy, and chattering excitedly to anyone who would listen. The only satisfactory conclusion Sacks could draw was that during their trance there had been no subjective duration for the victims whatever. It was as if the "current of being" (Sacks's phrase) had been abruptly turned off and, more than forty years later, turned back on again. In between, for the victim, time had stood still and memory remained intact. Nothing was added to it, but nothing was subtracted either.

We occasionally curse our memory when it lets us down. Yet overall, the powers of memory are prodigious. They enable a credible (though not necessarily objectively accurate) recollection of the life's journey of a particular human brain, built up from numerous perceptions, feelings, thoughts, actions, and conversations with other brains—a series of complex experiences stored coherently, so it appears, and in a form that corresponds with their actual chronological order. At the same time, most of us cannot remember anywhere near everything that has happened to us. And whatever we imagine might be the benefits of having an eidetic or photographic memory, those who actually possess one know that it can be a blight and a handicap—in fact, in its most extreme manifestation, a crippling neurological disorder. Jorge Luis Borges wrote a disturbing short story, "Funes the Memorius," about a young man who remembered every detail of his past:

> He knew by heart the forms of the southern
> clouds at dawn on 30 April 1882, and could
> compare them in his memory with the mottled
> streaks on a book in Spanish binding he had
> seen once and with the outlines of the foam
> raised by an oar in the Rio Negro the night
> before the Quebracho uprising.

Such exquisite retention might seem entirely fantastic. But the eminent neurologist A. R. Luria documented an actual case of total recall in his astonishing book, *The Mind of a Mnemonist*. The subject was a Russian man, Sherashevsky, who could remember—or, more to the point, could never forget—any detail, however small, of the experiences of his life: every sight, sound, taste, smell, and touch, every thought and impression, every way of looking at and analyzing a situation. And, of course, it was disastrous for him because he had no sense of discrimination. He could never focus on a specific problem or situation because as soon as he turned his attention to it, his mind was choked full of irrelevancies. Every trivial item spawned the recollection of a thousand others. He could not follow through a particular chain of reasoning, or make decisions, or take an interest in one topic over any other. In fact, he could not function normally at all and spent many of his days in abject depression and misery.

Recent research by scientists at the Cold Spring Harbor Laboratory, New York, suggests that photographic memory may have a genetic basis. Their work has centered on the so-called CREB gene in the fruit fly *Drosophila*. This gene is suspected of being the "master switch" that regulates other genes for synthesizing the key proteins involved in long-term memory. The Cold Spring Harbor team created a strain of fly carrying a modified form of the CREB gene which produced unusually large amounts of activator protein—the protein required for laying down memories. In addition, they arranged matters so that the altered CREB gene would only be turned on above 98 degrees Fahrenheit. Kept at room temperature, the genetically modified flies behaved normally, taking about ten training sessions to learn to avoid an odor associated with an electric shock. When warmed above 98 degrees, however, they learned the association after just one session. It seems likely that a similar "faulty" master gene, leading to the overproduction of activator protein, exists in people with exceptional powers of memory.

For survival reasons, a normal memory is selective and patchy, even if, to its owner, it doesn't seem to be that way. The brain holds on to what it needs and quickly forgets what is irrelevant. Having organized itself, during childhood, around a particular worldview, the brain tends to consolidate mainly those memories that appear to fit in with and enhance this system of belief. Normal memory, then, is heavily biased toward a particular conception of reality. It is gappy, but good in parts, and may be exceptionally good with regard to some specific life episodes.

Just how good it can be was graphically demonstrated by the Canadian neurosurgeon Wilder Penfield and his team in Montreal in the 1950s. While operating on people under local anesthesia, in an effort to cure focal seizures by excising damaged brain tissue, Penfield would cut and turn back a portion of their skulls, expose their cerebral cortices, and then touch an electrical probe to specific points on the surface of the brain. This allowed him to identify and map regions of special importance, such as the language centers, that it was crucial were left intact by the surgery. Depending on exactly where on the cortex the mild pulsing current from the probe was allowed to flow, the patient would react in a highly specific, often comical way. He might utter a short, incomprehensible sound, or be prevented from saying anything at all. He might twitch the index finger of his left hand. And if the probe made contact somewhere on the lateral side of the temporal lobe, it would often trigger in the patient a particular, vivid reliving of a past event, as if the play button of a tiny video recorder had been pressed. Touching one spot on the cortex might cause a patient to hear her mother and father singing Christmas carols around the piano as they did in her youth; stimulation of another point nearby might spark off the recollection of a winter walk through fresh-fallen snow, or of a childhood incident in the schoolyard, or of an encounter with a menacing stranger. Each episode would seem strikingly realistic and detailed (much more so than a normal recollection), and each could be played again from the start, exactly as before, by an identical touch of the probe.

Our sense of being someone, a distinct person in the world, depends upon the unique chain of experiences that connects the moments of our lives—and which, through memory, we carry into the present. In his poem "The Mother's Breast and the Father's House," B. Reed Whitmore writes:

Your seemingly small mind is in truth an enormous
warehouse devoted to documenting and buttressing the persistence of
you
Stuff with the dust of decades is in it
books, faces, tears, fears,
loves, hates, games, names

all in relation to

you

colors, odors, textures, travel incredible distances with us

even the weakest among us is a sort of god of preserving of that which

would be wholly trivial if it were not ours . . .

In the broadest sense, memory means more than just information stored in our heads. We "remember" about the past—even the very remote past—in our genes. And because of our onboard genetic program the stability of our selves is enhanced through the readily recognizable appearance, from day to day and year to year, of our bodies. Genes, too, inevitably have some influence on the basic architecture of our brains. But by far the most important contribution to personal identity and continuity comes from the memories our brains hold about what has happened to us during life.

Every day we gain some memories and lose others, have different sensations, and find ourselves in new situations, yet the brain copes with all of this change, adapts to it, and emerges at the end feeling as if it were the same person. This is its evolutionary legacy: the brain's primary urge (like that of our body's other systems) is to maintain the status quo. It works ceaselessly, automatically, to keep the impression it holds of itself constant and intact, whatever circumstances may prevail. To survive, biologically, means to stay the same, for if you change at all you become someone else, a new individual. So the brain is driven, relentlessly, to do everything it can to reinforce the feeling that it is unified, consistent, continuous. And in this mission, its ability to retain a chain of detailed past experiences is crucial.

Selves are defined by memories. But for many different reasons it is not always possible for a brain to maintain a complete or unbroken memory record. For instance, there is a certain kind of sleeping drug that induces a mild form of the effect known as retrograde amnesia. It does this by blocking the brain's ability to transfer memories from short-term store to long-term store: if you take this drug you cannot, upon waking, remember anything that happened in the hour or so before you fell asleep. That hour, as far as you are concerned, may as well never have existed.

Imagine, now, that you have just taken a dose of this drug. For an hour you feel perfectly fine, in no way different than you did before. But, knowing what the eventual effect of the drug will be, you decide to write a message to yourself. This describes all of the main events that happen during the next hour—the phone call from your friend, the sudden heavy shower of rain, the last minute touchdown you saw on TV that won the game for your team. Suddenly you feel an irresistible weariness creeping over you and decide it's time to lie down. Eight hours later you wake up. The last thing you remember is taking the sleeping pill. But where did this note come from by the side of your bed? The handwriting looks familiar. It's from you! Yet you have absolutely no recollection of having written it. You will never, at any moment during the rest of your life, remember having sent that message to yourself. It may as well have been written by a stranger. You are forever cut off from the thoughts and actions of the individual who lived through that missing hour of your life. He or she, though obviously *physically* continuous with you, is completely detached from your *psychological* continuum.

Blows to the head often produce a similar effect. A few years ago, my son fell down while playing in the street one evening and banged his head against the curb. For a short time he lay unconscious before coming round, clearly still dazed and groggy, with an unfocused look in his eyes. He came inside, sat down, and suddenly looked in surprise at what he was wearing. "Where did I get these clothes?" he asked. In fact, they had been newly bought that afternoon. Yet to this day he cannot remember having gone shopping or anything else that he did in the four hours prior to his accident. His memories hold none of the experiences that his body and brain had during that time. As far as he is concerned now, it may as well have been someone else who had these experiences.

Most instances of amnesia are short-lived and have no important lasting effects on a person. But as a result of certain kinds of serious brain injury or disease, a profound and permanent form of amnesia may overwhelm its victim to the extent that he or she is unable to lay down any new memories at all. Such was the predicament of a certain musician who suffered from Korsakov's syndrome. On one occasion, she had just completed, with three friends, a rendition of Beethoven's Quartet in E Minor, Opus 59, No. 2, having given a virtuoso performance on the violin. A few minutes later, the cellist urged that they try another piece to which the lady in question replied, "Let us play Beethoven's E Minor Quartet, Opus 59, No. 2." An embarrassed silence followed, after which a member of the company gently pointed out what had happened.

In one of his essays, Oliver Sacks gives a moving account of another victim of Korsakov's syndrome, whom he referred to as Jimmie G. When Jimmie first met Sacks in 1975 he was forty-nine years old but had no memory of anything that had happened for the previous thirty years (the damage to his brain having been caused by alcoholism). To him it was still 1945, World War II had just ended, and he was an ebullient nineteen-year-old working aboard submarines in the U.S. Navy. A moment of crisis and panic ensued when Sacks asked Jimmie to look into a mirror and describe what he saw.

"Jesus Christ," he whispered. "Christ, what's going on? What's happened to me? Is this a nightmare?"

Two minutes later, having left the room, Sacks reentered to find Jimmie cheerful again, the mirror incident entirely forgotten, greeting him as if for the first time. He had absolutely no recollection of their earlier meeting or conversation. In his notes, Sacks wrote: "He is, as it were, isolated in a single moment of being, with a moat or lacuna of forgetting all round him. . . . He is a man without a past (or future), stuck in a constantly changing, meaningless moment."

The problem for Jimmie and for others like him is not that life (in a caring, sheltered environment) need be impossible or even generally unpleasant, but that it is fraught with potential anomalies and contradictions. To believe with all your heart and mind that it is one time when it is really three decades later is to be in continual peril of confronting horrible, inexplicable inconsistencies. It is like living in an alien world—a world peopled by strangers who will always remain strange, and by relatives who appear unaccountably aged. Any moments of panic, it is true, are quickly and permanently forgotten— the syndrome at least ensures this degree of protection from itself. But to be in such a state, with no hope whatever of recovery, is to live permanently on the edge of an abyss of unreason.

We may think ourselves lucky that we are not afflicted with some such deep-seated neurological disorder. But none of us in truth stands far from the brink of personal chaos. Serious malfunctionings of the brain serve not to emphasize how much removed we are from the pathological but how frighteningly close we all stand to insanity's edge. They expose the fragile basis of our lives: the extraordinary importance of a carefully ordered repository of facts in defining the beings that we are.

For victims of Korsakov's syndrome, there is the continual problem of how to reconcile, how to make sense of, the crazy world in which they find themselves in terms of the only world they know— a world that may be many years out-of-date and that becomes increasingly anachronistic and irrelevant with each passing day. It is a problem that can be resolved or avoided in only one way: by confabulation, by making what (to others) seem facile and absurd rationalizations, "throwing bridges of meaning," as Sacks says, "over abysses of meaninglessness." The alternative, as when Jimmie was caught off guard and saw a middle-aged head on what he took to be a young man's body, is total disorientation, disbelief, and denial. Doubtless we all have, at one time or another, felt a momentary rush of panic when, for example, we wake up thinking we are in one place when, in fact, we are elsewhere. For us, the crisis soon ends as memories flood back and we remember the recent chain of events and how we came to be where we are. But for the Korsakov victim there is no such prospect of relief—only the complete failure, a few minutes later, to remember even the state of panic or its cause. And there is the danger with every new moment and every new incident of the experience being repeated.

As we age, our memories, especially for details such as phone numbers, place names, and other odd snippets of information, inevitably falter as a result of a general, modest neurophysiological decline. Our brains lose about 15 percent of their mass between the ages of twenty-five and seventy. And in the hippocampus, a structure vital to the laying down of new memories, approximately 5 percent of the neurons die for every decade in the second half of life. But this gentle decline doesn't seem to make much difference to us. We are born with a more than generous supply of around one hundred billion neurons (plus ten times as many glial or connecting cells), each of which becomes synaptically linked to as many as ten thousand of its neighbors. So we can well afford to lose several hundred million cells and their connections in a lifetime without being seriously inconvenienced. And, reassuringly, positron emission tomographic (PET) imaging has shown that the brains of spry eighty-year-olds are almost as active as those of people in their twenties. It seems that, along with many of the body's other organs, the brain has immense physiological reserves—more than sufficient to be able to cope with what seems like an alarming loss of its component parts.

For most of us, then, memory loss in old age will amount to no more than a minor nuisance, like nearsightedness or stiffness in the joints. The continuity of our life's story, the integrity of our brain's gallery of remembrances, is essentially uncompromised so that we have no difficulty in retaining a stable impression of our own identities or those of people with whom we are familiar. However, for a significant percentage of the population (about 11 percent of those over sixty-five in the United States), there is the prospect in later life of a fairly rapid and catastrophic loss of cognitive functioning, including all levels of memory, due to various forms of dementia.

Because of the devastating effects it has on both the victim and the victim's family, Alzheimer's disease has justifiably become one of the most dreaded of terminal illnesses. It is like a cancer that affects the mind rather than the body. Typically within two to five years, it reduces a person from a state of near normality to one of total mental and physical disintegration and helplessness. By stages, Alzheimer's patients become disconnected from their past. Their forgetfulness deepens until it becomes so profound that victims can no longer remember the names and faces of people they have known for many years, including their own children and spouses. Upon looking in a mirror they may be terrified to find that they can no longer recognize even their own faces. Unlike those afflicted by Korsakov's syndrome, Alzheimer's sufferers see not an incomprehensibly aged version of themselves, but a total stranger. Yet their terror at failing to recognize their own reflection is not due to a complete failure of the brain. On the contrary, it stems from the brain trying to struggle on; albeit beset with damage and decay, the brain still contrives to piece together and recall enough about the past and how the world *should* be that it inadvertently triggers a cataclysmic and irreconcilable inner conflict. The Alzheimer's patient, even when the disease is far advanced, remembers (though perhaps only at a subconscious level) that a person is supposed to *have* a face and that one is supposed to know what one's own face looks like. But the patient's memory of how his or her face actually appears has been lost.

The human brain, shaped and honed by powerful evolutionary forces over many millions of years, is a born fighter. Without prompting, without our conscious intervention, it does everything in its power to promote and prolong the survival of the organism that houses it. To this end, it works ceaselessly, and for the most part successfully, to integrate, accommodate, and reconcile all of the information at its disposal. Even in terminal decline, with the bulk of its neural equipment smashed or faulty, it engages in a titanic but ultimately futile attempt to make up for the devastating effects of massive cellular damage. It even tries to rewire and repair itself from within.

At the University of California at Irvine, Carl Cotman and colleagues examined microscopically the brains of people who had died from Alzheimer's disease and found that the loss of nerve cells in a region known as the entorhinal complex had been compensated for, to some extent, by the growth of other connections. Cells in the entorhinal complex analyze information about smells, but the region is also the site of the most important pathway from the cortex to the hippocampus (a structure crucial to the consolidation of new memories). In rats, cutting the pathway from the cortex to the hippocampus causes the input it receives from elsewhere in the brain (the so-called commissural-associational system and the septum) to rearrange themselves so that they partly take over from the layer of cells previously devoted to the terminals of the entorhinal cells. Cotman and his co-workers discovered that exactly the same kind of rearrangement took place in the hippocampi of Alzheimer's patients.

The brain, then, does not submit easily. Unfortunately for someone in the final stages of dementia, this grim struggle to retain the maximum degree of cognitive capacity possible under the circumstances is not really desirable. To feel yourself inexorably slipping away, to be gradually cut adrift from everything you believed yourself to be, is surely worse than the actuality of death. And in this situation, the sooner the brain gives over the fight to retain its self the better.

An erosion of memory is an erosion of selfhood. Thus, the victim of Korsakov's syndrome is still a person, but one whose evolution has come to an end—a person robbed of a future, trapped in stasis, without the possibility of further development or change. An Alzheimer's patient, on the other hand, is a person in rapid, irreversible decline, a person whose death is occurring bit by bit, to the distress of everyone concerned, during life.

Such conditions graphically expose the importance of our memories, insubstantial things that they are, in binding us together and helping maintain the impression that we exist as coherent, enduring selves. Deprived of them, as the eighteenth-century Scottish philosopher David Hume remarked, "we are nothing but a bundle or collection of different sensations, which succeed each other with an inconceivable rapidity, and are in a perpetual flux and movement." Hume recognized that personal identity—the one thing we so desperately want to believe is real—is no more than a masterful sleight of the brain. And modern neurology fully concurs.

We start out from the assumption that we are born, grow up, and live out our life as the same person. We have the strong impression of being a single, unchanging self. And all our dealings with other people and our conventional assumptions about our relationship to the world are predicated upon the notion that a fixed inner "I" exists— that personal identity is an inviolate fact.

Under equilibrium conditions—the normal, everyday situation in which changes to our warehouse of memories are small and gradual— the brain can easily sustain the illusion of self. So we who are this self are generally convinced of its permanence. But faced with a sudden or rapid depletion of its memory store, through accident or disease, the brain can no longer cope. It becomes deprived of the means by which to project a convincing feeling of selfhood, a feeling that by its very nature must be based upon security and stability. This breakdown of the brain's capacity to properly integrate the self triggers an inner conflict because the brain, compelled by its survival mandate, is bent upon avoiding change and reacts to it by generating the emotion of fear. In fact, the fear experienced by the Korsakov's victim or the Alzheimer's patient who can no longer recognize her own face or surroundings is simply a heightened form of the same fear we all feel when we contemplate the prospect of death. It is the raw fear of losing our selves.

Death would lose its sting if we had no fear of it. But how can we overcome this fear when confronted with the almost incontrovertible evidence that we are merely the narratives running inside our brains? It is bad enough that some of us may have whole sections of our life's story ripped away through illness. But in death we all confront the ultimate form of amnesia—total neurological destruction and, with it, the ending of everything we are. How can we possibly discover in advance what this implies and how, when it happens, it will feel?

5

A CHANGE OF MIND

"I can't explain myself, I'm afraid, sir," said
Alice, "because I'm not myself, you see."

"I don't see," said the Caterpillar.

—*Lewis Carroll*

In the 1960s, having been diagnosed as a schizophrenic, Linda
Macdonald was admitted to the Allen Memorial Institute in Montreal,
a psychiatric clinic and research center established by the psychiatrist
Ewan Campbell. Campbell had an interesting background and had
managed to acquire some rather extreme views. While working as an
adviser to the judges at the Nuremberg war-crimes trials, he formed
the opinion that the bitter rivalries of nationalism which had led to the
Second World War had to be eradicated. Nationalism, he decided, was
a product of people's distorted historical memories. Therefore it was
essential, in his opinion, to alter those memories in order to produce a
rational world, free of war.

Subsequently, Campbell joined Wilder Penfield's team and
became intrigued by Penfield's concept (erroneous, as it turned out)
of memories being stored in the brain as circuits which could be
turned on and off by external means, such as the touching of an electrical probe. From this, he envisaged the real prospect of applying
clinical techniques to the alteration of memory in mentally ill patients.
Sick memories, he concluded, could be wiped clean and replaced with

healthy ones. And it was with this extraordinary, disturbing goal in mind that he set up his Institute.

It was the chilliest period of the Cold War, and Campbell was not alone in being obsessed with mind control. The CIA had designs on it, too—but with the even more sinister possibility of using memory as a weapon. Paranoia was rife that the Soviets and Chinese had already developed powerful forms of mind manipulation that would enable them to program agents to infiltrate U.S. security. This fear was heightened by the observation that soldiers taken captive by the Communists showed evidence of altered behavior and often made false confessions, which they continued to repeat even after their release. Campbell became intrigued by how such mind control was being achieved, and whether it could be applied therapeutically. Not surprisingly, his efforts soon had the backing of CIA funds.

At the Allen Memorial Institute, Campbell subjected his patients to electroconvulsive therapy (ECT) on a massive scale. The shocks across the temples, often administered several times a day, day after day, progressively disrupted and erased the patients' memories, just as music recorded on an audiotape is reduced to a vapid hiss by repeatedly passing the tape through a powerful magnetic field. Drugs, including LSD, were also used in large doses in an effort to wipe out memory traces. And, as a further weapon in his fight to eradicate "sick" memories, Campbell pioneered what he called psychic driving—the interminable repetition, night and day, over headphones, of persuasive, positive-reinforcement messages. The end results of this blitzkrieg on the mind were human beings stripped down to the most primitive, vegetable state. Nothing of their old personalities, behavior patterns, or memories remained. As conscious selves, as beings with identities, they had, effectively, been destroyed.

Mercifully, Linda Macdonald recalls none of her traumatic therapy—the miasmic haze of ECT, the relentless psychic driving, and the long periods of drug-induced sleep. All of her experiences during her time at the Allen Memorial Institute were scoured clean from her tortured brain. But erased, too, were her memories of her parents, her childhood, her own children, her home. Her "depatterning" was so comprehensive that, in the aftermath, she had to learn again how to speak and to behave and respond appropriately in a society that seemed utterly strange to her. "I felt like an alien from another world," she commented in a television recording made years later. Of her old self, absolutely nothing remains.

The same is true of Patsy Cannon of Alabama, though for a very different reason. In 1986, a car crash left her with such severe retrograde amnesia that all of her past memories were rendered inaccessible to her. Whether, in fact, her brain still retains her old memories in some form is unknown—and entirely irrelevant. It may be that the principal damage is to connections to her hippocampus, in which case, even if the memories from before her accident survive in some latent biochemical form, they will never again be available to her conscious mind.

Patsy Cannon has had to discover how to speak again with the help of tapes and friends. But language is a subtle, complex affair, and its colloquial use especially can be bewildering to a neophyte. On one occasion a visitor casually mentioned to her that it was "raining cats and dogs," whereupon, in a panic, she rushed to the window expecting to find animals literally falling from the sky. Upon seeing her nine-year-old daughter for the first time after the accident, she felt nothing—no twinge of recognition, no sense of attachment. Even the ability to love her own child had to be relearned.

Patsy Cannon has had to acquire a completely fresh ensemble of memories in order to function once more as a normal human being. But what she has learned the second time around has not made her into the same individual. She has a different character and different interests, wears different types of clothes, and enjoys different foods than before the accident. Even in her dreams she recalls nothing of her former life. Having been told all about the "old" Patsy Cannon and having seen photos of her, she maintains with unshakable conviction: "That person is dead; I am a new person." And it seems for her, at least, there is no sense of loss.

Erode memories and you wear a person away, bit by bit. Erase *all* memories and you erase a person completely. Then replace the lost memories with fresh ones and you create someone new. In the event of such extreme memory erasure and substitution, there is surely justification in speaking of the death of one individual and the coming into being of another. And, most tellingly, it is precisely in these terms, and without any hesitation, that people to whom this catastrophe has happened describe their inner experience.

Selves are defined by memories. So, if a brain's memory chain is badly disrupted or destroyed, the brain will feel very different. It may feel afraid and even panic-stricken if the memory loss is severe but not total, because under such circumstances the brain may no longer be able to reconcile what it sees from one moment to the next with what it falsely believes (due to its damaged memory) the world and itself should be like. Such is the terrible predicament of the Korsakov's or Alzheimer's victim. On the other hand, if *all* of a brain's memories are lost, the accompanying self is lost too.

Instances of total, permanent amnesia challenge us to reevaluate our concept of death. For if we consider the most relevant aspect of death to be "what it feels like" (the subjective experience) rather than "what it looks like" (the objective view) then total memory loss does seem to qualify as an event remarkably similar—and, indeed, onto-logically identical—to death as we normally understand it. If the experience of being a particular person, say person A, is contingent upon having a particular stock of memories, then if this stock is irre-trievably lost the feeling of being person A must be lost as well. Person A, as a psychological entity, has effectively died—died, that is, as far as the victim and the victim's family and friends are concerned. Medically, genetically, legally—objectively—it is a different story, and someone whose memories have gone but who remains cortically alive is considered by society at large to be still the same person. However, to those who know the individual well, and, most impor-tantly, as actually experienced by the victim of total memory loss, it is clear that there has been a radical, irreversible change.

Yet the brain, as a result of its evolutionary heritage, is a resilient organ. And, if it remains fully functional, then no sooner has it been deprived of one complete set of memories than it begins to lay down a fresh set, like a camcorder that keeps on running. This reacquisition of memory takes place automatically, just as it does in the case of an infant. Moreover, it involves *an actual physical change in the brain*— a major regrowth and rearrangement of neural connections. As the brain that once generated the feeling of being a person builds up its new collection of archives so, at a conscious level, it begins to give rise to the feeling of being a different individual, person B. And, significantly, this is not a problem or a concern either for person A or for person B. At the time at which the old memories are lost (which in an accident is more or less instantaneous), person A ceases to exist and so cannot subsequently experience any regret, sadness, fear, or loss at what has happened. (These negative feelings can only be experienced by others who knew person A.) Person B, on the other hand, emerges gradually as new memories are acquired and, having no recollection or sense of attachment to person A, has no cause to be troubled by A's demise. B's main problem will be that, as an adult rather than an infant, she will almost inevitably have commitments carried over from her previous "life" to which she has to readjust. New attachments may have to be forged to children and to a spouse who, to begin with, may just as well be anyone else in the world. And it is during this period of recovery, this time of reentry into the human atmosphere, that the extent to which all of us are culturally conditioned becomes starkly apparent. A brain that has been wiped clean has lost its social acumen, its knowledge of how to behave and function appropriately in a particular "civilized" (and highly artificial) setting with other people. This cultural veneer has to be reacquired. And during the process of reacquisition, the new, emerging person, who looks like an adult but unfortunately acts like an infant, has ample opportunity to feel bewildered and out of place—a stranger in a very strange land.

Our awareness of others stems, in the first instance, from an awareness of their *physical* presence. We see and define a particular person by the physical continuity of their bodies. And so, however differently an individual may behave from one day to the next, we maintain that it is nevertheless the same person. Our society revolves around, and inculcates in us, this fundamental belief. Exceptions are rare: we sometimes make comments like "She's not herself today," but without any serious conviction that a new self has temporarily taken over. More importantly, the outcome of a criminal trial may hinge upon whether an individual is judged to have committed a serious offense while mentally disturbed and therefore not responsible for his or her actions. Yet, for the most part, our identification of other selves and our belief in their stability rests firmly upon bodily appearance and continuity.

As each of us perceives our own self, however, it is a very different matter. We naturally care about the looks and health of our bodies. But what is of paramount concern to us is the *psychological* continuity that we habitually feel. Most of us would probably not recoil in horror at the prospect of having a new (healthy) body and brain, providing that we could transfer to it our *mental* selves.

Now, under normal circumstances in life, we are not moved to think deeply about the distinction between our outer and inner conceptions of self. This is because there does indeed appear to be a one-to-one correspondence between particular bodies and particular selves. But abnormal and pathological situations compel us to reexamine this most basic assumption. These unusual situations reveal clearly that there *is* a difference, a very great difference, between the objective and subjective viewpoints of a person—one, moreover, that is pivotal to any exploration of issues surrounding death and individual survival.

When I talk about "you," I implicitly refer to a particular body and brain, and to what I perceive as being a certain, unique, reasonably consistent personality that is projected to the outside world. But as far as you are concerned, "you" are what it is like to be a certain stream of consciousness. My view (which forms part of *my* stream of consciousness!) is of a specific organic machine and its persona, its outward face. Your view—your direct experience—is of *being the subjective entity that the machine gives rise to*. It cannot be emphasized enough that these two phenomena—the machine and the feelings of this machine—must be considered with the utmost care with regard to both how they are distinct and how they interrelate. The brain and the mind belong to two different categories of existence, different facets of reality. And although all the evidence of science is that there is a clear dependent relationship (in particular, "you" cannot exist without a brain—or an adequate substitute for a brain) there is nothing prima facie that insists there must be a unique correspondence between the feeling of being you and a particular brain, or vice versa.

If we are to take both objective and subjective factors into account then our definition of what it means to be a specific person must involve two separate criteria. That is, given A at one time and B at some later time are both persons, it appears reasonable to suppose they are the same if (1) they have the same physical body, and (2) B, at the later time, has memories of A's activities and memories. This definition *seems* to be consistent with the belief we each individually hold that from birth to death we remain one and the same person. But the reality of the situation is not so simple.

There are, undoubtedly, times in the past of "your" body of which you have no conscious recollection. Indeed, if you are anything like me (which I assume in many ways you are), you can't actually remember *most* of what has happened during your life. So, from the apparently common sense definition of what is involved in remaining the same person, it appears to follow that there were many occasions in the past when you were not who you are now! The fact that we all suffer numerous minor bouts of natural amnesia every minute of every day suggests that despite the strong impression we have of smooth continuity and personal sameness we are actually, to a large degree, psychologically *dis*connected. And this being so, the possibility emerges of seeing our lives in a different way: not as one unbroken unit but as divided into the lives of many successive selves.

Again, focusing on examples beyond the commonplace helps us get to grips with this elusive problem of who we are. In the case of the amnesia-inducing sleeping pill, mentioned in the last chapter, there is clearly a break in psychological continuity caused by the drug's influence on the brain. Label as A1 the person who lived up to the point of taking the drug, A2 the person who lived through the subsequent hour up to the moment of falling asleep, and A3 the person who awoke eight hours later. At a casual glance, we would tend to assume that A1, A2, and A3 were one and the same person (and if it happened to us, we would *certainly* take this view). But A3 has no memories at all of what happened throughout the hour when A2 was alive. From the subjective viewpoint of A3, A2 never existed and may just as well have been someone else entirely. The criterion of bodily continuity has been satisfied. But if a person cannot remember anything about themselves during a particular waking period, then mentally the person who was conscious during this period is a being apart. Evidently, for as long as A2 existed he felt himself to be a continuation of the stream of consciousness of A1. But at the moment of falling asleep, A2 curiously disappeared from the chain of continuity to be replaced by A3. Who, then, in retrospect, *was* A2? Wouldn't it have felt a little strange to have been A2 and to have been told that all the fresh memories you were laying down during the hour the drug was taking effect would shortly be lost forever and that you were effectively traveling down a cul-de-sac of consciousness? Possibly, it might have felt strange. But it wouldn't have been a cause for great fear, like the fear of being some-one who knew he was soon going to die—for a simple reason.

If a brain suffers only a minor, localized form of amnesia then it still retains more than enough information about its past to be able to reconstruct a self virtually indistinguishable from the one in prior resi-dence. And so if you or I "lost" merely an hour from our memories we would not, *in practice,* be inclined to think of the person who lived during that missing hour as being someone else. We could conve-niently and easily gloss over the hiatus. But imagine now extending the period of amnesia back in time from a given point—a week, a year, ten years, twenty years, and, ultimately, to the moment of birth. This brings us back to cases of total amnesia such as those of Linda Macdonald and Patsy Cannon. And while it is true that these are extreme pathological examples, we can see now that *in principle* they are no different from instances of more confined memory loss. The fact is that *whenever* there is a memory loss, however great or small, there must inevitably be a corresponding break in psychological conti-nuity. So, what may seem from the inside to be a coherent, continuous self—the "I" with which we are all intimately familiar—is in reality highly disjointed. How can two such radically different perspectives on the self both be valid?

To make matters clearer, suppose I were to keep a diary of your con-sciousness in objective (clock) time. It might run something like this:

7:30 A.M.	After a good night's rest, you wake up.
3:00 P.M.	While doing work outside, you unfortunately stumble and bump your head, rendering you temporarily unconscious.
3:03 P.M.	You recover, take two aspirins for your headache, and spend the rest of the day indoors.

11:00 P.M.	You go to bed and quickly fall into a deep sleep.
2:15–2:30 A.M.	You have the first of three dreams during the night (as registered on an EEG).
4:00–4:20 A.M.	Second dream.
6:15–6:30 A.M.	Third dream.
7:30 A.M.	Your alarm goes off and you wake up.

According to these records, there were five periods (of three minutes, three hours and fifteen minutes, one hour and thirty minutes, one hour and fifty-five minutes, and one hour, respectively) during this twenty-four-hour span, when you were completely unconscious. And by referring to your watch throughout the day you would have been able approximately to verify these times. But this objective view of your day is not what you would actually have experienced. By definition, you cannot experience or be aware of the passage of time during spells of total unconsciousness. So, as it actually felt to you, you were *always* there. In subjective time, there are no breaks—there can be no breaks, otherwise there is no subject. If you are knocked out or faint or fall asleep (except for intervals of dreaming in which there is an attenuated form of self-consciousness), you don't notice any gaps. One instant you lose consciousness and the very next instant you regain it. Subjectively, there is no—can be no—hiatus. Subjectively, you never disappear, for who would there be on the inside to notice the disappearance?

It is easy to understand, then, why there should be such a great contrast between the objective and subjective views of self. The objective or conventional scientific notion is that the self is illusory in the sense that it doesn't correspond with anything definite either in substance or duration. Moreover, from an objective standpoint the consciousness of an individual is repeatedly punctuated. It comes and goes on a macroscopic level as a result of incursions such as sleep and general anesthesia. And there is every reason to suppose that it flickers in and out at a microscopic level, too. From your internal perspective, however, "you" are never unconscious—for this represents a contradiction in terms. There has never been a moment in your life when subjectively you have not been present. And nothing will or can happen in the future to change this fact.

"The feeling of being you" is a persistent phenomenon. It is simply not possible *from your point of view* to know or experience or even conceive what it would be like not to be you. And this applies to everyone else. It is true even for people who have suffered the most profound forms of amnesia. Before the onset of the amnesia there was "the feeling of being you" (in other words, a specific self-awareness). Then, an instant later in subjective time (though possibly months later in objective clock time), there was "the feeling of being you" again— only a different you based on a different set of memories.

The persistence of "you" is a phenomenon of vital concern to us. But at any given moment, what seems crucial to us is being and remaining precisely who we happen to be—not just any old "you." Our overwhelming desire is to stay who we are now, not to become some other "you" that our present self wouldn't be able to identify with and that would inevitably involve us becoming someone else. The thought of changing triggers our anticipatory fear of death, of losing our present selves. What we fail to properly recognize, though, is that we are always changing. And when we *do* become someone else—as happens every moment, whether we realize it or not—then we no longer hanker for the preservation of the self we used to be. The desire for self-preservation automatically transfers to whatever new "you" we have become.

We dread the prospect of becoming someone else because this would mean ceasing to be whoever we are now. Had Patsy Cannon, for instance, known in advance that she would be in an accident that would rob her of all her memories she would doubtless, like any normal person, have been just about as afraid of this as of actual physical death. But in the event, she had no such foreknowledge and therefore no anticipatory fear. Nor was there ever any internal feeling of loss of her "old" self, because there was never any break, subjectively, in her self-awareness. In subjective time, there was no experienced gap between the instant of her accident and the subsequent emergence of her new self—her new "feeling of being you." And this new self, like any self, wanted above anything else to continue as it was,* not revert to being the stranger who had lived before.

---

*Many people would like to change their *situation* (especially if they are poor, sick, or hungry) but without changing their inner feeling of self.

*   *   *

The dissolution and re-creation of personalities in the middle of a human lifespan following profound memory loss is remarkable enough. But there are even more bizarre and complex manifestations of this effect due to MPS, or multiple personality syndrome. In cases of MPS it is as if a group of individuals is vying for control of a single body. Different members of the group take it in turn to become conscious and decide what the body will do and say. Talking to someone with MPS can be disconcertingly like trying to hold a telephone conversation with a number of people fighting over a single receiver—you can converse with only one at a time and can never be sure who will answer next.

The story of one young man plunged into this extraordinary condition was told in Daniel Keyes's disturbing book *The Minds of Billy Milligan.* Billy was sadistically and sexually abused* by his stepfather when he was eight years old. As a result his schoolwork deteriorated, he began to suffer bouts of amnesia, and soon he was being accused of having done things he knew nothing about. Unbeknownst to Billy, he had developed alternative personalities who took over his body whenever Billy felt threatened. Eventually and incredibly, he was found to have acquired twenty-four distinct personalities who varied widely not only in character but also in nationality, age, and even sex. Billy himself was an American, but Arthur, who was normally the dominant personality, spoke with an English accent and was also fluent in Arabic. Ragen, a fiery Yugoslavian character, spoke both English (with a noticeable Slavic accent) and Serbo-Croat. His function, to take over in dangerous situations, was reflected in his name, which was a contraction of "rage again." Allen was outgoing and manipulative and was the only right-handed personality. Christene, a little girl, was English and dyslexic. And Adalane, another female personality, was a lesbian whose loneliness and longing for physical contact eventually led Billy to be accused of rape. Only after his arrest was Billy's problem discovered and, as a result, he was eventually found not guilty by reason of insanity. This situation can also work in

---

*A traumatic childhood, often including neglect and physical or sexual abuse, is a common precursor of MPS. It seems that the brain, in an effort to cope with extreme stress, compartmentalizes its life, behaving as different people in different contexts.

reverse. Recently in Oshkosh, Wisconsin, a man was arrested and put on trial for raping a woman with MPS by seducing one of her alternative personalities.

There was a period, earlier this century, when it was in vogue to criticize the status of multiple personality as a genuine clinical condition. But few researchers today seriously believe that all MPS sufferers are frauds or malingerers (though it certainly seems possible that additional personalities may be created by indirect suggestion from a therapist). The real point of contention is to what extent the various personalities are separate, given that they are obviously products of the same brain. In most cases, the original or root personality is seldom aware that the newer personalities exist, though the latter are often aware of each other and of the original. One way to check for true separateness is to look for consistently differing brain wave patterns among the separate personalities. At the National Institute of Mental Health in Washington, D.C., Frank Putnam did this and discovered differences as great as those between separate individuals in electroencephalograms (EEGs), visually evoked cortical responses, and galvanic skin responses (as used in lie-detector tests.) More controversial tests of personality and intelligence have produced similar results. And, most dramatically, 3-D scans have shown that entirely distinct regions of the brain are active depending upon which character is in charge.

There seems to be no getting away from the fact that the separate personalities inhabiting the brain of someone with MPS are real in the objective sense that they display measurable physiological states as diverse as those of a group of different people; and real in the subjective sense that they are *experienced* internally by the patient as distinct streams of conscious thought.

The core personality of someone with MPS may suddenly and alarmingly find that several hours or even days have elapsed without their knowledge. In an instant, it will seem to them as if they have leapt forward in time and been transported to a different, possibly unknown place. They may be wearing different clothes, be carrying unfamiliar objects, be facing strangers who act as if they are not strangers, and be somewhere they have never seen before. For a lost slice of their lives, they were literally not themselves; an alternative personality had taken control of their body, with a character and set of memories of his or her own.

One particularly astonishing and well-documented case of MPS, from around the turn of the century, was that of Miss Christine Beauchamp (a pseudonym) who was studied and treated by the American psychotherapist Morton Prince. As a child, Christine had been raised in a strict, stifling, puritanical atmosphere rent tragically by repeated abuses by her father. The fuse for MPS thus having been set in the most usual way, it took only a spark later on to lead to the explosion of her fragile personality. That spark came in 1893, when Christine was eighteen. She was working as a nurse in a hospital one terrible, stormy night when three separate events, any one of which would have proved unnerving, conspired to blow her world apart. A lightning flash illuminated a figure in white, a patient, who grabbed hold of her. Barely had she recovered from this when she caught sight of a face staring in at her through a second-floor window. It turned out to be her boyfriend, who had climbed up a ladder and peered in as a prank. Finally, and most devastatingly, the boyfriend entered the hospital and, according to Christine, ended up almost raping her in a darkness broken only by occasional flashes from the storm. The combined effect of these shocking, nightmarish incidents was to immerse her further in abject depression, accompanied by severe headaches, insomnia, and nervousness. So, in desperation, she sought the help of Morton Prince.

Under hypnosis, Christine, who was normally painfully reticent, relaxed and became less restrained. Prince, in his analysis of the case, referred to her waking state as B1 and her trance state as B1A. B1A knew of and claimed as her own B1's thoughts and actions, but B1 (in the usual manner of a hypnotized subject) could remember nothing of what she said and did as B1A. There was no reason, however, to suppose that B1 and B1A were different people. But then, one day, quite spontaneously, B1A started referring to B1 not as "I" but as "she." This was to mark the emergence of a new personality—one who chose to call herself Sally.

From then on, whenever Prince hypnotized B1, Sally would be likely to appear. And Sally, it turned out, was not at all impressed by B1. In her words, "she [B1] is stupid; she goes around mooning, half-asleep, with her head buried in a book; she does not know half the time what she is about." Sally claimed to have lived passively along-side B1 since early childhood. And then, finally, Sally emerged. During one particular hypnosis she opened her eyes and stepped out into the waking world as a vibrant, vivacious, energetic, and (Prince thought) likable person in her own right. As far as B1 was concerned, Sally did not exist. But Sally knew all about B1—her every thought, action, and dream. Sally could recall B1's dreams better than B1 could herself, because Sally was there all the time, in the background, watching and monitoring B1 even when B1 had control of the body.[*] By contrast, when Sally was in charge, B1 was not merely pushed aside, she was not there at all. Times when Sally was "out" were times completely lost to B1. On one occasion, for instance, B1 plucked up courage and admitted herself into hospital to get treatment for her severe depression. But almost immediately, Sally took over, pretended to be B1, convinced the hospital staff that she was much improved, and was discharged ten days later. When, shortly after, B1 "came back" it was as if the hospital stay had never happened, so that for all her efforts to improve her health she gained nothing.

B1 suffered terribly at Sally's hands. When Sally was in charge of the body she would spend B1's money on frivolous clothes, undo B1's knitting and sewing, stitch up the ends of her sleeves, tear up her let-ters, and even mail packages to B1 containing spiders. Furthermore, Sally drank and smoked (which B1, being very proper and deeply reli-gious, would never do) and kept her own circle of friends. And this often proved devastating and embarrassing to B1, who would abruptly regain consciousness in the midst of a social gathering with people she had never met, holding a cigarette in one hand and a glass of wine in the other.

Prince maintained that Sally's maliciousness to B1 was born of jealousy, because B1 was so much more refined and better educated (apparently Sally hadn't bothered to pay attention in class when they had attended school "together"). In fact, to confound Sally and pre-vent her listening in on conversations Prince didn't want her to hear,

*It is less confusing when discussing MPS cases to use terms like "the body" instead of "her body," since it is not clear who the "her" is referring to!

he would sometimes communicate with B1 in French, a language in which B1 was fluent but Sally could not understand a word.

Then B4* appeared—another personality with another highly individual set of character traits. B4 was impatient, short-tempered, and fiercely independent. It turned out that she knew nothing of what had happened since the traumatic night in the hospital six years earlier. In fact, on her first appearance in Prince's office she thought it was that very night. Then, realizing her mistake, she quickly withdrew, became reserved and curt, and subsequently fantasized to try to conceal her amnesia. The ever-present, ever-watchful Sally (she claimed that she never slept) reacted strongly to B4's arrival, regarding her as another, unwelcome rival for control of the body. Although Sally knew about B4's actions, she did not, as it happened, have access to her thoughts. Even so, from listening to what B4 said, it didn't take Sally long to realize that B4 was making up her own version of events from the last six years, and Sally started referring to her as "the idiot."

Prince discovered that by putting either B1 or B4 into a deep hypnotic trance, yet another personality, B2, emerged who claimed to be *both* B1 and B4. Because B2 appeared to combine the virtues of B1 and B4 without their excesses, Prince decided that B2 was in some sense the real or whole Christine Beauchamp. Therefore he explained to B1 and B4 that he wished to awake B2 from the deep trance as a unified, fully conscious individual. But this immediately created problems. Although B1 and B4 were components of B2, they effectively ceased to exist as independent entities when B2 was present. To B1 and B4, life as B2 *was the equivalent of death*. In characteristic fashion, B1 was ready to meekly accept extinction. But not so B4. She formed an alliance with Sally, who, although not deprived of consciousness by the arrival of B2, was in her own words "squeezed" back to her previous state as a passive, coexisting awareness. Sally much preferred her active existence, in which she could, at least sometimes, be in full control of the body. And independent Ms. B4 was certainly in no mood to die for the greater good. So, in order to thwart Prince's plans, both Sally and B4 broke appointments with him that B1 had pre-

*Again, I would remind the reader that this somewhat confusing notation is Dr. Prince's, not mine!

viously made, and B4 even went so far as to book tickets for a passage to Europe. However, in the end they were defeated. Sally confessed that in B2 she recognized the pre-1893 Christine Beauchamp and that it had been she (Sally) who split B2 back into B1 and B4 whenever Prince tried to draw B2 into normal waking life. She withdrew her influence, and, after completing her autobiography and a Last Will and Testament, voluntarily committed herself to what she regarded as extinction. And thus B2 awoke as Christine Beauchamp.

The epilogue is that B2 proved quite stable, though on occasions, at times of strain, she would temporarily split back into B1, B4, and Sally. And when B1 and B4 did reemerge, it was for them as if they had woken from a coma; months would have gone by as if in the wink of an eye. As for Sally, she returned to the state she had occupied since 1898—an intraconsciousness, a passive, aware cohabitant alongside Christine.

A century on, MPS is still not fully understood. In particular, it is unclear whether the syndrome generally starts when a single personality is broken up or when a still developing personality fails to coalesce. The latter possibility is suggested by some recent work by Peter Wolff at the Children's Hospital in Boston. Wolff's research shows just how rapidly and easily young children switch moods. They laugh one moment, then cry the next, as if they haven't yet learned how to integrate these different moods and feelings into a single self. It may well be that childhood abuse interferes with the normal process of integration, leading to fragmentary personalities that then evolve in isolation to become essentially separate (though pathological and highly depleted) selves.

The fast-changing moods of early childhood are indeed reminiscent of a mild form of MPS. But then so, too, are many examples of adult behavior. The psychologist Robert Jay Lifton pondered the mental state of doctors who committed atrocities on prisoners of the Auschwitz death camp in the name of science. How could these people, who had been trained to heal and cure, resume in the evening their role of kind fathers and husbands after hearing the screams of their victims during the day? Lifton concluded that they were essentially split personalities composed of

> two relatively autonomous selves: the prior
> "ordinary self," which for doctors includes

important elements of the healer, and the
"Auschwitz self," which includes all of the
psychological maneuvers that help one avoid a
conscious sense of oneself as a killer. The existence of an overall Auschwitz self more or less
integrated all of these mechanisms into a functioning whole, and permitted one to adapt oneself to that bizarre environment. The prior self
enabled one to retain a sense of decency and
loving connection.

It is hard to imagine what goes on in the minds of torturers or brutal dictators who seem at times capable of genuine compassion toward
their families. But to a lesser degree we are all split personalities,
capable of love and thoughtlessness, moderation and indulgence,
ambition and sloth. And our lives are further compartmentalized by
the different hats we are expected to wear—those of friend, lover,
partner, parent, child, leader, follower. Our behavior and personality
change markedly depending on the social roles we play.

We start out from the assumption that we are each a single person
with a definite, unique personality. We take our self to be a fixed
entity (like a soul) that endures from womb to tomb. But MPS and
various manifestations of amnesia, as well as apparently related conditions like sleepwalking, "automatic writing" under hypnosis, and
schizophrenia, throw into question this standard folk psychology
about who we really are. It seems that behind the stable facade we try
to present to the world lies more than a touch of Jekyll and Hyde. We
are far more fragmented and disconnected, less a single, smoothly
flowing river of consciousness, than we conventionally imagine and
project. And this realization has crucial implications for our quest to
penetrate the mystery of death. To understand what will happen when
we die we have to be clear about what it is that *can* die.

So far, the evidence presented that the self can be altered, fragmented, entirely destroyed, and remade during the course of life is primarily psychological. But there is also a wealth of intriguing data about
the nature of self from a very different source—from people whose
brains have been surgically partitioned or even partially removed.

6

DIVIDED OPINIONS

I have a splitting headache.

—*Patient's comment following
his cerebral commissurotomy*

Redundancy and symmetry in the form of duplicated organs are not uncommon in the human body. We each have two lungs, two kidneys, two ovaries or testes. And we each, effectively, have two brains. The fact that these two brains normally work in perfect accord as the cooperating hemispheres of a single brain is made possible by the band of connecting tissue that provides a natural information superhighway between them.

The main bundle of (about two hundred million) nerve fibers linking the brain's two halves, the corpus callosum,* is thought to have several functions, one of which is to allow memories and skills garnered during an individual's lifetime to be laid down simultaneously in both hemispheres. Because of this replication, if part of one hemisphere is damaged through accident or disease (such as a stroke), there is a reasonable chance that the matching portion of the other hemisphere may eventually be able to take over some or all of the lost mental functions for the whole brain. Normally, the corpus callosum supports a heavy two-way flow of data traffic so that each half of the

*A structure present in all mammals except the marsupials, which are considered the most primitive of the class.

brain is kept almost immediately abreast of what its partner is doing or thinking. But what happens if this communications link is broken?

During the 1940s, the American surgeon William Van Wagenen severed the corpus callosums of about two dozen patients who were suffering from grand mal epilepsy. In some cases, the condition was so severe that the victims would experience several violent seizures an hour, every hour, without respite. Epileptic attacks originate in a specific, small region of one hemisphere that may differ from one patient to another. The attacks quickly spread, invade the opposite hemisphere, and thereafter overwhelm the victim. By decoupling the hemispheres, Van Wagenen hoped to confine the seizures to the hemisphere in which they started and so allow the other hemisphere to continue functioning as normal. To his disappointment, his patients showed little or no improvement.

Twenty years later, two surgeons in California, Joseph Bogen and Philip Vogel, suggested that the earlier operations had failed because Van Wagenen had not cut through all of the commissures (the bundles of nerve connections) between the two halves of the cortex. As well as the corpus callosum there are other, smaller cortical links, including the anterior and hippocampal commissures. To test their idea, Bogen and Vogel carried out complete commissurotomies on sixteen grand mal epilepsy patients in the 1960s and 1970s, and achieved remarkable postoperative success. The epilepsy was cured. But it was for another, very different reason that many psychologists were intrigued by the surgery. What effects, they wondered, had there been on the patients' minds and behavior? To investigate this question, Roger Sperry of the California Institute of Technology and other researchers subjected several of the "split brain" patients* to a battery of ingenious tests.

The split-brain studies made use of the well-known but bizarre (and unexplained) fact that the left side of the body and the left visual field are controlled by the right hemisphere, and the right side of the body and the right visual field by the left hemisphere. (Control of the auditory fields is more complex, while our sense of smell, the most

---

*It is important to bear in mind that any epileptic patient ill enough to need such surgery very often has associated brain damage. In fact, fewer than half the total number of commissurotomy patients were competent enough mentally for the results of postoperative tests to be usable.

neurologically ancient of the senses, is not crossed over at all, each nostril being "wired" to the hemisphere on the same side of the body.) Under normal circumstances, any thoughts or perceptions first registered in one half of the brain are quickly relayed to the other half through the cerebral commissures. But following complete commissurotomy this is no longer possible, and extraordinary conflicts can ensue. One of the split-brain patients, for instance, found himself pulling on his pants with one hand while trying to take them off with the other. On another occasion, he attempted simultaneously to button and unbutton his jacket with opposite hands. With neither hand knowing what the other was doing, the patient was left bewildered as to why he seemed unable to perform so simple a task. In a particularly alarming moment, the same individual grabbed his wife with his left hand and shook her violently before his right hand could intervene. Another patient found each hand choosing different clothes to wear in the morning, and reported that every now and again her right hand would slap her awake when she (or, rather, her right hemisphere!) was in danger of oversleeping. Similar but even more startling behavior had been noted in a female patient in 1908 by the neurologist Kurt Goldstein. He described how the woman had been taken to the hospital because her left hand would repeatedly close around her neck and start to choke her. On each occasion her right hand would come to the rescue and she would then be compelled to sit on her left hand, which she accused of being bad and beyond her control. While in bed, she would throw the pillows on the floor and tear the bedclothes—but only with her left hand. On the basis of his examination, Goldstein surmised that she had suffered damage to the corpus callosum, and that the two sides of her brain had thus been disconnected from each other—a diagnosis eventually confirmed after the woman's death by a postmortem.

Given cases like these in which a patient's hands act in direct opposition to one another, it is hard to avoid the conclusion that the two hemispheres of the brain, when separated, can function independently and without each other's prior knowledge. In Sperry's words:

> Each hemisphere ... has its own ... private
> sensations, perceptions, thoughts, and ideas, all
> of which are cut off from the corresponding

experiences in the opposite hemisphere. Each
right and left hemisphere has its own private
chain of memories and learning experiences
that are inaccessible to recall by the other
hemisphere. In many respects each disconnected hemisphere appears to have a separate
"mind of its own."

One young woman, when asked whether she could feel her left
hand, shouted, "Yes! Wait! No! Yes! No, no! Wait, yes!" Her face
twisted as each of her two minds, only one of which could feel the
hand, tried to answer. A researcher then handed her a piece of paper
with the words "yes" and "no" written on it and asked her to indicate
the correct answer. After a moment's hesitation, the woman's left
forefinger jabbed at "yes" and her right forefinger at "no." The psychologist Norman Geschwind has gone so far as to say it is mislead-
ing even to talk of "the patient" in the case of disconnection of the
hemispheres. There are, he believes, really two people living inside
the same skull.

Clearly, this idea flies in the face of those who believe, as
Descartes did, that every human being has a unique seat of consciousness—a single mind that cannot be divided or fragmented whatever
happens to its host brain. But one objection can still be raised from
the Cartesian camp on the grounds of hemispherical asymmetry.
Among the chief critics of the idea that separating the hemispheres
inevitably leads to the creation of two separate minds is the English
neurophysiologist Sir John Eccles, one of the few remaining dualists
in his profession. Eccles has pointed to the well-known fact that, in
most people, the two halves of the human brain are not mirror images
of each other. At a casual glance they may give this impression, but in
fact they reveal subtle differences in structure and quite extensive differences in function. In particular, only one half of the brain normally
houses the regions equipped to deal with language at a high level. In
most people the left hemisphere is responsible both for speech and for
the majority of language comprehension skills, whereas the right
hemisphere is generally aphasic (speechless) and has only a childlike
ability to understand words.

That language processing is both localized and lateralized within the brain has been known for more than a century. It is well established that damage to specific regions called Broca's area and Wernicke's area, which are normally found only in the left hemisphere, impairs a person's speech and his ability to understand language, respectively. Because of the great importance of these regions, surgeons are especially anxious to avoid disturbing them if at all possible during brain surgery. A simple preoperative procedure known as the Wada test is carried out to determine in which hemisphere of a patient's brain the main language centers lie. This test exploits the fact that each cerebral hemisphere is supplied independently with blood via a carotid artery running along the same side of the neck as the hemisphere. If sodium amytal or a similar drug is injected into the artery on the same side as the hemisphere controlling speech, the patient temporarily loses the ability to talk and cannot answer any questions for several minutes until the effects of the drug wear off. By contrast, there is generally no loss of speech if the opposite hemisphere is anesthetized.

Studies have shown that around 99 percent of right-handers have their primary speech and language centers in their left hemispheres (the same side of the brain which controls their dominant hand), while, surprisingly, 70 percent of left-handers are *also* linguistically left-hemisphere dominant. Of the remainder of left-handers, about 15 percent have their main language centers in the right hemisphere and about 15 percent show evidence of speech control in *both* hemispheres.

Interestingly, research by Sandra Witelson, a psychologist at McMaster University in Hamilton, Ontario, has shown that left-handed and ambidextrous people have corpus callosums that are, on average, 11 percent larger than those of right-handers. This suggests a greater potential for communication between the hemispheres (assuming that the nerve fibers are equally dense) and, therefore, possibly a more equitable division of labor in many aspects of cognition, including language. It may be that we all start out potentially ambidextrous and with similar sized corpus callosums at birth but for some reason most of us rapidly lose twenty million or so neurons in the connecting body and develop a specialization in the brain that is associated with right-handedness. But why this should be is not clear.

Significantly, patients who are known to have suffered damage to the left side of their brain early in life are much more likely to show right-hemispherical or bilateral speech control. This backs up the view that, although we may have an innate, presumably genetic tendency to develop primary speech and language centers in just one hemisphere (usually the left), the other hemisphere can take over these functions if necessary. However, this plasticity of the brain falls off sharply with age so that by adolescence the capacity of one hemisphere to assume the specialized functions of the other is severely limited.

The objection of dualists, such as Eccles and his one-time colleague the late Sir Karl Popper, to the idea that commissurotomy creates two distinct minds or streams of consciousness rests on the grounds that one hemisphere—the dominant (and therefore usually the left) hemisphere—is overwhelmingly the better at handling high-level language. And it is the sophisticated use of language, the argument goes, that is the crucial ingredient in making us fully conscious. Eccles portrays the speechless right hemisphere as being primitive, bestial, and essentially unconscious. In his view, each human being has an indivisible self, a Cartesian ego or soul, that is associated exclusively with the left side of the brain. However, this argument does not bear up well under the weight of clinical evidence.

Dualists face a problem, for instance, in explaining the extraordinary postoperative recoveries of patients who have undergone hemispherectomy—the surgical removal of one entire brain hemisphere. This drastic procedure is now performed several dozen times a year in the United States, usually as a treatment for a rare condition known as Rasmussen's encephalitis, which afflicts its victims with rapidly recurrent life-threatening seizures. Extraordinarily, it is found that if hemispherectomy is carried out in infancy or early childhood, the remaining hemisphere, whichever it happens to be, can take over *all* of the functions usually lateralized to the other half.

Typical is the case of Matthew Simpson, a young American boy who at about the age of four began to experience violent seizures. Rasmussen's disease was diagnosed, and when medications failed to relieve his symptoms it was decided to proceed with a left hemispherectomy. With the removal of Matthew's left hemisphere went his principal language centers. Yet today Matthew is doing well in school and, with the help of weekly language therapy sessions, is rapidly making up for lost ground—and lost cortex.

Apparently, the normally aphasic side of the brain has just as good a *latent* capacity to mediate speech and to understand language at an advanced level as does the side which, if undisturbed, becomes language-dominant. This fact is demonstrated, too, by patients who undergo hemispherectomy later in life. Those who have had their right hemispheres removed (and were preoperatively left-brain language dominant) display no obvious language problems. But, remarkably, patients who have undergone *left* hemispherectomy show much less linguistic impairment than do individuals who have simply suffered lesions to their speech and language centers. It seems that not only is language represented to a considerable extent in both hemispheres but also that the left hemisphere *normally exerts an inhibitory influence over the right*. So, as far as language goes, we may actually be better off losing one entire side of our cortex rather than suffering localized damage to the language areas. Only when the left cortex is removed altogether can the full language potentialities of the right hemisphere be realized.

Patients who have had their language-dominant hemispheres taken out after early childhood do show some loss in the production of language, as would be expected, but are hardly impaired at all in comprehension. And even in language production, these people can still use the surviving half of their brain to convey messages in some oral form: they remain highly proficient at swearing (since the right cortex is largely in charge of strong emotional responses) and can continue to express themselves musically (again, a predominantly right-hemisphere skill). A female patient who underwent a left hemispherectomy could communicate much better in song than in speech after her operation. Some loss in oral skills may be inevitable, but those who are close to people who possess only a right hemisphere for a brain need no convincing that these individuals still possess a full, vigorous mind and a personality that can express itself in many different modes.

Of the split-brain patients studied, one, referred to as P.S., was unique in that *both* of his detached brain hemispheres had a pretty good command of language. He was sixteen years old when he had his commissurotomy, and was believed to have suffered damage to the left side of his brain when very young (causing the right side to compensate by becoming more language proficient than usual). For some time after his operation he could, like all of the other split-brain patients, communicate verbally only via his left hemisphere. But after two to three years, he acquired a useful language ability in the right side of his brain. Although his right hemisphere did not have access to the speech centers, P.S. could use his left hand to spell out words with Scrabble letters. This allowed researchers to establish a reasonable level of dialogue separately with each hemisphere—a breakthrough that was to lead to a striking confirmation of Sperry's dual mind hypothesis. The separate "conversations" revealed that each hemisphere did indeed appear to house an independent stream of consciousness, to the extent that the two halves of P.S.'s brain would often respond in completely different ways to the same question. Asked on one occasion about future ambitions, for instance, the right hemisphere expressed a desire to become a race-car driver while the left hemisphere said it hoped to pursue a career as a draftsman. On a scale of one to five ranging from "like very much" to "dislike very much," the right hemisphere frequently responded with a higher figure, though inter-hemispherical differences varied from day to day. Generally, it was found that on days when the two hemispheres gave more similar answers, P.S. was happy and relaxed, while at other times when the responses were in sharp disagreement, P.S. seemed more emotionally out of sorts.

Two of the researchers closely involved with studies on P.S., Joseph LeDoux and Michael Gazzaniga, concluded:

> Each hemisphere in P.S. has a sense of self and each possesses its own system for subjectively evaluating current events, planning for further events, setting response priorities, and generating personal responses. Consequently, it becomes useful to consider the practical and theoretical implications of the fact that double consciousness mechanisms can exist.

In a similar vein, in his book *The Bisected Brain*, Gazzaniga wrote:

> Just as conjoined [Siamese] twins are two peo-
> ple sharing a common body, the callosum-
> sectioned human has two separate conscious
> spheres sharing a common brain stem, head
> and body . . . A slice of the surgeon's knife
> through the midline commissures produces two
> separate, but equal, cognitive systems each
> with its own abilities to learn, emote, think,
> and act.

Only one observation, on the face of it, seems to pose a threat to the idea that commissurotomy results in a definite bifurcation of consciousness, the creation of two minds where previously there had been only one. Although on rare occasions, split-brain patients do, for instance, find their left and right hands working in opposition, *most of the time their behavior is bafflingly normal.* You could spend all day with a commissurotomy patient and never suspect the drastic change that had been wrought in his or her brain. In fact, as experience has shown, only sophisticated psychological testing can consistently reveal that anything unusual is going on. How can this be? How can someone have two hundred million neurons sliced clean through and continue to function more or less as if nothing had happened?

It is true that split-brain patients no longer have any *direct* con-
nections between the two halves of their cortex. But the absence of cerebral commissures can apparently be circumvented to a surprising degree by other linking mechanisms that are *not* affected by the operation. For instance, there are commissures in the lower parts of the brain. One of these, the superior colliculus, is involved in locating objects and tracking their movements. So, even after the higher commissures have been cut, the two hemispheres can continue to tap into the same primitive "radar" system giving the whereabouts of things in the outside world (albeit that they lack the means to reach a consensus

on what these things actually *are*). The brain stem, too, which is believed to play a vital role in generating basic emotional responses, continues to feed identical messages to the severed hemispheres.

Other ways of harmonizing the two disconnected brain halves are furnished by the senses. Each eye, for instance, projects to both hemispheres: the contents of the left visual field of each eye to the right hemisphere and the contents of the right visual field of each eye to the left hemisphere. As a result, eye movements initiated by one hemisphere to bring an object into direct view serve also to bring that object to the attention of the other hemisphere. A similar but more complex crossover of signals takes place with respect to hearing. And although the great majority of tactile signals are carried by *contra*lateral nerve fibers (that is, fibers crossing over from the opposite side of the body) there are also a few *ipsi*lateral fibers running from the left side of the body to the left hemisphere and from the right side of the body to the right hemisphere. All these subsidiary unifying mechanisms, which remain intact after complete commissurotomy, help the divided brain to continue to work as if it were a single unit.

That the brain should be so adept at keeping up the appearance of unity, even after it virtually has been sawn in two, is not really surprising. The brain has been exquisitely shaped and honed by evolutionary forces over many millions of years so that it is now perfectly tailored to protect and serve the interests of the organism in which it resides. It is the consummate survival machine. And one of the chief reasons for its phenomenal success is its ability to function so coherently. Despite the awesome complexity of activity among its two hundred billion neurons—a cell for every star in the galaxy—at the level of the whole organ it manages to act as a single, purposeful entity. In most situations, it presents to its owner and to the world at large a unified strategy. Why should we suppose, then, that it would start to behave differently, giving out conflicting messages, speaking discordantly with more than one voice, just because it had suffered some damage? Surely, the likelihood must be that whatever happens to the brain, whatever calamities it suffers, it will still make every attempt to stay true to its prime evolutionary directive. Like any effective committee, political party, or federation of states, it will continue to try to present a unified public face, to at least *behave* as if it harbored a single mind.

Apart from occasional instances when their left and right hands seem bent on different courses of action, split-brain patients don't report being aware of an inner conflict. They don't describe experiencing the presence of two different minds. But again this is hardly surprising. When a split-brain patient speaks, it is only his or her left hemisphere that is producing the speech and expressing itself. The right hemisphere, being mute, is compelled simply to listen. Even if it wanted to put forward an opinion of its own (and the right hemisphere seems much less strong-willed and focused than the left) it would be unable to. Therefore, asking a split-brain patient if he or she *feels* like two separate people living inside the same body resolves nothing. Even in the case of P.S., who has two "talking" hemispheres, one hemisphere is clearly more articulate than the other and, under normal circumstances, acts as the spokesperson for the whole brain.

Most of the time, then, a split-brain patient appears to have just one mind. Moreover, when the presence of the two minds *is* overtly revealed, the language-dominant hemisphere, confused by something it cannot readily explain, tries to cover up its ignorance of what the silent mind is seeing and doing. It resorts either to educated guesswork (based on cross-cueing) or confabulation. For instance, in one of Sperry's experiments a split-brain patient was shown a pencil in such a way that the image went only to his right hemisphere. When asked what he had seen, the patient (via his left hemisphere) replied "Nothing." However, when offered a tray of objects and asked to pick up with his left hand (connected to the right hemisphere) the object previously shown, the patient immediately reached for the pencil. Upon being asked why he had picked up the pencil, the patient (that is, his left hemisphere) grew confused and, not wishing to appear foolish, invented a story about the pencil resembling one he had once owned. On another occasion, Sperry showed a series of innocuous pictures in the left visual field of a female split-brain patient, and then slipped in a photo of a nude. Immediately, the woman felt acutely embarrassed, but couldn't explain why. Her talkative left hemisphere, not having seen the photo, had no idea why its owner was suddenly blushing and acting uncomfortably. So it contrived an answer to conceal its ignorance. When asked what the problem was, the woman complained simply that Sperry's machine was "very peculiar."

Why do we each feel single in spite of changing sensory impressions? Why don't we ever feel literally in two or three or more minds? The answer is simple: there are no conceivable circumstances under which a person could feel double—for *who* would there be to feel the doubling? Logic and intuition dictate that you can be only one person at a time. And this is a conclusion fully vindicated by the experiences of both MPS victims and split-brain patients.

In the case of MPS, though several personalities appear to inhabit the same brain, typically only one is active at any given time—as if a single searchlight of consciousness illuminated each character in turn. And even in situations where one of the personalities (like Sally) claims to have access to what one of the other personalities is thinking, the "supervisory" personality does not feel double. The situation is best thought of as a group of people sharing the same brain, with a few of the individuals being in a position to snoop on some of their cohabitants as if through a one-way mirror.

The case of split-brain patients is different (and less controversial) in that there are clearly two continuous, concurrent streams of consciousness in the same brain. Even so, there is no single entity that experiences dual awareness.

Consciousness, by its nature, is inevitably singular, unitary. Descartes gave the analogy of two one-eyed dogs fighting over a bone. The dogs would behave as if they saw one bone, not two! You cannot be two people at once. And no matter how hard you try to imagine your own stream of consciousness dividing, you always imagine the period after the split from the vantage point of one of the resulting streams.

In discussing such issues we quickly run into linguistic problems. We assume we know what words such as "you" and "person" mean. But it turns out that we normally use these terms in the Cartesian sense of being definite, indivisible objects. Our language therefore incorporates a philosophy of the self that fails to correspond with the reality science has now disclosed. What was one person can become two. What was "you" can become more than one you. Such bifurcations of the river of consciousness have happened. But the important fact is that when a "you" divides, or changes, or ends, or begins, it is not a problem for anyone concerned. From the point of view of the person you are now, change of any kind—especially death—*seems* to be a problem. But the only problem *in fact* is the advance fear of change itself. Once you actually stop being who you are now, the fear disappears, and you are free to continue life as someone else—a new you.

7

BEING SOMEONE AND
BECOMING SOMEONE ELSE

Our claim to our own bodies and our world is
our catastrophe . . .

—*W. H. Auden*, Canzone

I wake up. I wash and dress. I notice in the mirror with some alarm
a few more gray hairs, an unfamiliar wrinkle. I enjoy my morning
cup of tea. I venture out and feel the chill of a December morning.
Who or what is this "I" that does these things and has these experiences?

Each of us takes in the world from a unique vantage point. We see
our surroundings through one particular pair of eyes and feel our
awareness to be seated in one particular brain. We each think of ourselves as being unique and different from the rest. In your lifetime,
you have had many experiences, sensations, thoughts, and emotions.
But the one thing they all have in common is that they seem to be
specifically associated with *you*. To varying degrees you have felt
angry, happy, excited, in love, gloomy, anxious, and every other emotional state a person can feel. You have fallen asleep, daydreamed,
possibly had general anesthesia, probably been under the influence of
alcohol, and enjoyed who knows what other altered states of mind.
You have been different ages. Yet despite all of these extraordinarily

diverse experiences you are firmly convinced that you have remained, in some sense, one and the same person. You believe, as do those around you, that there is something—your "self"—that remains steady, secure, and identifiable amid the unpredictable flux of life. Furthermore, you believe that this self is distinct from all others. You feel, too, as if you did not exist before you were born, that your mind flickered into existence at some point, or over a limited period, in the not-so-long-ago past. And this raises the fear that you will similarly fade from existence in the not-too-distant future, when your body and brain stop working.

This feeling each of us has of unique individual consciousness and selfhood, of having an ego inside us, is both commonly accepted and, at the same time, profoundly mysterious. *How* did the conscious agency inside you come to occupy this particular body? *Why* were you born at a certain place and time, and not, for instance, two thousand years ago in Egypt or Rome, or a million years in the future in another part of the galaxy? Why is our personal existence unique?

If we think only about other people, it hardly seems surprising that there should be different selves, different eddies of being, characterized outwardly by different personalities. Each of us has a unique collection of genes and is exposed to a unique set of circumstances, so it would be unreasonable to expect any two people to turn out the same. But as soon as we focus on our own particular consciousness, mind-boggling paradoxes seem to arise. Of all the billions of centers of human (and nonhuman) awareness that have existed and do exist and will exist throughout time and space, why are you the one individual you are, in *this* body, here and now?

You would hardly expect to wake up tomorrow and find yourself, literally, stepping into someone else's shoes. You don't expect to be looking out, from one moment to the next, through the eyes of a succession of unfamiliar people. Your consciousness doesn't flit around like a hummingbird from one place and time to another. Why should that be? We can breathe the same air and eat the same food, so why can't we share or swap consciousness? Why can't you be me, and I be you?

There's no reason to suppose that the day-to-day experiences in your life are very much different from mine or anyone else's. In matters of detail, it is true, they may differ quite a bit. But if you and I were to look at the same tree together, it's reasonable to assume that we would inwardly perceive pretty much the same thing. Your experience of the tree—your feeling of its "treeness"—would, in all probability, closely match mine. We can say this with some confidence because the way the human senses and brain work doesn't vary much from one person to another, so there are no grounds to suspect that our inner perceptions differ much either. It seems as safe as it possibly could be to conclude that a lot of what goes on inside our heads is not unique to us as individuals. The warmth of the sun, the smell of a rose, the throbbing pain of a toothache, and innumerable other sensations almost certainly feel more or less the same to you as they do to me. What, then, if two people in the same place could stop thinking for a moment about anything to do with themselves—the money *he* owes on his car, the itch *she* has on her arm, and so on—and instead simply take in their surroundings. What would happen?

Imagine, for instance, you are sitting on a boulder on the shore of a remote lake in the Canadian wilderness, a place little changed since the end of the last ice age. You see the sun glinting off the cool blue water, the rocky shoreline, the tall pines stretching away on either side. You have let your mind settle into a state as clear and tranquil as the cloudless sky, undisturbed by any personal thoughts or concerns. Beside you is a friend, and together you simply absorb and enjoy all the rich sensations this wild place has to offer—the cry of a bird overhead, the exhilarating feel of a fresh breeze, the gentle lapping of waves on the shore, the aroma of leaf and flower. Both of you experience the same scene, thinking no other thoughts, just letting the sights and sounds of your immediate environment wash over you. How is your consciousness, in this entirely open and receptive state, any different from that of your friend? How *could* it be different if the only aspect of experience that distinguishes two people—thoughts to do with themselves—have been suspended? Two bodies, two sets of sense organs, two brains, there might be—in objective space. But what matters, and is of primary importance to each of us, is the view from the inside. How can two minds differ internally if they are experiencing, purely and simply, the same underlying reality? When experience is exclusively of what is happening *here and now,* uninfluenced by personal memories, then it is—and must be—the same for everyone.

Now imagine that, a thousand years ago, another person sat on this same boulder savoring this same view of the lake and shoreline under the same bright sun. How is your consciousness, your immediate experience of this situation, any different from this other individual's? You might argue that he was a different person who lived a different life at a different time and so inevitably had different thoughts from your own. But, again, leave aside these circumstantial differences, *the very differences that define individual selves,* and focus only on what you and this other fellow have in common—the unadulterated awareness of sitting on a boulder by an ancient lake, with no other thoughts intruding. Under these circumstances, what distinguishes your consciousness from his?

We are brought up to suppose that the consciousness of a particular person is entirely separate and distinct from the consciousness of anyone else, that we each inhabit our own little bubble of awareness. We are led to believe that the inner experience of being a particular person, a "you" or an "I," is an exclusively private affair. And so we accept without question that this inner experience must be associated uniquely with one particular body and brain—the one that happens to be "ours." But this belief is groundless, a mere social convention.

Most of the elements of what you and I experience are the same. So why do we regard ourselves as being utterly different? Why does it *seem* as if you are only conscious of what goes on inside your own head and not mine, or anyone else's—or, for that matter, *everyone* else's? It would be easier to accept that consciousness is a partly shared affair if it were not for the fact that you and I acutely feel as if we are looking out on the world from particular vantage points. Everything apparently comes not just to any observer, but constantly and unremittingly to you or to me. If you stub your toe, the whole population of the planet doesn't groan along with you. If you have a long, cold drink after a long, hot game of tennis, the rest of humanity doesn't share in your moment of bliss. As William James remarked:

> Other men's experiences, no matter how much
> I may know about them, never bear this vivid,
> this peculiar brand.

We are alike, and therefore able to communicate with each other, inasmuch as part of our consciousness is the same. But we are different and distinguishable in that everyone has a unique life story. I know what it is like to feel pain, but I didn't feel pain at the same times or in the same physical surroundings or in the same psychological contexts as you did. I know what it is like to fall in love, but not with that certain blond-haired girl or boy with the out-of-state accent you met at your high school dance when you were seventeen.

For most of the time we have an overwhelming impression of there being a central unifying agency inside us that remains steadfast and secure. This agency is the power that relates sensations, from one moment to the next, as if they were experienced by the *same* person, that seems to will actions, erects boundaries between itself and the outside, and seeks self-preservation. The brain, in effect, appears to have a resident storyteller that works ceaselessly to link everything that comes to its attention into a single coherent narrative. And even as you read this, the story is continuing. Your brain is drawing upon a knowledge of its own history to generate the feeling of being you, interpreting every new idea and sensation it receives in terms of the information it already has stored.

The brain manufactures us, integrates us, moment by moment, from bits and pieces it finds in its database of memories. So inevitably the contents of this database are crucial in fashioning the particular persons we become. Childhood circumstances, especially, play a vital role in laying down the basic infrastructure of our brains. However, the process of brain modification continues throughout our lives; the network of neurons, the pattern of synaptic links, alters and evolves over time in response to the demands placed upon it. Our brains change—and so, as a result, do we.

We are never the same, objectively, from one moment to the next. As sensations and emotions fluctuate, as the brain's repository of memories is added to or depleted, we change too. And yet the change is not apparent from within. Every moment the brain is bombarded with fresh sensory data, and every moment, without fail, it filters, sorts, and merges this data with past recollections *at an unconscious level* to give a single, coherent, conscious experience. Across time, too, the brain unites, building bridges between its separate conscious experiences to create the impression of a smoothly running narrative. And, as its pièce de résistance, the brain conjures up the illusion of a character as its story's heart—the self.

All the evidence of neurology suggests that you are nothing more than what it feels like to be a particular brain at a particular moment in time. And although this experience is determined by what has happened in the past, through the influence of memory, who you were in the past is not who you are now. It is one of the cleverest and most beguiling of the brain's tricks to foster the belief that this is so—but you do not feel now as you did ten years ago, or even ten minutes ago. You are the feeling of one brain at one moment in time, *this* moment, no more. And part of this feeling, the illusory part, is that you are identical and continuous with what has gone before.

We are brought up to take pride in our individuality, to value being a particular person with a mind of our own. But however well this belief serves us in many ways, it comes at a heavy cost. Our tendency to accept unquestioningly the existence of a distinct, unchanging, private ego makes us terrified at the prospect of its loss. How, in the light of what science and psychology have revealed about the self, can we come to terms with the inevitability of death?

Suppose that neurosurgery develops to the stage where whole or partial brain transplants become possible. And suppose, for some reason, that you and I decide to have our brains swapped. After the operation, your brain, and therefore your continuing sense of self, would have taken up residence in my body, and my brain and sense of self in your body. A *total* brain transfer like this seems to pose no serious dilemma in deciding what happens to each person involved. We instinctively accept that "you go where your brain goes," though it might well be that having a new body and appearance would eventually lead to marked changes in how you thought and felt. This would be especially so if the new body was very different from the original—say, a man's body instead of a woman's, or an adult's instead of a child's (as comically portrayed in the movie *Big*).

More problematic, though, would be the case where instead of a whole brain transfer we opted for a *gradual* swap of our brains. After the first operation, small clumps of cells from corresponding parts of the two brains would have changed places. How would this feel for you and for me? One possibility is that, upon regaining consciousness, we might notice the presence of a few new memories, the loss of some others, and perhaps a hard-to-define feeling of being not quite ourselves. If so, then if more such operations were carried out a point would presumably be reached at which you had become me and I had become you. Is this a reasonable theory?

Of course, no progressive transfer of healthy brains is ever likely to be carried out in practice. However, the surgical repair of damaged brains through the grafting on of healthy tissue from donor brains *is* a possibility. And some preliminary work in this area has already been done.

As long ago as 1903, Elizabeth Hopkins Dunn, an anatomist at the University of Chicago, showed that small groups of cells or fragments of nervous tissue could be successfully grafted from the brain of one newborn rat onto that of another. The brain, it turns out, is surprisingly unfussy about having foreign material patched on to it (though it may, after several weeks or months, reject it). But the graft will not take at all unless it consists of very young cells, because only these have sufficient plasticity to form viable connections with the host brain.

Like their human counterparts, old rats tend to be forgetful. They have trouble, for instance, remembering their way around mazes that they have previously negotiated. But a graft of cells from a rat fetus, providing it comes from a specific little region of the brain known as the septum, serves dramatically to boost an aging rat's maze-solving ability. This is because the septum regulates how much of a neurotransmitter (a chemical by which nerve cells communicate) called acetylcholine is fed to the hippocampus. And the hippocampus, as already mentioned, plays a vital role in helping lay down new memories. In an old rat—or an elderly person—the supply of acetylcholine in the hippocampus dries up because the necessary signals no longer come through from the septum. Fresh septum cells grafted onto the hippocampus help restore the supply—and hence the ability of the animal to remember.

Since the 1980s, brain grafts have been given to several hundred human patients around the world in an effort to relieve the symptoms of Parkinson's disease. Parkinson's victims face acute problems in exercising voluntary muscle control. Although not paralyzed (at least in the early stages of the disease) they may have great difficulty in initiating or controlling movements. Their limbs may tremble violently one moment and be stuck in frozen immobility the next, and the normal gait of walking may be replaced by rapid shuffling steps. Unlike Alzheimer's disease, which is characterized by a catastrophic loss of cells from virtually all parts of the brain, the effects of Parkinsonism can be traced principally to the death of cells in one specific structure—the substantia nigra. This part of the brain regulates the amount of the neurotransmitter dopamine reaching an important motor-control center called the striatum. The experimental transplant treatment involves taking substantia nigra tissue from aborted human fetuses and attaching it to the striata of affected patients in the hope that it will trigger the production of dopamine and so suppress the symptoms of Parkinsonism. It is far from being a cure, and in many cases it produces little or no improvement. But for some Parkinson's patients, brain grafts have led to a marked recovery of independence and mobility.

The important point about this type of graft is that the connections formed between the transplanted cells and the existing brain cells *don't have to be precise*. The substantia nigra just modulates the activity of the striatum like a volume control, so the details of the circuitry aren't crucial. All that matters is that the right amount of dopamine gets through to where it is needed. This is obviously a very different form of communication from, say, that between the eyes and the visual cortex, in which the exact plan of the neural circuitry is absolutely critical.

More extensive brain grafts may be carried out in the future. But they will continue to involve immature cells that have the capacity to bind to existing tissue. Obvious ethical problems surround the use of brains from aborted fetuses, particularly as several fetal brains are needed to provide sufficient dopamine-producing neurons for a transplant. This process will become much more efficient—and less ethically contentious—as it becomes possible to grow large numbers of dopamine neurons in the laboratory from a tiny amount of fetal brain material. But the necessity for using foreign tissue at all is likely to be short-lived as techniques are evolved to generate new brain cells in situ through tissue and genetic engineering.

Whatever method is used for future brain repairs, there is no conceivable threat to the identity of the patient. The new tissue will simply become integrated into the structure of the existing brain without introducing foreign elements into the recipient's memories or character.

In fact, even if it were possible to transplant tissue from one mature brain to another, this would not raise the specter of memory transfer. Neurologists no longer subscribe to the idea that specific memories are carried by specific neurons or clusters of neurons. Instead, the modern view is that memories depend upon the overall associational network of connections within the cortex.

Reality, then, precludes a would-be Dr. Frankenstein from gradually changing one person into another by progressively swapping bits of their brains. But we can still envisage another method of achieving the same end. Suppose that it becomes possible to map a living brain down to the level of every neuron and synapse. And suppose further that we develop the means to reconfigure a brain's connections by as little or as much as we desire. This would allow us, for instance, to make any number of the connections in one brain identical with those in another brain. Thus equipped we are ready to ask again: what would such a progressive change feel like?

A contemporary philosopher who has done a great deal of ground-breaking work using thought experiments like these is Derek Parfit of Oxford University. Imagine, then, to borrow from one of Parfit's own gedankenexperiments, that the two brains involved are those of Parfit himself and Napoleon Bonaparte. The question is, at what stage in the rewiring procedure would Parfit start to think of himself as being Napoleon rather than his old self? It would be ridiculous to suppose there would be a sudden switchover of identities. Clearly, we would be dealing with a continuous spectrum of possible mental states ranging from the feeling of being 100 percent Derek Parfit (a feeling that only Parfit is privy to) to that of being 100 percent Napoleon (a feeling known only to the emperor). In between these two extremes, memories from both individuals would be present together and so, for instance, Parfit/Napoleon might be ambiguous as to his loyalties to

England and France or to Mrs. Parfit and Josephine. The storyteller in
the Parfit/Napoleon brain would be working overtime trying to reconcile the conflicting bits of narrative at its disposal and doubtless
around the midpoint of the operation, Parfit/Napoleon would be seriously confused as to his true identity. However, there is absolutely no
reason to suppose that at any stage in the neural reconfiguration there
would exist the feeling in the Parfit/Napoleon brain of being *two* people at once. Observers would certainly be forced to agree that the person who emerged from the operation, behaving exactly like Napoleon,
was very different from the original Derek Parfit. On the other hand,
as experienced by the Parfit/Napoleon brain, there would never have
been a moment at which the "I" inside ceased to exist or at which this
"I" experienced a dual or fragmented consciousness. The "I" inside
may have felt disoriented, unsettled, afraid, or uncertain as to its identity, but it would nevertheless have experienced a single continuity of
awareness.

Who should we think of as being the individual who walks away
from the operation? He looks like Parfit and has Parfit's old brain
(extensively rewired, but with all the original atoms). Yet he acts like
Napoleon. He talks in immaculate French of his military campaigns,
his love for Josephine, and his despair at being sent into exile. He is,
legally and biologically, the father of Parfit's children and the husband
of Parfit's wife, but he retains not a single memory of *being* Parfit.
Who then is this person? As experienced internally he is Napoleon
(though an extremely confused Napoleon, having suddenly found
himself in twentieth-century Oxford in an unfamiliar body!). But as
far as others are concerned, he has the appearance of Derek Parfit
apparently having gone mad and now doing a ludicrous (but brilliant)
impression of the French emperor. What label should we pin on this
person?

Such a question may prove difficult or impossible to resolve
unless we are prepared to adopt a radically new outlook. We have to
accept that there is a difference—a very great difference—between
what we conventionally believe to be true about people, including
ourselves, and what is actually the case. We have had it drummed
into us that particular selves exist and that personal identity is all-
important. We have been conditioned, both by evolution and by the

society we live in, to think that the "I" inside us is clearly defined, extremely special, and worth preserving at almost any cost. As a result, we imagine ourselves as being at a privileged focus of the world, at the center of a special bubble of awareness that is different and more significant than any other.

So intently focused are we on our own self-centered domains that we consistently overlook the fact that the "feeling of being you" is universal. Everyone has to be someone, and everyone happens to be the particular someone they are right now. Say to a crowd of five hundred people, "Put up your hand if you feel like you," and five hundred hands will go up. The simple but underrated fact is that *we all feel like you*. Right now, six billion people are busily "being you"—and not one of them is anyone special.

You might argue: "But there's only one *me,* one self that's exactly like me. Why is it that, of everyone I might have been, I happen to be me?" Yet, the fact is that anyone else could reply: "I think exactly the same way—and so does *she,* and so does *he*." So where is the problem? I may not be having exactly the same thoughts or seeing the same things or experiencing the same emotions as you are right now, but what does that matter? Neither did you feel the same way last year or yesterday or even five minutes ago. The fact is that the range of subjective experiences you have been through in your life is as great as the range of subjective experiences being felt by many different people at any given moment in time. How can you claim to be a unique, definitive thing, this supposedly immutable "you," when the succession of many past yous and the present you are as different from each other as a large collection of totally different individuals? It may be that at this moment (the moment at which you are reading this sentence) you have more in common with the way I am feeling right now than the way you yourself were feeling at this time yesterday. How then can we avoid the conclusion that conscious experiences are much more communal, much more commonly shared among everyone, than we normally suppose?

We have to realize, difficult as it may be, that there is absolutely nothing special about any of us. Only when we can grasp at the deepest level that *personal identity is not what matters* can we make progress toward understanding our true nature. The fact is, you could have been anybody. If your mother had conceived five minutes later than she did, a different sperm cell from your father would almost certainly have fertilized your mother's egg, and a child having a different genetic makeup from your own would have developed. Ask yourself: would you have been that child? Or would you instead have been the brother or sister of who you actually turned out to be? The child that might have been conceived five minutes later would have grown up to think of itself as being a particular person, would have had an inner world of experience as rich and as coherent as anyone else's, and would have been referred to by others as "you." Its unique genetic constitution would have made it different from you in some ways (including possibly its sex), though its almost identical upbringing and environment would inevitably have made it similar to you in other ways (just as brothers and sisters are similar). Since the child would effectively have taken your place, is it reasonable to say it would actually have been you?

Or take a different example. Imagine you have an identical twin and that your parents divorced when you were three years old. Your mother and twin went to live in New York, while your father and you remained in San Francisco. Thirty years later, having been out of contact for all that time, you learn that whereas your own upbringing, while happy, was materially modest, that of your twin was extremely privileged. He or she attended a private school, won a scholarship to a first-rate medical college, had the opportunity to make all the right social connections, and is now a successful cardiologist. You, on the other hand, sell seafood on Fisherman's Wharf. Though content with life, you wonder aloud to yourself one day what might have happened if you had been able to take your twin's place. I overhear and in my newly constructed time machine travel back three decades to the moment at which your mother is about to leave for New York. I surreptitiously swap her twins around. Subsequently, the twin who goes to New York becomes a cardiologist while the other twin finds eventual employment as a purveyor of clams and crabs. One question we might ask is, given this new situation, would you now be your twin (the cardiologist) or would you still be you (the seafood seller) in spite of the exchange? A more meaningful question, however, might be: *does it matter?* In the end, there are still two people—one a heart surgeon, the other a food merchant—who are conscious and happy and have complete, continuous sets of memories and other characteristics that help define the individuals they are. They are not confused about their own identities. Nor, to go back to the earlier example, would the person who might have been conceived inside your mother five minutes later have grown up confused about his or her identity. Why then should we make such an issue of who is who?

You chose to read this book. It may revolutionize your life, or it may not. But what is certain is that, simply by having absorbed these words—whether you believe them or not—you are, in at least some small way, not quite the person you would have been had you decided to do something else instead. This is a *physical* fact. As a result of processing the ideas about self and consciousness and death that this book has already invoked, your brain has acquired a slightly different atomic and neurophysiological configuration than it would otherwise have done. Therefore, since you are undoubtedly influenced by the state of your brain, you are not quite the same person you would have been had you never started reading. Ask yourself: does this matter to you? Would it matter to you if I said I was going to throw a switch and turn you into this "other you" who would have existed if you had not picked up this book? Why *should* it matter to you? The person you would then become would still have a complete chain of memories and a secure sense of identity—a feeling of being "I."

The future, on a human scale, is almost totally unpredictable. For example, I have no idea what I shall be doing in three years' time. If this book sells well, I may be sunning myself on some warm Caribbean beach marveling at how wonderful a writer's life can be. On the other hand, if you are my only reader, I may be pawning my computer and ruing the day I ignored by parents' advice to find a real job. I know that, in any event, I shall continue to be me because I can never be anyone else (or, to put it another way, even if I *did* become someone else, in an existential sense I wouldn't be aware of it and would therefore still think of myself as being me). However, I also feel sure that the me who might be basking on some faraway desert isle would not be quite the same me who, if fortune fails to smile, ends up impecunious and untanned.

Even if we think we know who we are now, we haven't a clue

who we are going to be tomorrow or next year. Whatever happens, you will still *think* of yourself as being the same person—a continuation of the "old you." But you will *in fact* have changed. You will be composed of different atoms, your body will have aged, your brain will be wired up somewhat differently, and your feelings about the world will have matured and evolved. Despite the fact that received wisdom tells us we retain the same personal identity throughout life, the reality of the matter is different. Personal identity *does* change, all the time. You are not the same "you" that you were a week ago or even a second ago. You, as a fixed entity, are an illusion that we have been persuaded to believe is real. Personal identity as a constant, enduring thing is a myth—a myth that on a day-to-day basis, it is true, serves a useful purpose. But to grow in understanding we need to move on, both individually and as a society, in the direction of laying less stress on the particular people we think we are—because being particular is not important. You and I are nobody special. We are simply brains having thoughts and that is all there is to it.

8

YOU AGAIN

What is a friend? A single soul dwelling in two
bodies.

—Aristotle

So here we are: brains in conversation, trying to understand and come
to terms with death. We want to know what it will involve, what it
will feel like, what will happen after the last shallow breath and feeble
heartbeat, after the sheet is finally drawn over our still features. Of
this much we can be certain: within a matter of minutes, at some
future time, our brains will become terminally starved of oxygen and
will cease to function. All of the memories they so recently held,
together with the power to integrate two selves—you and I—will be
lost. Put this way, it sounds catastrophic. It sounds hopeless, terrifying, terrible. But how will it *really* be for us when the time comes?

   Our great difficulty in thinking about death is that we can see it
only in others, never in ourselves.* And viewed objectively it does
look depressing—lifeless corpses, despair, mourning, decay, loss.
Since our only contact with death is as an outsider this is our natural basis for envisaging what our own death will be like. But our
own death will be special and unique, because we shall be part of

---

*I am reminded of a quote from a dying student nurse in Allegra Taylor's book
Acquainted with the Night: "Death may get to be a routine to you, but it is new to me.
You may not see me as unique, but I've never died before."

it, inside it, the one who actually dies. And as experienced, rather than observed, death is a very different proposition.

Witnesses regularly report that in the last days or hours of life, a dying person will appear serenely calm and at peace with the world, and even, on occasions, extraordinarily joyful and elated. And there are the reassuring testimonies, too, of people who have been through near-death experiences in which reference is often made to almost indescribably blissful sensations. The final passage leading to death is evidently, in the great majority of cases, not at all unpleasant. Indeed, for those who have suffered from a long, painful, or debilitating illness, such as cancer, the immediate prelude to death can be anticipated as a time of welcome deliverance from suffering. As for the moment of death itself, if we take this to mean the total breakdown of cognitive function (brain death) at the end of a person's life, then, as experienced, it will be over in a painless, trouble-free instant.

To those who knew and loved a person who has just died there is obviously great regret and sadness at his or her departure. But, if we are being honest (and it is especially hard to be objective about such matters following a bereavement), at least a part—and perhaps a very large part—of the sadness we feel is for ourselves because we have lost someone dear, like a cherished possession. We will no longer have the pleasure of their company, and so we are consumed, understandably, by self-pity. Moreover, the death of another, especially a close family member like a parent or spouse, reminds us keenly of our own mortality.

The terrible thing about death, then, is not the actual experience that awaits us—we all *know* what it is like to lose consciousness—but the angst and feeling of insecurity it instills in us *now*. It preys on our mind that, despite all the assurances of religion and the many tales of people who claim, in all sincerity, to have glimpsed wonderful visions of the other side of life, there may, quite simply, be nothing to come. And however irrational, however futile it may be to fret about death, we are psychologically paralyzed by the thought of a timeless, mindless void.

We seek comfort. But what does science do? It rejects the soul as an implausible and unnecessary hypothesis and reduces what is left of us to the musings of a moist, cauliflower-like (though nonetheless remarkable) lump of tissue. Have general anesthesia, go comatose, faint, or just fall into a deep, dreamless sleep, it asks, and where are you? You are nowhere, because in such situations the brain temporarily stops generating the feeling of being someone. The brain makes you, it dissolves you, it brings you back again. And, as psychology and neurology have emphatically shown, when the brain's workings are altered or impaired, the sense of self they give rise to is correspondingly changed or diminished so that you become no longer the person you were. The scientific evidence for an intimate brain-self link is overwhelming. But the problem seems to be that if we are persuaded by such no-nonsense materialism, and if at the same time we abandon faith in a higher, spiritual domain, our hopes for the future will be dashed. Such is the brooding and pervasive concern of contemporary Western society. But it is a concern that is wholly unjustified.

What most of us instinctively hope for is to be able to continue, after we die, as the person we are now. We may be happy to accept a change of scenery and circumstances, but our overwhelming desire is to survive death with our current selves intact. There is a general assumption that, in denying the existence of the soul, science precludes such a possibility. But it does not. On the contrary, science can supply an astonishing variety of scenarios, any one of which amounts to nothing short of secular reincarnation.

To take just one example: we know from experience that we carry on thinking we are the same person throughout life despite the ceaseless turnover of our constituent particles. And this is just what theory would predict. Because all atoms of a given type are identical, it doesn't matter which particular ones happen to temporarily form part of our bodies and brains. Therefore, it follows that if your brain were to be reconstituted, at some point in the future, down to the last atom (and perhaps the replication wouldn't need to be anywhere near this precise), *you would live again*. The chance of such atomic level re-creation taking place might seem incredibly remote. But set against this improbability is the fact that the universe is extremely large and long-lived. It may also be cyclic, alternating repeatedly between epochs of growth and collapse. Some cosmologists have recently gone further and proposed that our cosmos may be just one of count-less universes that exist like bubbles in an inconceivably vast ocean of foaming space-time. In any event, since no one has yet come near to circumscribing the bounds of physical reality, we cannot rule out the possibility that *any* specific collection of matter, however complex, will recur—and recur many times over—in the distant future. Our uncertainty as to the full extent of the universe leaves open the prospect of a given brain being re-created, and therefore the possibility of its associated conscious mind coming back into operation. The same argument applies, with equal strength, to the past of an indefinitely old universe, or collection of universes. If your brain has existed before, then in some sense it must be that "you" have existed before—perhaps an infinite number of times.

Were this mind-boggling scenario of recurring yous to be enacted in reality, the jump from one "phase" of your existence to the next, as experienced by you, would be instantaneous. Since you would not be conscious of anything in the intervening periods (you would after all be dead during these times!), you would not be aware in the slightest of any passage of time between when you last existed, even if tens or hundreds of billions of years had gone by. Any periods during which your brain was not (reasonably) accurately configured would be time-less instants from your subjective point of view.

This may seem like a stratospheric flight of speculation. Never-theless, it is true that given the limitations of our current knowledge of cosmology, there is as much reason to suppose that materialism leads to a prediction of eternal life as it does to a prediction of nonexistence. And neither need give us any cause for concern. The Epicureans and the Stoics realized more than two thousand years ago that there was nothing to be afraid of in permanent extinction. Now, without assuming anything more than an indefinitely long-lived and varied cosmos, we have arrived at an alternative scenario of eternal life.

Yet it may be premature to start uncorking the champagne. We need to consider carefully what "eternal life" on these terms might mean. Nowhere in the picture of recurring yous just outlined is there a mecha-nism, an escape pod (like a soul), for transferring memories between successive phases of your existence. So, apparently, there is no way you could know or build upon the fact that you had lived before. Any previ-

ous yous might as well have been different people with differently patterned brains. As far as you were concerned, at any moment in time, it
would be as if you had only one life, bounded by a single birth and
death, not a series of more or less identical lives scattered across different epochs in cosmic history. Frustratingly, you would not be able to
carry on where you had left off in your last life, or enjoy interphase
continuity of any kind, because you could not inherit or benefit from
what your previous incarnation had achieved. At the same time this
wouldn't matter to you since you wouldn't know about it.

Eternal life punctuated by bouts of total amnesia seems to offer
no advantage over an ordinary mortal life followed by permanent
extinction. What most of us hope for after death is something quite
different—a chance to live forever under circumstances not unlike
those of the popular Christian notion of heaven. We fantasize about
spending the rest of eternity in a gardenlike Eden, fraternizing with
other kindly souls, without the inconvenience of having to die again at
some point. Genuine eternal life on this basis sounds idyllic. But,
again, looked at more closely, it rapidly loses its appeal. Imagine
spending endless eons—trillions upon trillions of years—with the
same people in the same place doing the same things (but not, rumor
has it, involving such diversions as sex or alcohol). If this is paradise,
one can scarcely conceive what hell might have in store.

In Jonathan Swift's *Gulliver's Travels,* the hero discovers what a
curse everlasting life can be during his stay in the land of Luggnagg.
Every so often in this country, a child is born with a distinctive mark
on its forehead indicating that it is a Struldbrugg—an individual who
can never die. Gulliver supposes, naturally enough, that the
Struldbruggs must become steadily wiser and wealthier than anyone
else since they have all the time in the world to accumulate knowledge and riches. But, in fact, it turns out that the Struldbruggs, though
normal until about the age of thirty, thereafter become increasingly
dejected, opinionated, peevish, vain, unsociable, and envious—especially of the dead. Eventually, they lose their teeth, hair, appetite,
memory, and ability to communicate. They become, in other words,
permanently and unpleasantly senile—and are universally despised.
Gulliver learns that only in those countries not having Struldbruggs is
death considered to be an evil to be delayed as long as possible.

Not having journeyed with Gulliver, we tend to have a superficial and, therefore, exceptionally rosy view of what eternal life would be like. And there is no doubt we have a powerful urge, at least while we are healthy and active, to go on living as long as possible. How many of us would spurn the offer of a safe drug that guaranteed, barring accident, an additional fifty years of top-quality life? That extra half century might allow us to survive to a time when still more powerful drugs, or other techniques, become available for extending life for much greater periods. Gerontologists are already suggesting such breakthroughs may happen in the early part of the twenty-first century. And so we might continue, indefinitely, leapfrogging down the generations. The trouble is that, under such circumstances, we might well become obsessed with clinging on to life, dissatisfied with whatever time was left to us, frightened even to go outdoors in case death came by accident, concerned only with the quantity of life and not its quality.

Voltaire was another who understood well that a longer life is not necessarily a better one. In his comic, cosmic satire, *Micromegas,* an inhabitant of Saturn complains that the people on his planet live only to the age of fifteen thousand years.

> So, you see, we in a manner begin to die at the
> very moment we are born: our existence is no
> more than a point, our duration an instant, and
> our globe an atom. Scarce do we begin to learn
> a little, when death intervenes before we can
> profit by experience: for my own part, I am
> deterred from laying any schemes. I consider
> myself a single drop in an immense ocean.

In reply, a creature from Sirius points out that the folk of his world live seven hundred times longer than on Saturn. Moreover, he adds, there are some places where people live a thousand times longer than Sirians, and still complain about the shortness of life.

A long or endless life grounded in perpetual routine and repetition could become a weary treadmill—an existence from which we would be only too glad to escape, even if it meant death. In just such a frame of mind must the aging Jefferson have been when he wrote to a friend: "I am tired of putting my clothes on every morning and taking them off every evening."

And there is another potential problem with life everlasting. We are all familiar with the worrying sensation that time seems to pass by more and more swiftly as we age. Could it be that the human brain keeps track of the passage of time by the frequency of novel additions to its memory? In our youth, most of the experiences we encounter during the course of a day are new or have some element of newness. This makes them memorable, in the sense that there is potential survival value in the brain adding them to its store for future reference. It seems reasonable to assume that our subjective experience of the passage of time is linked to the availability of fixed objective reference points. And this is evidenced by the absence or gross distortion of time sense which people report when they spend extended periods in total isolation. When we are young, all sorts of events in the outside world catch our attention and are subsequently ferreted away in our brain. With so many novel entries being made in our daily memory diary, the experience of time is stretched out. But as we grow older, more and more of the things we do and see are mere repetitions of what has happened before. Habituated actions, sights, and sounds fail to register in our consciousness: the loudly ticking clock that its owner no longer hears, the daily drive to work that is done on mental autopilot, there are many such examples. As our lives revolve increasingly around set routines so there is less need for the brain to lay down fresh memory traces—our "novel event density" falls dramatically while, at the same time, the passage of our lives alarmingly speeds up.

We seem to be faced with a dilemma. We have a strong urge to remain the same, either by staying alive or by surviving death as the person we are now. Yet the enjoyment of life, and indeed the very experience of life in a fully conscious way, seems to hinge upon novelty and change. We don't want to die, to stop being who we are now. But continued existence of any meaningful kind seems to demand that we eventually become someone else. How can we make sense of this apparent contradiction?

Science has revealed that we are the products of an evolutionary process that goes back billions of years. Everything that is part of us—

our cells, tissues, organs, and organ systems—has come about because it proved successful in the great survival stakes. And the brain is no exception. The brain evolved, at least in part, as a means to allow a creature to learn from what happens in its life, to retain key elements of experience so that they are available for favorably influencing future action. A physicist might liken the brain to an instrument that automatically records the most relevant parts of its own "world line," its unique private meanderings through the four-dimensional realm of space and time. We don't find this difficult to believe in the case of brains in general. But when it comes to our own brain we are reluctant to accept that it is "just" an information processor—and one, moreover, with a depressingly short mean time to failure. We want to equip it with a soul that offers us a way of escape when the brain dies. We will do anything to avoid facing the possibility that who we are now *cannot* continue. And it is not difficult to see why this should be so. As Rick Blaine, Humphrey Bogart's character in *Casablanca,* put it: "I'm the only cause I'm interested in." Everything about us—our bodies, our brains, our selves—is geared for self-preservation. If this were not so, if the self were not wholly preoccupied with the business of staying alive (ultimately to propagate its genes) then we humans would not be here today. In fact, it is no overstatement to say that *the prime biological function of the self is to be afraid of death.* Only by being so contrived can the self play its crucial survival role.

This seems to put us in a difficult position. Awareness of self and awareness of mortality effectively go hand in hand. Self and the death-fear almost certainly came into existence together, both during the evolution of the human race and during the evolution of each human being from birth to adulthood. They are inextricable. And, as a consequence, only together can they disappear. Nothing that "we"—our selves—can say or do or think will quell our terror of dying. The self can never come to terms with its own extinction. And yet, having said this, the situation is far from hopeless. In fact, we now hold the key to the solution of our problem: to understand what lies beyond death we need only understand what lies beyond self.

And what are selves other than the sum of our differences? At the beginning of our lives, we are all, from a subjective standpoint, equal and undifferentiated. A newborn does not and cannot distinguish itself from the world around it—there is no self, no person, no firm sense of boundary. Only *we,* as mature selves looking on, make a distinction between the latent individual and his surroundings. Even during childhood, perhaps until late adolescence, the feeling of selfhood is not completely well defined. One indication of this is that young people can be remarkably stoic and even sanguine in the face of impending death, a fact that shines through from the deeply moving, uplifting statements that many children make when faced with terminal illness. It is only as we age that we start to think more and more of the particular brain and self we "own" as having a special, privileged status—of being a unique, treasured possession that we are desperate not to lose. Increasingly we become, in the most basic sense of the word, selfish. And once the self is fully installed, as "you" and "I" are now, feeling secure, confident of its own inner story, then it becomes impossible for it to conceive of its own demise. The psychological barrier preventing us from coming to terms with death, *from our self's point of view,* is utterly impenetrable. In fact, it becomes impossible for the self to contemplate *any* kind of change in itself, because to change is to become someone else, and to become someone else is to cease to exist as the person you are now. Logically and practically, change to the self is the *exact equivalent* of death. Even to go back and become the child you once were would seem frightening, unless you could take your present cargo of memories with you—in other words, transfer who you are now into your former body. To obliterate the memories of the intervening years would be to destroy an essential part of your current self. And the self, here and now, is satisfied by nothing less than the prospect of having continued access to all the memories that define it.

Yet the scientific evidence is clear that the brain never stops changing throughout life. Its neural configuration is in a continuous state of flux, the pattern of synapses shifting, individual connections forming and breaking, the dendrites (nerve cell endings) and axons (nerve cell bodies) extending and retracting like the pseudopodia of amoebae in response to every new thought and sensation. And since *we* arise, at any given time, from the particular configuration and state of our brains, we also, viewed objectively, are subject to continual change. We are forever gaining new memories, losing old ones, having different feelings—or, rather, *being* different feelings—so that the permanent creature we take ourselves to be is in reality a marvelous artifice of the brain.

For the vast majority of the time, the brain assimilates change so adroitly, its primal urge to maintain coherence and internal consistency is so strong, that the change appears to take place exclusively in the outside world. It seems not to affect "us" at all. As far as the self is concerned, it feels like a rock against which the waves of external change relentlessly and harmlessly break. But there is a limit to how much flux the brain can handle and still maintain the illusion of a constant inner "I." Once this critical threshold has been passed, the self senses the threat to its continued existence and reacts by becoming afraid. For this reason, although we are not apprehensive about ordinary day-to-day experiences, we become very nervous indeed about situations that represent a sudden significant shift from our normal way of life. Leaving home, embarking on a new career, getting married or divorced, having children, losing a loved one, all generate internal stress because they confront the brain with a degree and rapidity of change from which it cannot shield the self. These, then, are transformative experiences, sudden twists and jumps in the inner narrative, that alter the self to such an extent that it goes through a period of uncertainty, instability, and doubt before settling down into a new equilibrium state. During such disturbances to the self, a person is launched along a new trajectory in life, surrounded by very different circumstances, and suddenly inundated with fresh memories and ideas. We acknowledge marked outward changes in character that may ensue in phrases such as "Marriage has made a new man of him" or "She has never been the same since her husband's death." However, because the individual who has been through the change still looks the same and appears to us to have access to all of his or her old memories, we don't conventionally go so far as to say that an entirely new person has been created. But this is where we make our mistake. A new person *has* been created, and it is only by challenging preconceived notions, by bringing our view of self into line with contemporary scientific evidence, that we can hope to properly understand the implications of death.

In physics, the classical mechanics of Newton provides a perfectly workable model for most everyday applications. Only in exceptional situations, for example at very high relative speeds or in very strong gravitational fields, docs the Newtonian approximation break down and need to be replaced by the more precise formulations of Einstein. A parallel exists with our conception of the self. In most ordinary circumstances the self approximates well to the Cartesian ideal of a fixed ego, both from an objective and a subjective point of view. But as conditions deviate increasingly from the norm, it becomes necessary to switch to a new, more realistic conception of the self as a dynamic process subject to continuous and unpredictable change.

The problem we face is that unlike in physics, where Einstein's notions of space and time have superseded those of Newton, our conventional ideas about the self remain strictly "classical" and very outmoded. Despite the startling progress made by neurology in uncovering the mechanisms of the brain, as a society we have not yet moved on from the body-soul dualism of René Descartes. This leaves us as nonplused as the classical physicists were at the end of the nineteenth century when they were confronted with observations—such as the constancy of the speed of light—that their theories were unable to explain. The old generation of physicists invented the ether. We cling to the idea of the rock-solid self, the indestructible ego, and the possibility of a spirit that will carry away our true essence at the moment of death. But just as the ether failed in the end, so too our antiquated notions about the self have proved inadequate to account for cases in which the inner world of an individual is damaged, fragmented, divided, rejoined, destroyed, or remade.

The crucial point to realize is that the death, or changing, of the self from one moment to the next and death as we normally understand it differ only in degree. In nature, in essence, they are identical. Like radio waves and gamma rays, they simply lie at opposite ends of the same continuous spectrum. Thanks to numerous psychological and neurological case studies we now have the ability to mark off points virtually all the way along this spectrum, so that physical death need no longer be seen as a unique, isolated, inexplicable, phenomenon. At the "little death" end of the spectrum, for example, are cases of minor memory loss that chip away, by varying amounts, at the supposedly immutable thing we think of as personal identity. Further along come more profound cases of amnesia or other manifestations of brain damage—especially to the prefrontal lobes—that can affect the brain's power to integrate a clear and secure sense of self. Somewhere in the middle of the "death spectrum" are conditions such as MPS in which a person may fragment or flicker in and out of subjective existence or even (as in the case of "Sally") effectively die by merging with other personalities. Finally, near the "big death" end of the spectrum are found instances of total, permanent amnesia that completely obliterate one person and are followed by the emergence of a different person as new memories are laid down.

It might be objected that total amnesia differs fundamentally from actual death because in the former case a physical body and brain survive. This survival is recognized objectively by others and can subsequently be pointed out to the new person who arises, even though all memories of the previous occupant of the body have been internally erased and replaced. By contrast, when a person dies in the conventional way there is no functional body or brain left to provide any outward sign of continuity. But this physical continuity is irrelevant, for two reasons. First, although the brain survives overall (and, if we could see it, would superficially look the same) it is almost certainly altered beyond recognition at the level of synaptic connections. In its microscopic details, the post–total amnesia brain, following recovery, can be expected to be as different from the preamnesia brain as it is from any other brain. In computational terms, it is an entirely different neural network—and it is the specific wiring pattern of a brain that is pivotal in determining the characteristics of the self. This, then, represents a definite prediction based on the ideas being advocated here that is, in principle, testable.

The second reason that bodily continuity is irrelevant is that it makes no difference at all to the new postamnesia "person" that there was once some other mind, some other self, occupying the head in which it now resides. And for confirmation of this, one need only reflect back to the comments, recorded earlier, of Linda Macdonald and Patsy Cannon.

Objectively, the extinction of a person following complete memory loss and the physical death of an individual appear very different. But what matters to each of us, in the final analysis, is the inner experience. And from this perspective there is absolutely no difference whatever between, on the one hand, losing all your memories and gaining a new set *during life* and, on the other hand, the death of one human being followed by the birth of another.*

If this argument is valid, and I firmly believe that it is, then from the reported experiences of people who have had unusual and extreme subjective experiences during life we can begin to build a picture of what the experience of physical death is like. And, in broad outline, what emerges is remarkably simple, straightforward, and familiar. In brief: the act of dying is like falling asleep, the effect of dying is to forget all about being one particular person, and the sequel to dying is the gradual laying down of new memories in a new brain, which will define another particular person. What is crucial is that, from the subjective point of view, although one set of memories (and life circumstances) is completely replaced by another, and one brain by another, there is no cessation of experience, of consciousness, of being. One story ends and, in the wink of an eye as felt from within, another story begins.

You might reply: "But this is no consolation because I happen to be *this* story, here and now. It does *me* no good at all that other stories, other people, will follow after my death." The philosopher Leibniz put it like this:

> Of what use would it be to you, sir, to become
> king of China, on condition that you forgot
> what you had been? Would it not be the same
> as if God, at the same time, destroyed you and
> created a king in China?

This objection, however, comes from—who else?—the self. The only vantage point *we* have from which to think about death is the current self, and this is the very entity whose principal biological function is to avoid death at all cost. The fact is, if we die and some-

---

*In fact, in some ways actual physical death is to be preferred, since it does not require the new person to assume a particular, and perhaps unwanted, role or set of responsibilities that, in the case of a victim of total amnesia, is expected by society, family, and friends.

one else is born who has no memory of us, then it is perfectly true that it does *us*—meaning the person who once existed—no "good" at all. But the person you think is going to die is not the person you are now. Who you are now is impossible to lose—and this will be true at all future moments at which you exist. You fear death because you imagine your self to be a static thing which will continue unchanged (amid an ever-changing world) until the dreaded moment at which your brain stops working. But it is logically impossible for you—the feeling of being one brain in the present—to die. And what else can you ever be except the feeling of being one brain in the present? Death only marks a limit to what new experiences can arise based on the memory chain that a brain has access to.

We assume that if death terminates a particular "you," then it must mean the end of all subjective experience. But, on the contrary, what death actually involves is a new start. And here it is essential to keep in mind the parallel between physical death and actual clinical cases of total amnesia and related syndromes. A certain concatenation of memories disappears. And after this very minor loss, the world continues as before, life carries on, a new neural network comes into existence, and as this new support system for the mind develops, a new self begins to emerge—a new narrative, a new "you."

Still, you may argue: "I accept all this. There's nothing revolutionary in the idea that as some people die, others are born. But if, as you claim, we—our inner selves—die when our brains die, then surely that's it. We can't somehow become one of these new yous because there's nothing to transfer over to the next person in line."

And this also is perfectly true. There is indeed nothing about "us"—our selves—that can pass into the future for the simple reason, as we have seen, that there is nothing substantial about us during life. The self will do anything to find a way out, to stay alive in some form. So, as soon as it starts to contemplate the period after death, it wonders, "What will happen to *me*?" and "Who will *I* be next?" But such questions represent an effort by the self to seek reassurance about its future. The self will not and cannot admit that it is going to perish, that its story is bound to reach an end. It has to believe that, after death, its essence will live on in some new guise, that perhaps it will appropriate some new brain in which to live again. However, this is not going to happen. There is no direct connection between person A who dies and person B who follows. Whether we are talking about total amnesia or physical death, nothing of the old person transfers to the new (as Patsy Cannon remarked, "That person is dead; I am a new person"). And yet, such a transfer is not important or problematic, once it happens, either to person A (who never stops existing as far as *she* is concerned) or to person B (who has always existed as far as *she* is concerned). All that is relevant is that, subjectively, after death, *the feeling of being continues*—a feeling that, as a new individual condenses, becomes once again the feeling of being a person.

The difficulty we face is in appreciating why this is a conclusion we should be happy about. And again the answer is that *we*—our present selves—can never be happy about it because the one all-consuming goal of a self is not to end. It is pointless—literally self-defeating—to attempt to understand death while in our typical "selfish" frame of mind. The "I" cannot abnegate itself because it cannot operate outside its own particular field of memories and projections. The "I" may go from level to level seeking release, but its efforts will always take place within the sphere of its own making. This leaves as our only viable alternative to try to adopt a less self-centered mode of thinking—a nondualistic mode—in which it *is* possible, I believe, to grasp the idea that the continuity of consciousness in general is more important, more fundamental, and ultimately more desirable than the continued existence or identity of the person we imagine ourselves to be right now.

A determined effort, involving the intuition as much as the intellect, is called for if we are to adjust to this seemingly offbeat way of seeing death. And since our thoughts unavoidably take place within the context of our self-awareness, it is not possible for us to logic away entirely our deep-seated thanatophobia. Even so, I can attest from personal (or, rather, impersonal) experience that the effort is worthwhile and can at least lead to a more philosophical and sanguine attitude to our own mortality.

To be a person is just to have the feeling of being part of an ongoing story, to experience being within a narrative. But what needs to be appreciated is that *any narrative will do*. While we are in the midst of one particular story we naturally don't want that story to end; we dread the approach of the final chapter, the final paragraph, the final line. And yet it is important to realize that the very obvious discontinuity and impression of finality associated with the objective view of death (seeing someone die) are not what is felt from within. Subjectively, there is never—and never could be—a break in awareness. As experienced, rather than observed, death is not the end of life, but rather the point of entry into a new phase of existence, the coming back into being as someone else. Inevitably, this implies the loss of your current identity. But to have a sense of identity means just to have a continuity of memory—a life history to date. It makes no difference in the long run whether this life history is the one we happen to have now, or whether it is a completely different autobiography that may exist in the future. Whatever happens, whenever it happens, it *will* happen in the present. And in the present moment there will be a you with a narrative and a secure feeling of self.

What will it be like, though, to be someone else after we die? Our language makes it impossible for us to frame questions that do not seem to imply the direct continuity of who we are now. But as long as we are aware of this limitation, we can attempt an answer.

As neurological studies of living brains using PET and MRI scanners have shown, we are not as different from each other as was once supposed. The individual experiences and perceptions we have, as the nearly identical measured reactions of different brains to identical stimuli attest, are almost certainly very similar indeed. Therefore, in terms of the kinds of distinct sensations, emotions, and feelings that humans can and do have, being one person is much like being any other. The differences between us lie in contexts—in the particular situations and in the particular combination and order of circumstances that accompany our lives. We tend to emphasize our differences precisely because "we" are the *result* of our differences. The process that begins in infancy with distinguishing "my hand" and "my foot," the bodily-I, extends by degrees to identifying a whole complex of feelings, experiences, thoughts, ideas, impulses, desires, hopes, and fears as "mine"—a complex that constitutes the self. However, when we look closely at these components, it becomes clear that they are derived from our environment and culture; they are the common building blocks from which we are all made. Yet in ordinary life we don't see this. And the more actions we perform imagining that the self originates and executes whatever is felt, the more substance seems to be endowed to this wholly insubstantial entity. This ongoing process of self-discrimination makes us overlook, or neglect, how remarkably alike our inner worlds really are. Society and the way the self has evolved lead us to place undue stress on the importance of the individual, on the differentiation and separation of selves, when in truth the basic "feeling of being me" is much the same for us all. Our different-looking faces, our varied *personas* conceal the fact that under it all we are pretty much alike, and therefore need no great leap of the imagination to put ourselves in someone else's place.

Consider the actor who studies his part so well that he feels himself to have taken on a new personality. Play Othello well enough, and in some sense for a while you *are* Othello (or, rather, Shakespeare thinking about Othello!). And consider identical twins who, although they may not have seen each other in many years, turn out to have lived incredibly similar lives. They may have almost identical jobs and hobbies; they may even have children and spouses with the same names. And there are many well-documented instances of twins apparently having sensed when their co-twin was unwell or in danger. On such occasions, it is as if the walls separating one self from another have, for a short while, been breached, allowing the awareness of the individuals involved to become shared, overlapped, or merged. More disturbing cases are on record, involving schizophrenics, who seemed to experience directly what another person was thinking. One patient complained to the Canadian psychiatrist Clive Mellor that the thoughts of a television presenter kept coming into his head: "There are no other thoughts there, only his. He treats my mind like a screen and flashes his thoughts onto it." Another patient said, "They project upon me laughter, for no reason, and you have no idea how terrible it is to laugh and look happy and know it is not you, but their emotions." In such cases it is almost as if the resident self has been displaced or become merely a mirror for reflecting the consciousness of an outsider. Finally, there are numerous examples of the differences between people disappearing almost completely, both subjectively and objectively, when mobs, gangs, or mass movements form. How easily, for instance, the individual's sense of personal identity was submerged and melded with terrifying effect in the all-pervading, tribal identity of the *Volk* (Nation) of Nazi Germany.

Everyone's life story includes numerous lacunae when we are not our normal selves. We may play at being someone else—empathizing with, imitating, or adopting a specific role (such as that of a parent or child) for another. We may join groups of individuals with a common interest or cause and so, to a certain extent, allow our identity to be subsumed in the cooperative effort. In the most intimate of dialogues and associations with others, we may well feel as if we are less a distinct self and more a part of a larger consciousness, a communal awareness, that is not localized within any one brain. Such experiences make it much easier to conceive of what becoming someone else is like. But as soon as we slip back into our normal I-mode again, we lose this ability to see beyond our present selves.

Most of the time, with the apparent solidity and uniqueness of the self at the forefront of our minds, we suppose there can be only two possibilities for the future. These are that we carry on as we are, albeit possibly in some less material form, or that after death there is nothing. However, as we have seen, science and logic point compellingly to a third option—that while particular personal identities come and go, subjective continuity, the feeling of being someone, does not end with our death. A useful analogy is to think of a chain of volcanic islands in the middle of the ocean. At surface level, the islands appear completely separate and distinct. But at a deeper level, under the ocean, it becomes clear that the islands are part of a single mass and have a common origin—their individuality is an illusion.

Do these ideas amount to a theory of reincarnation? The answer depends very much on what we mean by this term. The picture of death being presented here is not one in which "we" survive or carry through any memories whatever of our present existence. Death is total amnesia *plus* total dissolution of our bodies and brains. As a result, when we die, not only will there be an internal break with who we once were, as there was for Patsy Cannon and Linda Macdonald, but there will also be no physical link between the old self and any new one that follows by which an objective observer might trace a lineage of "yous." The experience of physical death could be closely simulated, for example, by a total amnesia victim who, after her accident, recovered in a place surrounded by people who had not known her previous self and who, therefore, could not "re-mind" her of who had previously occupied her body. In fact, situations like this do sometimes arise when people have "fugues"— passages in their lives when they suddenly forget who they are (or were) and find themselves (if the pun can be excused) in an unfamiliar place among people they have never seen before. To the victim of a fugue it is as if they had been suddenly born as an adult with a general understanding of language and the world but without any inkling of their own identity.

So, reincarnation? Yes and no. Death defines the ultimate limits of selves and exposes how fragile, artificial, and essentially unimportant these creations of the living human brain really are. Will you live again? Once more, it is the present self-in-charge that wants to know. And perhaps the best, most reassuring answer we can give it is that death is like a spring cleaning of the mind, a replacement of body and brain—the opportunity to start again and see the world through a fresh pair of eyes. You *will* live again. But it will seem, as always, as if it were for the first time.

People often wonder: Is there a purpose to life? Are we here for a reason? Or are we trivial bystanders—brief, tiny sparks of awareness in a universe so vast and ancient that it is wholly indifferent to our presence? In seeking the answers to these questions we shall need to broaden the scope of our inquiry, beyond brain science, to include two seemingly very disparate worldviews: those of modern physics and of mysticism. This will lead us to consider more deeply the nature of consciousness and its relationship with the cosmos as a whole. And so, eventually, we shall come back to look at ourselves—but perhaps in a new light, not as frail individuals limited by small, uncertain lives, but as eternal participants in a much greater adventure that extends throughout time and space.

Part II

BEYOND THE FRONTIERS OF THE SELF

Who need be afraid of the merge?

—*Walt Whitman*, Leaves of Grass

9

SCIENCE AND THE
SUBJECTIVE

> Matter is less material and the mind less spiritual than is generally supposed. The habitual separation of physics and psychology, mind and matter is metaphysically indefensible.
>
> —*Bertrand Russell*

We live in a culture dominated by scientific thinking: by analysis and the partitioning of knowledge. So it is curious to find that science has never really taken root except among peoples who were strongly influenced by the Greeks. All of the other great cultural traditions around the world, particularly those of India and China, have evolved along quite different lines from our own. And while they have spawned artists, philosophers, and poets in great abundance, they have produced no Darwins, no Newtons. It seems strange to us, as if these otherwise marvelously talented folk suffered from some kind of racial myopia which prevented them from seeing how to properly understand the universe, to take it apart, as we do, to reveal the cogs, levers, and springs that make it tick. Shouldn't it be obvious to any intelligent, civilized person—to any child who has dismantled an old clock—that science is the best way, perhaps the *only* way, to discover how things really are? Yet we need to remember the extent of our own conditioning: from an early age, we are inculcated with a certain approach to looking at nature. We have a very specific attitude and perspective on the world encoded in our brains. And this makes it hard for us to appreciate that there may be other, perhaps equally valid ways of apprehending reality.

The wellspring of science can be traced to Ionia (in present-day Turkey), on the east coast of the Aegean, in the sixth century B.C. Here the sages of the Milesian school of philosophy established as their goal the discovery of the essential nature, or true constitution of things, which they called *physis*. Yet they were certainly not physicists in the modern sense because their speculations roamed freely over subject matter that today would be considered not only scientific but also philosophical and religious. To later Greeks they were known as "hylozoists," or "those who believe that matter is alive," since as far as the Milesians were concerned, life and nonlife, matter and spirit, were all one. Such a unified outlook is unmistakably mystical in flavor. And it is especially interesting and appropriate, in the light of recent developments, that physics, and Western science in general, should have had such a source.

The mystical attitude to understanding the world was even more evident in the work of Heraclitus of Ephesus. Although Heraclitus accepted the Ionian "physicists'" idea of the wholeness of nature, he was strongly opposed to the reality of Being—the endurance of objects—which they upheld. For Heraclitus, there was only Becoming, a continuous flow and change in all things which he saw as arising from the endless cyclic interplay of opposites. Two opposites comprised a unity which Heraclitus called the Logos. But this was a unity soon to be broken—and with it the monistic and organic tradition of the first period of Greek philosophy.

The split was started by the Eleatic school in southern Italy, which assumed that above all gods and men a divine principle operated. To begin with, this principle was equated with the totality of the universe, but later its identity shifted to that of an intelligent and personal God who orchestrated the cosmos from outside. So began a trend of thought which was to have far-reaching consequences. It would lead, in time, to the divorce of mind and matter, of subject and object, and to a profoundly dualistic mentality that pervaded all future Western culture.

A further step along the road to dualism was taken by Parmenides of Elea, who rejected Heraclitus's notion of continual Becoming. Parmenides argued that change was logically impossible and that its appearance was a mere illusion of the senses. It then fell upon the Greek philosophers of the fifth century B.C. to try to reconcile the sharply contrasting views of Parmenides (unchangeable Being) and Heraclitus (eternal Becoming). This led to the idea that Being is represented by certain indestructible substances that form the material basis of the universe, while Becoming—change—comes about as these substances mix and separate. A further development was the notion of the atom as the smallest indivisible unit of matter. And the key point here is that the Greek atomists, led by Leucippus and Democritus, drew a sharp distinction between spirit and matter, depicting the latter as being made up purely of passive and inanimate particles moving in the void. Any spiritual element was thus effectively sucked out of the material universe and confined to a realm of its own.

In the Hellenistic age which followed the Classical period of Greece, in the fourth and third centuries B.C., opinion tended to polarize around two principal worldviews. The Epicureans favored a radical form of atomism, rejecting any need for spiritual intervention and placing the gods in the empty space between worlds where they were aloof from the affairs of man. The Stoics, on the other hand, taught that the world is governed by unbreakable natural laws that were laid down by God. Furthermore, they held that the soul is what makes a human being cohere: that it is some subtle essence diffused throughout a person's frame, much as God, according to their belief, is diffused throughout the world. In the Epicurean view, perception, not the soul, is the source of true and indisputable information. Against this the Stoics maintained that the soul is what both observes and reasons. These contrasting positions can be seen as an early stage in the development of the debate that continues to this day between science and religion about the fundamental nature of the world.

From the Greeks in general, then, we have inherited a deeply dualistic mind-set, an instinctive, urgent tendency to divide everything into two contrasting, often mutually exclusive, aspects: matter and mind, actual and ideal, observed and theoretical, and, more generally, this and that, and right and wrong. But the specific direction of Western thought for many centuries to come was determined largely by one man. Aristotle, tutor to Alexander the Great and founder of the Lyceum school in Athens, whose ideas inspired the Stoics, was an energetic collector and organizer of facts, especially biological facts. Much of his time was spent studying the various forms of animals and plants in minute detail with a view to classifying them, and his "scale of nature" became a standard taxonomic reference for many future generations.

Aristotle's genius and contributions were immense. But for two reasons he is judged, perhaps unfairly, to have had a disastrous effect on the progress of science. First, he believed passionately in teleology, the doctrine of final causes, which maintains that all things—people, lower forms of life, and inanimate objects alike—move unerringly toward a predetermined goal, a perfect final state (like one of Plato's Forms). With this notion in mind it would have seemed pointless to him to try to uncover relationships in nature because, as he saw it, causes and effects were inherent properties of things. Therefore, whatever conclusions he drew, whatever theories he held—and he held many—he never bothered to check them by experiment. Second, despite all the work he did in classifying the material world, he regarded this to be of far less importance than problems related to the human soul and the contemplation of God's perfection. Not surprisingly then, in constructing its own cosmology and scheme of nature, the Christian Church found Aristotle's views both appealing and appropriate. And so it was through the Church's all-pervasive and intimidating power that the seriously flawed doctrines of Aristotle survived, as fossilized relics, through to the end of the Middle Ages. Effectively, the pursuit of science was put on hold for two thousand years.

Those who eventually began to challenge Aristotelianism, in Renaissance times, placed their very lives at risk. And, indeed, Giordano Bruno, a Dominican monk, was executed for daring to voice his liberal cosmological views. But in the end, despite the threats of torture and death made to other freethinkers of this time, the new spirit of inquiry proved impossible to extinguish.

Spearheading the revolution, in the early years of the seventeenth century, was the Italian Galileo Galilei, the first true scientific researcher. In fact, he was never referred to as a scientist in his day for the simple reason that the word "scientist" only entered our vocabulary in 1834, courtesy of the Cambridge University philosopher William Whewell. Galileo, like Newton and the other great investigators around this time, considered himself to be a natural philosopher. But Galileo *was* a scientist in the contemporary sense in that he exposed his hypotheses to the possibility of being falsified through carefully controlled experiments. He directed his attention upon a little bit of the world that interested him—a pendulum, perhaps, or a falling object—and then strove to limit or simplify all extraneous influences on his chosen experimental setup.

Central to this methodology was Galileo's precise distinction, first made public in 1623, between "primary" and "secondary" qualities. This was a vital step in establishing a clear future direction for science, but it was based upon a reaffirmation of the old Greek way of splitting the world in two. Primary qualities were those, such as mass, distance, and time, that could be measured by some suitable instrument. Only these, Galileo maintained, were amenable to scientific study because only these could be treated as if they were independent of the observer. A primary quality can be measured and therefore described by a number in some appropriate system of units—ten grams, six thousand miles, 58.3 seconds, and so on. By contrast, secondary qualities, such as color and love, cannot be reduced to an empirical form and so were deemed to fall outside science's domain.

Galileo's cleaving of nature was manifestly Greek in origin. But he and the other new-wave Renaissance thinkers of sixteenth and seventeenth century Europe tightened the focus of science to mean the systematic study of the *material* universe—the universe of things presumed to exist independently of the mind. Henceforth, if science did refer to color, it would not officially be in terms of red or yellow or blue, but in terms of the wavelength of light, a measurable property. And if science did eventually attempt to analyze human emotions, then it would be in terms of quantifiable, physiological events in the brain—electrical potentials, the timings of synaptic firings, the rate of movement of chemicals, and so on. The same sharp distinction between primary (objective) and secondary (subjective) qualities that Galileo brought to science, Descartes, with his separation of matter (*res extensa*) and mind (*res cogitans*) introduced to philosophy. And so the scene was set for the emergence of the worldview commonly held in the West today.

Previously, in ancient and medieval times, the universe had seemed organismic; all matter had been held to be living and interconnected. But the clear Cartesian division between subject and object allowed scientists to treat matter as dead and completely separate from themselves, and to envision the universe as a plethora of different objects assembled into a huge machine. At the same time, this was paralleled by the concept of a supervisory God who ruled the world externally and remotely. The laws of nature sought by scientists were thus seen, ultimately, as being the laws of God, eternal and inviolable, to which the world was subjected. This religious component was important because the influence of the Church, though weakened, was still far-reaching. And men such as Newton and, later, Pascal and Mendel, to name but a few, were devout Christians (as, too, are a considerable number of present-day scientists). The separation of matter and spirit allowed them to keep faith both in science and God, without the risk of compromise to either.

That the human body itself was nothing more than an object, a machine, amenable to scientific investigation was an idea promulgated by the English philosopher Thomas Hobbes, who had met Galileo in Italy in 1635. Hobbes's view was inspired to a large extent by the discovery of the circulation of blood by William Harvey, physician to Elizabeth the First. Previously, people had believed in Aristotle's and Galen's theory that the blood ebbed and flowed to and from the same vessels, giving rise to "animal spirits" that differed in different organs. But Harvey's new mechanistic portrayal of the heart as a pump, and blood vessels as a complex system of tubes and valves, had a deep effect on philosophers of the time. Hobbes simply generalized the image to the whole human being. And thus man took on a new appearance, as a complex mechanism, his behavior potentially explicable in terms of mechanical laws.

There is, undoubtedly, a cold and remote feel to the universe as cast by post-Renaissance science. Though perfect and beautiful in its way, it is an austere abstraction, devoid of "reality tone"—of the vibrant sensations and feelings that are the most immediate aspects of our concern. And this sterile scientific depiction of the cosmos has remained with us to this day. As one of the leading theoreticians of the twentieth century, the Austrian physicist Erwin Schrödinger, remarked:

> [The scientific picture] gives us a lot of factual information, puts all our experience in magnificent order, but it is ghastly silent about all and sundry that is really near our heart, that really matters to us. It cannot tell us a word about red and blue, bitter and sweet, physical pain and physical delight; it knows nothing of beautiful and ugly, good or bad, God and eternity. Science sometimes pretends to answer questions in these domains, but the answers are often so silly that we are not inclined to take them seriously.

In confining its attentions exclusively to the objective world, science has become detached from the inner, experiential world of the mind. It may tell you *how* you see but is mute on the topic of *what it is like* to see. In *An Experiment with Time*, an intriguing book about dreams, time, and immortality, first published in 1927, the English writer John William Dunne imagines a situation in which a person who has been totally blind since birth is trying to learn about *redness* through the language of physics. As Dunne points out:

> You might talk to him of particles . . . and describe these as oscillating, spinning, circling, colliding, and rebounding in any kind of complicated dance you cared to imagine. . . . You might speak of waves—big waves, little waves, long waves, and short waves. . . . You might hark back to the older physics and descant upon forces . . . , magnetic, electrical, and gravitational; or you might plunge forward into the newer physics. . . . And you might hold forth upon such lines until exhaustion supervened,

> while the blind man nodded and smiled appre-
> ciation; but it is obvious that, at the end of it all,
> he would have no more suspicion of what it is
> that . . . you immediately experience when you
> look at a field poppy than he had at the outset.

Science has yielded startling insights into the mathematical infrastructure of the world—the hidden rules by which stones fall, planets
orbit, electrons whirl, and stars explode. But in order to do this it has
had first to expunge everything that refuses to succumb to description
by formulas. From the start, then, science renounces all interest in
such matters as are essentially dependent on the presence of a human
observer. It sets out to investigate what is assumed *would* be the case
if we didn't exist. Yet the underlying weakness of this approach was
exposed a long time ago. As early as 420 B.C., Democritus realized
that in studying nature both reason *and* the senses must be brought to
bear. In the case of atoms, for instance, they are assumed to have none
of the sensual qualities which are the common everyday experience of
human beings. Yet it is precisely *because* of these qualities that we are
able to infer the existence of atoms. Schrödinger again:

> So we are faced with the following remarkable
> situation. While the stuff from which our world
> picture is built is yielded exclusively by the
> sense organs as organs of the mind, so that
> every man's world picture is and always
> remains a construct of his mind and cannot be
> proved to have any other existence, yet the
> conscious mind itself remains a stranger within
> that construct, it has no living space in it, you
> can spot it nowhere in space.

Two and a half thousand years have taken us from Greek intellec-
tualism to technological mastery over the planet. But this impressive
conquest of nature has been at the cost of estranging us—our conscious selves—from the universe that is our birthplace and home.
Galileo and the other early scientists portrayed the world of nature as

being a realm of objects set over and against the mind. And yet it is clear that every datum used by science in formulating its supposedly objective worldview comes in through the human senses. Every attempt at making an impartial objective observation is foiled at the outset and becomes, instead, a *subject* of our personal attention. The human observer cannot be left out of the reckoning or be reduced to insignificance, because he or she is the very means by which science is prosecuted. Scientific experimentation and theorizing are conducted necessarily within the emotion-filled, perception-charged, *conscious* environment of the human mind. And this is a fact that scientists readily admit. Einstein, for instance, often acknowledged his debt to intuition, inspiration, and a sense of irrational awe in the wonder of things. "In every true search of Nature there is a kind of religious reverence," he once said. And again: "Imagination is more important than knowledge." Nevertheless, as a society, we find ourselves in a strange situation. To comprehend the nature of things, our reason has proposed a view of the world which fails to account for the sense impressions upon which its conclusions rest.

Nor is this omission of the subjective something that we can conveniently overlook. The experience of being conscious, of having perceptions and emotions, is an experience with which we are all intimately familiar. It is central and indispensable to our lives. Imagine if you could never again smell a rose, or fresh-cut grass, or newly baked bread. Would you feel adequately compensated for this loss if instead you could fully understand the chemical and physical processes taking place in the olfactory regions of your brain? Would you be willing to trade your ability to perceive sounds and enjoy music for a knowledge of what happens to your neurons when auditory signals arrive from your inner ear? The science of neurology may be fascinating. But what really matters to us (even to neurologists!) at heart is the act of being aware and perceiving—of being conscious in the universe. And it is this whole vital aspect of the world that science simply fails to address. We are cast by science as mere observing machines, convenient tools for gathering data about a universe so vast and ancient that by comparison we seem utterly insignificant.

Science seeks to uncover patterns and connections in nature by treating the world as if it had entirely distinct objective and subjective components. Only the objective component, the universe presumed to exist independently of the human mind and senses, is considered accessible to scientific analysis. But more than this, the objective aspect of the world is taken by science to be the world *as it actually is,* undistorted by the act of bringing "outside" phenomena into our awareness. Small wonder, then, that we, as experiencing beings, are missing from our physical portrait of nature; we intentionally leave ourselves out from the start.

Yet, oddly enough, we tend to forget this. We begin by purposely exiling ourselves, our feelings, the whole of the subjective, from the scientific cosmos, but then we wonder why science has nothing to say about us, other than that we are sophisticated, motile lumps of matter. We fail to grasp properly the fact that this is bound to happen, that once the world has been translated or reduced to pure number it will inevitably be devoid of human value and meaning. Nor is there anything wrong with this, providing we appreciate the bounds within which contemporary science operates.

Science deals with measurable quantities as if they exist independently, "out there," irrespective of whether we choose to observe them or not. But we need to keep firmly in mind how we came to know about these quantities in the first place. Clearly, it was by *experiencing* them. Our ancestors didn't build clocks on the off chance that there might be something like time which they would then be able to measure. They *felt* change and progression in their daily lives, they felt duration, the cycle of the seasons and of life and death; the clocks came later. And likewise, distance wasn't discovered by chance with yardsticks. It was *sensed,* it came into people's awareness as a feeling of the separation between things. Thus, that whole aspect of the world which science tries so assiduously to ignore—the subjective—is in fact the very means by which the phenomena explored by science are initially brought to its attention. Viewed in this light, Galileo's categorization seems curiously reversed: our primary and immediate experience is actually subjective, this experience being then projected outward as the expression of a mental model upon which our culture is generally agreed. The subjective cannot be dismissed as a mere derivative or aside. On the contrary, it is inextricably bound up with the world in which we find ourselves—a fact that has recently been demonstrated in the most startling and unexpected way.

10

MATTERS OF CONSCIOUSNESS

I think I can safely say that nobody understands quantum mechanics.

—*Richard Feynman*

A century ago, science might still have claimed confidently that, as far as the universe as a whole is concerned, consciousness appears to have no special relevance. But not any longer. By peering into the workings of nature at the very smallest of scales—at or below the dimensions of the atom—physicists have uncovered what appears to be an intimate connection between the mind of conscious observers and the bringing into being of what is real.

Around the end of the nineteenth century, it became clear that classical, Newtonian science was in serious trouble. It appeared unable to account for some of the observed properties of radiation given off when matter is heated. The only way to bring theory back into line with this aspect of the world seemed to be by making an astonishing and, at the time, seemingly ad hoc assumption: namely, that energy could only be traded back and forth in discrete packets. An electron, for instance, in the outer part of an atom, could not just gain or lose energy indiscriminately. It had to do so in definite, pre-scribed amounts that came to be known as "quanta." The man who first made this bold proposal in 1900, the German physicist Max Planck, was not at all happy with the idea of quantized energy. Nor were his contemporaries, and, to begin with, Planck's quantum theory, which was simply patched onto classical physics in an effort to repair the dangerous hole that had opened up, failed to make much of an impression. It was only in 1905, when Einstein brilliantly accounted for the so-called photoelectric effect in terms of quanta of light kicking electrons out of a metal surface, that the idea really caught hold.

Einstein showed that although light generally behaves as if it were made of waves, it can at times behave instead as if it consists of a stream of particles—quanta of light, or photons. His successful explanation of the photoelectric effect using this idea focused the attention of physicists on Planck's quantum theory and led to its rapid development into an entirely new and revolutionary field of modern science known as quantum mechanics.

Soon, researchers found themselves staring into the maws of a monstrous paradox. For not only light, it transpired, revealed this curious wave-particle duality. So, too, did particles of matter. Electrons and every other material constituent of the subatomic world apparently exhibited a schizoid nature. Whereas on some occasions an electron would act as a tiny speck or bullet of matter, on other occasions it would just as obviously manifest itself as a wave.

At first, it was suspected that the wave associated with a subatomic particle might be a physical effect—a kind of smearing out of the particle's substance or of the electrical charge which it carried. According to this idea, the smeared-out particle would have to condense in an instant at a single point as soon as any attempt was made to detect it. But such instantaneous shrinkage would run counter to Einstein's special theory of relativity, which forbids matter and energy to be accelerated to a speed greater than that of light. Therefore an alternative proposal was put forward by the German physicist Max Born in 1926. Born suggested that the wave associated with a subatomic particle was not physical at all but *mathematical;* it was a wave of probability. It could be described by a mathematical artifact called the "wave function," which effectively gave the odds of finding the particle at any given point in space and time should an attempt be made to look for it. Einstein railed against such a blatant probabilistic notion at the heart of nature and issued his now-famous proclamation "I shall never believe that God plays dice with the world." But most of his contemporaries disagreed with him, quantum uncertainty won the day, and mainstream science began to acquaint itself with the bizarre idea that, at its most basic level, the material universe is not concrete and well determined but, on the contrary, is curiously abstract and conditional.

It was no longer meaningful to think of an electron, for instance, as always being definitely somewhere and "somewhen" in between the times when it was being observed. Unless an attempt was made to detect it, the sum total of what was and could be known about the whereabouts of a particle was contained in its wave function—a purely statistical description.

It could not be claimed, in the new quantum picture of the world, that particles even truly *exist* outside of our observations of them. They have no independent, enduring reality in the familiar classical sense of being like tiny beads of matter with a definite (if not necessarily known) location in space and time. The distinguished American physicist John Wheeler has expressed the central quantum mystery in these terms:

> Nothing is more important about the quantum principle than this, that it destroys the concept of the world as "sitting out there," with the observer safely separated from it by a 20 centimeter slab of plate glass. Even to observe so minuscule an object as an electron, he must shatter the glass. He must reach in. He must install his chosen measuring equipment. . . . The measurement changes the state of the electron. The universe will never afterward be the same. To describe what has happened, one has to cross out that old word "observer" and put in its place the new word "participator." In some strange sense the universe is a participatory universe.

Somehow, through the act of observation, subatomic particles are briefly summoned out of a kind of mathematical never-never land of potentiality and possibility into the solid world of tangible things and events. In quantum parlance, an observation results in the "collapse" of the wave function—the instantaneous telescoping-down of the probability spread to a localized point, a real particle. But what counts as a valid observation in this respect? Who or what qualifies as an effective quantum observer—a measuring instrument such as a Geiger counter, a human being, a committee of people? No one is sure. But the most widely accepted viewpoint, first advocated by the Danish physicist Niels Bohr and referred to as the Copenhagen interpretation, is that the sudden change in character or collapse of the wave function is brought about, ultimately, by *conscious* observership—the registering of an event, such as the reading of an instrument, in the mind.

This is a staggering conclusion. And it appears the more so when one remembers that *all of the material universe is comprised of sub-atomic particles*. Not one of these particles, according to modern physics, can be "actualized," or made properly real, without an observation that collapses the wave function. Almost unbelievably, our most fundamental branch of science implies that what had previously been assumed to be a concrete, objective world *cannot even be said to exist* outside of the subjective act of observation. Furthermore, if the Copenhagen interpretation is correct, then it is the mind—the mirror in which the object is reflected and becomes the subject—that serves as the essential link between mathematical possibility and physical actuality.

The intervention of mind in the affairs of the subatomic world was spectacularly demonstrated a few years ago. In 1977, B. Misra and George Sudarshan at the University of Texas showed theoretically that the decay of an unstable particle—say, a radioactive nucleus—is suppressed by the act of observation. Like any quantum system, an unstable particle is described as fully as it can be by its wave function. Initially, this is concentrated around the undecayed state. But as time goes on, the wave function spreads out into the decayed state so that the probability of decay gradually increases. Misra and Sudarshan showed that every time an observation is made it causes the wave function to snap back, or collapse, to the undecayed state. The more frequent the observations, the less likely the decay. And if the observations come so close together that they are virtually continuous then, as in the case of the proverbial watched pot that never boils, the decay simply doesn't happen. This astonishing prediction was verified by measurements carried out by David Winehead and colleagues at the National Institute of Standards and Technology, Boulder, Colorado, in 1990, using a sample of beryllium ions.

An even more remarkable insight into the strangeness of the quantum world is provided by a modified version of the famous double-slit experiment. The original, "classical" form of this experiment was first conducted in the early nineteenth century by the English physicist Thomas Young. He showed that if a beam of light is split in two by shining it onto a pair of narrow slits, an interference pattern of alternating light and dark bands is created when the beams recombine on the other side and are allowed to fall onto a screen. Interference is exclusively a wave phenomenon and so its appearance clearly reveals light to have wavelike characteristics. But the same experimental setup in a more sophisticated form can be used to show light behaving either in a wavelike or a particlelike way.

Quantum mechanics makes a remarkable prediction about the double-slit experiment. It says that even if photons are allowed to pass through the slits *one at a time*, an interference pattern will still gradually build up. This prediction is perhaps *the* outstanding quantum mystery because, no matter how we try to imagine what is going on in the interval between when a single photon leaves its source and when it arrives at the screen, we cannot make sense of the situation that reality presents us with. In our minds, a photon *must* be either a particle or a wave. If it leaves its source as a particle and passes through just one of the slits as a particle, then how on earth, we wonder, can it subsequently manage to interfere with itself as if it had gone through both slits as a wave? We might suppose that we could get to the bottom of the mystery by closely monitoring the progress of each photon through the apparatus—and, in particular, if we arrange to detect which of the two slits each photon passes through. But nature forbids us to peek behind the scenes in an attempt, as we see it, to find out what is "really" happening without irreversibly *changing* what is happening. If we arrange to track the path of each photon, quantum theory predicts, the interference pattern will be destroyed. In other words, simply by pinning down which slit each photon passes through, we force the experimental system as a whole to make a definite decision between particlelike and wavelike behavior in favor of the former. Our intrusion causes the interference pattern to vanish and be replaced instead simply by two bright lines corresponding to the images of the slits formed by photons striking the screen as if they were particles traveling in straight lines from the source. The American physicist Richard Feynman put forward this basic rule: if the paths of photons are distinguishable, then light behaves as particles; if they are indistinguishable, then light behaves as waves. And every experiment carried out in recent years to test this fundamental prediction has upheld it beyond a shadow of a doubt.

What does this mean? Apparently, just by inquiring into the state of a system we inevitably and profoundly affect the very nature of that system. The desire to have a yes-no, either-or, particle-wave determination actually influences reality in a most fundamental way. More to the point, our intervention fragments the continuous wavelike nature of the world into separate, discrete particles. Just as with words and analysis on a macroscopic scale we break our surroundings down into isolated objects, so with our objective intrusions at the subatomic scale we force a dualistic split from the normal, ongoing state of continuity to a transient state of individualism.

Such a conclusion is far-reaching enough. But recent experiments have led to even more sensational revelations about the world in which we live, again in full accord with the expectations of quantum theory. These experiments have demonstrated that not only is observership a mandatory requirement for making reality tangible, but every component of the universe—down to the level of each individual subatomic particle—is in some peculiar sense immediately "aware" of what is going on around it. The very idea of subatomic particles having an elementary form of consciousness strains credibility to breaking point. And although there is great excitement among the physicists involved in this field, there is also profound bewilderment at the implications of the results they are uncovering.

Among the most extraordinary dramatizations of quantum weirdness to date have been a number of experiments involving what physicists have dubbed "quantum erasers." These are extensions and elaborations of the basic double-slit apparatus, the first of which was successfully implemented at the University of California, Berkeley, by Raymond Chiao and his team in 1992.

The idea behind the quantum eraser is to make the paths of photons initially distinguishable, but then erase that "which-path" information before the light actually reaches the screen. If an interference pattern reappears then it is a clear indication that a photon approaching the slits somehow "knows" whether or not there is an eraser further down the line, so it can decide whether to pass through both slits as a wave or through only one slit as a particle. The existence of this advance knowledge or remote sensing was precisely what the Berkeley team confirmed in its inaugural quantum eraser experiments.

More recently, a team at the University of Innsbruck, in Austria, has taken work in this direction an important step further. In particular, these researchers have shown clearly that the "which-path" information is not carried by what might be called the interfering photon itself. Rather it is carried by a second photon created, in the first stage of the apparatus, as a twin of the first and directed along a different path. The Innsbruck experiment was conducted in such a way that it elegantly demonstrated not only that the second photon somehow knew what lay ahead, but also that it had instantaneous access to information about its twin's physical status. This latter remarkable property is known to quantum physicists as "nonlocality."

Bluntly, nonlocality amounts to zero-delay communication between two particles no matter what their separation distance. It was first derived by Einstein as a fundamental prediction of the equations of quantum mechanics—and was used, in fact, by Einstein as an argument against the completeness of quantum theory. It was absurd, Einstein said, to imagine that one of a pair of particles, which might be light-years away from its partner, could effectively react immediately to a change in the state of its twin. This led to a statement of the so-called Einstein-Podolsky-Rosen (EPR) effect and the throwing down of a gauntlet to quantum physicists to demonstrate its reality.

Say an atom emits two photons simultaneously and in different directions. One way to define the state of these photons is by their polarization, that is, the direction in which the electric field associated with them is vibrating. Quantum theory predicts that, as soon as an observation is made, one of the photons emitted from the atom would be found to have a definite "up" or "down" polarization. This would also fix the direction of polarization of its twin, since, for conservation reasons, this would have to be in the opposite sense. However, unless and until such a measurement is carried out, the quantum state of the photons would be undefined—not just unknown, but physically undetermined. The EPR effect is that the fixing of the state of polarization of one of the pair of photons instaneously causes the polarization state of its partner to be decided, irrespective of the distance between the particles. Einstein argued that such an effect, implying faster than light travel, is nonsensical and would never be vindicated. But as the Innsbruck quantum eraser experiments and other recent investigations have shown it is real and inescapable. The quantum world is in practice every bit as outrageous as its mathematical formalism suggests.

Slowly, and reluctantly, science is trying to come to terms with the truths it has found at nature's heart. Out of matter is made mind, which sees and interprets the world and thereby makes matter real. The universe creates itself out of itself, moment by moment, through a mutual interaction between subject and object. Sir Arthur Eddington put it this way:

> We have found that where science has progressed the furthest, the mind has but regained from nature that which the mind has put into nature. We have found a strange footprint on the shores of the unknown. We have devised profound theories, one after another, to account for its origin. At last, we have succeeded in reconstructing the creature that made the footprint. And lo! it is our own.

Incredibly, modern physics, which is the most advanced product of our dualistic way of thinking, has shown that dualism is no longer tenable. Consciousness is an inextricable and essential property of the real world. Subject and object cannot be treated apart; there is no gap, no delay, no *difference* in the real world between being and experiencing. There is no existence without the conscious act.

Nor, it seems, can there be existence without contingency. Everything and every event is meaningful only in how it stands in direct relationship to the rest of the cosmos. Whereas previously, under Newtonian physics, we were able to sustain a belief in the separate reality of particles and waves, rest and motion, energy and mass, time and space, now we have no such confidence. Einstein showed that rest and motion are relative concepts, while energy and mass, and time and space, are interchangeable. Quantum physicists have discovered that, at its most fundamental level, the world cannot be accurately viewed as a complex of distinct things. What we took to be sharply bounded objects—particles of matter—have turned out to be interwoven, overlapping aspects of each other. Every thing and every event in the universe seems to be attached to an all-embracing, quivering web that interconnects it with every other thing and event. Nothing stands apart. The cosmos as now portrayed by relativity and quantum mechanics is less like a loose collection of jiggling billiard balls and more reminiscent of a single, giant universal field—an unbreakable unity which Alfred North Whitehead dubbed "the seamless coat of the universe."

Physicists have caught a glimpse of the infrastructure of the *real* world. Yet oddly enough, they have been able to do this only through the use of advanced technology. And all of our technology—the panoply of tools and devices at our disposal—has been developed starting from the assumption that the world *can* be taken apart and analyzed. Our map-making, bounding, and classifying is what has given us power over nature. But now, because of the sophisticated technology that has allowed us to experimentally probe the subatomic domain, we have found that reality has no boundaries.

11

EAST WORLD

Anthropology has taught us that the world is differently defined in different places ... The very metaphysical presuppositions differ: space does not conform to Euclidean geometry, time does not form a continuous unidirectional flow, causation does not conform to Aristotelian logic, man is not differentiated from non-man or life from death, as in our world. ... The central importance of entering into worlds other than our own ... lies in the fact that the experience leads us to understand that our own world is also a cultural construct.

—*Carlos Castaneda*, The Teachings of
Don Juan

The basic oneness of the universe as revealed by quantum mechanics is also the central characteristic of the mystical experience. And so, after more than two thousand years, we Westerners have come back full circle to a unified vision of the world that a holistic Greek thinker such as Heraclitus would have recognized immediately. More to the point, twentieth-century physics has finally caught up with the philosophy of the Far East—a fact not lost on some of the founding fathers of modern subatomic theory, including Bohr, Schrödinger, and the German physicist Werner Heisenberg. Bohr, for example, wrote:

> For a parallel to the lesson of atomic theory
> . . . [we must turn] to those kinds of episte-
> mological problems with which already
> thinkers like the Buddha and Lao-tzu have
> been confronted, when trying to harmonize our
> position as spectators and actors in the great
> drama of existence.

Similarly, Heisenberg remarked:

> The great scientific contribution in theoretical
> physics that has come from Japan since the last
> war may be an indication of a certain relation-
> ship between philosophical ideas in the tradi-
> tion of the Far East and the philosophical sub-
> stance of quantum theory.

And the mystical roots of contemporary subatomic theory may extend even further back. In his book *The Emperor's New Mind,* Oxford mathematician Roger Penrose points to the eccentric sixteenth-century mathematician Gerolamo Cardano, who discovered, almost without any help from others, the basic laws of probability and complex numbers that now underpin quantum mechanics. "Perhaps," writes Penrose, "Cardano's curious combination of a mystical and a scientifically rational personality allowed him to catch these first glimmerings of what developed to be one of the most powerful of mathematical conceptions."

In a sense, quantum mechanics has brought the conscious observer—ourselves—back into the universe with an important and potentially decisive role to play. This has profound philosophical implications. At the same time, the goings-on of the subatomic world seem very far removed from everyday life. We don't feel personally touched by them. And so, in practice, the revelations of the new physics of the ultrasmall, strange and wonderful though they may be, have had little effect on the common psyche. Nor, as a matter of fact, have they influenced much of the way that science in general is carried out. The standard scientific approach—even in experimental particle physics—is still to proceed as if there were an objective world out there independent of our senses and experience.

From an early age, our minds are rigorously conditioned to think of the world and ourselves in a highly specific way. And at the heart of our traditional Western outlook is dualism. It seems so natural, so right to us, because of our cultural and social training, to believe that the world has both an inner, mental component and an outer, material one. So we tacitly assume that through our (mental) will we move our (material) bodies and, by means of them, other material objects in the outside world. Likewise, objects coming into contact with our bodies give rise through the nerves to the experience of touch; vibrations in the air, when they reach the ear, cause the sensation of sound; and light particles, striking the eye, lead to the sensation of sight. It appears so transparently clear to us that this must represent the true state of affairs. But we forget, or never really consider, the depth of our conditioning. Being a product of a Greek-inspired culture and upbringing, we are programmed at the very level of our neurons, in the arrangement of our dendrites and synapses, to think in a dualistic way.

Every second of our lives we are constrained in what we see and in how we interpret and react to our surroundings by the biological and cultural mind-set we have inherited. We suppose ourselves to be very advanced in thought. But our thinking has matured only in certain specific directions, notably the scientific and technical, which are concerned with manipulating aspects of the objective world. We have become masters at understanding the relationships between different things. Yet this mastery has been won only at the cost of shattering the unity of nature. A passage from Lewis Carroll describes our predicament well:

"We actually made a map of the country, on
the scale of a *mile to a mile*!"

"Have you used it much?" I enquired.

"It has never been spread out, yet," said
Mein Herr: "the farmers objected: they said it
would cover the whole country, and shut out
the sunlight! So we now use the country itself,
as its own map, and I assure you it does nearly
as well."

In the West, we are very keen and adept at making maps—scientific maps of the reality in which we find ourselves. Boundaries, names, and labels have assumed with us enormous power. So we find ourselves inhabiting a world of bits and pieces, a world of apparently irreconcilable differences. And one of our principal misunderstandings stems from our use of the words "you" and "I." For what we fail to recognize, or have forgotten, is that "you" and "I" are purely constructs of our language, and of our linguistic interactions with others. "You" come about because we happen to be speaking English (or some similar tongue) and are therefore conforming to the rule that a verb must have a subject, and that processes are mysteriously initiated by pronouns. The syntax of Western language demands a clear indication of the subject-object relation. Therefore, every time we speak we reinforce our belief that every situation can be analyzed into a subject-predicate-object form. Our language forces us to be compulsive analyzers, to break down our experience of the world into composite elements. The fact that there might be entirely different modes of thinking usually escapes our attention. And yet such modes do exist.

A language that encourages less frequent use of "I's" and "yous" tends to downplay the role of the individual. In Japanese, for instance, the first or second person is often omitted as the subject of a sentence. Instead, it has to be inferred by context. The Japanese approach is not to point explicitly to the subject of an action, unless necessary, but rather to locate the individual in experience.

In Japanese, a single word may serve as a complete and sufficient statement. For example, a man might be walking in the quiet countryside, surrounded by tranquil autumn scenery, when a feeling comes to his mind—that of solitude. In our language, we would instinctively analyze this feeling, identify a subject and an object, and make a comment such as "I am feeling lonesome," or perhaps "The scenery is lonesome." Our expression of the sentiment would involve an immediate distancing of the perceiver from the perceived, or of the actor from the action. But this is not the way in Japanese. The man on his walk might simply say *"samishii"* (lonesome), thus projecting the experience immediately, nonjudgmentally, without analysis. Of course, in Western languages, too, people sometimes speak in abbreviated form. But when they do so, they are always conscious of the fact that what is being said is a shortened version of a more detailed description. The syntax of a language like English demands a subject-object declaration, either explicit or implied. Japanese, by contrast, does not insist upon the specification of an individual or an independent performer of deeds.

Language, culture, and a people's general mode of thought are bound up together in close, complex symbiosis. And whereas our Western upbringing teaches us to see the subject, the self, in sharp relief, the Japanese style is to give precedence to interconnectedness, to human relationships over the individual. This is reflected in the fact that personal pronouns are much more complicated in Japanese than in other languages. Special pronouns are required for superiors, equals, inferiors, intimates, and strangers, and if an improper choice is made, then confusion, difficulty, and that worst of all disasters for a Japanese, loss of face, may ensue. Therefore, every time a native speaker uses a personal pronoun, he or she must have at the forefront of their mind such relationships as rank and intimacy.

Number is not always made explicit in the grammar of Japanese sentences. Nor is a distinction always made between the singular and the plural forms of words. On the other hand, when a statement definitely *is* expressed in the plural, several kinds of plural may be used to suit different occasions. For example, *domo* and *tachi* are used for persons of equal or inferior status or for intimates, as in *funo-hito-domo* (boatman), *hito-tachi* (people), and *tomo-tachi* (friends). When respect must be shown, the suffix *gata* is used—*anatagata* (you), *sensei-gata* (teacher), and so on. In short, the use of plural suffixes is determined by the relationship of social ranks and the feeling that the speaker entertains for the persons of whom he is speaking. Again, this reveals the Japanese trait to think in terms of human connectivity or embeddedness rather than of separate selves in an objective world.

When this type of thinking has the upper hand, consciousness of the individual as a distinct entity becomes less clear-cut. There is a shift away from regarding each person as an objective unit and a greater tendency to emphasize the concrete immediacy of experience. The individual becomes not so much a distinct object or even a subject in the world, but rather an integral and inseparable part of life's ever-rolling stream.

With the self seen not in isolation, and individuality regarded as more of a negative than a positive trait, the character of a nation is fundamentally influenced. The Japanese have a favorite saying: "The nail that sticks up will be knocked down." Yet rather than being a sign of oppressiveness, this is intended to sum up the essential undesirability of acting in a self-willed way. Children are taught not to be different (rigorous conformity being especially obvious in the Japanese educational system) and not to express their emotions too openly or to make a fuss, even when confronted by considerable hardship or even disaster. The Japanese "poker face" is well known and the inscrutability of Orientals, in general, has become almost a caricature. But in fact, this quality of equanimity is a real and essential part of life in the Far East. The Japanese call it *gaman* and it was most evident recently in the aftermath of the Kobe earthquake. Outsiders watching the scenes of devastation on television were amazed at how calm and composed the victims of the quake remained and at how little looting took place. The behavior of the victims may have appeared unemotional and unfeeling, but it was in truth a remarkable demonstration of the inner strength and sense of quiet fatalism this people draws from its non-egocentric perspective of the world.

Death is regarded with none of the fear or despair that it often invokes in the West. Instead, the Japanese see it as a natural, integral part of life and are raised to approach death in a manner of calm, resigned dignity. This attitude has led, in the past, to some extraordinary Japanese customs including, in the most extreme case, that of hara-kiri (literally, "belly-cutting"), a ritual form of suicide practiced by members of the ruling class. An official or noble who had broken the law or been disloyal received a message from the emperor, couched always in sympathetic and gracious tones, courteously intimating that continued life was no longer an option. A jeweled dagger usually accompanied the message, and with this the custom was enacted with scrupulous formality. In his own baronial hall or in a temple, a dais three or four inches high was constructed. Upon this was laid a mat of red felt. The suicide, clothed in his ceremonial dress and accompanied by his second or *kaishaku,* took his place on the mat, with officials and friends arranged around him in a semicircle. After a minute's prayer the dagger was handed to him with many obeisances by the emperor's representative, and the doomed man made a public confession of his wrongdoing. He then stripped to the waist and tucked his wide sleeves under his knees to prevent him from collapsing onto his back, for it was only considered honorable for a Japanese noble to die falling forward. A moment later he plunged the dagger hard into his stomach below the waist on the left side, drew it across to the right, and, turning it, gave a slight upward cut. At the same time his faithful *kaishaku* leapt forward and brought his sword down on the outstretched neck. Obligatory hara-kiri like this became obsolete in the middle of the nineteenth century, and was abolished in 1868. However, voluntary hara-kiri continued and occasionally is carried out today. With such stoicism and selfless bravery in the face of death a deeply ingrained national trait, it becomes easier to understand how the infamous Japanese suicide pilots were able to complete their devastating missions during the war in the Pacific. Nowhere in the world is the ego kept smaller and weaker than in Japan; nowhere, therefore, is there considered to be less to lose in death.

This makes it hard, very hard, for us to penetrate fully the Japanese mind. And, failing to understand properly a system of thought and culture that is so totally different from our own, we tend to criticize it because it doesn't measure up to our standards. To us, the Japanese seem lacking in new ideas and individualism. We characterize them as being great copiers and adapters but poor innovators. And it is often pointed out how few Nobel prize–winners Japan has produced considering its technical prowess. Indeed, the Japanese have recently begun to find fault with themselves on these accounts, but only because they are becoming increasingly Westernized in their outlook. Traditionally, Japanese language and culture are rooted in man's direct experience of the world, so it naturally leans away from theoretical or systematic thinking. Whereas we put a high value on logic, analysis, and abstraction, in Japan there is more of a tendency toward the aesthetic, the intuitive, and the concrete.

And not just in Japan. Across the East, in India, China, and other neighboring lands, a traditional way of life has evolved that is remarkably at variance with our own.

*   *   *

To pick up but one strand in the labyrinthine history of Eastern thought: twenty-five hundred years ago, in China, lived Lao-tzu (pronounced "Low Dzoo"). In a sense he was the world's first dropout— an anticonventional, independent thinker. Very little is known of him, not even his proper name, since Lao-tzu means simply "old philosopher," or even "old child." He may, for all we know, have been more of a lineage, as perhaps Homer was, than a single person. What matters, though, is not his identity but the book he wrote, which for the past two millennia has been called the Tao Te Ching ("Dow they Jing")—the Tao Virtue Classic. Though only five thousand Chinese characters long, it gave birth to Taoism, shaped Buddhism, spawned Ch'an meditation, and encouraged the development of Chinese landscape painting. The fact that we know virtually nothing about its author is particularly appropriate since of the things Lao-tzu rejected, including violence, oppression, superstition, and imposed authority of any kind, he rejected none so insistently as the self.

At the heart of Lao-tzu's message is Tao, which translates as "the Way." By its nature, Tao is held to transcend description. As Lao-tzu said: "The Tao that can be expressed is not the eternal Tao." And so, if Lao-tzu's words are read with a view to logically analyzing them, the effort is bound to end in frustration. No matter how our intellect tries to sneak up on Tao we are ultimately repelled by a "not this, not that" force field. The Tao of Lao-tzu is reality as a whole—not a patchwork of diverse theories such as we have in the West to try to *explain* the universe. Tao is considered to be on top of everything as well as in everything. It is the nothing as well as the something; the nothing that penetrates all reality from the space inside atoms and between stars to that inner space of the human mind. Above all, Tao is not anything that we can apprehend or appreciate by thinking about it. In fact, Lao-tzu is at pains to reject learning and intellectual effort as a waste of time. Give up learning, he urges, and you will have no anxieties—a philosophy echoed in the Bible's plea for us to be as little children.

Tao stresses "nothing-doing," which means not projecting one's self as the center of all that happens, not manipulating people and things, not imposing one's will on events, not trying to control reality. And with regard to this last point, Lao-tzu counsels against naming things. Giving names is seen as an effort to subjugate reality through abstraction and analysis. To live in harmony, we shouldn't name things but intimate with them. Reality can never be captured in words, or as Lao-tzu put it: "He who speaks does not know, and he who knows does not speak."

Lao-tzu introduced a method of posing logical paradoxes as an antidote to naming and rational thought. Sometimes these are taken for subtle witticisms, but their purpose is not to entertain or even to state profound truths. Instead, it is effectively to bypass the intellect and illuminate by sudden flashes—to rend the veil of words.

Lao-tzu contrasts the contentment and effortlessness of moving with the flow of events in nature, with the tension of always acting *on* the world. He proposes an attitude toward life that is full of warmth, amusement, awe, and acceptance, and not a reaction against nature that continually strives to control, improve, and make the self the focus of attention. His philosophy, in fact, is the diametric opposite of that to which most Westerners adhere.

Even among those in the modern West who profess to be anti-establishment, who devote themselves to personal meditation, communal living, unorthodox appearance, and fighting environmental issues, the underlying ethos remains that the meaning of life is to be found through self-expression. In our culture, egocentrism is as much a trap for the outs as for the ins. From a Taoist perspective, we are the "do something" set. We fight against each other and the elemental forces of nature; we mess up the environment and then strive to fix it; we struggle to teach our children, to make them conform, and wrestle with the problems of delinquency and drugs; we match violence against society with organized violence sanctioned by society; we praise, blame, manipulate, and restrain. We even try to do good by controlling—by seeking peace and eliminating oppression. Lao-tzu's way, by contrast, is not to exert the will at all but to go with the flow, to simply experience reality—all of man's being and all of nature's working. In modern times, this approach was perhaps most conspicuously and successfully adopted by Mahatma Gandhi and his followers in their nonviolent resistance to British imperialism.

Presumably, the Way came about as a reaction to the patterns of self-willed violence, authoritarianism, and deceit that emerged as civilization took hold in ancient China. At the time of Lao-tzu there would still have been many people living under essentially Stone Age conditions, following a simple lifestyle based on daily sustenance and intimacy with nature. And Lao-tzu would have been able to compare firsthand this unforced approach to life with the problems that arose when people adopted a more self-centered, control-over-nature attitude in the towns and cities of Bronze Age culture.

In any event, Taoism took root and evolved to become one of the two principal Chinese worldviews, alongside Confucianism. In it, the universe was seen to be organic rather than mechanistic, spontaneous rather than contrived, circular rather than linear, synthetic rather than analytic. Unlike the conventional Western conception of God as someone or something "out there," Tao is inherent and pervasive. From a Western perspective, Tao may seem to be a negation of existence—a vacuum or void. And such an interpretation appears superficially justified by comments like those of the Taoist philosopher Chuang-tzu: "In the great beginning, there was nonbeing. It had neither being nor name." However, we have to be careful when judging other outlooks on life with our rigid dualistic mind-set. In the Western sense, being and nonbeing are mutually exclusive and opposed, whereas in the Chinese view they are mutually inclusive and complementary. As far as Taoism is concerned, the universe was not created or ordered by some external power. There is nothing external or apart from Tao. All exists together, at once, and the universe is considered to be inherently self-generating.

Because in Taoism man is embedded in nature, traditional Chinese art, culture, and language became imbued with this sense of identity between the experiencer and the experienced. The individual saw himself, as it were, wedded to his surroundings. And Taoist poetry and painting reflected this direct perception and conscious experience of nature's integrity. Chinese landscape painting, in its wonderful economy of brushstrokes, its subtlety, its sense of timelessness, and, above all, its use of space, portrays life as going beyond human definition and limits. Emptiness is seen to have as much importance as the scenery and the characters. As in the verses of William Wordsworth, the Taoists, in their art, grasped the world as a living organism, its streams and groves infused with a mysterious spirit, its rocks and mountains possessed with a life of their own.

Chinese religion and philosophy, if these terms are not too mis-
leading, reflect a "one-in-all" appreciation of the nature of reality and
self. In Taoism this view reached its most developed form before
migrating further East, to the islands of Japan. And in Japan we find
at last our true antithesis to Western analytical thought—that extraordinary thing which is not a philosophy or a religion, and which is
known as Zen.

12

NOW AND ZEN

There is something in Zen which we never
meet anywhere else in the history of human
thought and culture. It begins with rationalism
since it deals with such religio-philosophical
concepts as being and non-being, truth and
falsehood, the Buddha and *nirvana*; but after
the beginning is once made, the matter is
strangely switched off in a most unexpected
direction. To judge Zen by the ordinary standard of reasoning is altogether out of place, for
that standard is simply inapplicable. We must
acknowledge that our Western world view is
limited and that there is a much wider world
beyond our mentality.

—*Daisetz Teitaro Suzuki*

Zen is . . . difficult to talk about. So alien, indeed, is Zen to the analytical Western mind that it is perhaps easier to say what it is not. Zen
is not a faith because it doesn't urge the acceptance of any form of
dogma, creed, or object of worship. Nor is it antireligious or atheistic;
it simply makes no comment on the matter. Zen is not a philosophy or
even, to the Western mind, a form of mysticism. As we normally
understand it, mysticism starts with a separation of subject and object
and has as its goal the unification or reconciliation of this antithesis.
But Zen does not teach absorption, identification, or union of any

kind because all of these ideas are derived ultimately from a dualistic conception of life. If a label is needed that best approximates to the spirit of Zen then "dynamic intuition" is perhaps as close as we can come.

There is a saying in Zen: "The instant you speak about a thing you miss the mark." So, presumably, this saying has also missed the mark—and *this* one, too. Our endless analysis can lead us into all sorts of difficulties. But how can we break free of it? Living in a world of words and concepts and inherited beliefs, says Zen, we have lost the power to grasp reality directly. Our minds are permeated with notions of cause and effect, subject and object, being and nonbeing, life and death. Inevitably this leads to conflict and a feeling of personal detachment and alienation from the world. Zen's whole emphasis is on the experience of reality *as it is,* rather than the solution of problems that, in the end, arise merely from our mistaken beliefs.

Because it eschews the use of the intellect, Zen can appear nihilistic (which it is not) and elusive (which it is). Certainly, it would be hard to conceive of a system that stood in greater contrast with the logical, symbol-based formulations of contemporary science. More than any other product of the Oriental mind, Zen is convinced that no language or symbolic mapping of the world can come close to expressing the ultimate truth. As one of its famous exponents, Master Tokusan said: "All our understanding of the abstractions of philosophy is like a single hair in the vastness of space."

Zen claims no thought system of its own. Yet it is undeniably Buddhistic in origin and essence. And so before trying to appreciate its final flowering, it is worthwhile digging down to examine Zen's roots—roots which are set firmly in Indian soil, in the fertile ground of Mahayana Buddhism.

The Indian mind was, and is, different in character from the Chinese or Japanese. It is more expansive, more austerely intellectual, less concerned with practical, everyday affairs, and more inclined to complex exposition and exploration of ideas. Nowhere is this more evident than in the writings of the monk-philosopher Nagarjuna, a central figure in the development of Mahayana Buddhism and the founder, during the second century A.D., of the Madhyamika ("Middle Path") school. Nagarjuna wrote two key treatises, *Madhyamika Sastra* and

The Discourse of Twelve Sections, in he which probed the nature of reality with remarkably sophisticated dialectic and rigorous arguments. In a dazzling display of polemic against the prevailing metaphysical ideas of his time, he argued strongly that the basic quality of existence is relational. There is no soul, no thing, no concept independent of its context; all things are devoid of absolute reality and exist only relative to conditions. In Nagarjuna's view, the universe is a true unity of inter-penetrating processes: a continuous, interpenetrating flux.

Through such deep, technically brilliant philosophical inquiries, Buddhism acquired a rich intellectual base. Profound questions were asked about the nature of the body and of the mind. Possible solutions were considered from many angles, not dogmatically but critically—and they were discarded if found to be unsatisfactory. The data for these theoretical studies came from what might be called "subjective empiricism" or, alternatively, "participatory observation"—that is, a methodical, progressive, introspective inquiry into the domain of direct, nonsensory experience.

Parallels may be discerned, then, between the goals, the rigorous application of technique, and the lively skepticism of Buddhist "researchers" on the one hand and, on the other, modern scientists. Both arrive at tentative conclusions and build theories based on experience, and both reject or modify those theories as further experience demands. But we Westerners are not so inclined to give credence to the results of subjective inquiry—in fact, we instinctively react to them with downright suspicion. In the West, the emphasis is almost exclusively on objective methods, on the primacy of what is taken to be an independently existing outer world, and on the dualistic logic of Aristotle as later formalized by Descartes and Galileo. We tend to suppose that this is the best and proper way of acquiring systematic knowledge. Yet the sole reason for this is that it is the way to which we are accustomed. Our lifelong conditioning makes us balk at the very different, subjective approach that has been favored in the East and that is unique to Asian culture. Participant observation is simply not a recognized part of the experimental model of contemporary science. However, to dismiss the Eastern approach as being either ill-founded or illogical would be a mistake equivalent, say, to rejecting non-Euclidean geometry (which provides our current relativistic description of gravity and space-time) on the grounds that it falls outside the familiar, "common sense" axioms of Euclid. The logic and methodology of Buddhism, and other related philosophies, may appear alien, and perhaps even impenetrable, upon first contact. But a careful reading of the classic mystical literature, as well as recent studies of altered states of awareness (see Chapter 11), leads to the conclusion that the terrain of subjective phenomena is genuinely scientific. It contains within it lawful processes pertaining to a mode of consciousness that is as valid and mature as the one to which we are accustomed. If our Western logic and system of thought is Aristotelian, then that of Buddhism is non-Aristotelian, but no less worthy of our serious attention.

Of course, the pioneers and patriarchs of Buddhism had no access to high technology. They lacked the powerful, sensitive instruments and well-equipped laboratories of modern science. Nor did they know much, by today's standards, about mathematics. However, such facilities would not have been helpful in the quest upon which they were embarked. Their monasteries were their laboratories, their own minds the only equipment needed for their studies. Their method of research was not to focus on some particular aspect of the outer world but to turn inward, to systematically explore states of consciousness to a depth virtually unknown in the West. And it was as a result of this intense and highly disciplined introspective investigation, carried out over a period of many centuries, that the central tenets of the Buddhist worldview, which amount to a genuine science of consciousness, came about.

Among the notable features of Buddhist cosmology is the doctrine of *Dharmadhatu*—the Universal Realm or Field of Reality. In this scheme there are no dividing boundaries between things, no separation between subject and object; every entity is seen to interpenetrate every other—a view strikingly in keeping with the ideas of interconnectedness that have emerged from modern quantum mechanics. Here, for example, are two descriptions, one by a Buddhist philosopher, the other by a quantum physicist:

> The world thus appears as a complicated tissue
> of events, in which connections of different
> kinds alternate or overlap or combine and
> thereby determine the texture of the whole.

*   *   *

Things derive their being and nature by mutual
dependence and are nothing in themselves.

But which is which? The first quote is actually from Werner
Heisenberg's book *Physics and Philosophy,* the second, almost two
thousand years earlier, from Nagarjuna. Coming from very different
directions, using very different techniques, Buddhism and quantum
mechanics have converged on virtually the same underlying description of reality.

Buddhist belief is also remarkably in sympathy with our modern,
macroscopic conceptions of space and time. Eastern philosophy,
unlike that of the Greeks, has always maintained that space and time
are constructs of the mind. A passage in the *Madhyamika Sastra,* for
example, reads:

> [T]he past, the future, physical space, . . . and
> individuals are nothing but names, forms of
> thought, words of common usage, merely
> superficial realities.

The French physicist Louis de Broglie, outlining the new view of
the universe as revealed by relativity theory, holds out a similar concept:

> In space-time, everything which for each of us
> constitutes the past, the present, and the future
> is given *en bloc* . . . Each observer, as his time
> passes, discovers, so to speak, new slices of
> space-time which appear to him as successive
> aspects of the material world, though in reality
> the ensemble of events constituting space-time
> exists prior to his knowledge of it.

Both these commentaries point out the essential unreality of the
present moment and the passage of time. There is no "now," no real
barrier between the past and the future, and no flow of time outside

the observer's ego-centered awareness. These are concepts relevant only within the context of our personal, I-focused existence. Upon this, both Buddhism and the General Theory of Relativity agree, and both espouse a much grander, four-dimensional scheme of the universe in which all of space and time, in a sense, already exists—past, present, and future laid out in complete topographical detail for anyone who can command the vantage point from which to see. Einstein himself well understood our personal limitations in coming to grips with the true nature of reality. Indeed, he might have been acting as a spokesman either for mysticism or for physics when he said:

> A human being is part of the whole, called by us "Universe"; a part limited in time and space. He experiences himself, his thoughts and feelings as something separated from the rest—a kind of optical delusion of his consciousness. The delusion is a prison for us, restricting us to our personal desires and to affection for a few persons nearest to us. Our task must be to free ourselves from this prison by widening our circle of compassion to embrace all living creatures and the whole of nature in its beauty. Nobody is able to achieve this completely but the striving for such achievement is, in itself, a part of the liberation and a foundation for inner security.

Einstein grasped what other visionary minds have done before: that a principal aspiration of mankind should be to see beyond ourselves, beyond the parochial self-oriented here and now, to a wider, cosmic panorama. But how to do this? The very reason human thought has progressed as far as it has is by virtue of having access to a sophisticated language. And all of human language, Oriental and Occidental alike, hinges upon the use of words, names, labels, and symbols—the purposeful fragmentation of the whole and the substitution of tokens for the pieces into which we have broken reality. Removal of the wall between ourselves and the cosmos at large, dissolution of the subject-object barrier, can only come with the cessation of thought based on language. Yet, try as we might, we cannot stop thinking. The very act of attempting to shut out thought involves thought, so that this approach is defeated from the start. If we apply our intellect to block our intellect we only make matters worse—we simply end up distancing ourselves further from an innocent awareness of how things actually are.

All human beings the world over face this same dilemma. Evolution has made us into inherently self-centered individuals bent on survival. But our conscious experience of selfhood, of our individuality—which is ultimately the creation of language and rational thought—can lead to suffering and anxiety and, in particular, a preoccupation with death. Easterners harbor the same concerns about self, survival, and mortality as we do. Yet, in the West, our difficulty is made more acute by the belief in the supremacy of the intellect. Our immediate reaction to any problem is always to try to think or reason our way to a solution: an approach that, being predicated on the notion that the self is separate from the world, can never in itself lead to the *experience* of selflessness. Our dogged objective probing of the world has finally led, it is true, to the discovery that at the subatomic level all divisions and boundaries imposed by us on the universe are in fact illusory—including the split between mind and matter. But although we have discerned this at an intellectual level, we still *feel* ourselves to be apart from—rather than a part of—the universe as a whole.

Philosophers everywhere have long known that the human mind is capable of two contrasting modes of consciousness, the rational and the intuitive. But whereas the West has favored the former, in the East the latter has always been given priority. Buddhism, as a case in point, reveals this bias in its distinction (made in the sacred texts known as the Upanishads) between "higher" knowledge, or *prajna,* also referred to as "transcendental" or "absolute" awareness, and "lower" knowledge, or *vijnana,* identified with analytical or scientific thought. Thus, although Buddhism has a rich intellectual base and body of philosophical teachings, it uses these not as an end in itself but as a way of pointing to the greater truth that can only be attained by a suspension of logic and symbolism.

As that branch of Buddhism known as Mahayana (Sanskrit for

"Great Vehicle") spread out of its original homeland into neighboring China, two main developments took place. On the one hand, the translation of the Buddhist *sutras,* or expository texts, stimulated Chinese thinkers to interpret the Indian teachings in the light of their own philosophies. On the other hand, the more pragmatic Chinese mentality fused the abstruse spiritual disciplines—the meditation techniques—of Indian Buddhism with Taoism to give birth to the system known as *Ch'an.** This, in turn, was acquired by the Japanese around 1200 A.D. and reached its final fruition as Zen.

In a sense, what modern physics is to the history of Western thought, Zen is to the development of the Eastern worldview: the ultimate refinement of more than two thousand years of incisive debate, discussion, and critical development. Yet the difference between the two could hardly be more marked. Whereas physics is interested above all in theories, concepts, and formulas, Zen values only the concrete and the simple. Zen wants facts—not in the Western sense of things that are measurable and numerical (which are, *in fact,* abstractions!) but as living, immediate, and tangible. Its approach to understanding is not to theorize because it recognizes that previously accumulated ideas and knowledge—in other words, memories of all kinds—block the direct perception of reality. Therefore, Zen adopts an unusual approach. Its buildup involves language—which is unavoidable. Any method, even if it turns out to be an antimethod, has first to convey some background in order to be effective. But the way Zen uses language is always to point beyond language, beyond concepts to the concrete.

Two major schools of Zen exist in Japan: the Rinzai and the Soto. Both have the same goal, of seeing the world unmediated, but their approaches are different. In the Soto school, the emphasis is on quiet contemplation in a seated position (*zazen*) without a particular focus for thought. The method in the Rinzai school, however, is to put the intellect to work on problems that have no logical resolution. Such problems are known as *koans,* from the Chinese *kung-an* meaning "public announcement." Some are mere questions, for example:

**Ch'an* is the Chinese transliteration of the Sanskrit word "dhyana," which signifies the mystical experience in which subjectivity and objectivity merge. Zen is the transliteration into Japanese of Ch'an.

"When your mind is not dwelling on the dualism of good and evil, what is your original face before you were born?" Others are set in a question-and-answer (*mondo*) form, like: "What is the Buddha?" Answer: "Three pounds of flax" or "The cypress tree in the courtyard" (to name but two of the classic responses). According to tradition there are seventeen hundred such conundrums in the Zen repertoire. And their common aim is to induce a kind of intellectual catastrophe, a sudden jump which lifts the individual out of the domain of words and reason into a direct, nonmediated experience known as *satori*.

Zen differs from other meditative forms, including other schools of Buddhism, in that it does not start from where we are and gradually lead us to a clear view of the true way of the world. It is not a progressive system in this respect. The sole purpose of studying Zen is to have Zen experiences—sudden moments, like flashes of lightning, when the intellect is short-circuited and there is no longer a barrier between the experiencer and reality. Sometimes its methods can seem bizarre and even startling. To catch the flavor, if a Zen master found you reading this book he might grab it from you and hit you over the head with it, saying: "Here's something else for you to think about!" Such shock tactics, however, are intended not to offend but rather to wake us up from our normal symbol-bound frame of mind.

Zen may seem chaotic and irrational (often infuriatingly so!). Yet traditionally it is pursued and imparted in a highly formal, doctrinal way. Students at a Japanese Rinzai monastery must abide by strict rules and follow a precisely prescribed path of development, involving regular periods of meditation and private interviews with the Zen master (*roshi*), in which koans are given and discussed. When the student attains, in the master's judgment, the correct insight into a koan, he or she will be given a new koan designed to open up a further appreciation of the true nature of reality. In this sense, enlightenment comes as a result of a succession of *satori*s, some more profound than others.

Zen uses language to point beyond language, which is what poets and playwrights and musicians do. But, less obviously, it is also what modern science does if the intuitive leap is taken beyond its abstract formalism. The deep, latent message of quantum mechanics, for instance, codified in the language of mathematics, is that there is a reality beyond our senses which eludes verbal comprehension or logical analysis. And this is best exemplified in the central idea of "complementarity"—an idea introduced by Niels Bohr to account for the fact that two different conditions of observations could lead to conclusions that were *conceptually* incompatible. In one experiment, for example, light might behave as if it were made of particles, in another as if it were made of waves. Bohr proposed, however, there is no *intrinsic* incompatibility between these results because they are functions of different conditions of observation; no experiment could be devised that would demonstrate both aspects of a single condition. The wave and particle natures of light and matter are not mutually exclusive, they are mutually inclusive—necessary, complementary aspects of reality. Bohr gained his inspiration for this concept from Eastern philosophy, in particular from the Taoist concept of the dynamic interplay of opposites, *yin* and *yang*. And so, one of the central principles of modern physics is coincident with, and actually derived from, one of the most basic doctrines of the Eastern worldview.

Intuition has ever been the handmaiden of science. And although science presents its theories and conclusions in a "respectable" symbolic form, its greatest advances have always come initially not from the application of reason but from intuitive leaps—sudden flashes of inspiration very much akin to Zen experiences.

Zen and physics, then, seemingly so different, are not so different after all. They are themselves complementary—the waves of Zen to the particles of physics. And the truth of this symbiosis is further revealed by the fact that the branch of physics that is closest to the bedrock of reality, quantum mechanics, now appears to be as profoundly paradoxical and enigmatic as Zen. Physics even poses riddles that, like koans, make a mockery of our logic: "Does a particle that is not watched exist?" Trees, like everything else, are made of subatomic particles. So, does an unwatched tree exist? If it falls in a forest, when no one is around to "observe it into being," can it meaningfully be said to make a sound? Physics and Zen, pragmatism and poetry, conceptualization and creativity, meet at such points—and become one.

But what does this mean for the ordinary man and woman? We

cannot all sit cross-legged in Japanese monasteries, hour after hour, day after day, year after year, preparing our mind for the flash of Zen lightning that will hopefully show us the meaning of life, the universe, and everything. Nor can we all immerse ourselves for a similar lengthy period in the complexities of higher mathematics and quantum field theory so that we might someday fully appreciate the new scientific vision of a unified cosmos. We have children to raise, jobs to go to, mortgages to pay. How can we, in our everyday lives, discover our true place in the universe? How can we see beyond the narrow confines of our individual existence to the timeless, deathless, frontierless place that, the sages of both the East and the West now tell us, is the one true reality?

13

TRANSCENDENCE

> Our normal waking consciousness, rational
> consciousness as we call it, is but one special
> type of consciousness, whilst all about it,
> parted from it by the filmiest of screens, there
> lie potential forms of consciousness entirely
> different.
>
> —*William James*

Throughout history, and in many different situations, people of all
backgrounds and beliefs have enjoyed spontaneous mystical experiences. Suddenly the individual feels, beyond any shadow of doubt,
that she is fundamentally one with the universe. Her sense of identity
expands to embrace the cosmos as a whole.

Following the publication of an earlier book, *Soul Search,* I
received many letters from individuals telling me of extraordinary and
unprecedented experiences that had left them with a radically changed
view of the world. One particularly fascinating account came from a
young woman, Tina W., in Portsmouth, England. She wrote:

> What happened could be explained as an hallu-
> cination or a dream, but in all my life I have
> never had an experience remotely like this one.
> Since it happened . . . I have found it difficult
> to concentrate on anything else.

It was around 10 P.M. in my bedroom in Portsmouth on my first day home after a long holiday. I had spent the previous month in the U.S.A. with my partner who lives there. I had the most wonderful, relaxing time living in a trailer in the countryside of West Virginia. . . .

Holiday over, I flew out of Washington, D.C., on the evening of the 17th of September. The flight was awful, I didn't sleep, and though I had flown several times before with no concerns at all, on this occasion my mortality came very clearly into focus. Anyway, we landed safely at 7 A.M. and I went straight into work, where I stayed all day. At 9 P.M. I went to bed with a book—M. Scott Peck's *Further Along the Road Less Traveled*. At this time, I had been awake for over thirty hours. About halfway through the book Mr. Peck relates an anecdote of a dinner companion asking him to explain his latest book in a sentence; he failed—but then he went on to relate how Jesus encapsulated the Christian message: "Love the Lord thy God with all thy heart, with all thy soul and with all thy might and love thy neighbour as thyself." Although these words were familiar, the depth of their meaning hit me then for the first time.

It was as though something clicked in my brain . . . I felt unbounded love for everyone and every living thing—just an immensity of love, so that it was almost unbearable—I totally abandoned myself to that feeling. What happened next is difficult to describe because words become inadequate. . . .

I felt overwhelmed by something, some pure clear clean cool essence . . . pouring into me . . . then somewhere around this point the

experience occurred. All I can do is list impressions, thoughts and feelings I was able to store.
The real thing is way beyond description or
even logical recall. . . .

Joy, ecstasy, love, I was immersed in it and
saturated with it. Understanding of what was
going on came intuitively . . . we are all in
but not aware of this dimension all the time.
We are all one light but separate also. This
doesn't make sense in our regular consciousness but did in that state. . . . I identified my
boyfriend's essence . . . [and] remember
thinking, "It doesn't matter if I never see him
again in the physical earthly sense because at
this level we are always together." . . .

Material things and our desire for them
seemed totally idiotic and unimportant. . . . All
the human defenses and facades we create to
hide from each other are nonsense because we
are all one. All the things we do to sustain our
self-image are redundant here.

Death is a release. Our body is anchoring us
in space and time. . . . Life as we know it is
only the tiniest bit of what comes after. . . .

I consciously decided to leave that mode (I
thought I could get back again). . . .
Afterwards, I cried a little, a combination of
joy and shock, I think. . . . It totally changed
the way I feel about a lot of things—faith,
death, life.

The pivotal moment in Tina's adventure was when "something
clicked in my brain," because this was clearly the point of switchover
from the normal dualistic mode of thinking to the selfless experience
of transcendence. To a Zen practitioner it would be *satori,* the flash of
lightning. A Muslim might have recognized it as "the Supreme
Identity." And there are other names: *nirvana*, Tao, enlightenment,

zoning, bliss. So widespread is this fundamental mystical feeling that it has, along with the doctrines that purport to explain it, been called "The Perennial Philosophy." For some, it comes only after years of asceticism, study, and devotion to some particular religious or meditation system. But for most ordinary folk, like Tina, it arrives out of the blue, unbidden and unsought. In fact, the very act of seeking may block or hinder the experience of enlightenment. As Tina mentions later in her letter, "I haven't yet been able to get into that mode again." The problem is that she is now *trying* to rekindle the feeling through an effort of intellect and self-will, whereas the original experience arose spontaneously as a result of a freak series of events—a long period of relaxation, followed by complete exhaustion and, finally, an enigmatic biblical quotation (like a koan)—which caught her reasoning mind off guard.

Tina comments that her experience was "way beyond description." And this sums up the difficulty people have always faced in trying to convey to others this ultimate state of selfless being: by its nature it is ineffable. The whole point about transcendence is that it is the experience of reality, pure and simple, without any of the symbolic interpretation normally placed on it by the rationalizing human mind. It is not something amenable to linguistic or logical analysis. This impossibility of putting the transcendent into language is why the different forms of religious instruction that have sprung up around the world vary so much. It is also why so much superfluous dogma has become attached to what is basically a very straightforward message: stop thinking and start experiencing.

All the most prominent sages throughout human history, including Buddha, Lao-tzu, Jesus, Muhammad, and Isaiah, apparently saw through the artificiality of the world of symbols to the true ground of existence. And subsequently, they each strove to put their experience and their method of achieving it into words that others might understand. The feeling of transcendent unity is the same for everyone when it happens, since there is only one reality. However, problems ensue in translating this feeling into words. Even greater difficulties arise when others, who have not had the experience themselves, try to convey secondhand or thirdhand what the fundamental teaching consisted of. And so, for instance, from the reasonably clear and simple message of Gautama Buddha, the vast and intricate system of religious philosophy that is Buddhism has sprung. Thousands of books and many millions of words have been set down on the subject, often in a style that only a lifetime devotee or learned academic could penetrate. But the irony is that language and symbolism are anathema to the basic message of Buddha, which is all about direct experience, unadulterated being. And the same is true of Christianity. The central teaching of Jesus—who, if he was any one man, was surely a flesh-and-blood human being like you and me—is to forget yourself and get in touch with the real world.

Every principal religion and moral code from around the world has this notion at its core: that we should aspire to be selfless. The admonition to "do as you would be done by" or "love thy neighbor as thyself" or "be as little children" is universal. To achieve the best, most natural, most worthwhile, state of existence we are urged to lose ourselves and merge with the whole. As the Christian mystic Meister Eckehart said:

> As long as I am this or that, or have this or that, I am not all things and I have not all things. Become pure till you neither are nor have either this or that; then you are omnipresent and, being neither this nor that, are all things.

Another great mystic put it this way:

> Still there are moments when one feels free from one's own identification with human limitations and inadequacies. At such moments, one imagines that one stands on some spot of a small planet, gazing in amazement at the cold yet profoundly moving beauty of the eternal, the unfathomable: life and death flow into one, and there is neither evolution nor destiny; only being.

His name was Albert Einstein.

The true and sole aim of all deep religion and of all deep science is the same—to point past the personal, survival-oriented self to the boundless reality that has always been there. Jesus said, "The Kingdom of Heaven is within you." Buddha said, "Look within, thou art the Buddha." And what they meant was the same.

When the brain is relaxed enough to take time out from projecting the self, we become, in those brief mystical interludes, aware suddenly of a greater world stretching away on all sides beyond our small, personal, finite lives. The writer Aldous Huxley frequently expressed his view that the function of the human nervous system is to filter and limit the amount and intensity of the experience that our minds have to deal with. To him the brain was actually an impediment, a "reducing valve," that restricted what we would otherwise be able to see. And in *The Doors of Perception,* published in 1954, he described his personal attempts to open up the reducing valve in his head using the hallucinogen mescaline.

Psychedelic drugs, most notably LSD, have been regarded by some as shortcuts to higher states of consciousness, as have the extreme states of exhaustion induced, for instance, by repetitive, anaerobic forms of dance. Nor is this a recent trend. Whether it be through eating magic mushrooms, licking the psychoactive secretions of certain types of toad, walking on red-hot coals, whirling like dervishes, or simply imbibing alcohol, people have been seeking artificially induced transcendent experiences for thousands of years. For others, music, poetry, prayer, quiet contemplation, or a walk in the woods or the hills can trigger the same effect. In a remarkable variety of ways, it seems that we all at times try to break free from our normal mode of self-centered awareness.

One of the most interestingly consistent times at which a very profound transcendent experience is reported to occur is when people come near to death. Studies and surveys reveal that the so-called near-death experience (NDE) is surprisingly common and, in its essential elements, is remarkably consistent. Many millions of individuals around the world claim to have had NDEs and, although interest in the phenomenon is greater today than it has ever been before, descriptions of such experiences are to be found in diverse records going back hundreds and even thousands of years.

Among the most common elements of NDEs are the sensations of leaving and floating away from the body, traveling down a tunnel toward an intensely bright light, an all-pervasive feeling of rapture and love, and seeing one's life recapitulated in vivid detail. Most significantly, NDEers often relate having had a most extraordinary feeling of unity, an acute awareness of everything being there all at once, with a concomitant loss of self-boundaries. Subjects sometimes recall having felt as if they were really alive for the first time. And this, remember, during a period when, objectively, their bodies and brains were totally inert. Indeed, in some cases, profound transcendent experiences apparently took place after the person had been pronounced clinically dead.

It is possible to explain some aspects of the NDE, including the tunnel and the light, in terms of hallucinatory-type events taking place in the distressed brain (though other explanations cannot yet be discounted). But conventional neurological wisdom is at a loss to account for the astonishing broadening and deepening of consciousness reported by people who have, albeit temporarily, crossed over the threshold from life into death. Some of these individuals went through all of the stages of dying up to and including cardiac arrest and the cessation of breathing for several minutes or more. They entered briefly into that uncharted region where all of us are destined eventually to go—but then, thanks in the main to modern resuscitation procedures, came back to tell their tale. *Except that there should not have been any tale to tell.* How can a brain in which virtually all neurological activity has ground to a halt be capable of giving rise to an awareness of unprecedented depth and acuity?

The most reasonable explanation is that the unity feeling which is the central mystery of the NDE is not a product of brain activity at all. It results instead from the removal of the brain's restricting influence. For the first time in a person's life, at the moment of death the selecting and limiting effect of the brain is eliminated, the psychological walls of the self are broken down, and the individual is set free to meld again with the whole unbroken field of reality.

If it were but one aspect of experience that pointed to a cosmic dimension of consciousness then we might easily choose to ignore it. But there is now compelling evidence from physics, psychology, Eastern philosophies, and numerous reported episodes of transcendental awareness in ordinary people for us to take this matter very seriously indeed. What is being suggested is not a new scientific paradigm, but a revolution in the metaphysical underpinnings of our worldview. The simple materialistic notion that consciousness can continue only as long as there is a brain to support it is becoming increasingly untenable. Quantum mechanics and our modern conception of space-time has made nonsense of the Newtonian mechanistic cosmos in which man was effectively divorced from the processes going on around him. We now know—and every experiment quantum physicists carry out further bolsters our knowledge—that we are deeply, intrinsically bound up with reality as a whole. Subject and object are one. The only reason we see it differently is that the self puts up artificial barriers, and creates the feeling of difference and distance between itself and the rest of nature.

This same core truth was appreciated directly by those mystic-philosophers, principally in the East, who, through circumventing the self, saw directly the way things really are. And this same truth, it is clear, does not even require special training or effort for it to be grasped. At any moment, for one reason or another, a person can suddenly come into direct, unmediated contact with the cosmos—can, to all intents, *become* the cosmos.

14

I, UNIVERSE

Like the waters of a river

That in the swift flow of the stream

A great rock divides,

Though our ways seem to have parted

I know that in the end we shall meet.

—Twelfth-century Japanese verse

One simple change in our worldview would have the most profound and dramatic effect on our lives. And it is this: to see, as Eastern philosophies have long seen, that *the brain does not give rise to consciousness*.

The brain is an organ of thought and memory, and has evolved as such for a variety of reasons. It pays for an animal to be able to remember what has happened to it so that it has a better chance of repeating its successes and avoiding its failures. It pays to know how to respond most appropriately to fellow members of your species or clan, especially if you have to fit in with a social structure in which complex interrelationships play a central role. It pays to be able to speculate about the future, analyze situations, and work out novel strategies. It pays—if you are to stay alive and prosper in a niche as incredibly intricate as that of *Homo sapiens*—to have inside your skull a two-hundred-billion-unit neural net of unprecedented power for processing and storing information. You have to be able to think and remember extraordinarily well. But the point so often overlooked is that *there is absolutely no reason why you should have to be conscious.*

Consciousness, in survival terms, is an irrelevancy. It is perfectly possible to conceive of a world inhabited by all sorts of life-forms, from the simplest bacteria to the most spectacularly cerebral of creatures, in which there never stirred a single conscious feeling or experience. In fact, such a world could be imagined that was outwardly indistinguishable from our own. It might appear to be full of diversity, sophisticated behavior, intelligence, and even wit and charm, and yet involve no subjective experience, no inner feeling of being, whatsoever.

Many attempts have been made by evolutionary biologists to explain why consciousness should have come about and what possible advantage it might have bestowed on its owners. For example, it has been suggested that being conscious allows us to understand how other members of our social group feel so that we can better interact and communicate with them. Consciousness, it is sometimes said, helps us to see the world from each other's point of view. But the circularity of this argument is readily apparent. It might indeed be a survival advantage to appreciate how the other fellow feels if conscious feelings and experiences are *already* a fact of the world, but this offers no explanation of why consciousness should have come about in the first place. Exasperated by their failure to discern an obvious purpose for consciousness, some researchers have dismissed it as peripheral and almost accidental—an inconsequential spin-off of the brain's other activities.

The same problem that evolutionary biologists invent for themselves in trying to find a credible survival function of consciousness, neurologists face in their attempts to explain how consciousness stems from the workings of the brain. Consciousness-explainers are currently going to all sorts of lengths to weave a viable theory—studying the development of neurons, tracing the precise pathways and stages of visual processing, drawing inspiration from artificial intelligence research, and, in the case of Roger Penrose and his followers, proposing that quantum effects inside the microtubules of cells will somehow do the trick. How long this tilting at windmills will go on before the necessary basic paradigm shift renders it all unnecessary is anyone's guess. But old habits die hard. And, meanwhile, the present crop of brain researchers continue to be encouraged in their ultimately futile quest by the numerous successes they are achieving along the way in understanding the *true* workings of the brain.

Viewed superficially, the explaining of consciousness as a derivative of the physical workings of the brain has a ring of plausibility about it. After all, the history of science is replete with examples of large conceptual gaps being bridged by new developments and sudden flashes of insight. Life and nonlife, for instance, once considered fundamentally irreconcilable, were eventually seen to have a common basis thanks to the advent of molecular biology. In physics, magnetism and electricity were unified by Maxwell's field equations; mass and energy, and space and time, were linked through Einstein's monumental work. But the divide between neural events and consciousness, brain and mind, is of a different order entirely. As Konrad Lorenz described in *Behind the Mirror*:

> The "hiatus" between soul and body . . . is indeed unbridgeable. . . . I do not believe that this is a limitation imposed just by the present state of our knowledge, or that even a utopian advance of this knowledge would bring us closer to a solution. . . . It is not a matter of a horizontal split between subjective experience and physiological events, nor a matter of dividing the higher from the lower, the more complex from the more elementary, but a kind of vertical dividing line through our whole nature.

There is an interesting parallel—and it may be more than a parallel—between the attempts of neurologists to explain how consciousness is produced by the brain and the efforts of cosmologists to show how the material universe was created or why it should even exist at all. At first sight, these programs seem poles apart. But in both cases, there is a persistent failure on the part of the investigators to recognize one simple truth beyond the complexity and ingenuity of their theories. And this simple truth is that what they are trying to do is not just difficult but *fundamentally, categorically impossible.* Even if physicists eventually discover their Holy Grail—the long sought after Theory of Everything—it will not be possible to deduce from this *why* there should be an actual, material universe instead of the potential, abstract universe described by mathematical equations. Why should there be actuality instead of mere potentiality? Why should the equations have come to life? Why should there be both a script *and* a play? There is no way—and there never will be a way— to breathe fire into the formalism, to understand the existence of reality from theory alone. And, in exactly the same way, it will never be possible, even in principle, to explain why physical activity in a brain—however intricate, however well integrated—should give rise to the subjective experience of consciousness. If, in the next thousand years, we discover how the brain is organized and functions on every level, from the individual cell to the entire central nervous system, we shall not be a scintilla closer to comprehending why a person should feel and be aware and experience a whole fantastic inner world instead of being just a complex, unconscious automaton. To try to explain consciousness in terms of the mechanisms of thought, the activities of neurons, is to miss the whole point about consciousness. As Milan Kundera wrote in his novel *Immortality:* "I think, therefore I am, is the statement of an intellectual who underrates toothaches."

For the past several hundred years, Western humanity has embraced the view that to be real is to be material. Matter's what matters. And mind? Never mind. Science has upheld this position for so long now that it has become an axiom of our culture. We take it as given that matter exists "out there" whether or not there is a mind present to experience it. And we take it as given that the cosmos has always had an objective aspect and that only later, as conditions allowed, did the raw, nonconscious building blocks of the universe come together in such a way as to allow the emergence of subjective experience. This makes it easy and natural for us to believe that if only data is handled by a system (like a brain) in a sufficiently and suitably complex way, consciousness will arise, like steam over a hot stew. So deeply embedded is this notion in our collective psyche that to challenge it may seem outrageous, contemptuous, and just plain wrong. Yet the moment we stand back, shake off our conditioning, and look at the issue anew, we can begin to appreciate that the scientific tenet that matter—the entire objective world—is primary is an arbitrary and totally unsubstantiated claim. There is no prima facie reason at all to go along with the assertion that mind is an emergent property of matter—that, at some point, mind came into being when matter, in the form of brains, acquired some critical level of complexity. On the contrary, it is the *material* world which is very evidently conditional, for it is just one among many objects of our experience, and an object, moreover, that is not strictly given but known only through interpretation.

In time, no doubt, we shall come to understand the brain very well in computational or mechanistic terms. And there is no compelling reason to suppose that we shouldn't eventually be able to duplicate or even exceed all of its capabilities using artificial neural networks. But we shall never, in a billion years, be able to explain how the brain gives rise to consciousness. Because consciousness is *not* a product of the brain, nor did it come about at some point during the development of life. The time is ripe for us to reexamine the metaphysical foundations of our worldview.

Out of the heart of quantum mechanics, that most basic branch of science, has come the realization that consciousness can never be divorced from matter, that every aspect of the universe—and indeed the universe as a whole—has both an objective and a subjective nature. "Things" have no reality independent of their location in experience; they require the intimate involvement of mind to be given substance. And so, quantum physics insists, consciousness has to be seen in a radically new light—not as some quirky, local by-product of matter but as the very groundswell of creation. Only our stubborn, outmoded attachment to Newtonian reductionism and Cartesian dualism—an attachment that, not surprisingly, remains strongest among many scientists, despite recent developments—is blocking the acceptance of this fundamental truth.

Consciousness is not new, isolated, and relatively unimportant; it is ubiquitous and essential. It is a permanent, inherent property of the universe, a fact that becomes most immediately obvious to us when we escape temporarily from our normal, egocentric state of mind during mystical or transcendental interludes. At such times, "we" vanish altogether and in our place is simply consciousness. As soon as the analytical activity of the brain is suppressed or circumvented, pure consciousness—the background consciousness of the universe—floods in. The barrier is removed, the partition between subject and object dissolved. And of all the occasions when this happens none is more profound or revealing than at the point of death when, with the brain almost totally disabled, a condition of the most indescribably profound and expansive awareness takes hold.

Without the brain, it is true, there cannot be selves. And our preoccupation with the self is perhaps the main reason for our long-standing confusion. In the West, we have tended to equate having thoughts and memories and, above all, selves, with being conscious. But this is a serious mistake. As long as the self is in residence we can never truly be conscious, for while "we" exist we are trapped in a kind of fantasy—Einstein's "optical delusion"—in which memories and conditioning cause us to put a private and false interpretation on the world. Only when thought and self come to an end, when symbolizing, analyzing, boundary-defining, and ego-building cease, can genuine, unfettered consciousness begin.

It is one of our greatest misconceptions to suppose that somehow the brain produces consciousness by integrating all of the perceptions and information that come in from the outside world. But the world is *already* integrated. It is already as perfect, whole, and well conceived, throughout all of space and time, as it will ever be. What the brain really does is to sample extremely narrow aspects of reality through the senses and then subject these to further drastic and highly selective reinterpretation.

To grasp the truth about the universe we need to adopt a new, broader perspective. We have to see that reality is an unbroken unity, and that within this unity are aspects of the whole that think of themselves as being separate. Despite how it may seem, there is no paradox or inconsistency here: the development of living organisms has necessarily involved the development of selves—the feeling (albeit, in most cases, only at a very primitive level) of *being* those organisms. And all of this has taken place within the undivided totality of what is real. It seems unusual and puzzling. But nothing is contradictory in the "feeling of being apart" existing within an overall system that actually *has* no parts. This, as it happens, is the situation in which we find ourselves.

Human beings have reached what may well be a pivotal stage in their evolution. They have been created by the universe, in the universe, as an integral part of the universe. They have passed through a difficult period when their strong day-to-day experience of selfhood and their cultural conditioning have made them feel detached from the reality in which they are permanently embedded. And now they are beginning to see beyond the self again to the truth of their condition. They are beginning, on a planet-wide, intercultural scale, to appreciate that, as Freud put it:

> Our present I-feeling is . . . only a shrunken
> residue of a much more inclusive—indeed, all-
> embracing—feeling which corresponded to a
> more intimate bond between the I and the
> world about it.

We are coming back, experientially, into the universe again—slowly, nonuniformly, slightly uncomprehendingly, and, in some cases, begrudgingly. The signs of emergence of a new, as-yet-uncertain cosmic perspective are evident in a number of seemingly diverse areas: in the esoteric philosophy of quantum physics, in the study of NDEs and other altered and transcendent conscious states, in the work of poets like Whitman and Eliot, in the ecology movement, in various aspects of youth culture and counterculture, and in the growing appreciation of the timeless truths of the world's major religions.

It is likely to be a testing time for us, not least because we are beginning to discover that the universe is entirely natural. The only reality that exists, it is becoming clear, is right in front of us; nothing is hidden, nothing is beyond our ken. As Ralph Waldo Emerson wrote: "Other world! There is no other world! Here or nowhere is the whole fact."

Perhaps it is one of the definitive signs of a sentient species reaching maturity when it finally manages to let go of the security blanket of the supernatural. This we are gradually starting to do. We have peered inside ourselves, into the depths of the human brain, in search of a soul and have found . . . nothing. We don't have souls. There is no deeper, further fact to being a person than being a thinking brain— a small, temporary whirlpool of memories and thoughts in the larger river of life. And science and religion, despite superficial appearances, actually agree on this point: science quite clearly, but religion, too, quietly and insistently. No major religion, from Christianity to Buddhism, professes in its core a belief in the existence of personal souls. On the contrary, the aim of all sincere religion is, and always has been, to go beyond the self and its putative spiritual counterpart— both of which are seen as illusory—to the boundless consciousness of reality. The core message of the world's great religio-philosophical systems, Eastern and Western, is to forget about yourself, lose yourself, and so, in the process, make contact with the much more important truth of the timeless awareness of the universe.

If this sounds more than a little mystical and starry-eyed, then I make no apologies. The universe *is* one and to see it as such *is* the goal of mysticism, as well as of science. And our eyes are indeed starry, being composed of atoms whose nuclei were manufactured inside the intensely hot cores of giant stars that exploded in the remote past. Waxing lyrical about our relationship with the cosmos is entirely appropriate at a time when science, religion, and mysticism are finally converging on a unified worldview, by contrast with which our old anthropocentric perspectives are going to seem extraordinarily parochial. We are nothing less than the universe in dialogue with itself and our words do sometimes need to rise above the prosaic, the practical, and the scientifically correct to catch a hint of the drama of our situation. This is why music and poetry so often touch us more deeply than the anodyne pronouncements of reductionist science, why so often we choose to rely upon intuition and unspoken feelings above intellect. We know inside what the truth is, without being told. Even a hardened pragmatist like J. B. S. Haldane felt moved to write that

> if death will probably be the end of me as a
> finite individual mind, that does not mean that
> it will be the end of me altogether. It seems to

me immensely unlikely that mind is a mere by-product of matter. . . .

But as regards my own very finite and imperfect mind, I can see, by studying the effects on it of drugs, alcohol, disease, and so on, that its limitations are largely at least due to my body.

Without that body it may perish altogether, but it seems to me quite as probable that it will lose its limitations and be merged into an infinite mind or something analogous to a mind which I have reason to suspect probably exists behind nature. How this might be accomplished I have no idea.

But I notice that when I think logically and scientifically or act morally my thoughts and actions become those of any intelligent or moral being in the same position; in fact, I am already identifying my mind with an absolute or unconditioned mind.

Only in so far as I do this can I see any probability of my survival, and the more I do so the less I am interested in my private affairs and the less desire do I feel for personal immortality. The belief in my own eternity seems to me indeed a piece of unwarranted self-glorification, and the desire for it gives concession to selfishness.

In so far as I set my heart on things that will not perish with me, I automatically remove the sting from my death.

It may seem as if I have reached two very different and incompatible conclusions in this book. Earlier, I reasoned that after death the feeling of being a self continues. I argued that this can be thought of as a form of reincarnation: the death of one brain followed by the birth of another being functionally and experientially equivalent to a person in life forgetting who they are and subsequently remembering they are someone else. How can this conclusion be squared with the idea that at death we effectively rejoin the unbroken sea of consciousness that lies outside us? Surely, when we die, there can be only one outcome.

But, in fact, there is no incompatibility. We simply need to appreciate that we are dealing with two complementary aspects of the universe. And I use the word "complementary" here advisedly to highlight a comparison with the wave-particle complementarity of modern physics and the subject-object complementarity of Eastern philosophies. The cosmos exists *en bloc* and yet within it individual selves have evolved. The one does not preclude the other; in fact, the two appear to be in some kind of extraordinary, intimate symbiosis, the significance of which will doubtless become clearer as our species further matures.

New selves emerge as new brains emerge, because what a brain does is to act as a funnel, a filter, a limiter of consciousness, and therefore a shaper of self—a separator of subject and object. The brain effectively pinches off a little bubble of introverted awareness and stores and manipulates information relevant exclusively to the survival needs of the individual so created. Using its archived memories, the brain builds and subtends the myth of personality and self, its onboard programming working ceaselessly to substantiate and immortalize this phantasmic inner being. And such a fine job does it do that the projected self not only feels itself to be tangible, but it fails to appreciate, or even suspect, that it is never the same from one moment to the next.

Selves come and go, as brains come and go. And at the subjective, human level what this amounts to is a continuous state of "being you." "You" don't have to worry about dying, because the moment you stop being associated with a particular brain and a particular narrative, the feeling of being you reemerges in a new guise. It has happened before and it will happen again. And it is not a case of you becoming one person and me becoming someone else in the traditional sense of transmigrating souls. We have to see that "being you" is just a general phenomenon. There is no actual, objective link that determines who you will become. You will not become anyone. There is just a continuously experienced condition of you-ness.

Through such ongoing reincarnation—if we choose to use this term—the human race evolves, the efforts and achievements of individuals being stored both extrasomatically and in the living memories of others so that in every life we each contribute, to a greater or lesser extent, to humanity's overall progress. Viewed in this way, it is true that we appear to be far from the masters of our situation. Our brains are in thrall to the automatically encoded programs in our genes, and "we" are shaped not by our own efforts but by the influence of our brains and our environments. It is a sobering realization that, in an important sense, we don't really own or exert will over our bodies and minds; we are simply part of an endlessly unfolding process. It is sobering, and yet it is also strangely exhilarating and liberating to think that there is more to us than brief, solitary lives. Each of us, in the broader scheme of nature, is the latest representative of a lineage of individuals that stretches back to the dawn of mankind and before, and will continue, indefinitely, into the future. Moreover, if we can embrace a still wider panorama, we can begin to see that the differences between us are so slight and the similarities so great that all of us alive today are really just minor variations on the *same* person. The fragmentation or plurality of consciousness is only an appearance, like the hundreds of little pictures that a multifaceted crystal reflects without multiplying the object in reality. The physicist Erwin Schrödinger understood this well when he wrote:

> Thus you can throw yourself flat on the ground, stretched out upon Mother Earth with the certain conviction that you are one with her and she with you. You are as firmly established, as invulnerable as she—and more so. As surely as she will engulf you tomorrow, so surely she will bring you forth, just as every day she engulfs you a thousand times over.

We have a future, then, beyond death, as new individuals—as participants in "I-mode" continuity, or what amounts to secular reincarnation. However, standing behind this is the unfragmented consciousness of the universe. And, in some ways, this is the ideal and only genuine state in which to exist. It is that to which we ultimately aspire—the timeless, all-knowing condition in which subject and object, life and death, you and I, God and man, are one.

In his novel *Childhood's End,* Arthur C. Clarke referred enigmatically to the "overmind"—a higher entity with which, he speculated, the individual minds of many advanced species, at some crucial, metamorphic point in their development, begin spontaneously to merge. And it is at least interesting to speculate that, in this particular instance, fact may be on an intercept course with fiction.

Death of the self is seen as the gateway to what Buddhism calls *nirvana* and Christianity refers to as heaven. Buddhism urges us to escape the Wheel of Life, the cycle of death and rebirth, by achieving enlightenment through meditation—by becoming a new Buddha. Zen goes a step further and tells us, effectively, not to even bother trying to escape; we should simply stop thinking about it, because there has never been a time when we haven't been free. In Christianity, the same message is couched in different terms. All we need do, it says, is become like little children (whose selves are not yet well defined) in order to enter God's kingdom.

Every deep moral and religious system around the world has intuitively grasped this truth—that we must endeavor to transcend the self. Death of the self, either through the physical death of the brain or the bypassing of its analytical mode during life, breaks down the psychological walls that contain us, leaving us free to meld again with the whole unbroken field of consciousness.

We may not think we want this to happen. The idea of being, at one moment, a small speck of humanity in the vastness of space and, at the next, becoming one with the universe may seem terrifying. But this is only because we are compelled to try to understand everything from our limited personal perspective. The plain fact is we are *already* one with the universe; we have never really been apart from it. And only the presence of the self prevents us from seeing this. Through techniques such as Zen, which bring a temporary halt to thought, we can directly experience the consciousness of the cosmos—have a taste, as it were, of death during life. Or a transcendent awareness may, for one reason or another, simply happen. Or, without having any dramatic experiences, we may simply through quiet contemplation become accustomed to the idea of who we really are. As Bertrand Russell wrote:

> The best way to overcome [the fear of death]—so it seems to me—is to make your interests gradually wider and more impersonal, until bit by bit the walls of the ego recede, and your life becomes increasingly merged in the universal life. An individual human existence should be like a river—small at first, narrowly contained within its banks, and rushing passionately past boulders and over waterfalls. Gradually the river grows wider, the banks recede, the water flows more quietly, and in the end, without any visible break, they become merged in the sea, and painlessly lose their individual being. The man who, in old age, can see his life in this way, will not suffer from the fear of death, since the things he cares for will continue. And if, with the decay of vitality, weariness increases, the thought of rest will not be unwelcome.

Death is not the end. In the truest sense, it is the essential prelude to change and new life. Death is the point where the individual and the cosmos meet, where differences are reconciled, and where physics and Zen, so long held apart in uneasy tension, merge effortlessly in a realm beyond words and thought.

Our revels are now ended. These our actors,

As I foretold you, were all spirits and

Are melted into air . . .

. . . We are such stuff

As dreams are made on, and our little life

Is rounded with a sleep.

—*Shakespeare,* The Tempest

To die will be an awfully big adventure.

—*James Barrie,* Peter Pan

REFERENCES

Books

Abe, Masao. *Zen and Western Thought*. London: Macmillan, 1985.

Anderson, Walt. *Open Secrets: A Western Guide to Tibetan Buddhism*. New York: Viking Press, 1979.

Aries, Philippe. *Western Attitudes Toward Death: From the Middle Ages to the Present*. Baltimore: The Johns Hopkins University Press, 1974.

Ayer, Alfred J. *The Concept of a Person, and Other Essays*. London: Macmillan, 1963.

Bancroft, Anne. *The Spiritual Journey*. Shaftesbury, Dorset: Element, 1991.

Barber, Paul. *Vampires, Burial and Death: Folklore and Reality*. New Haven: Yale University Press, 1988.

Bardis, Panos D. *History of Thanatology: Philosophical, Religious, Psychological, and Sociological Ideas Concerning Death, from Primitive Times to the Present*. Washington, D.C.: University Press of America, 1981.

Barglow, Raymond. *The Crisis of the Self in the Age of Information*. London: Routledge, 1994.

Bates, Brian. *The Way of Wyrd*. London: Century, 1983.

Baumeister, Roy F. *Identity: Cultural Change and the Struggle for Self*. New York: Oxford University Press, 1986.

Bendann, Effie. *Death Customs: An Analytical Study of Burial Rites*. London: Dawsons, 1969.

Bishop, Peter. *Dreams of Power: Tibetan Buddhism and the Western Imagination*. London: The Athlone Press, 1993.

Blakemore, Colin, and Susan Greenfield, eds. *Mindwaves: Thoughts on Intelligence, Identity and Consciousness*. Oxford: Blackwell, 1987.

Blofeld, John. *The Secret and the Sublime: Taoist Mysteries and Magic*. London: Allen and Unwin, 1973.

Bohr, Niels. *Essays, 1958–1962, on Atomic Physics and Human Knowledge*. New York: John Wiley, 1963.

Borges, Jorge Luis. *Labyrinths*. New York: New Directions, 1964.

Bowker, John. *The Meanings of Death*. Cambridge: Cambridge University Press, 1991.

Burnet, John. *Early Greek Philosophers*. London: A. & C. Black, 1908.

Carrithers, Michael, et al., eds. *The Category of the Person: Anthropology, Philosophy, History*. Cambridge: Cambridge University Press, 1985.

Carse, James P. *Death and Existence: A Conceptual History of Human Mortality*. New York: John Wiley, 1980.

Choron, Jacques. *Death and Western Thought*. London: Collier-Macmillan, 1963.

Churchland, Paul M. *Matter and Consciousness: A Contemporary Introduction to the Philosophy of Mind*. Cambridge: M.I.T. Press, 1988.

Clark, David. *The Sociology of Death: Theory, Culture, Practice*. Oxford: Blackwell, 1993.

Collins, Steven. *Selfless Persons: Imagery and Thought in Theravada Buddhism*. Cambridge: Cambridge University Press, 1982.

Confer, W. N., and B. S. Ables. *Multiple Personality: Etiology, Diagnosis, and Treatment*. New York: Human Sciences Press, 1983.

Corballis, Michael C. *Human Laterality*. New York: Academic Press, 1983.

Cornwell, John, ed. *Nature's Imagination: The Frontiers of Scientific Vision*. Oxford: Oxford University Press, 1995.

Crook, John H. *The Evolution of Human Consciousness*. Oxford: Clarendon Press, 1980.

Cullman, Oscar. *Immortality of the Soul or Resurrection of the Dead?* London: The Epsworth Press, 1958.

Cupitt, Don. *What Is a Story?* London: SCM Press, 1991.

Darling, David. *Deep Time: The Journey of a Single Subatomic Particle from the Moment of Creation to the Death of the Universe and Beyond.* New York: Delacorte, 1989.

―――. *Equations of Eternity: Speculations on Consciousness, Meaning, and the Mathematical Rules That Orchestrate the Cosmos.* New York: Hyperion, 1993.

―――. *Soul Search: A Scientist Explores the Afterlife.* New York: Villard, 1995.

Davies, Martin, and Glyn W. Humphreys, eds. *Consciousness: Psychological and Philosophical Essays.* Oxford: Blackwell, 1993.

Davies, Paul. *The Mind of God.* London: Heinemann, 1992.

Ducasse, Curt J. *Nature, Mind and Death.* LaSalle, Ill.: Open Court, 1951.

Dunne, John W. *An Experiment with Time.* London: Faber, 1939.

Eccles, John C. *Evolution of the Brain, Creation of the Self.* New York: Routledge, 1990.

Enright, D. J., ed. *The Oxford Book of Death.* Oxford: Oxford University Press, 1983.

Evans-Wentz, W. Y., ed. *The Tibetan Book of the Great Liberation.* Oxford: Oxford University Press, 1954.

Flew, Antony G. N. *Body, Mind and Death: Readings.* New York: Collier-Macmillan, 1964.

Fulton, Robert. *Death and Identity.* New York: John Wiley, 1966.

Gazzaniga, Michael S. *The Bisected Brain.* New York: Appleton-Century-Crofts, 1970.

―――, and Joseph E. LeDoux. *The Integrated Mind.* New York: Plenum Press, 1978.

Gittings, Clare. *Death, Burial and the Individual in Early Modern England.* London: Routledge, 1988.

Glover, Jonathan. *I: The Philosophy and Psychology of Personal Identity.* New York: Penguin Books, 1988.

Gordon, David Cole. *Overcoming the Fear of Death.* Baltimore: Penguin Books, 1970.

Gregory, Richard. *Mind in Science*. London: Weidenfeld and Nicolson, 1981.

Grof, Stanislav. *The Human Encounter with Death*. London: Souvenir Press, 1979.

————. *Beyond the Brain: Birth, Death and Transcendence in Psychotherapy*. State University of New York Press, n.d.

Hacking, Ian. *Rewriting the Soul: Multiple Personality and the Sciences of Memory*. Princeton: Princeton University Press, 1995.

Harpur, Tom. *Life After Death*. Toronto: McClelland & Stewart, 1991.

Harre, Horace R. *Personal Being: A Theory for Individual Psychology*. Oxford: Blackwell, 1983.

Hilgard, Ernest R. *Divided Consciousness: Multiple Controls in Human Thought and Action*. New York: John Wiley, 1986.

Hinton, John. *Dying*. Harmondsworth, England: Penguin, 1967.

Hockey, Jennifer L. *Experiences of Death: An Anthropological Account*. Edinburgh: Edinburgh University Press, 1990.

Humphrey, Nicholas. *A History of the Mind*. New York: Vintage, 1993.

Iserson, Kenneth. *Death to Dust: What Happens to Dead Bodies?* Tucson, Ariz.: Galen Press, 1994.

Jaeger, Werner. *The Theology of the Early Greek Philosophers*. Oxford: Oxford University Press, 1947.

Josephson, B. D., and V. S. Ramachandran, eds. *Consciousness and the Physical World*. Oxford: Pergamon Press, 1980.

Kapleau, Philip. *Wheel of Death: A Collection of Writings from Zen Buddhist and Other Sources on Dying-Death-Rebirth*. New York: Harper & Row, 1971.

Kastenbaum, Robert, and Ruth Aisenberg. *The Psychology of Death*. New York: Springer-Verlag, 1972.

Keyes, Daniel. *The Minds of Billy Milligan*. New York: Random House, 1981.

Kübler-Ross, Elisabeth. *Questions and Answers on Death and Dying*. London: Macmillan, 1974.

Laing, R. D. *The Divided Self: An Existential Study in Sanity and Madness*. London: Tavistock, 1960.

Lee, Philip R., Robert E. Ornstein, et al. *Symposium on Consciousness*. New York: Viking Press, 1976.

Lewis, Hywel D. *The Self and Immortality*. New York: Seabury Press, 1973.

Lorenz, Konrad Z. *Behind the Mirror: A Search for a Natural History of Human Knowledge*. London: Methuen, 1977.

Luria, Alexander R. *The Mind of a Mnemonist: A Little Book About a Vast Memory*. New York: Basic Books, 1968.

——— (trans. Basil Haigh). *The Neuropsychology of Memory*. Washington, D.C.: V. H. Winston, 1986.

McCarthy, James B. *Death Anxiety: The Loss of Self*. New York: Gardner Press, 1980.

McCrone, John. *The Myth of Irrationality: The Science of the Mind from Plato to Star Trek*. London: Macmillan, 1993.

Marcus Aurelius. *Meditations*, trans. by G. M. A. Grube. Indianapolis: Bobbs-Merrill, 1963.

Marks, Charles E. *Commissurotomy, Consciousness, and Unity of Mind*. Montgomery, Vt.: Bradford, 1980.

Maurer, Herryman, trans. and ed. *Tao: The Way of the Ways*. Aldershot, Hampshire: Wildwood House, 1986.

Mazlish, Bruce. *The Fourth Discontinuity: The Co-Evolution of Humans and Machines*. New Haven: Yale University Press, 1994.

Metcalf, Peter. *Celebrations of Death: The Anthropology of Mortuary Ritual*. Cambridge: Cambridge University Press, 1991.

Moore, Charles A., ed. *The Japanese Mind: Essentials of Japanese Philosophy and Culture*. Honolulu: University of Hawaii Press, 1967.

Nagel, Thomas. *Mortal Questions* ("Brain Bisection and the Unity of Consciousness"). Cambridge: Cambridge University Press, 1979.

———. *The View from Nowhere*. New York: Oxford University Press, 1986.

Negroponte, Nicholas. *Being Digital*. Alfred A. Knopf, 1995.

Nozick, Robert. *Philosophical Explanations*. Cambridge: Harvard University Press, 1981.

Parfit, Derek. *Reasons and Persons*. Oxford: Clarendon, 1984.

Pelletier, Kenneth R., and Charles Garfield. *Consciousness: East and West*. New York: Harper & Row, 1976.

Penelhum, Terence. *Survival and Disembodied Existence*. London: Routledge and Kegan Paul, 1970.

Perry, J. *A Dialogue on Personal Identity and Immortality*. Berkeley: University of California Press, 1975.

Philips, D. Z. *Death and Immortality*. London: Macmillan, 1970.

Piaget, Jean. *The Construction of Reality in the Child*. New York: Basic Books, 1954.

Polkinghorne, John. *Quarks, Chaos and Christianity*. London: Triangle, 1994.

Popper, Karl R. and John Eccles. *The Self and Its Brain: An Argument for Interactionism*. London: Springer International, 1977.

Prince, Morton. *The Dissociation of a Personality: The Hunt for the Real Miss Beauchamp*. London: n.p., 1905.

Quen, Jacques M., ed. *Split Minds/Split Brains: Historical and Current Perspectives*. New York: New York University Press, 1986.

Richardson, Ruth. *Death, Dissection and the Destitute*. London: Penguin, 1988.

Rinpoche, Sogyal. *The Tibetan Book of Living and Dying*. San Francisco: HarperSanFrancisco, 1992.

Rosenberger, Nancy R., ed. *Japanese Sense of Self*. Cambridge: Cambridge University Press, 1992.

Russell, Bertrand. *New Hopes for a Changing World*. London: Allen and Unwin, 1951.

———. *History of Western Philosophy*. London: Unwin, 1961.

Sacks, Oliver. *The Man Who Mistook His Wife for a Hat*. London: Duckworth, 1985.

———. *Awakenings*. New York: HarperCollins, 1990.

Schrödinger, Erwin. *Mind and Matter*. Cambridge: Cambridge University Press, 1958.

———. *My View of the World*. Cambridge: Cambridge University Press, 1964.

Scott, William T. *Erwin Schrödinger: An Introduction to His Writings*. Amherst, Mass.: University of Massachusetts Press, 1967.

Sekida, Katsuki. *Zen Training: Methods and Philosophy*. New York: Weatherhill, 1975.

Shibles, Warren. *Death: An Interdisciplinary Analysis*. Whitewater, Wis.: Language Press, 1974.

Sidtis, J. J. "Bilateral Language and Commissurotomy: Interactions Between the Hemispheres with and Without the Corpus

Callosum." In A. Reeves, ed., *Epilepsy and the Corpus Callosum*. New York: Plenum Press, 1985.

Springer, Sally and Georg Deutsch. *Left Brain, Right Brain*. New York: W. H. Freeman, 1993.

Suzuki, D. T. *The Field of Zen*. London: The Buddhist Society, 1969.

Tipler, Frank. *The Physics of Immortality: Modern Cosmology, God and the Resurrection of the Dead*. New York: Macmillan, 1994.

Toynbee, Arnold J. *Man's Concern with Death*. London: Hodder and Stoughton, 1968.

———, Arthur Koestler, et al. *Life After Death*. London: Weidenfeld and Nicolson, 1976.

Vesey, Godfrey. *Personal Identity: A Philosophical Analysis*. Ithaca, N.Y.: Cornell University Press, 1974.

Wagner, August H., ed. *What Happens When You Die?: Twentieth Century Thought on Survival After Death*. London: Abelard-Schuman, 1968.

Walton, Douglas. *On Defining Death: An Analytic Study of the Concept of Death in Philosophy and Medical Ethics*. Montreal: McGill-Queen's University Press, 1979.

Wiener, Philip P., ed. *Ways of Thinking of Eastern Peoples*. Honolulu: University of Hawaii Press, 1964.

Wilber, Ken. *No Boundary*. Boston: New Science Library, 1981.

———. *Eye to Eye: The Quest for the New Paradigm*. Boston: Shambhala, 1988.

Wilkes, Kathleen. *Real People: Personal Identity Without Thought Experiment*. Oxford: Clarendon Press, 1988.

Williams, Bernard. *Problems of the Self: Philosophical Papers, 1956–1974* ("The Self and the Future"). Cambridge: Cambridge University Press, 1973.

Wilson Ross, Nancy, ed. *The World of Zen: An East-West Anthology*. London: Collins, 1962.

Articles

Baillie, J. "Philosophical Problems of the Self." *The Psychologist: Bulletin of the British Psychological Society* 2 (1989): 279–281.

————. "Identity, Survival and Sortal Concepts." *Philosophical Quarterly* 40 (1990): 2.

Berman, A. L. and J. E. Hays. "Relation Between Death Anxiety, Belief in Afterlife, and Locus of Control." *Journal of Consulting and Clinical Psychology* 41 (1973): 318.

Bogen, Joseph. "Identity and Origin." *Analysis* 26 (Apr. 1966).

Brennan, Andrew A. "Personal Identity and Personal Survival." *Analysis* 42 (Jan. 1982).

Cotman, Carl, et al. "Plasticity of Hippocampal Circuitry in Alzheimer's Disease." *Science* 230 (1986): 1179–1181.

Curran, Charles. "Death and Dying." *Journal of Religion and Health* 14 (1975): 254–64.

Dennett, Daniel. "The Origin of Selves." *Cogito* 3 (1989): 3.

Dimond, Stewart, Linda Farrington, and Peter Johnson. "Differing Emotional Responses from Right and Left Hemispheres." *Nature* 261 (1976): 690–692.

Feifel, H., and A. B. Branscomb. "Who's Afraid of Death?" *Journal of Abnormal Psychology* 81 (1973): 282–88.

Fine, Alan. "Transplantation in the Central Nervous System." *Scientific American* 255 (Aug. 1986): 42–50.

Fodor, Jerry. "The Mind-Body Problem." *Scientific American* 244 (Jan. 1981): 114–123.

Frankfurt, H. "Freedom of the Will and the Concept of a Person." *Journal of Philosophy* 68 (1971): 5–20.

Gates, A., and J. L. Bradshaw. "The Role of the Cerebral Hemispheres in Music." *Brain and Language* 4 (1977): 403–431.

Gazzaniga, Michael S. "The Split Brain in Man." *Scientific American* 217 (Aug. 1967): 24–29.

Geschwind, N. "Disconnexion Syndromes in Animals and Man." *Brain* 88 (1965): 636–639.

Horgan, John. "Can Science Explain Consciousness?" *Scientific American* 271 (Jul. 1994): 72–78.

Huttenlocher, Peter. *Brain Research* 163 (1979): 175.

Joynt, R. J. "Are Two Heads Better Than One?" *The Behavioral and Brain Sciences* 4 (1981): 108–109.

Kavka, Gregory. "The Paradox of Future Individuals." *Philosophy and Public Affairs* 11 (1982): 93–112.

LeDoux, J. E., D. H. Wilson, and Michael S. Gazzaniga. "A Divided Mind: Observations on the Conscious Properties of the Separated Hemispheres." *Annals of Neurology* 2 (1977): 417–421.

Lifton, Robert Jay. "Medicalized Killing in Auschwitz." *Psychiatry* (1982).

Mackay, D. M., and Valerie Mackay. "Explicit Dialogue Between Left and Right Half-Systems of Split Brains." *Nature* 295 (1982): 690–691.

Penelhum, T. "The Importance of Self-identity." *The Journal of Philosophy* 68 (1971), no. 20.

Penfield, W., and P. Perot. "The Brain's Record of Visual and Auditory Experience." *Brain* 86 (1963): 595–696.

Puccetti, Roland. "Remembering the Past of Another." *Canadian Journal of Philosophy* 2 (1973): 523–532.

———. "Brain Bisection and Personal Identity." *British Journal of the Philosophy of Science* 24 (1973): 339–355.

Putnam, Frank W. "The Psychophysiologic Investigation of Multiple Personality Disorder: A Review." *Psychiatric Clinics of North America, Symposium of Multiple Personality* (1984).

Raichle, Marcus E. "Visualizing the Mind." *Scientific American* 270 (Apr. 94): 36–42.

Rasmussen, T., and B. Milner. "The Role of Early Left-Brain Injury in Determining Lateralization of Cerebral Speech Functions." *Annals of the New York Academy of Sciences* 299 (1977): 355–369.

Rowan, J. "The Self: One or Many." *The Psychologist: Bulletin of the British Psychological Society* 3 (1990): 302–305.

Serafetinides, E. A., R. D. Hoare, and M. V. Driver. "Intracarotid Sodium Amylobarbitone and Cerebral Dominance for Speech and Consciousness." *Brain* 88 (1965): 107–130.

Shoemaker, S. "Persons and Their Pasts." *American Philosophical Quarterly* 7 (1970): 269–285.

Shorter, J. M. "More About Bodily Continuity and Personal Identity." *Analysis* 22 (1961–2).

Van Wagenen, W. P., and R. Y. Herren. "Surgical Division of Commissural Pathways in the Corpus Callosum." *Archives of Neurology* 44 (1940): 740–759.

Wada, J., and T. Rasmussen. "Intracarotid Injection of Sodium Amytal for the Lateralization of Cerebral Speech Dominance." *Journal of Neurosurgery* 17 (1960): 266–282.

Witelson, Sandra F. "The Brain Connection: The Corpus Callosum Is Larger in Left-Handers." *Science* 229 (1985): 665–668.

INDEX